THE REDWING SAGA

— BOOK ONE —

BLOOD LIES

SHARON K. GILBERT

She2collages 20

BLOOD LIES

BOOK ONE OF THE REDWING SAGA
BY SHARON K. GILBERT
WWW.THEREDWINGSAGA.COM

First Print Edition April 8, 2017
Kindle Edition April 8, 2017

ISBN-10: 0-9980967-0-9
ISBN-13: 978-0-9980967-0-4

514 ROSE AVENUE, CRANE, MO 65633

Published by Rose Avenue Fiction, LLC
514 Rose Avenue, Crane, MO 65633

TABLE OF CONTENTS

FROM THE AUTHOR

I love history, and I love to write, so it's not a surprise that a merging of these two great loves would eventually produce this series of novels. For decades, I've read (devoured in some cases) the works of great British writers like Doyle, Dickens, Austen, Stoker, Shelley, and more recently Wilkie Collins and G. K. Chesterton. Though the style and formality of these 19th century writers are no longer in vogue today, I find them both beautiful and edifying, for they remind me of a time when gender roles seemed rooted in firmer soil, and religion and religious teaching were almost universal.

Today's young reader is awash in a sea of social media and net-speak that—for me—would soon make of my brain a grey soup, fit for neither creativity nor compassion. And so, I have decided to immerse my poor brain in phrases and polite conversations of a less technologically advanced time, that of late 19th century England and Scotland. Since I always write from a Christian worldview and hope to use fiction as a means to teach others about spiritual warfare, I have decided to commence this *Redwing Saga* with a seminal event in London's criminal archives: Jack the Ripper. Many writers have used Ripper as a springboard for fiction, however my tale—whilst providing a solution to the crimes—will wander far afield of traditional interpretation.

History purists will likely find my version of the Ripper murders disappointing if not infuriating, but wherever possible, I have included true facts, embroidering them only as needed to fit with my plot, and I have depicted historical persons as clearly and truly as my research permits (again sprinkling in additional traits or opinions to fit the plot), but also adding a few whose names most readers may have never before heard. One such example is American journalist Harry Dam, who actually did work for *The Star* during the time of the Ripper slayings.

The grammar and spelling of this novel are primarily British, and much of its style would be considered antiquated and formal now. Despite my best efforts to faithfully represent both 19th century British phrasing and spelling, I'm sure that somewhere within these pages—and in the books to come—I will fail in this attempt. For this, I beg your indulgence and forgiveness. Other strange inclusions to my American readers will be references to housing units. In Britain, our 'first' floor would be the 'ground floor', and our 'second' would be their 'first', so I have maintained a British point of view, in keeping with my characters. In short, if you find a phrase, spelling, or reference that seems odd or out of step, look it up, and you'll most likely discover yet another difference 'twixt British and American English'.

As to the secret history of monarchs, there is (to my knowledge) no such true parallel, however, histories are written and codified by those who control media, so I shall leave such to your discretion and discernment, gentle reader. As with the Ripper murders, I have endeavoured to keep to the facts where I must, but use my imagination and perhaps literary licence (yes, that's how the British spell it) for the remainder. The characters in this series of books have already grown upon my mind and heart, and I hope they will yours as well.

I have visited England and Scotland, but of course never in the 1880s, so I have done my best to provide a picturesque but earnest representation of that pivotal time in history, when the industrial age, like a spirit doorway, opened its mechanical gates into a vast increase in knowledge and the mass transport of peoples across the globe—in fulfillment of Christ's prophecy. The peoples of London and Scotland spoke with a wide variety of dialects and accents, so you will find conversations which include speakers whose speech patterns and pronunciations differ from those of the main characters, and quite possibly from your own, dear reader. I've done my best to convey their interesting rhythms and sounds in written form.

Redwing is a fictional name, but it is based upon those many human/demonic alliances that are even now preparing the way for AntiChrist. The white bird (dove) represents the Holy Spirit, of course, and the 'red spot' on one wing indicates the dark desire of every Redwing member, whether human or spiritual, to forever murder the Spirit of Christ upon the Earth. This symbol is a sign of their intent, but you and I know that such a goal is doomed to failure from the start. Christ is the beginning and the ending—He created all, and all humans and fallen entities who now oppose His Spirit will find themselves judged and sentenced to eternal death, no matter how intricate their war plans.

Our Saviour is returning soon, but as Christians, living in a world ruled—for now—by His enemies (who know their time is short) we must daily follow St. Paul's admonition in Ephesians 6 to always be dressed for battle:

Put on the full armour of God, so that you will be able to stand firm against the schemes of the devil. For our struggle is not against flesh and blood, but against the rulers, against the powers, against the world forces of this darkness, against the spiritual forces of wickedness in the heavenly places. Therefore, take up the full armour of God, so that you will be able to resist in the evil day, and having done everything, to stand firm.

Finally, I'd like to thank my husband for reading through this manuscript *twice.* Is that not love? Also, a huge thanks goes to Karla Akins, who was kind enough to read the manuscript as well. You are a wonderful friend and a gifted writer, Karla. And to each of you who buys this book—many, many thanks and prayers.

Sharon K. Gilbert
February, 2017

For the love of my life...

My treasured husband has always been and will ever be both my Paul and Charles, and he has always treated me like his very own Princess, so it is to him that I dedicate this book. Derek, you are my heart and soul, and your sweet voice and gentle eyes have revealed Christ's love to me every day since first we met.

PROLOGUE

3, March, 1879—East End, London

It was well past midnight by the time Annie Donovan had finally earned enough to pay for a night's lodging in the dosshouse. As she stumbled through the dark, the choked backstreets and alleyways of Spitalfields teemed with an eclectic mix of nightlife: drunks by the dozens; gaunt beggars in bug-ridden rags with outstretched, bony hands; bleary-eyed dockworkers staggering home from their wharf-side labours; exhausted chars and pale-faced, hourly wage house-maids who scrubbed and polished middle-class homes by day but scrounged for a warm place to sleep each night; and the occasional silhouette of *ad hoc* lovers pinned against sooty brick walls or broken windows, heaving rhythmically to the sad, symphonic strains of weeping and public house revelries. All around this east end sea of flesh, floated a silvery mist, rising into the miasma like dragon's breath on a winter's evening.

Annie's blue dress, once her Sunday best, was ripped at the shoulder seam, thanks to the excited pawing of an impatient trio of Russian sailors, but she walked with her chin held high, a music hall tune playing in her head, and she imagined herself to be a regal queen without a care, a silken pocketbook heavy with silver, dangling from her bejeweled fingers. Each footfall of Annie's worn boots echoed against the thick fog as she walked along the muck-stained cobbles. Passing by a street corner, she could just make out the familiar form of a quick-paced duo, a greasy sailor's cap sliding off the man's balding pate, his excited grunts spilling a cloudy mist into the night air: customer and product, sharing a bit of warmth and a sip of cheap gin before exchanging a coin or two. Sighing, Ann Marie Donovan wondered how she'd ended up in such a dismal, doom-ridden place.

Married at sixteen, the bright-eyed daughter of a lawyer's clerk had taken the train from Manchester toward a fresh start in metropolitan London with her new husband, a handsome young cartwright named Bill Donovan. Six months later, Bill had been charged, found guilty, and sentenced to ten years in Pentonville for theft and counterfeiting, leaving his desperate wife to scratch out a meagre living on the miserable streets of Whitechapel. Finding respectable employment for a girl with few skills had proven impossible, so Annie had set up a back alley 'shop', selling the only commodity she owned—her body—earning small sums by offering nightly entertainments to anyone willing to pay. Now, twenty years old and looking twice that, Annie had learnt the tricks of staying alive from her street sisters. She slept in a rented bed when she could, on the street or in doorways when she couldn't. Lift your skirts if you must, but never be too proud to beg a penny from a passing Christian. Tonight, a warm bed awaited at Flower and Dean Street, if only Mr. Cooper hadn't already sold it.

"Posies, Miss? Buy a posy from a blind girl," came a pitiful call from around the next corner. Annie's weary steps slowed as she reached Fashion Street, little more than a connecting lane that ran south of Christ Church. With Spitalfields now serving as refuge for the mass exodus of beleaguered Jews fleeing the Russian Empire's deadly pogroms, the Anglican church building seldom housed a congregation, unless one counted the peddlers and prostitutes that littered the lawn and cemetery day and night.

Donovan stopped and gazed at the girl, who sat all alone on the steps of the church's main entry. *She can't be more than six*, Annie thought with a sharp pang.

"Buy a posy, won't ya?" the girl called sweetly, her blind, blue eyes hidden behind dark green glasses.

Annie fetched out a pearl button from a tobacco tin, and handed it to the child. "I've no money to give you, luv, but here's a pretty button for your dress."

The girl reached out timidly. Her small, soot-covered fingers closed around the offering, which she then slipped quickly into her apron pocket. "God bless ya, Miss," she smiled. "What colour?" she asked, touching the wilted carnations in her basket. "I fink I go' pink and yellow still. Pick your favourite. Nuffin' cheers like yellow—so said me mum afore the typhus took 'er las' year."

Annie wiped a tear and brushed at the girl's dirty curls with her own bony hand. "No need, pet. You keep it. You got a place to bed tonight?"

"Yes, Miss," the girl lied. "Thanks, Miss. Keep safe."

"You, too, pet. You, too." Annie returned the rusty tobacco tin to her own pocket, gazing up at the dim light of the gas lamp near the church's doorway. With a sigh, she turned north toward Brushfield Street and 'Cooper's Rooms and Rents', a miserable heap two blocks west of Commercial. She could still hear the flower girl's plaintive call as she disappeared into the rising fog. Her mind on the child and her own sorry life, Annie suddenly cried out. Her ill-fitting, right boot had struck something in the lane, causing her to trip, and she tumbled forward onto her face.

"Lord 'elp us!" Donovan gasped, slowly picking herself up from the rough cobbles and brushing her hands. As she did so, she noticed her hands felt slick, wet. Fearing she'd cut herself, Annie checked her palms in the pale light of the street lamps, finding dark stains on both. "What in the name of…?" she asked aloud, her left foot still caught in something soft and wet that blocked the path.

Looking down, Annie realised with horror just what it was that lay upon the rough dirt and cobbled surface. Something beyond imagination. "Oh, merciful heaven! Help! *Help!*" she shouted, tears sliding down her dirty face as bile rose to the back of her throat.

"Murder! Police! *Help, it's murder!*"

Police Constable Thomas Wenderly blinked to clear his eyes. "Coffee, sir?" he asked the desk sergeant, an imposing Irishman named Taggart, who appeared half asleep himself. "Sir? Would you like some o' this coffee? I made it myself, sir."

The older man took the stoneware mug of steaming, black liquid and sipped, licking at his lips as he pondered the strong taste. "Well, lad, at least you can make coffee," he noted with a paternal grin. "It's a start. How 'bout doing a bit o' real police work, Constable? Here comes Sergeant Littlefield. Lend a hand with that door. Look sharp now!"

Taggart's peppery moustache twitched as Wenderly pulled the police station door open wide to admit one of Leman Street's fifteen CID detectives. His pale face and bloodied hands told a dark story.

"It's murder! Like I ain't never seen before!" the detective shouted to Taggart, gasping for breath. "Over on Commercial. A woman's been ripped apart. Head torn clean off. And there's more..." He paused a moment, holding the door and stepping to one side as a uniformed policeman approached, carrying an unconscious child in his arms. "There's a witness!"

CHAPTER ONE

Chief Inspector Robert Morehouse gazed thoughtfully at the sleeping girl in his office. After DS Littlefield's shock announcement of murder and a witness, the entire H-Division police station had gone into nonstop motion. As CID commander of the division, Morehouse had been roused from a deep sleep at 1:13 a.m., hastily dressed, and then followed Police Constable McMillan to the crime scene, one of the most vicious he'd seen in nearly twenty-five years of policing. Morehouse's second-in-command for CID, Inspector Charles St. Clair, had served as an expert set of eyes in the gloom and fog, whilst sixteen uniformed police constables and their sergeant maintained a modicum of order amongst the curious citizenry, all the while pinching a pickpocket or two found working their way through the densely packed crowd of voyeurs.

The victim's savaged body had fallen into several pieces and required two wagons to convey it to Morehouse's morgue, a modestly furnished examination parlour used by Dr. Alan Dollarhide, a London Hospital physician whose scientific curiosity and forensic skill had solved many a crime for Morehouse and often found publication and praise in *The Lancet*.

Now, what to do with the little girl who had, one presumed, witnessed the crime?

"I've given her a drop of laudanum to help calm her nerves. Still, I'm amazed at her overall condition. She's sleeping when no other child could," observed Dollarhide from the office doorway. "However, Chief Inspector, if you wish to hear my conclusions regarding our unfortunate victim, that will require time. I've only just completed my gross examination. I've given all the clothing and other personals to PC France. He's shown promise with fine work, so I might second him as an autopsy assistant—with your permission, of course."

"Fine work as in sewing?" Morehouse remarked with a raised eyebrow.

"Fine work as in evidence collection," the doctor replied with a suppressed grin. "Lord, will it never warm up? This station house is freezing!"

Charles St. Clair sat at the end of a long, well-worn damask sofa, that served as an emergency bed for Morehouse, but also as visitor accommodation. "She's a pretty thing," he said aloud as he gazed at the sleeping girl. "Has she said anything yet?"

Morehouse struck a match and relit his pipe, tapping the bowl to force it to draw. "She called out for her mother at one point, which makes me wonder if our victim might be this child's mother, or if she had some other role to play—assuming the girl is involved at all. She could be a complete stranger."

"We'd better get a matron up here," St. Clair said, his eyes on the girl's footwear. "Dollarhide, have you ever seen a Spitalfields waif with such shoes as these? They are new and made of fine grade leather. Italian, I'd say. And her stockings, silk ones by the look of it, are soiled at the knees, but clearly done very recently. And they are torn just in the one spot. Her clothing alone would cost more than my entire month's wages."

The doctor leaned in, touching the child's pale hand. "Her skin's quite good, too. Though the hair is matted with straw and dirt, the scalp is clean and in healthy condition. I'd say this child's hair was recently washed and regularly so. We don't see that often hereabouts. And she's dainty, not half-starved. I sorely doubt this girl is local."

Charles St. Clair had lost his only child, a son, to smallpox a little over three months earlier, and neither he nor his grieving wife had recovered emotionally. The young inspector contemplated the girl's heart-shaped face and dark lashes, and he longed to help her if he could. "Did the woman have anything about her that might provide a clue to identifying either her or this child?" he asked.

Dollarhide flipped through a small, leather-bound notebook, kept constantly in his right coat pocket. "Let me see. A jeweled cross, gold—high quality gold, mind you—on a box chain. A wedding ring set with three good-sized diamonds and two sapphires. All superior quality, which makes one wonder why the murderer didn't take them, because they appear to be expensive cuts. I imagine a jeweler could tell us more. And her skin, what there is that's left undamaged, is well-cared for, like the girl's. I'd say both our victim and this child reside in a more prosperous part of London. Perhaps even a wealthy section. A west end kidnapping, you think?"

"What do we have?" Morehouse mused. "A woman with apparent access to money and a girl who might be related to her or not." The chief inspector leaned back in his office chair, his dark eyes glancing upward. He puffed on the briar thoughtfully, and tendrils of silver smoke rose to the ceiling as he considered the situation. "I suppose it might be a kidnapping," he continued, "but it is premature to make such a guess as that, Doctor. However, such crimes have become all too common of late, have they not, St. Clair? Shanghaied businessmen and bankers, ransomed for money and all that."

Charles couldn't take his eyes off the girl's pale cheeks as she breathed rhythmically, sleeping peacefully beneath a happy haze of laudanum, courtesy of the good doctor. He felt a strange connexion to her, which made no sense, but then many things in policing made little sense in this modern age. "Is it possible I know her?" he muttered to himself, then looking to his superior, snapped back to the present. "A kidnapping? I suppose that's one possibility, sir, but it explains neither the woman on our autopsy table, nor her unspeakable condition. I've never seen anything like it—as if a wild animal tore her apart! Yet this child, except for a few stains of blood upon her dress and hair, is untouched so far as I can tell. Mother and child, you think?"

Morehouse tapped his pipe on the desk in irritation. "Damnable place, this borough! Mother? Who can say? The dead woman cannot speak, can she? However, she is fair-haired, and this girl has raven tresses. I'd not pick them out as mother and child if I saw them on the street, would you? A governess, perhaps? St. Clair, since you appear to have taken a shine to her, I'll leave the girl in your care. You might ask Dr. Limerick to keep watch on her in his clinic. He has a nurse on duty tonight, does he not?"

"I will not leave her there," St. Clair responded firmly. "That place is a sea of lice and not much better than Bedlam. Amelia can care for her at our home. With your approval, of course, sir."

Morehouse waved a hand and stood as if to dismiss his officers. "So long as she is watched. Write down anything she may say, and have her back here tomorrow if she can bear questioning."

"Certainly, sir. If no one objects, I shall take her home now," he said, bending to lift the child into his long arms.

Her eyelids twitched and flickered open for just a moment. "Paul? Where's Paul?" she asked, snuggling in close to St. Clair's chest. "I... I... Mother?"

"Don't worry, little one," he assured her. "We'll contact Paul and your mother." Then to Morehouse, he observed, "Her accent is certainly not Spitalfields. Far too refined. Little one, what is your name? Can you tell us where you live?"

The girl's eyelids closed, and she returned to sleep, her head against the young inspector's shoulder.

"Fair enough," St. Clair said, stroking her dark curls. "For now, let's go see if we can find you a place to sleep, all right?"

She nodded, as if dreaming, pulling in close to share his warmth. "She's shivering," he remarked, wrapping his overcoat around her shoulders. "Littlefield, would you fetch me a hansom, please? I'd rather not walk with such a precious cargo."

The sergeant nodded and rushed down the stairs to hail a cab. St. Clair followed slowly and carefully, making sure the child did not awaken as he descended the steps.

Sergeant Liam Taggart waved to the inspector. "Mr. St. Clair, sir. Your hat," he said, handing the policeman a grey Homburg. "She's a right sweet nipper, isn't she, sir?"

"She is at that," St. Clair said, taking the hat. "Until tomorrow, gentlemen. Should you learn anything more about the dead woman, please, send word to me at my home."

Outside, in the mist, Sergeant Littlefield opened the folding, wooden doors that protected the interior of the hansom, and then held the girl whilst St. Clair stepped inside. "I'll take her now, Sergeant. Thank you." Charles rapped on the trap door above to signal to the driver, who opened the hinged flap and peered down through the opening.

"Yes, Inspector St. Clair? Your home, I take it," the middle-aged man said. "That your girl, sir?"

"Not mine, Edgar," he said in return, stroking her cheek. "Just a lost waif. Yes. My home, if you please."

The child stirred as the hansom jerked forward. The cold night air chilled the interior, and the police detective spread his woolen overcoat across her as a blanket. In a few moments, the carriage sped past Christ Church, and St. Clair noticed several constables and thirty or more locals still wandering the gore-streaked crime scene.

"Little one?" he asked. "Are you awake?"

She reached out and took his hand, her eyes shut, and she turned toward him, moaning in her sleep. "Paul...?"

"I'll find him for you, darling," St. Clair promised. "Can you tell me your name?"

"Who are you?" she whispered, her teeth chattering in the biting chill of the dawn.

"A friend," he said. "Where is your coat? It's not wise to venture into the night 'round here without warm clothing."

Her dark brows furrowed into a frown. "Around here? Where is this? This doesn't look like... You're a friend? Do you know Paul?"

"No, darling, but I shall find him, if you can tell me more about him. Is he your brother?"

She began to tremble, and the policeman wondered if her shivers might be more than just the cold. If this girl witnessed the woman's murder and dismemberment, she might be in shock. "I'm sorry, little one. I shan't ask anymore questions just now. Sleep, if you wish. We've plenty time to learn all about each other, don't we? For now, let's get you home."

It was nearing seven by the time St. Clair carried the small child into the parlour of his red brick, two-storey home. The rent on the house was modest, and the location provided him quick access to most of the H-Division police district whilst still living in relative safety and comfort. Amelia St. Clair had never liked living in the east end quarter, preferring the smarter areas of the London metropolis. In fact, she had pressed Charles to seek placement in D-Division, which would have allowed them to live with her parents in Marylebone, but Charles hadn't wished to begin life as a married couple indebted to his wife's snobbish family.

St. Clair's only servant, a live-in housekeeper and cook bustled into the hallway, carrying a hand-painted coal scuttle. "Mornin', Mr. St. Clair. The missus is still sleepin'. It's sure cold, ain' it? I'll be ready for spring soon enough." Then noticing the little girl, she tilted her large head, grey eyes squinting curiously. "An' who's this then?"

St. Clair held the girl with one arm and used the other to hang his coat and hat on a wooden rack by the door. "Allow me to break the news to my wife, Mrs. Wilsham. This child is witness to an unspeakable crime in Spitalfields this night. We've not yet learnt the victim's identity or this girl's name, so she's nowhere else to go."

The kind woman smiled. "Poor thing! You're a lovely man, you are, sir. I'll say naught, but we should have summat for the wee thing to eat, when she wakes. She's all mucked, it looks like. Her clothes is bloody, too, an' Mrs. St. Clair won't want her leavin' stains all about. I can help 'er wash up, if you like, but I don't reckon we have anythin' that would fit 'er."

"How about one of my old shirts?" he suggested. "She's been asleep nearly the entire time since we found her, so she may require a bit of rousing."

The kind-hearted housekeeper nodded and led the way to her modest sleeping quarters, where St. Clair left the dozing child on a small wooden chair, propped up by Mrs. Wilsham. It took half an hour before she called him back, but the detective found the child clean, half awake, and wearing one of his work shirts, taken from the mending basket, over top of her own petticoats and chemise. The blue and white striped shirt reached to the floor on the girl, and St. Clair smiled as he picked her up and carried her into the sitting room.

"I think my old shirt's a bit too large for you, little one. That's much better, don't you think? Clean and dry, though still very sleepy it seems. Here we go," he whispered as he carefully laid her into the curve of a velveteen settee and covered her with a knit shawl. "Thank you, Mrs. Wilsham."

"Shall I wash her little clothes, sir? They're beautifully made, and the material's sure expensive. Will you need them as evidence?"

"We might, Mary, so just put them into a safe place for now. No need to wash them. Most likely I'll need to take them with me when she and I return to the station house. It's possible that the clothing contains bits of evidence missed by Dollarhide. Did you happen to notice if there's a maker's label inside either the dress or the jacket? Or perhaps a laundry mark?"

"The label in the jacket said 'House o' Worth', but I don't know where that might be. Do you, sir?"

"No idea," Charles admitted. "I imagine it's a high end couturier whose prices lie well outside of my budget, Mary. But how did such finery end up on a child in our borough?"

"It's a right mystery," the housekeeper remarked. "Oh, but there's a bit of embroidery inside her petticoats, sir. It's just the letter *E*, followed by the word *Anjou*. You suppose she's French, Mr. St. Clair?"

"She didn't sound French to me. Oh, I am tired," he said, rubbing his eyes.

"I reckon you're hungry, too. I'll fetch that tea now, sir," the woman said, bustling back toward the kitchen.

"Tea sounds divine." St. Clair dropped wearily into a flower-covered armchair, every muscle in his body screaming for sleep.

In a few moments, the housekeeper returned with a pot of strong black tea and a plate of toast and cold ham with two fried eggs. "You reckon she'd eat, sir?"

"I'll give her some of this when she awakens, Mary. Thank you."

The woman whistled to herself as she swept out the grate, then added fresh coals and a few crumpled newspapers before carefully lighting the fire. In minutes, the room cheered and warmed considerably. The mantel clock chimed eight bells, and Charles St. Clair stared into the dancing flames, mentally sifting through the crime scene and what few facts he and Morehouse had been able to discern from the pitiable victim's remains.

The dead woman had been strangled, or so thought Dr. Dollarhide. Only after death, presumably, had the unthinkable dismembering occurred, but yet there had been blood—*lots of blood, as if sprayed*. Impossible. How could a dead heart exert the force to cause so much posthumous bleeding? The girl's clothing had shown a few bloodstains, but had been spared for the most part. Had she witnessed the murder? If so, she may have escaped an even greater crime.

"Captain Nemo," a small voice whispered softly.

St. Clair turned toward the girl, whose dark eyes now stood open, her gaze fixed upon a tall bookcase in the far corner of the room.

"Captain Nemo?" he asked, leaning toward the girl. All weariness fell away as the young detective prayed for answers.

She continued to look toward the case, her right hand raised as if to point. "Jules Verne," she explained. "Second shelf down, third from the left. It's one of my favourites. Captain Nemo is such a lonely man; don't you think?"

"You know, I've never given it a thought, but I suppose he is," St. Clair replied softly. "Do you know the book?"

"I've read it twice. The second time in French. The French is much better."

Seldom had words so stunned the seasoned policeman. This child could read French? Could Anjou be her name, then?

"Is it? I've not read the French version myself," he answered matter-of-factly. "My French is rather poor, I'm afraid, much to the dismay of my Cambridge don."

The girl smiled—and the change lit up her entire face. "Cambridge? That is a university, isn't it? Like Oxford?"

"It is much like Oxford, yes. A rather dull school. Where did you learn French?"

She sighed. "It's strange. I'm not sure where I learnt it. Shouldn't I remember that? I think from my governess. Or perhaps my cousin."

"Your governess?" he repeated. "Do you recall her name? Does she have golden hair?"

She shook her head. "No, I don't believe so. Her name is… No, it's Miss…" She sighed. "I am sorry, Captain. I cannot remember."

"Captain?" he asked.

"You look rather like a Captain, I think. My memory isn't very good today. Where am I?"

"My home, little one. Can you tell me where you live?"

She nodded. "Yes, of course. No... Wait." Her dark brows pinched together, and her cheeks flushed with effort. "It is a very large house," she said at last. "Though, I think there is more than one. I can see the pictures in my mind, but it's as if all the words have gone."

"Don't worry about it now," he whispered, leaning toward the sofa and touching her small hand. "So, have you read many books in French?" he asked, deciding to use what she could remember as a fulcrum to pry open the rest of her memories.

"A few. Mother says my French needs improvement, but it's getting better. Paul says I shall go to Paris with him one day when I am older. Do you know Paul? Are you a policeman?"

St. Clair thought for a moment. As a CID detective, he wore no uniform or insignia that identified him as police. Had she been listening at the station? Had she feigned sleep?

"I am. How did you know?" he asked.

"I overheard you talking to another man…and a doctor, I think. I don't really like pipe smoke, but it seemed impolite to mention it."

He smiled, wondering how Morehouse might react to such a frank observation from a child. "I'm not mad about it either, to be honest, but I expect Chief Inspector Morehouse would find my mentioning it more than impolite; he might, in fact, consider it impertinent. If I may ask, little one, who is Paul?"

Her face grew soft, and she settled back into the satin cushions, the fire dancing in the deep mirrors of her dark eyes. "He is my cousin, and he is quite handsome, and very kind, and altogether wonderful. You remind me of him. Are you related to Paul?"

"I doubt it. My name is Charles," he said, noting a small shaking in her hands. "Are you cold?"

"Yes. A little. Did Paul bring me here?"

"No, but I shall contact Paul for you, if you know how I might do that."

"And this is your home?" she asked, her eyes taking on a somewhat faraway look.

"Yes. You're in my home. We found you in the streets not far from here."

She thought about this revelation for a moment, her face growing slightly pale again. "I think... I think something happened. Someone took me. I thought I saw Paul, but now, I don't know. I cannot remember very well. My head—oh, it *hurts*," she said with a pained expression.

Charles left his chair and sat on the edge of the settee to better reach her head. "Dr. Dollarhide may have missed something. Where does your head hurt, little one? Above your eyes?" he asked, touching her gently with one hand, stroking just above her dark brows.

She shook her head. "No, it hurts…here," she said, indicating the back of her head, just above the neck. He reached behind, deftly feeling beneath the raven curls. She twitched, a sharp moan escaping her lips.

"Sorry!" he cried out, drawing back his hand and finding it stained with dried blood. "Can you sit up for me?" he asked, helping her to do so. Lifting her thick hair, he examined the contusion. She had been struck at least twice with something heavy, but the blood had clotted. He worried about a concussion. *No wonder the girl slept, Dollarhide, you old fool!* he thought, making a mental note to upbraid the physician later that day. "Can you tell me your name? Is it Anjou?" he asked at last, hoping she might now feel safe enough to share it with a stranger.

She thought about this, opening her small mouth once or twice as if to speak, and then her face grew pale, worried—her eyes widening. "I—I'm not sure. Paul would know. Why don't I remember, Captain? Am I dreaming?"

Tears played at St. Clair's sea blue eyes, and he shook his head. "No, darling. You're not dreaming, but I think the headache you feel and your memory loss may go hand in hand. You'll remember it all soon. Trust me. Now, Mrs. Wilsham will bring you a cup of tea and perhaps a biscuit, and then you must sleep if you can."

She nodded and lay back against the pillows. "All right, Captain."

As the girl fell asleep, the detective kissed her forehead. "I suppose that's as good a name for me as any," he said with a smile. "Sleep now, little one. Sleep."

CHAPTER TWO

Amelia Marie Winstone St. Clair had grown up the youngest child of a large middle-class family, who proudly lauded their distant, if not entirely believable, connexions to the crowned heads of Europe via their second cousin on Margaret Winstone's side, Sir Albert Wendaway, a practically penniless baronet with a notorious gambling habit. Blood ties outweighed pecuniary shortfalls to the Winstones, and they proudly reminded all who would listen that Sir Albert's finances were not nearly as dire as many claimed, and besides they were due to reverse at any moment.

Amelia, who refused to be called Amy, had met her husband three years earlier, in 1876, at one of a whirlwind series of spring parties attended by London's marriageable, middle-class sons and daughters. Having just joined the police force at the age of twenty, fresh from receiving a degree in mathematics, Charles St. Clair's keen instincts, deductive reasoning, and dogged determination immediately impressed his superiors, and he'd been assigned to act as security at one of these occasions. During a break between dances, Amelia had struck up a conversation with the handsome police constable, bringing him a cup of punch and complaining about the close air inside the ballroom. The pair soon found themselves engrossed in conversation, causing Amelia to forget three of the young gentlemen on her dance card, but by then Charles had lost his heart to the lovely young woman with the dove grey eyes and bright smile.

The Winstones had, at first, objected to their daughter's choice in a husband, but genealogical research had turned up tenuous hints at the St. Clair family name, including a distant, though improbable, connexion to a certain Chief Inspector Hamish St. Clair, a retired Scotland Yard detective who lived in Edinburgh and was rumoured to have the queen's 'ear'. Upon making this tantalising discovery, both parents had heartily consented to welcoming Charles into their exclusive family. The couple married that August, and the following year, on the tenth of December, 1877, Amelia had given birth to a perpetually smiling baby boy—the spitting image of his father—whom she named Albert after her game-loving, baronet cousin. When smallpox ravaged through Whitechapel in December of 1878, Albert had been one of the youngest to succumb. Amelia had never forgiven her husband for forcing her to bring up *her* child in what she perceived as 'penury and squalor'.

It was past ten when Amelia at last came down for breakfast that morning in March, and she now listened as her husband explained the mysterious child she had found sleeping in their parlour. After being startled by the formidable Mrs. St. Clair, the girl had been removed to Mrs. Wilsham's tiny room behind the kitchen, so the couple now spoke without fear of being overheard.

"This girl. You say she reads French?" Amelia asked pointedly.

"So she told me," Charles explained. "She certainly reads English. I suppose she's older than Dollarhide surmised. He guessed her age to be seven, perhaps eight, but what child reads Jules Verne in French at such an age?"

"Assuming she reads at all," Amelia replied acerbically, doing little to hide her irritation. She sipped tea—black, no sugar, as she always watched her slender figure—whilst gazing out the parlour window, which looked southward onto Columbia Road. "Charles, how is it we are saddled with this girl?"

"Saddled?" he repeated, his blue eyes turned to hers in shock. "Saddled? Amelia, she needs but a little caring, a day or two of someone watching after her whilst Morehouse and I investigate. It's possible that whoever murdered the woman in her company may yet wish to do the same to this girl. Frankly, I am appalled by your callous attitude and perplexed by your complete lack of heart!"

"Are you? Then your memory is poor, Charles. My heart died four months ago, or have you forgotten Albert's death?"

Hearing his son's name used as a verbal weapon stabbed at St. Clair's tender soul, and he lowered his head, his hands clenched into tight fists as he tried with all his might to keep his temper. "No, of course, I have not. How can I? I see that empty crib every day and think of him, Amelia. Every day. And I know you do the same. Yet, surely your mother's heart can find a reason to help a child in need, can it not?"

"No, it cannot," she replied simply. "Do not look at me with such a face, Charles St. Clair. You've no idea how I've suffered, so do not pretend you do! Can she not go to a work house?"

"A work house? Amelia, such a place would be her death! This girl is delicate and shows no sign of ever having worked a day in her life."

Amelia sighed. "She is a street beggar, then, I imagine. Oh, Charles, you are such a fool sometimes, and perhaps a bit too much in love with your Whitechapel citizenry to know when you are being duped. The girl will no doubt rob us blind as soon as our backs are turned."

St. Clair started to respond angrily, but he paused a few seconds, struggling to regain his composure. Even before their son's death, Amelia's stone-cold attitude often bewildered the young detective, but her current obstinacy had opened a floodgate of emotions he had kept dammed up for many months. However, before he could reply, a small voice spoke from the hallway.

"Why should I wish to rob you?"

Mrs. Wilsham appeared, taking the girl's hand. "I'm so sorry, Mr. St. Clair, she just slipped away as I was dryin' the dishes. I can take her back. Come wi' me now, dearie."

St. Clair jumped to his feet, startled at the girl's sudden appearance, but infuriated with his wife. "No, she will be fine with us, Mrs. Wilsham." Then, he turned to the child, his face soft. "Of course, you wouldn't take anything, little one." He guided her into the room, his large hand gently holding her dainty fingers. "This is my wife, little one. Mrs. St. Clair."

The girl gazed into the woman's cold grey eyes without one word in reply.

"Cat got your tongue?" Amelia asked sharply. "Is it true you can read? Tell the truth. I shall know if you are lying, girl!"

The child's dark brows knit together, and her lower lip trembled, just a tiny bit, just once, but then her small back straightened, and she pointed to the top row of books on the shelf. "*Little Women, Oliver Twist, The King James Bible, Wuthering Heights, Pride and Prejudice, Manners for Women, Manners for Men, France by Night, Capitals of Europe, Crowned Heads of Europe, Debrett's Guide to*

Entertaining, Landed Gentry of England, and on the far right *Whispers in the Dark* by Reginald Greene, though I've never heard of that author before."

Charles laughed and broke into applause. "Well done, oh, very well done, little one! Many grown men could not have read out those titles so swiftly, and all without one mistake. Well done indeed!"

Clearly unimpressed, Amelia St. Clair glared at the child, her cold eyes clouding like a rising storm. "It is a trick, no doubt. Mrs. Wilsham may have taught her the titles by rote—or perhaps you did, Charles! Either way, I'll not be duped. What is your name, girl?"

The child showed no anger, no fear, but took a deep breath as if to remind herself of something long before taught about dealing with obstinate adults. "I cannot remember. Not now, but the Captain says I shall; therefore, I shall." She gave Charles a wide smile.

"Captain? Who on earth is that?" Amelia asked with a laugh. "Surely, she doesn't mean you, Charles! My dear child, this policeman husband of mine is hardly that. He is to be addressed as *Detective Inspector*, which does have its privileges and burdens, but he has never been on a naval vessel that I can recall, nor has he served in the military—which is to be understood at his age. Why do you call him such?"

The girl winked at St. Clair, her small mouth widening into a grin, and then she moved to the window, watching the passersby. "He looks like a Captain; don't you think?"

Amelia said nothing, merely glared. "Charles, I expect this girl to be gone when I return from my committee meeting at Mrs. Etherington's home. We're selecting a new chairwoman for the church bring-and-buy sale, and then I've an appointment with my dressmaker. That gives you until four this afternoon. Mrs. Wilsham, call a hansom, please. Charles, walk me to the door."

St. Clair kissed the child's cheek and placed her on the settee. "Wait here, little one. I shan't be long."

"All right," she said. "May I read?"

Amelia turned back toward the girl. "We've nothing in French," she remarked sarcastically. "You will have to make do with English, girl."

The child smiled, deep dimples creasing her cheeks. "That's all right. I could teach you French, if you like."

Amelia's eyes rounded. "Impertinent child! Charles, if she is still here when I return, I shall..." she began, but St. Clair soothed his wife's temper by handing her three, one-pound notes, all he had left from that week's pay packet.

"For your trip to the dressmaker's," he told her. "Perhaps, a new bonnet, too," he added with a handsome smile.

Amelia had thought her husband's dimpled smile dashing and irresistible three years before, but now she found it annoying. Regardless, she took the bank notes and tucked them into her handbag. She then let Charles place a velvet cloak around her shoulders as she fastened an electric blue hat against her upswept hair with a pearl and silver pin.

"Remember, Charles. I want her gone. If she is not, then I shall find a place for her myself. I will not see this house turned into an orphanage!"

"I shall endeavour to comply," he said. "Take an umbrella, Amelia. It's supposed to rain later."

"I shall decide if I wish to take an umbrella. You see to that girl. Goodbye, Charles. Kiss me now."

He leaned forward and kissed her cheek, noting its coolness, wondering just how it was that he'd ever found her warm. "Be careful," he said, walking his wife to the coach and helping her into the seat. "Say hello to Mrs. Etherington for me."

"I will, Charles. Remember, I shall be home no later than four. Make certain that girl is gone."

The coachman's whip snapped, and the horse trotted forward. Turning back toward the house, Charles found the child waiting for him inside the open doorway.

"She seems very sad," she said, taking his hand as he returned to the small foyer. "Shall I read to you?"

Charles felt weary to his bones, but he feared that his wife's demands had set a clock ticking that left him with little time. "That would be lovely. So, could you teach me French?"

"I thought you studied it at...Cambridge? Was that the school?"

"Yes, that was it. Come in here by the fire, little one. Did you eat breakfast?"

"I did. Mrs. Mary gave me some tea and a thick slice of toast that she helped me to bake myself. I've never made toast on a fire before."

"Really?" he asked, sinking into a large, comfortable chair near the hearth and setting her onto his lap. "How do you make toast in your home?"

She thought for a moment. "I'm not sure. I don't think I've ever made it. I've eaten it many times, though. And I think my cook... No, another cook... No, I'm not sure."

"Your hair is very pretty since Mrs. Mary washed it," he told her, deciding to move to a new topic. "Is your mother's hair dark like yours?"

"No. At least, I don't think so. Was your mother's hair dark, Captain? Yours is black like mine. My father's hair was very dark."

"His hair *was* dark? Has your father passed away then?"

She nodded, her smile disappearing, and her eyes downcast. "Yes. It makes me very sad to think about it. He was wonderful, Captain. Really wonderful, and he laughed nearly all the time— well, mostly. It's strange that I can recall his death so clearly, yet other things are...it's like they're not there. I cannot even recall his name, yet I can see him in my mind. He was very tall and quite handsome with black hair and dark eyes. He called me his lassie."

"He did? Was your father Scottish?"

"Yes, I think so. Does that help?"

"It might. And his eyes were dark, like your own? Your eyes are quite dark. You have beautiful eyes, little one."

She blinked, but the smile did not return. "Do I? Someone else told me that recently, but... No, I don't want to remember that."

She had pulled close, and he felt her tremble. *Dare I pursue this? Perhaps, it relates to this crime. Is it possible that her father also lies murdered somewhere near Christ Church?*

"I'm sorry to upset you, little one. It's just that I want to help you, if I can. What else do you recall about your father? You said he was tall. Do you know how tall?"

Her face pinched, as she struggled to dredge up memories, and he noticed she'd begun to breathe heavily. "I cannot remember. Quite tall, I think. Taller than you, perhaps. I—I cannot..." she finished, the last words catching in her throat as large tears gathered on her eyelashes.

"That's all right, little one. I don't remember my father or my mother," he said with a deep sigh. "Both died long ago when I was quite small, I'm afraid, and I've no photographs or paintings, so I do not know if their hair was dark or light. My aunt and uncle raised me. They are kind enough, but I often wonder about my true parents."

"I'm very sorry," she said, her eyes growing large as she touched his face. "Where are they? Your aunt and uncle, I mean."

"They live in Lambeth. Do you know where that is?"

She nodded. "Yes, it's not far from Westminster."

St. Clair's brows rose in surprise. "Have you been to Westminster?"

She nodded. "Yes, of course. Many times. It's quite crowded, but not like it is here. Your street is filled with very interesting people, isn't it? The men in Westminster wear different clothes from the ones worn here, and there are lots of horses in the park—riding horses, I mean. Have you ever visited our park?"

"Your park? St. James's Park, you mean?"

Her dark brows worked together as she struggled to remember. "No. I don't think so. It's *Queen* Something, I think."

"Queen Victoria? Is this park close to the palace?"

She lay her head against his chest, sighing. "I cannot remember. I'm very sorry, Captain. I don't believe it's Queen Victoria. There was a man in our park, though. Last month and even before. He kept watching me, and he frightened me, so I ran to... I ran to someone. Paul, perhaps. No. My cousin wasn't in London then. A man then carried me back into the house." She shivered. "Has it gotten colder?"

"Yes, I imagine it has," St. Clair replied gently, and he drew a thick blanket from a basket near the fireplace and spread it across her shoulders. "Does your head still hurt, little one?"

She nodded. "A bit."

Realising that the strain of trying to force memories might be causing her more pain, he changed to something less strenuous. "What else did you and Mrs. Mary do this morning?"

"I helped her to make a bed," she whispered, brightening. "It was quite fun, actually. I don't think I've ever done that before either. And she taught me to roll out biscuits and bake them in the oven. And we added sugar on top. Do you know how to do that, Captain?"

"I'm afraid not. Have you ever helped with any other chores around the house?"

She thought about this, leaning against his chest. "I don't believe so. Although, I have pictures in my mind of horses and stables.

31

And long staircases and lots of books. And something else… Something that…" She tensed up, beginning to tremble. "I don't want to think about it."

He held her close, stroking her long curls. "Does it frighten you?"
She nodded.

"Can you describe it? I will keep you safe, little one. Nothing will harm you here. Not whilst I live. Nothing. Not ever."

"I know, Captain. I trust you..." Her small fingers traced the shape of his nose. "You remind me of someone, I think. Do I know you?"

"No, darling, you don't. Not until now, anyway. Can you tell me about this thing that frightens you?"

She sat still for many moments before replying, and Charles watched her eyes as she weighed her response. "I'm not supposed to talk about it."

"Who told you that?" he asked.

Again, she appeared to be considering her reply very carefully, and the lower lip began to tremble again. "You will protect me?"

He nodded, taking her small hand. "Always. I promise."

"It is an... *An animal*," she whispered at last, trembling once more. "It snarls and bites, and it watches me. It knows me. It knows my name. It has red eyes, and it... *It talks to me.*"

"Talks to you? An animal?"

She nodded again. "Mother doesn't believe me. She says I imagined it. Paul doesn't believe me either, but you will, won't you, Captain?"

"Of course, I believe you, little one. Can you remember anything else, about your mother perhaps?"

"I think... I think that she is dead," the child whispered, and she began to shiver. "May I go to sleep now, please?" she asked, her voice choking and her eyes closing. Tears traced her cheeks, and Charles dried them with his handkerchief, kissing her as he held her close to his chest, pondering her words about an animal. Was the woman at Leman Street this girl's mother? If so, did an animal kill her? The injuries were certainly consistent with such an attack, but if so, then who strangled her? Or was it something else, someone else. A man who *behaved* like an animal? The man from the park?

Charles found his own eyelids growing heavy, and within a few minutes, he, too, fell asleep.

Three hours passed, and St. Clair's body jerked, as someone tapped him on the shoulder.

Mary Wilsham stood beside the detective's chair, her face flushed and beaded with sweat. "Oh it's all my fault, Mr. St. Clair! While you was sleepin' with the girl, I went out to buy a chicken and some potatoes, an' when I come back she was gone!"

St. Clair's heart sank at these words. The child had vanished. He leapt to his feet, running into the hallway to don his overcoat and hat. "She's nowhere inside the house? You checked everywhere? Even closets?"

"I did, sir. She's gone. Oh, I am so sorry!"

"How long were you away, Mrs. Wilsham?" he asked, struggling to maintain a sense of calm.

"Not more'n an hour, sir. Not even that. The girl was sleepin' right peaceful when I left."

An hour! He thought for a moment, imagining all the dreadful things that could have happened to the beautiful child in that space of time and forcing them from his mind. "Stay here, in case she returns, Mary. I'll walk the neighbourhood. If anyone from the station house comes by, have him join me in the search."

"I will, sir. Oh, I pray the Lord helps you to find her!"

Charles raced into the street, looking in all directions for any sign of the child. To his left, he could see several costermongers plying their wares along Columbia and eastward toward Birdcage Walk. To the right, he noticed two hansoms and an elegant coach parked near a three-storey house he knew to be an upscale brothel called the Empress Hotel. Two well-dressed women stood near the door to the bawdy house, one looking in his direction. Charles crossed Columbia and made for the women, keeping his manner light, for everyone here knew him to be with the police, and he had no wish to alarm them.

"Good afternoon, ladies," he called pleasantly. "Has either of you seen a young girl in the past hour? A little under four feet tall, dark eyes and hair?"

The shorter of the two women wrapped a blue printed shawl around her shoulders and squinted into the afternoon sun. "Wearin' naught bu' a man's striped shirt o'er top 'er personals?"

"Yes!" Charles exclaimed as he reached their door. "Forgive me, Miss Irene, but she might be somewhat disoriented. The child is part of a murder investigation, and she came home with me this morning, for we do not yet know her name or address."

"I said she looked all muddled, didn't I, Ida?" the woman answered, glancing up at her tall companion. Turning toward the detective, she continued, "She run out no more'n quarter of an hour past, Mr. St. Clair. Walked that way. Over toward Johnny Pete's place."

"Thank you, Irene. And you as well, Miss... Oh, I'm sorry I don't think I've met you," he added, speaking to the taller woman.

"Ida, Mr. St. Clair. Ida Ross. I'm new. I just started two days ago, sir." She appeared embarrassed. Ross looked no older than fifteen, perhaps younger, and St. Clair wondered what the girl's story might be. *Another tragedy waiting to happen*, he thought.

"Thank you, then, Miss Ida," he replied, bowing slightly. "If you see the child again, will you take her to my home? It's right across the street. Number twelve. My housekeeper is there waiting."

Ross nodded, clearly self-conscious. "Uh, yes, sir, Mr. St. Clair." Her strawberry blonde hair seemed to redden as her cheeks crimsoned beneath a sea of pale freckles.

"We will, sir. I hope you find 'er, Mr. St. Clair!" the shorter woman called as Charles ran west toward the public house known as Johnny Pete's.

Once the detective had reached the next block, the taller girl pulled her emerald green jacket tightly about her shoulders. "He's right nice for a copper."

Irene Lester struck a match and lit her cigarette. "A real looker, too. And all over muscled, I'll wager. Mrs. Hansen moons over 'im all the time, she does, but don't let 'er know I told ya. Mrs. St. Clair, though. She's a right piece o' work. Never did understand how come he took up wif the likes o' her. Come on then, Ida. We best go back in an' earn our keep."

"I'll wait out here in case the little girl walks past, Irene. I did tell the inspector I'd keep watch."

Lester laughed and sucked on the cigarette. "Watch all ya like. It won't make no difference. Mr. St. Clair's too nice ta step ou' on 'is missus, even though she does naught to keep 'im. So, put them thoughts outa yer noggin'."

"I'll just keep watch. That's all. You go on in, and I'll come inside soon."

The shorter woman laughed again as she re-entered the house, noticing that the new girl's eyes continued to follow the policeman's progress until he disappeared from their view.

The Greenway public house stood opposite the Mission School at the corner of Columbia Road and Gascoigne. Even with his long legs, it took St. Clair several minutes running at top speed to reach the pub, and he pushed through the heavy, glass and oak door, instantly recognised by everyone in the establishment.

"You 'ere on business, Inspector?" asked a pretty barmaid as she distributed pints of ale to a table of four, middle-aged men.

Charles stopped to catch his breath, gulping for air. "I haven't come to roust anyone, Myrtle. I'm searching for a small child. A girl."

"Real sweet an' pretty, wif dark hair?" the waitress asked. "She's back there, Mr. St. Clair. Talkin' wif Johnny Pete."

Charles passed through a collection of postal workers, goods yard men, and several coopers on their lunch break from the Hanbury & Co. Brewery. "Gentlemen, I am not here to make trouble. I'm just looking for..."

"Hello, Captain," the child called at seeing him. She sat on the pub's sturdy brass and oak bar, her bare feet peeking from beneath the curved hem of his work shirt. "I saw this man walk past your window, and he looked familiar. I tried to wake you, but since you kept sleeping and I couldn't find Mrs. Mary, I followed him on your behalf."

John Peter MacArthur gulped at seeing the policeman. "Inspector St. Clair, sir, I ain' done nuffin' wrong. She jus' come in, all on 'er own, she did!"

"That's true. I did," she agreed as St. Clair picked her up from the counter. "Are you cross with me, Captain? I'm sorry to worry you, but I thought I ought to investigate."

He felt such relief at finding the girl safe that his previous terror had dissolved into a mixture of elation and anger, but Charles shook his head, unwilling to cause her any distress. "No, little one. I'm not cross, but you did frighten me. I'd feared you'd gone, and that would make me very sad."

She kissed his cheek. "We cannot have that," she said with a bright smile.

"Thank you, Mr. MacArthur," St. Clair said, and then to the girl, he asked, "Darling, what about this gentleman looked familiar? John, do you know her?"

"No, sir, I do not. Yet, she seemed to think me someone she knows."

"I thought he was the man from the park," she explained.

"The man you mentioned to me earlier?"

"Yes. The tall one with the funny accent," she said. "But he isn't. Should we go back to your house, Captain?"

He nodded. "Yes, I think we should, little one, else I shall have to issue you a warrant card," he said, proudly. "You'd make a fine detective."

"Would I?" she asked, giggling.

"You would indeed." Charles wrapped his overcoat around her shoulders as the pair of them left the pub, neither noticing a curious man who watched from a corner near Columbia and Gascoigne Place. The man was quite tall, wore a colourful, plaid vest and walked with a limp. He scribbled something into a leather notebook as he observed the policeman and the girl, before vanishing into thin air.

Within a few minutes, the twosome passed the brothel, and the girl waved to Ida, who smiled and waved in return. "Glad you found 'er, Mr. St. Clair!" she called, and the child tapped her protector on the shoulder.

"May we say hello?" she asked him. "She looks cold."

"As do you, little one. Might it not have been wiser to put on your boots before rushing out to investigate?"

She giggled. "I didn't wish to lose him, and my shoes were still drying by the fire in Mrs. Mary's room. May I talk to her? Please?"

With Amelia due home by four, Charles had no wish to lose any more time, but he admired the child's compassion for others. "Yes, we should say hello. Miss Ida, my houseguest would like to say thank you."

The girl jumped out of his arms and ran up to the prostitute. "Do you live here?" she asked innocently.

The young woman bent down and touched the girl's dark curls. "I do. It looks like the inspector is taking right good care o' you, little miss." Then she bent forward and whispered something to the child.

The girl's face grew pale. "Really? How do you know?" she asked, and Ross touched the child's cheek and whispered something in return. The girl nodded. "I shall, but you must be careful, too."

"Oh, I'm all right," the young prostitute said aloud. "But you've nothing to fear, luv. You put your trust in Mr. St. Clair, my girl. Keep near him, and you'll be all right."

"Yes, I know," the child replied. "He will take good care of me. I shan't worry. He is the Captain, you know. Shouldn't you go inside, Miss Ida? It's quite cold out here without a coat. Do you need a coat? Perhaps, we could bring you one."

"I'm plenty warm," Ida lied. "She's a right sweet thing, sir. I can see why you was worried. Thank you, little miss. You take care now, an' mind wha' the inspector says—I mean wha' the Captain says."

"Thank you again, Miss Ida," Charles said, touching her hand briefly. "If you hear or see anything amiss, I hope you will tell me. I should get her back into the house. We're on a bit of a deadline. It was a pleasure to meet you."

She wanted to say more, but the detective had already lifted the child into his muscular arms and turned back toward his home. Ida Ross wished she had the courage to tell him the truth, but it was too late, so she climbed the steps back up to the doorway and returned to work.

Arriving back at his home, St. Clair carried the child inside, where both were greeted by a very relieved Mrs. Wilsham.

"Oh, sir, you found her! May the Lord be praised! Where was she then?"

The child ran forward and kissed the housekeeper, as St. Clair hung up his hat and coat. "I worried you both. I am sorry," she said. "I thought I saw the man from the park."

Charles carried her back into the parlour, where the fire had nearly burnt out. "Do you remember which park, little one?"

"The one near..." she started, but then her brows pinched together, as if she had reached a mental roadblock. "I'm not sure. It's all rather mixed up. I could almost see it in my mind, like recalling a dream, but it's gone now. I am sorry, Captain. Is it important?"

"Possibly," he told her honestly. "Darling, I think someone tried to hurt you, and I only wish to find that man and arrest him.

You say the gentleman in the pub looked familiar. Like the man with the accent."

"A very strange accent. Not English," she said as Wilsham brought in a fresh pot of tea and served a cup to the detective.

"Thank you, Mary," he said kindly. "It's already three, so if we're to find a solution to this puzzle before four, then we'll need to hurry. I should not have fallen asleep."

The girl bit her lip, her eyes round with fright. "Will I have to leave when Mrs. St. Clair comes home?"

"Not if I can help it," he promised her. "Darling, what else can you remember? Anything more about your cousin?"

"Paul?" she asked. "He's tall and handsome, much like you, Captain. I think he's somewhere else now, but I cannot remember where."

"And what about this other memory? The one about the animal?"

"I... I don't want to think about that," she whispered, trembling, her eyes grown wide with fear.

"Yes, I know, darling, but it's very important. Can you tell me what the animal did? Did he try to hurt you? You said he talked to you. What did he say?"

"He...uh, he... No, I do not wish to remember! He'll... He'll *do things* to me—awful things!" She tensed up, terror filling her dark eyes, and her head dropped backward, her mouth open wide. "I mustn't tell! I mustn't! I promised! No!" she screamed, kicking her legs. "Please, no!"

Wilsham rushed over, kneeling beside the chair, whilst St. Clair did his best to calm the child. "Little one, you are safe. He will not harm you. I shan't let anyone hurt you—not ever again!" Her entire body had gone rigid, and her breathing increased into a rapid-fire, staccato pattern. Charles held her close, kissing her forehead. "Darling, it's all right. We won't talk about the animal. You're safe. You are completely safe," he whispered to her lovingly.

The detective prayed silently, beseeching the Lord for aid and intervention, and after several minutes, the girl began to relax, but her breathing remained shallow and swift, her small fists clenched. "Mary, would you fetch me a warm towel, please?" he asked.

Wilsham disappeared into the kitchen, and in a few moments returned with a moist linen towel she'd warmed in a pan on the stove. St. Clair took the cloth and placed it on the child's forehead. Again he prayed, terrified that he'd caused her harm. Tears slid down his face as he held her, and the detective fought rising panic.

"You are safe, little one," he whispered, kissing her cheek. "That animal will *never* touch you. Not here. Not whilst I live."

Ten more minutes passed, an agonizingly long time, but at last the girl began to relax, and she pulled herself close to his chest, sobbing.

"No one will hurt you, little one. I promise," he assured her.

She trembled still, and her breath caught as she wept. "And if—if I have to—to leave here?" she asked in gasps, her dark lashes beaded with tears.

"You will not leave here until we can send for Paul, and I will not desert you, little one. Not ever. Not so long as you need me."

She continued to sob but soon fell asleep in his arms, and St. Clair, though weary, remained awake to guard her until Amelia returned at four. Whilst he waited, he talked with Wilsham, hoping the housekeeper had noticed anything that might help to identify the girl.

"Mary, sit, won't you? You've been a great help with this child. She trusts you and likes you very much."

"As she does you, sir, if I may say so. She talked about you often whilst we done the mornin's chores. She's a good little helper, though she don't seem to know much 'bout cleanin'."

"About that, Mary," he probed, "the girl told me that she'd never baked toast or even made a bed before. Did you learn anything else about what she has or has not experienced?"

Wilsham sat into a small armchair, the warm towel in her hand. "Well, sir, I'd say she's done no cleanin' nor bakin', which is odd. Even at her age, most girls I know has done some housework. Her hands is smooth and soft, so I don't think your missus is right about the girl bein' a beggar. She'd have rough hands from sleepin' on the streets an' all, an' she'd be right scrawny, I think. Bu' she's real healthy, though petite, you know."

"Yes, that's what I think, too. She recognised Westminster as being near Lambeth, even describing the businessmen, and she says she's been there many times. Her accent and speech patterns are quite refined, don't you think?"

Wilsham nodded. "She knows some fairly big words, too. She even spoke to me in French a bit."

"Did she? I say, Mary, surely this girl isn't part of some child procurement operation?"

"What is that, sir?"

He gazed at the girl's serene, sleeping face, and kissed her forehead. "She is heartbreakingly beautiful, is she not? I fear a beautiful child like this is precisely the kind these procurers look for. Without being too descriptive, for it's possible she may awaken and I'd not want her to be alarmed, it is an organisation that provides very young girls, often raised from infancy and kept pure and lovely, to, well," he explained, clearing his throat, a trifle embarrassed. "Well, you see, these girls are sold to... Well, to evil men for their *personal* use. Do you understand what I mean?"

Wilsham's face went white. "Surely, you do not mean that this precious girl may have been used in such a way? Might tha' be this *animal* she speaks of? Would she remember it as such?"

"That is just what I fear, Mary. These men are evil. Pure evil, and a child might interpret such aberrant behaviour as animalistic in nature."

"Do you find such in London, sir? Men wha' uses girls such as this dear child?"

"Such men exist all across the world, I imagine, and yes, in London as well. This child seems to recall a man with a strange accent who frightened her in a park. Perhaps the woman found dead beside her tried to interfere—perhaps even came to her rescue. It's important that I learn all I can before..."

"Before Mrs. St. Clair returns. Yes, sir. I'm sorry she said such to you about this child. It weren't right. No, it weren't. She's been tore up since little Albert—I mean, well, you know what I mean, sir. Weren't your fault, sir. No, it weren't, an' I know how much you miss that boy, sir. Each and every day."

A flash of regret darkened his face for a moment, but St. Clair offered the housekeeper a weary smile. "You needn't explain, Mary. I understand what you mean. Albert's passing tore all our hearts, did it not? But God has given me a chance to help another child now, and I shan't fail her as I did my son. Now, is there anything else you noticed or heard?"

Wilsham thought for a moment, then her eyes widened. "She's got a bad scar on her little leg, sir. Like some animal tore it. Looks like it's a year or more old, though."

"Perhaps, that's the source of her terror, but you say it looked older?"

"Aye, sir, but I saw some bruises on her back that looked real new."

"Bruises sometimes take a day or two to emerge, do they not, Mary?" he asked.

"Yes, sir, they do. She's a sweet child. She sung me a song in French whilst she tried her hand at workin' a broom. She'd never swept afore neither, I reckon."

St. Clair blinked, his eyes dry and weary. "Did she eat anything besides toast?"

"Not much. A bit of cheese and an apple. She said somethin' though about havin' lots of apple trees in her yard. Does that help?"

"I don't think so, but it is one more reason to rule out the east end. Few houses here have fruit trees. The yard space is too limited. Did she say anything about someone named Paul?"

"Aye, sir, she did. Many times. She talked abou' him like he were right special, but then she talked abou' you a lot, too, sir. Callin' you Captain."

St. Clair smiled. "Really? Funny, I rather like that nickname. And she always takes on a happy look when she talks about this Paul person. At first, I'd thought this man might be involved in transporting or grooming her, if indeed she is part of such a dark operation as these procurement circles are, but she seems to trust him, does she not? So, what else did she say about him?"

"That he's tall and handsome, and that he goes to Paris a lot. Oh, sir, your wife's back!"

A black hansom cab had pulled in front of the home, and Amelia St. Clair alighted, planting her feet upon the sidewalk, a grim expression on her face as she gazed at the blue-painted, front door.

Charles had risen to his feet, the girl still clutched within his arms, and he prayed Amelia had reconsidered her harsh demands whilst away. A moment passed, the front door opened, and Charles held onto the girl tightly, determined she would not be evicted.

"Why is that child still here?" his wife shouted as she entered the parlour.

"Keep your voice down, please, Amelia," he whispered. "She is sleeping."

"All the more reason to raise my voice, Charles. Girl! Wake up! It is time you left for a place more in keeping with your age and social status!"

Amelia handed her hat and cloak to Wilsham and then walked straight to her husband. "Give her to me, Charles."

St. Clair, usually compliant if not conciliatory toward his wife, refused to back down this time. "I will not. She is here because she needs tending and protection, Amelia."

"Others with more experience and less to lose may tend to her, Charles. That is the purpose of orphanages and work houses, is it not? Now, hand her to me."

"No!" he shouted angrily. "Do not say more! I will not abandon this girl; do you hear me? Now, if you worry about silverware, or jewelry, or anything else in this house, Amelia, you are free to hide them or remove them. However, if you ask me again to remove this child, then I shall do so, but I will go with her, and you will not see me more."

Amelia started to reply, but her husband's stern expression kept her silent—for now. The raised voices had wakened the girl, however, and she looked up at St. Clair's wife.

"I shan't take anything," the girl said simply. "Why are you always so sad?"

Mrs. St. Clair's face paled, and her mouth flew open. "I am not—that is, I'm—what impertinence! Charles, I shall be upstairs until your temper returns to normal."

She turned to leave, but the girl spoke again. "I'm sorry," she said. "I am not any help to you, am I? I didn't intend to hurt you, Mrs. St. Clair. The Captain says…"

"The Captain! Child, you are rude and disrespectful! My husband is not to be addressed with such insolence!"

Charles set the girl onto the floor. "Go sit by the window, little one," he whispered. "Amelia, I will speak with you in the kitchen."

"I have a headache," she countered, turning toward the staircase.

"*Now*," he whispered tightly, taking her arm to stop her.

St. Clair guided his wife down the hallway, pausing only when they had reached the passageway betwixt the dining room and the small kitchen. "I will not have you speak to that little girl in such a way, Amelia. No, do not say one word more, else you will find my temper flaring far more than you ever thought possible. I have

42

tolerated much from you because of Albert, but I will not have you endanger the life of another child because of it!"

"That girl is not our problem," the woman countered angrily.

"She is without a home, so for now, this will be her home until I say otherwise. Is that clear?"

"You would order me about in my own home?"

"It is my home, too, Amelia, and for the foreseeable future, it shall be hers. If you press me on this, then I will leave this house to you and find a new place to live—for myself and for this girl, should she need one. Do not test me!"

He turned around, fearing his own rising tide of anger, because, for the first time since marrying her, Charles suddenly wished he had never done so. He walked back into the parlour, gazing at the small girl who stood near the window, her face pressed against the panes. Amelia had followed, and she was about to continue their argument, when the child turned toward them.

"Is that one of your policemen coming this way, Captain?" she asked as a young man in blue splashed through the cold winter mud to cross the busy street, dodging a beer wagon, a costermonger selling imported vegetables, and a dog cart.

The policeman knocked, and Mrs. Wilsham, still in the parlour close to the girl, rushed into the foyer and opened wide the front door. "If it isn't PC France," she said with a motherly grin, happy to see the lad for many reasons, not the least of which being that his arrival had prevented the St. Clairs from escalating their argument further. "Come in, lad, before you catch yer death. Where's yer coat? It's the Devil's own out there, and that's no mistakin' it."

Arthur France removed his helmet and tucked it beneath his left elbow. "Thank you, Mrs. Wilsham. Inspector St. Clair, sir?"

St. Clair crossed to the constable. "France, I assume that Morehouse has sent you to fetch us. Sorry, we got involved and lost track of the day. We're just about to have tea," he lied, wishing to avoid further sharp words with his wife. "Won't you join us?"

France took a breath. "No, thank you, sir. Chief Inspector Morehouse did send me, sir, but not as he thinks you're late or any such, but because we've had a visit. There's a gentleman—a right angry one, if you ask me, sir. He's at the station house and claims he's the girl's father."

The child joined the two men in the narrow hallway, her dark brows knit together. "My father?" she asked France, "No, that cannot be."

Amelia motioned to the servant. "Fetch the girl's shoes and other clothing, Mrs. Wilsham. She may keep the shirt, of course, as a gift. Our good deed is finished. Let the father remove her to his own home; we've more pressing matters to attend. Charles, I would speak to you privately once you've returned," she said, casting an angry glance at her husband. "Good afternoon, Constable France. Thank you for your news. I will see you at the hospital fundraiser next week, I take it? Yes? Well good. I shall say good day to you all then."

With that, the lady of the house left the hallway and glided upstairs as if she'd won the entire battle and now dismissed them all from her presence.

The child's eyes followed the woman's retreat with fascination. "She seems very unhappy," she said softly.

Charles finished putting on his coat and hat and swept the girl into his arms once more. "So she is, little one, but Mrs. St. Clair's mood is my fault, not yours. Now, let us see who this man is that has come to claim you. Remember, I will let no one harm you. Do you believe me?"

She kissed his cheek, her arms around his neck. "Yes, I do, Captain. I truly do," she whispered, and PC France led them all back across the road and into a waiting hansom.

"Well?" bellowed the tall, imposing gentleman. "Is she here, or isn't she?"

Chief Inspector Morehouse showed no ruffling at all, but kept his eyes fixed on the pacing man. Their visitor rose well beyond six feet tall, and his physique was that of a man accustomed to outdoor pleasures. He looked to be no more than forty and wore a charcoal grey vicuna overcoat with an astrakhan collar and matching hat. His black boots shone like mirrors, and his chin bore the slender, dark stubble known only to those accustomed to daily shaving, but having missed one or two days. He wore no spectacles, but his vision appeared to be sharp, as he had signed for the child's personal items without so much as a squint at the small typewriting on the form. His left hand bore a curious signet ring, and his trousers and waistcoat were made of finest Merino wool and fit as if tailor-made. The man had access to wealth, of that there could be no doubt, but was his tale a true one? Morehouse's 'inner voice' had been screaming *no* for nearly an hour.

"Where is she?" the man shouted to the entire station house. In the nearby cells, several street urchins, who'd been arrested for pickpocketing the previous night, began to imitate the man's strident calls. A quick word from Sergeant Taggart sent them all scurrying back to the corners of their cells in subdued silence.

The street door opened, and St. Clair brought the girl in just as PC France appeared to be finishing a joke. "And so, the monkey said his would be the last *tail* they'd ever tell!" he said with a wink. The girl broke into musical peals of genuine laughter, and she giggled as St. Clair set her down onto the floorboards, her large eyes riveted to France's crazed 'monkey' face.

"Look at *me*, Elizabeth!" the well-dressed man shouted, stomping the floor with a gleaming, black boot.

The girl jumped, spinning 'round toward the man, whose pale grey eyes quickly assessed the disapproval of the policemen who now saw themselves as the child's guardians. Recovering himself, the tall man's face softened, and he bent down and whispered, "I've come to take you home, Elizabeth. Won't that be nice?"

Her face blanched, and her bottom lip trembled. The girl's right hand shot toward St. Clair's reflexively, and she stepped close to the inspector's side. "You are not my father!" she said emphatically.

The man nearly shouted back in return, but he again purposefully made his demeanor kinder, softer—his voice silken and inviting. "Dear, sweet Elizabeth, I might not be your actual father, but I've been like one to you for almost two years now. Come with me, darling. Your mother is waiting for you."

Like lightning, as if these last words snapped her to reality, the girl's dark eyes grew round, and she stood directly in the man's face as he bent beside her. "You are a liar! You are a detestable liar! Murderer! You shall hang for what you did!" she cried out, her entire body quivering.

Her words split the air like cracking ice, but the man would not allow her to continue. Upon hearing the accusation of 'murderer', he'd seized the child by the shoulders and begun to shake her violently.

Immediately, St. Clair and Morehouse intervened. Morehouse pulled the man to his feet and toward the booking desk whilst St. Clair scooped up the girl and held her tightly, protectively. Outraged, the tall man nearly struck Morehouse, but two officers restrained him, and Sergeant Taggart held up a set of iron manacles.

"There now," Morehouse said simply. "Shall we continue this conversation in one of my cells, Sir William?"

Charles held onto the girl, who had begun to weep into his shoulder. "He lies, Captain! He is not my father," she whispered. "He killed her! He killed my mother!"

Sir William Trent's teeth ground in disgust. "You are the liar, little brat! Prove to me that your mother is dead, you wretched child. I have only done my best for you—and for your mother—since the day I came into your lives! How have you repaid me?" he asked, hoping to gain sympathy but failing. "I am battered and belittled by an upstart *girl!* Prove to me that Patricia is gone, and I shall be the first to demand justice for her!"

The entire police station stared at him in unison, and the air grew thick with the rising tide of blue-uniformed anger. Once again, the man's manner altered, becoming deceptively soft, and he began to whisper in a beguiling tone. "Elizabeth, your mother is in Paris. Just as I said she was two days ago, when you ran away from me."

Sir William then turned toward Morehouse and the others, trying to elicit sympathy. "Chief Inspector, if you must know, I was boarding the S.S. *Plymouth*, bound for Calais, when I looked away—just for a moment—and this one ran off. I sent my man to find her, but Elizabeth is like a little snake in a crowd, and she eluded us both. It was only because my valet learnt of a child being held for questioning at your station house that we came here at all. I showed her photograph to this officer," he said, looking toward Taggart, "and he agreed that it resembled the child you had taken in. Now, Elizabeth," he continued, looking at the girl, "you are my wife's daughter, which makes you my stepchild, and legally, I may take you. Prepare now to leave this place, and we shall meet your mother in Paris in three days. She is terribly worried about you."

St. Clair glared at Sir William. "We will not release Elizabeth, if that is her name, without more than that! Come, little one, let's go up to Mr. Morehouse's office, shall we? I think he has some sweets in his desk drawer."

Morehouse nodded, and St. Clair carried her up the steep staircase and out of Sir William's line of sight. Once inside the office, Charles shut the door and took her on his knee. "Is your name Elizabeth?"

The girl nodded slowly. "Yes. It is. I remember now. And I know that man. He did marry my mother, but she is not in Paris, Captain. She is dead. I remember that, too—sort of. It's like a dream, you know? A terrifying, awful nightmare. William murdered her! I saw him do it! He put his hands 'round her throat, and she cried out—falling, falling into…into something. I cannot remember all, but I did see it, Captain, I did! I saw it! But…there was…more, and someone else, I think. The animal…with great, sharp teeth, and… oh, why is it so hard to remember?" she continued, tears streaming down her cheeks. "I have a very good memory, usually," she whispered, choking on the last word. "Would you find Paul for me? He will know what to do."

St. Clair wanted to shoot the man below, and he expected he'd one day have the chance considering the man's temperament. "Paul is your cousin. Is that right? Elizabeth, do you remember anything more about Paul yet? I shall find him for you if you can just tell me more about him."

"Beth," she said softly. "My family always calls me Beth."

Tears played at his eyes, and he wondered how anyone could hurt such a precious child. "Beth it is then. And you must call me Charles, all right?"

"Captain Nemo," she said, wiping the tear from his face. "You're my lonely Captain, and I shall always be your friend, so you won't be lonely or sad." She sighed, playing with a lock of his dark hair. "You have very nice eyes, Captain. Honest eyes. You're very kind, and I shall never forget you. My cousin will want to thank you, too. His name is James Paul Ian Stuart, and he is the Viscount Marlbury. His father is my uncle, the Earl of Aubrey."

Arthur France, who had quietly entered and now stood inside the office doorway, whistled as his eyes grew round. "Blimey, sir! An earl! Just who is this little girl?"

CHAPTER THREE

It was nearly three hours later when Paul Stuart, 5th Viscount Marlbury and only surviving son of the 11th Earl of Aubrey arrived at the Whitechapel station house to collect his young cousin. The viscount apologised to St. Clair for not arriving sooner, explaining that he'd been in Oxford when the message arrived at Aubrey House, and it had taken some time to make travel arrangements and contact the rest of Beth's family.

Marlbury was a polar opposite in disposition to the pretender stepfather who had earlier tried to remove the girl from St. Clair's care. Stuart stood about the same height as St. Clair, several inches over six feet. He had a muscular build, laughing blue eyes, and shoulder length chestnut hair that danced as he moved. It was clear from the moment he arrived that he loved the child dearly, and that she in turn loved and trusted him.

For their part, St. Clair and Morehouse not only needed to deliver the girl into safe and proper hands, but they also had a murder to solve. They had been unable to charge Sir William with any crime, based solely on the word of a young girl known to have suffered a concussion, so the angry gentleman had disappeared as mysteriously as he had appeared, leaving no trace for the police to follow.

Sitting now with the viscount in Morehouse's office, St. Clair sought answers whilst Elizabeth enjoyed lemonade and sandwiches with PC France in another room.

"You found her like that? Torn apart like some animal and then dumped onto your streets?" the viscount asked.

"I fear we did, Lord Marlbury. A local woman came upon her— the dead woman, I mean. Your Cousin Elizabeth lay unconscious nearby. You recognised the victim then?"

Tears rolled down his honest, open face, and the viscount wiped at them as he remembered the savaged body—literally torn into pieces—that he'd been shown in the police morgue. "God help her! Patricia was so beautiful in life, Inspector. Nothing like what you found. Nothing. And Beth says she saw him do it? So help me, if Trent did that—which would not surprise me in the least—then I shall drag him from here to Scotland and hang him myself!"

"You will have many honest officers with you, my lord. But we must know our victim's name. You called her Patricia. Is the girl her daughter? Beth is your cousin, correct?"

He nodded, regaining his composure. "She is, and I am proud to call her such. Beth's full name for your records, Inspector, is Elizabeth Georgianna Regina Stuart. Her mother, who was once beautiful and will now be remembered only as the pitiable victim in your morgue is, no...I fear, that she *was* Patricia Regina Charlotte Linnhe Stuart. Trish married my cousin Connor Stuart, who died two and a half years ago, following a hunting accident. I say accident, because I have no proof otherwise, but if I did, I would add it to my list of accusations against the scoundrel who came here claiming his right to take Beth with him. Trent's only interest in my cousin is mercenary, as it ever was, but Patricia did not always make the wisest choices. She will be much mourned and sorely missed."

Charles admired the young Scottish nobleman, and he suspected that every word he'd said would be fulfilled should Sir William ever cross the viscount's path. "Beth has asked for you many times," St. Clair told him. "My Paul, she would say, as if somehow you belong to her alone."

The viscount laughed, fond memories teasing at the corners of his bright eyes. "And so I do. It's a long story that I will gladly tell you one day, Inspector. You've shown true colours in your care for her. Beth told me how you protected her. If ever there is anything I or my family might do for you, it is but for you to ask it. My Uncle James is meeting us at Drummond House when he arrives. I hope you will come by there tomorrow evening to meet him."

"Drummond House? Your uncle is the Duke of Drummond?" St. Clair asked, imagining what his wife's family might make of this moment. A viscount inviting a lowly police detective to a duke's London house!

"He is, and he is also Elizabeth's grandfather. Uncle James will want to thank you in person, I know it. And my father will also be there. You might have guessed it, Inspector St. Clair, Elizabeth is our most cherished gift, and we are but her guardians—and now you have joined that happy club!"

"Thank you, sir. I consider that an honour. Beth's surname is Stuart, you say? We noticed that monogram in her clothing said *E.*, which I assume stands for Elizabeth, but the other name written there was *Anjou*. May I ask if that is the name of a clothing maker?"

"It is her title," Marlbury replied. "Beth is the Marchioness of Anjou."

"Her title?" St. Clair echoed, flabbergasted. "Elizabeth is a marchioness?"

"She is that and more. Much more," Marlbury replied, pulling on his cloak. "The Anjou marquessate is a *suo jure* title, and Beth has used it as her courtesy title since birth. But, now that her mother is dead, Elizabeth will inherit that title as well. Patricia was Duchess of Branham in her own right, and now it will pass to her only child. It is the sole remaining *suo jure* ducal title in England. Does it now begin to make sense, Inspector? Trent cares nothing for Beth. Only for her titles and inheritance. The Branham estate is considerable."

"It does make sense, my lord," the detective answered thoughtfully. "I would speak to you more about this, at your convenience, of course. I'm sure you wish to take your cousin home."

The viscount nodded. "Yes, I do. Again, Inspector St. Clair, thank you many times over for keeping Elizabeth safe. You are her true hero today. Her knight errant."

St. Clair smiled. "And she is a dazzling damsel, Lord Marlbury. And she has forever won my heart."

"Well said," Marlbury agreed. "Beth wins the hearts of all who meet her. Ah, but she is amazing for one who has not quite seen eleven years, is she not?"

"Eleven? I would have said less considering her small stature, but her vocabulary and reading skills told me that could not be."

Paul glanced at the girl waiting for him on the other side of the leaded window that overlooked the station's main police lounge. "Well, she is nearly eleven, but you must call her petite. Never say she is 'small'. She will never let you forget it. Now, I must take Beth to her true family. Please, come to Drummond House tomorrow evening for supper. And bring your dear wife as well. We shall welcome you both like family!"

CHAPTER FOUR

Drummond House was a sprawling, three-storey ducal estate near the western edge of Westminster. The house and grounds covered just over sixty acres, which included a mews, formal gardens, and a recently installed 'glass house' for growing year-round fruits and vegetables. The mews was a collection of six stables and two carriage houses, each with living quarters above for groomsmen plus tack storage. In addition to the primary staff of a butler, underbutler, housekeeper, cook, footmen, and a variety of maids, the estate employed half a dozen gardeners, two drivers, a farrier, and a blacksmith.

As their hansom pulled into the long gravel drive, Charles St. Clair's wife took his arm and whispered excitedly, "It's like I've always dreamt!"

"I'm glad, Amelia. And I am sorry for my harsh words at our home yesterday," he said, taking her hand and kissing it. "It was unkind of me. And thoughtless."

"Think nothing of it, Charles," she said sweetly.

In truth, St. Clair still felt his wife's attitude had been heartless, but he had no wish to hurt her further. He had, in fact, done all he could in the past twenty-four hours to make up for his outburst. In those same twenty-four hours, Amelia St. Clair had transformed from a defiant harpy into a compliant kitten, purring now as she accompanied her policeman husband into the grand mansion's front entry.

St. Clair had never dreamt about the rarified life of the landed gentry, but he knew his wife had done so nearly every waking moment of her life, so he welcomed this chance to fulfil her dreams, especially if it helped to restore calm in his household. The detective wore his best Sunday suit, and Amelia had borrowed her mother's jewels and a gown of cornflower blue silk from her eldest sister for the evening. The couple now entered the enormous foyer like a pair of ducks in a swan pond.

"Inspector and Mrs. St. Clair, my lords," the butler announced, once he'd led the couple into a large salon near the southwest side of the enormous mansion. The gleaming paneled walls bore dozens of paintings from centuries past, visages of Scottish dukes reaching back to the 1400s, many whose strong lines and forms of face bore striking similarities to James, Duke of Drummond and his kind-hearted nephew, Paul Stuart.

The latter rose to greet the St. Clairs and offer introductions. "Inspector, it is so very good to see you again," he said warmly, shaking the detective's hand. "Mrs. St. Clair, I am Paul Stuart, and we are honoured by your presence. Thank you for helping to keep our Elizabeth safe."

Amelia curtseyed and let the viscount kiss her gloved hand, not bothering to mention that her welcome to his cousin had been far less than courteous.

"Inspector and Mrs. St. Clair, allow me to introduce my father, Robert Stuart, the 11ᵗʰ Earl of Aubrey, who has forgotten more about politics than I shall ever learn."

The earl bowed as he kissed her hand, and Amelia fairly blushed as Aubrey's eyes met hers. "Charmed," he whispered. He then shook St. Clair's hand, his grip firm. "Inspector, it is a genuine delight to make your acquaintance. I feel as if I know you already. Our Beth has not ceased to speak of you both."

Charles smiled, wondering just how the little duchess had described her encounters in Whitechapel, particularly her treatment at his wife's hands. "You are too kind, sir," he managed. "Though our time with your niece was brief, she made an indelible mark on both our hearts."

Aubrey's son cleared his throat as he tapped the detective on the shoulder. "Beth does that with everyone, Inspector. Now, if I may," he continued, leading the couple to a man near to the earl's age, who wore a grin as wide as his entire face. "This is my most unique and worthy uncle, James Stuart, 10ᵗʰ Duke of Drummond, who is perhaps, the most notable and handsome of all ten to hear him tell it. One day, I expect his exploits and my father's will find publication in some learned history book, but even such a massive tome could never contain all the truths regarding their remarkable service to our country, and of course to our little Beth."

"A pleasure, son. A true pleasure!" Drummond said as he shook St. Clair's hand, and he also kissed the hand of his wife, who suppressed bashful blushes as she curtseyed, hoping later to recall every word and gesture to regale her parents and sisters until all were green with envy.

Lord Aubrey was a tall and magnificently handsome man of sixty-five and the more subdued of the two elder statesmen, who had served in numerous positions in the Foreign Office as well as in the House of Lords. Charles recognised him at once, for he'd often seen the earl's photograph appearing alongside timely quotes in the city's leading newspapers as an authority on finance and world politics. He appeared far friendlier than Charles would have imagined.

"Welcome, Inspector," the earl said with a wide smile. "Since our arrival here this morning, Elizabeth has not ceased to speak of you both, and she asks after a Mrs. Wilsham—I hope I remember the name correctly. Beth says that we must have her to our home to bake cakes for her."

"You're very kind, Lord Aubrey," St. Clair replied. "Mrs. Wilsham would, I am sure, bake your niece all the cakes she should ever desire. We are honoured that you would mention it."

"My cousin is Sir Albert Wendaway, Lord Aubrey," Amelia said, and though he'd felt certain his wife would bring up her layabout cousin, Charles dearly wished she had not.

The duke, however, eased the gaffe without so much as a wrinkle. "Ah, yes, I know this young man. A fine fellow," he lied, with a wink to Charles, whose blue eyes openly expressed his undying gratitude for the duke's thoughtfulness. "You must have him look me up next time he's in Glasgow," Drummond continued, sending Amelia into shower of giggles and six shades of rosy blushes.

The duke was a very young sixty and stood a few inches shorter than his nephew, and where the viscount was clean-shaven, Drummond wore a black moustache salted with grey, and his hair was close-cropped and neat. He seemed a man of high contrasts: a sense of refinement mingled with the mirth of a man without a care. His tanned face revealed a love of the outdoors, and he laughed with abandon whenever a joke was told. His dark eyes, however, sparkled with keen insight and high intelligence like those of his grand-daughter Elizabeth. Clearly, the young duchess had inherited her Scottish relative's best qualities.

"Inspector," the duke continued to Charles with a massive grin crossing his broad face, "you are the hero of the hour to us! Elizabeth cannot stop talking of you and your kindness to her. I tell you, that if we were not so much in grief over the loss of her dear mother, we'd be hosting a parade in your honour, my friend. I hope you will always consider yourself welcome under this roof. And you must come to Scotland! London's fine if you want to play about in parlours with dancing ladies, but if you want to hunt and fish, there's no place like Glasgow!"

"You give me too much credit, sir," St. Clair objected, realising at once, as she squeezed his hand, that his wife loved the attention and praise, mostly for herself, for she hadn't even considered the dangers her husband had faced in standing up to Sir William; dangers that may yet unfold. "Your nephew, perhaps, exaggerates just a bit, but I appreciate your kindness nonetheless."

"Paul never exaggerates," came a refined voice from the doorway to the salon. All turned to see the young girl at the centre of their gathering. No longer wearing bloodied, torn, or borrowed clothing, her hair matted with straw and blood, her face slack with shock, this Elizabeth, the newly proclaimed Duchess of Branham, was arrayed in a royal blue velvet dress with a rose-coloured sash, and her dark eyes and gleaming black hair made her look as if she were a princess of the realm. Her face, ashen and sad during the past day's nightmare, now glowed with serenity; her skin, more cream than white—her cheeks pale pink with an adolescent blush.

"Paul speaks only truth, as do you, Inspector. He is my darling cousin, but you are my Captain Nemo," she said with a bright smile that lit up the room. "And I shall ever be in your debt."

St. Clair stepped toward her, bending down to one knee as he kissed her small hand. "It is I who am in your debt, Your Grace. Your gentle manner and bright eyes have forever lightened my heart. I am grateful to our Saviour for protecting you and returning you to your rightful family."

Elizabeth's eyes looked into his, and she cupped his chin with her small hand. "And I thank Him for sending you to my aid, Captain. You served as His protective hand when I needed it most. I shall never forget you for that. Nor shall I ever forget the kindness shown me by all the brave men at your police station. And I pray that tonight begins a long and close friendship twixt our family and yours."

St. Clair stood and bowed, gallantly. Amelia stepped forward next, eager to greet and be greeted by the child she had so scorned the previous day, but rather than remind her former hostess of this slight, Elizabeth took Amelia's hand and walked her to the centre of the room. "Uncle Robert," she said, calling Lord Aubrey by his Christian name, "Paul, Grandfather, we all must cherish our time with the St. Clairs. And we must always be their friends, as they have been friend to me."

"Hear, hear!" the Stuart men said in concert.

Elizabeth looked up at Amelia and smiled. Amelia smiled in return, convinced that the girl had simply forgotten or not noticed any unkindness whilst in her home. Elizabeth, for her part, felt sorry for the inspector's wife, for she seemed very unhappy, and the little duchess had determined to do her best to bring a smile to the woman's lips.

As canapés were served by two liveried footmen, Beth sat down beside the duke, talking now with him and Amelia St. Clair, whilst the young inspector spoke quietly with Lord Aubrey and his son in another corner of the enormous drawing room.

"We can never thank you enough for keeping her safe," Aubrey said. "James and I feared the worst when Paul wired us in Scotland. Believe me when I tell you, Inspector, this man Trent is an evil one. Do you think you'll be able to arrest him, assuming he shows his face again in London?"

"I hope to," St. Clair replied. "Sir, Beth—the duchess, I mean— she told me that she saw a man in a park. She was unable to tell me which park she meant, but she thought its name had the word Queen in it. Do you know which park this might be?"

Paul nodded and leaned in to answer. "The Branham estate here in Westminster is called Queen Anne House, Inspector. There is a sizeable, private park behind that beautiful home, and Beth often walks or rides there whenever she is in London. She was last here in January, two months past. Her mother came here for a friend's wedding, I believe. Is that right, Father?"

The earl nodded. "So Patricia said, but I know of no one in her circles who married in January. I suspect that she had other business in London," he finished mysteriously.

The viscount showed surprise. "Really?" His father's severe glance indicated that he would say nothing further to enlighten his son, so the young nobleman continued. "Inspector, I was working in Paris until last week, so I fear I can only speculate, which would do little to help solve Patricia's murder. I wonder if Elizabeth recalls any more regarding this man in the park, now that she's recovered some of her memory. Father, do we dare ask her?"

Robert Stuart's light blue eyes narrowed as he considered this question for several moments. Before replying, he smiled at his niece, who had turned to wave happily to the trio of men. "She seems content, does she not?" he noted. "So brave yet so very innocent. Paul, to your question, it may be best to give Beth some time to reconcile all that has happened before we subject her to interrogation."

"Yes, Father, but dare we risk losing an opportunity? If Elizabeth wants to discuss this matter, then..."

"Then, you want to help her. Is that it, son?" the earl replied. "She might recall more, now that she's around those she loves and trusts—not that she did not trust you, Inspector. Indeed, Elizabeth has told all of us, many times, how much you protected her," he explained, "but I wonder if we dare risk it. I worry about her mind, you see. She is still in shock over the death of her mother. I'm not sure the reality of all this has truly sunk in, if you get my meaning."

St. Clair sipped a glass of white wine, his gaze upon the young duchess. "She is remarkably brave, my lords. Please, I hope you will forgive me for making our conversation centre on police matters, but I wish only to find the man who murdered Elizabeth's mother. I cannot explain it, but she—Beth, I mean—well, she has found a permanent place in my heart, and I would seek justice for her and for her mother, if I am able."

"Your affections and persistent spirit do you credit, Inspector," Aubrey replied, "but our Beth has suffered memory lapses before, and when she does, we've found the buried events are, more often than not, harmful to her mind. Consequently, we have learnt to tread carefully when questioning her."

"Yes, I think I understand, sir, but what if this man she mentioned is involved in the murder, or something far worse? Elizabeth spoke of an animal that terrified her."

"An animal?" the younger Stuart asked, his face becoming intense and worried. "Did she say what kind of animal?"

"No, I do not think she did, but when I pressed her on it, she—well, sir, she had a seizure of some kind."

Suddenly, Lord Aubrey stood. "Let us move this conversation outdoors. It's a somewhat chilly evening, but I would not risk Beth's overhearing us, Inspector."

They left the magnificent drawing room and followed the taciturn butler through the main doors and onto a spacious, south-facing, covered portico, that overlooked a dense line of oak and ash trees.

Beyond the treeline, through the main gates to the estate, Charles could see the northern edge of St. James's Park. There, on the rolling green, the gaslights and round moon shone upon couples who walked together despite the chilly evening. The wooden benches were filled with primly attired governesses, laughing children, deal-making businessmen, prostitutes, peddlers, politicians, and a wide variety of London's diverse humanity—most with money, but a few seeking to beg enough for a night's bed and a bit of breakfast come morning.

"Please, Inspector, sit," the earl said, his blue eyes fixed on movement near the dark trees. "Paul, is that one of your men near the edge of the park?"

Marlbury's sharp eyes scanned the area. "No, Father. I've no one stationed in St. James now. Forgive us, Inspector, you must wonder what we mean. Like my father, I also work for the Foreign Office, and I've only just returned from a difficult, field assignment in Paris. I think my father worries that I'm being followed."

"An old habit," the earl said, his eyes continuing to assess the shadowy figure beyond the trees. "Mr. St. Clair, my niece is somewhat fragile when it comes to certain memories. I'd spare her further injury, if I could. You say she suffered a seizure whilst in your care?"

"That is the only way I know to describe it, my lord. I had asked her about the animal, and I fear I persisted, for I wanted to unmask her mother's murderer. You see, I'd feared that your niece might have been victim to a procurement operation. One that specialises in the young."

Paul's clear blue eyes flashed angrily. "Merciful heavens! Is it possible Trent planned to sell her? If so, I shall find that miserable excuse for a man now and save the queen's hangman a day's work!"

The earl's handsome features remained calm, and the policeman could see years of experience and wisdom written in small creases along his face as well as in two, old linear scars that paralleled his jawline, which St. Clair surmised to have been caused by a very sharp knife. He wondered just what 'political' activities might have left such permanent imprints on a peer of the realm.

"Sit down, Paul," the earl said gently, a strong, reassuring hand touching that of his son. "It will help no one if you allow emotion to define your actions. The inspector is correct to suspect such, for that sort of foul organisation is all too common, Paul, as you surely know. Inspector, my niece has suffered from seizures before, but it has been more than two years since her last episode. This man in Queen Anne Park. Did Beth describe him?"

"She said he spoke with a funny accent. That he frightened her and wrote in a book. I assumed him part of such an operation, and that he made notes regarding her appearance."

"Ah. That would make sense, but the description provides very little to go on," the older man replied.

St. Clair suddenly brightened. "But wait! Beth also told me something else about this man. I hesitate to admit this, sir, but I fell asleep whilst she napped, and when I awoke, your niece had disappeared. I rushed out to find her, and she was several blocks from my home in a public house."

"What? You found her in a pub?" the viscount asked. "Why on earth would she go there?"

"In truth, I wish now I'd taken more time to speak with her about it, but at that moment, I was so relieved to find her well and unharmed that my policeman's senses failed me. She did tell me, however, that she'd followed a man who looked like the one in the park. It turned out that the man she followed was the publican."

Aubrey broke into a wide smile, and he began to laugh. "So she decided to investigate on her own whilst you slept? How like our Beth! Inspector, when you get to know our little duchess better, you will realise that she can be somewhat difficult to control. She is highly intelligent and curious, but also somewhat headstrong. Do not blame yourself for her rash behaviour. Only praise the Lord for keeping her in His care whilst she escaped yours."

St. Clair sighed. "That is kind of you, sir, but Whitechapel is neither Westminster, nor is it Scotland. Rash behaviour there may lead to disasters beyond imagining."

"True. True, but even country life has dangers beyond your imagining, Inspector. One day, you will understand, but for now, would you describe this publican for us? Perhaps, my son and I have seen a man similar."

"He is tall. Quite tall, actually," St. Clair said. "I am six-foot-three, and John's easily two or three inches taller than I. He's muscular as well. He once boxed in Manchester, but one too many punches left him rather weak in limb, so he took over his father's pub."

"Hair colour?" Paul Stuart asked.

"Dark. Like mine, but long. Similar to the length you wear your own, Lord Marlbury. Just at the shoulder. Does this strike as at all familiar?"

"No, I fear that it does not," Aubrey said. "Inspector, Beth does not always have clear recall, as I'm sure you observed. Her concussion most likely caused her to suffer memory loss, but there might also be other factors at work. As I said, she is highly intelligent and kind and thoughtful and resourceful, but also very sensitive. And she has endured many hardships in her young life. I would know that William Trent can no longer reach her, if that can be made possible. How might we aid your investigation without further risking my niece?"

St. Clair watched the play of life in the park, thinking of the many dangers facing children in London, his fears for Elizabeth painting a dark picture. "I would not wish any harm to come to her, sir. She is a precious young lady. I can see why she is dear to you all."

Paul stood. "She is more precious than you can imagine, Inspector. Father, we should not remain out here long. Elizabeth will wonder why we linger. Her independent nature might bring her through those doors any moment, in fact. Shall we rejoin the others? Inspector, my father and I shall speak more of this with you tomorrow. At Leman Street."

The three men returned to the drawing room, and Charles walked in just as Elizabeth was reading an article from the latest edition of *Le Figaro* to Amelia. St. Clair winked as he entered, and the little duchess winked at her Captain in return and then continued to translate the difficult political articles for the woman who had scorned her claims at reading Jules Verne in the original language. Seeing her rescuer returned, the little duchess excused herself and approached the detective, who now sat near the window, alone.

"I take it that my uncle and cousin did not wish me to overhear your conversation, Captain," she said, sitting next to him on the sofa.

St. Clair smiled as he helped her to sit. "They were showing me the view from your grandfather's front portico. It's breathtaking. Your Grace, is that the park you told me about, or were you speaking of the one behind Queen Anne House?"

She paled slightly, and he instantly wished he'd said nothing. She leaned in close to whisper. "You promised to call me Beth," she reminded him.

The inspector smiled, noticing his wife's easy manner and laughter as she sat talking with the duke. "I did promise. Beth it is. I'm very sorry that my wife treated you so unfairly. She isn't a bad person, but she... Well, Amelia has been through much that has left her scarred and bitter."

The girl sighed. "Yes, I can see that. She has the same look my mother used to wear. It is strange that she is dead. I know that I should be weeping, but I find it difficult to do. I did love my mother, Captain, truly, I did—I do," she corrected, her eyes downcast. "The funeral will take place at Branham, of course."

"That is your family seat, correct? In Kent?"

She nodded. "Yes. Branham Hall is my home, when I'm not in London, that is. I'm not sure when it will all happen, though. There's to be a public service here in London first. The queen has sent her condolences and will likely come to the funeral."

"You know Her Majesty?" he asked, realising at once how naive the question sounded.

"Yes. She's a lovely person. Her grandson, Prince Albert Victor, is a friend of mine. He'll come, I know. In fact, I'm certain that hundreds of peers and royals and politicians will be there. I'd prefer it to be private, but then my grandfather is making all the arrangements. My Aunt Victoria's been ill, but she hopes to come." She paused, her brows pinching together as if something disturbed her. "Tell me, truly, how does your investigation affect her funeral? Will you need to—to keep her body whilst you look for her murderer? I've already told you that it is William. Do you need more than that?"

Charles knew that the police surgeon had not yet completed his work on the torn and bloodied corpse, but he had no wish to disclose too much. "Sadly, Beth, I fear the courts will not accept your testimony—not just because of your age, but because of your head injury."

She sighed. "I'd thought that might be the case."

"Beth, I shall do all within my power to see that Trent answers for his crimes. As to your mother's body, I imagine we'll need to keep it for a little while longer. My superior will be the one to decide when we might release her back to your family. Beth, I am so sorry for your loss. If I could reset time and change it for you, I would."

She gripped his hand and moved closer, setting her small head against his shoulder. "You are quite wonderful, Captain. Will you come to the funeral?"

"I will, if you wish it."

"I do. It would help me more than you could possibly imagine." She swallowed, as if forcing down dark thoughts. "I think that there is more I'm not remembering, and..."

"Do not try to stir up the memories, little one," he said, kissing her cheek. "Give your heart time to work through it all."

She turned to gaze out the window, her fingers gripping his. "You asked me about the park. It is the one behind our house. I saw the tall man there, but not just once. Many times. He would always wait until after my mother had gone, and then come over to talk to me. I remember more about him now, but much of it is still rather like a dream, Captain."

"And it is a dream that troubles you, is it not, little one?"

She smiled, relaxing a bit. "I like it when you call me that," she confessed, her dark eyes fixed on his. "It makes me feel protected and safe." Lord Aubrey had been watching them, and the young duchess offered him a slight smile. Apparently satisfied that his niece was in good hands, the earl returned to his conversation with his son. "Uncle Robert does not want you to ask me questions, does he?"

St. Clair had also noticed Aubrey's gaze. "He'd prefer you not remember experiences that frighten you. Is that wrong?"

"It is understandable," she countered. "Uncle Robert has been like a father to me since my own died—that is whenever my grandfather is away on business. Did I mention my father to you? I cannot recall."

"You did, though that memory seemed to trouble you."

She grew quiet for a moment, turning again toward the window that overlooked the front lawn. "I loved my father very much. More than... Well, more than I loved my mother. I'm not proud of that, but it is true. His death..." she began, but he noticed her lower lip tremble, and she blinked back tears. "His death broke my heart, Captain. But mother's death, well, it...forgive me, I'm not sure how to put it."

As she struggled for words, he marveled at her command of language and social rules. Most children in Whitechapel could barely read English at eleven, but this young lady spoke and read in several languages and behaved with the decorum of a woman twice her age.

"Beth, perhaps, you should not think about it just now. Your uncle believes you are still in shock, and I agree."

She wiped tears from her cheek and took his hand. "You are kind, Captain. Very kind, and I wish... That is, I hope that you will visit me now and again."

"I should enjoy that," he said honestly.

"Good. The man from the park," she began, and he could see that same, small tremble of her lower lip. "He whispered things to me, Captain. Strange things that made no sense. They still do not."

"Do you recall what he said?" he asked, noticing Lord Aubrey had begun again to look their way. "But then perhaps you'd best not think on that now."

"My uncle worries," she said, "but I want to speak of this. Somehow, telling you about it helps. The man spoke of children and kept repeating something about blood and history. And he took notes in a strange book, covered over with very odd symbols. I told you that he talks strangely, I think. Did I say that?"

"You did. I thought perhaps it was a foreign accent. Is it?"

"No. Not an accent. A language."

"French?"

"No, not French. Nor German. Nor Spanish. I'm still not fluent in Italian, but I would have recognised that easily. Though no longer spoken outside of some churches, I know enough Latin and Greek to have discerned those languages as well. I've learnt a few things in Russian, and I know how that language sounds. It may have been Russian, but I cannot say for sure."

Her breathing had accelerated, and St. Clair could tell that re-counting the tale brought her great distress. "But Beth, if he spoke in a language you do not speak, how is it you understood his words?"

She visibly shuddered. "I don't know, but I did understand them."

"Elizabeth, perhaps, you shouldn't think on it now."

She moved closer to his side, her hand on his. "Captain, you said you would always believe me."

"Yes, little one. I will always believe you."

Her hand began to tremble, and the lower lip quivered. "The man in the park. He is something quite different. Not like anyone on earth. He...he...is...*not human*. He is a..." she whispered, but a sudden interruption meant St. Clair would wait nearly ten years to hear the rest. The butler, a thin but kind looking man named Booth, had quietly entered the room to whisper to the duke.

"Everyone!" Drummond announced as he stood. "I'm told supper is served. Mrs. St. Clair, would you do me the honour?" he asked, giving his arm to Amelia, who fairly gushed as she accepted. Paul and Lord Aubrey followed.

Lastly, Charles St. Clair put out his hand toward Elizabeth and asked, "May I be your escort, Duchess?"

Beth's face had gone pale, but she smiled at him, the slight tremor in her lower lip slowly disappearing as she placed her hand into his. "I should very much like that, Captain," she said with all seriousness. "Forget what I said a moment ago. I'm sure it was all a dream."

He led her into the magnificent dining hall, her dainty arm through his, and he wondered just what it was she'd been about to say. The little duchess spoke no more of her memories that night, but over the years, the detective would learn the dark secrets behind Trent and the strange man from the park.

Little did St. Clair imagine how the years would play with this simple gathering of new friends. Nor could he foresee just how much Sir William Trent and *his* friends would influence policing in and around London, particularly in Whitechapel; the deaths to come, the horrors to arise, the terrible and even wonderful future in store, nor could he imagine that it would all proceed out of this moment: when he took the small, trusting hand of an eleven-year-old girl.

CHAPTER FIVE
2, October, 1888

Nearly ten years had passed for Charles St. Clair. Remaining friends with the Stuart clan, the St. Clairs—or Charles at least—met often with the Stuart men and attended numerous family events, including Elizabeth's birthday party each year in April until she turned fourteen. Two years later, the duchess left to live with her aunt in Paris. Paul and Charles continued to work together in pursuit of Sir William Trent, but the trail grew cold in early '86, and St. Clair received orders to discontinue the investigation by newly appointed police commissioner Sir Charles Warren.

Less than a year after the party at Drummond House, Amelia decided her marriage to Charles could no longer be sustained, and she decamped to Ireland with a cocaine addict named Harold Lowry, whom she had secretly been seeing for many months. Lowry had been a close gambling friend and accomplice to Amelia's baronet cousin, and once he perceived a shift in the harmony of the St. Clair marriage, the vulture Lowry had swept down upon his prey and conveyed Amelia to her doom in Dublin. Though still legally married to St. Clair, Amelia miscarried two of Lowry's children—both sons—the second in '85, and she died of a severe typhus infection in June of '86.

Despite all he'd endured after she'd left him, upon learning of his wife's death from the Dublin constabulary, Charles arranged for Amelia's body and those of her dead children to be returned to England and buried in a single grave in her parents' church cemetery in Marylebone. The detective then sailed to Dublin and tried to locate Lowry, but the degenerate gambler had fled Ireland the moment Amelia had died.

Robert Paul Ian Stuart III, 11th Earl of Aubrey passed away peacefully in his sleep seven years to the day following the Drummond House gathering, joining his beloved wife Abigail in a graveyard near their Glencoe castle, overlooking Loch Leven. Paul Stuart, who had now become the 12th Earl of Aubrey, continued a successful career in diplomacy, serving as special envoy to Paris and then Vienna on behalf of the Foreign Office. Many at Whitehall assumed the young Aubrey would eventually become Foreign Secretary, for his shrewd backroom negotiations and quick thinking had more than once saved England from making serious international blunders, but the energetic earl had no desire for public office. During his travels, Paul also served more secretively as an espionage agent, though most in Whitehall had no idea such was the earl's true mission when abroad. He'd used these excursions to continue his search for Sir William Trent, a man he still considered the most dangerous in all England.

Though his personal life had fallen into shambles, professionally, Charles St. Clair continued to climb the career ladder within the Criminal Investigation Department of the Metropolitan Police, progressing from Inspector underneath Morehouse to Chief Inspector in charge of H-Division and finally to Superintendent in charge of the entire east end. Operating now from Scotland Yard most days rather than Whitechapel, it was to this office, that he received a surprise letter, addressed to *Captain Nemo of the Yard, c/o Superintendent Charles St. Clair, Whitehall.* He smiled as he recalled the nickname from so long ago, noting the beautifully engraved notepaper that read 'Branham Hall, Kent'.

"Not another Ripper letter, I hope," teased his friend and fellow superintendent, George Haskell. "Seems like the public knows a sight lot more than even Abberline and Reid do. Jack! No more, I say. No more!"

St. Clair's nose caught a whiff of delicate perfume as he opened the letter. "I doubt it," he said happily. "Most Ripper letters don't come with such lovely scent upon them."

He shut his door, much to Haskell's chagrin, and took the letter to his desk, eager to see what it might say. It had been over four years since he'd seen or spoken to the duchess. Four long years of policing, politics, and policy-making. How had she changed? She had not written once during those years, so why write now?

He opened the letter.

30th September, 1888

My Dearest Captain,

Before I begin, let me express my most sincere apologies for the long silence. The last time I saw you was four years ago at my cousin's London home, and I may have seemed out of sorts. I assure you that you had nothing whatsoever to do with my mood—in fact, I was delighted to see you. I had other matters on my mind that day, but seeing you brought me more joy than you can possibly imagine. I pray that you will not hold my four-year silence against me. There is much behind that silence, and one day—when we are able to speak in person—I promise to explain it all. Believe me when I tell you that I have missed you, my Captain. Missed you very, very much.

I know from my Cousin Paul that the two of you have remained in touch, so he has no doubt informed you that I have spent much of the past four years in Paris with my Aunt Victoria. Tory is my grandfather's youngest sister, and she has accomplished what she tells me no school or tutor could have done; that is, she has turned me into a finished lady with proper respect for the system of noble houses in our fair land. In short, I have learnt to disregard all propriety in favour of doing whatever I deem is best!

I cannot tell you what a relief this has been to me, for I have no great desire to lead the life of a typical society woman, who exists only for 'the season', and spends each week looking for opportunities that best show off the latest Paris fashions—behaviour I find tiresome to say the least. Most men would probably find my attitude shocking, dear Captain, but I pray you do not, for I long to use my brain rather than my social position. My aunt admires that resolve, and she has actually encouraged it. I dearly love Aunt Victoria!

Now, my dear Captain, I also wish to say how very sorry I was to hear of your Amelia's passing. Paul kept this from me until very recently, for his own reasons I presume. Dear Paul has become rather secretive of late concerning many things; he oft repeats to me that 'it is for your protection, Beth'—and though this angers me just a bit, I love and respect him, so I forgive him this easily. I would have attended Amelia's funeral to support you, my dear friend, had I but known. She always struck me as a lonely woman in need of affirmation from others, a trait my own dear mother shared with her. I pray both women are now at peace.

And so it is to my mother that I come at last. It was her tragic end that brought me to your door nearly ten years ago, and it is that very same kind of tragedy that now echoes throughout the streets of your beloved Whitechapel. The Paris newspapers have written of little else since late August, but there were stories of crimes beginning as early as December last, which must concern you greatly. I expect your desk is stacked with letters and witness reports, each attesting to a singular truth, but what I have to tell you—what I must tell you—would, if it were known to the public, shake the very foundations of England, and it would then echo throughout the entire realm of Christendom.

Therefore, as you must now suspect, I shall say nothing of it in this letter. This missive serves only as a means (I pray) to bring you once again to my side, dear Captain! There is more danger in my world now than ever before, and I would again claim your protective hand.

Beginning tomorrow, I shall be in residence in London until three weeks before Christmas, when I must return to Kent to celebrate with our staff and the wonderful farmers and shepherds who tend our lands. Would it be possible to meet with you soon, perhaps, even this week?

You may send word to me at Queen Anne House, Westminster.

Until then, I shall remain ever and always…

Your very own,
Elizabeth

As Charles read the final words, he suddenly realised he could not hear his heart—he had stopped breathing, and his face had grown warm. 'Your very own', she had signed it. What might that simple line imply? Dare he imagine such a thing?

"So, is it another crank letter about old Jack?" his friend asked, shutting the door behind him as he entered.

Charles turned, completely startled. He had been so absorbed by the extraordinary letter that he'd not heard the door open. "Wh— what?" he stammered, hastily returning the letter to its envelope. "No—I mean, yes. No. Actually, no. It's from an old friend, who mentions the Ripper murders in passing. No clues, no suggestions. None. So, I... Well, I'd best be off to Leman Street. Reid's expecting me for a late morning chat about the Eddowes and Stride cases. If anyone asks, I shall be out for the remainder of the day."

Taking the letter with him, Charles then left to find a hansom.

The old city of Westminster had originally grown up as a service area for the well-known abbey and eventually the Palace of Westminster. Formerly known as Thorney Island, an eyot, which had once risen above the old Tyburn River where it met the Thames, the area had eventually developed into a palatial estate with surrounding parks, administration buildings, and of course Buckingham Palace. With so many ancient buildings now used by government, including the recently rebuilt Palace of Westminster, now called Parliament, the old city had become a common equivalent to English government, law, and all its entails.

Queen Anne House had been designed and completed in 1625 by Inigo Jones in his signature 'Palladian' style by order of James I, also known to the Scots and to the Drummond and Aubrey houses as James VI. The king had built the palace for his Danish bride, Anne of Denmark, and it was subsequently passed to Charles I and later to James II, who then gifted the magnificent mansion to Anne Hyde before their official marriage but in honour of their 'secret' nuptials after the lady had fallen pregnant with the king's child. Queen Anne, the king's second daughter, eventually gifted the palace to her child-hood friend and Lady of the Robes, Katherine du Bonnier Linnhe, Duchess of Branham, who proclaimed that the house would always bear the name of her friend and benefactor at court: Queen Anne.

More a palace than a London ducal estate, the home was cross-shaped and featured a large, rectangular main section, two extensive wings, and three full storeys with a ballroom comprising the northern half of the main section's second floor. Servant quarters and storage rooms were located just above the ballroom, making it rather noisy for any charmaid or footman hoping to catch a good night's rest during the raucous parties once given by the king. The south entrance was central, formal, and imposing, reaching upward throughout the entire height of the building and ending at the roofline in a dazzling glass dome that spanned the length of the foyer and bathed the rich Roman tiles below in sunshine during the morning and permitted stargazing at night.

Jones had experimented with cantilevered, spiral design by constructing a matched pair of graceful staircases that rose up in gentle curves throughout the centre of the main section, leading up to an expansive balcony landing and thence into the apartments of each wing as well as the wide, central ballroom staircase. Frescoes and elaborate brushwork decorated all the walls and coffered ceilings throughout, featuring Bible scenes and famous mythologies, save for one room: an elegant two-storey private library in the far, northwest corner of the house, which held mahogany shelving from floor to ceiling, and was crammed to bursting with Shakespeare folios, original manuscripts by Dee and Bacon, first editions from Pepys to Dickens, and one entire section specializing in ancient cartographies.

Standing now in this imposing library, Charles St. Clair thought of the adolescent girl who read out the works on his meagre bookshelf, and he laughed. "And Amelia actually wondered if you could truly read," he whispered to himself.

"Looking for your book, Captain?" a sweet voice asked from a doorway to his right. The entrance had been hidden, formed from a reference shelf, and it now provided a frame for a woman more beautiful, more radiant than Charles had ever imagined she would become.

He held his breath and allowed his eyes to sweep over her. She had retained her petite form, but grown round in all the correct places. He guessed her height to be a few inches beyond five feet— though he observed that she wore one inch heels, peeking just from beneath the hem of her skirts. Rather than wearing the tight chignons and fussy upsweeps now favoured by high society women, Beth's raven hair was arranged in chic waves that cascaded down her back, leaving her exquisite ears to act as gateways to a heart-shaped face. And oh what a face! Unlike the garish white preferred by many noble women, hers was a naturally sweet combination of cream and pale rose. Her brown eyes, always dark and mysterious even as a child, now held a light in them that both froze and warmed his heart. Her mouth was like a kiss of peaches, and she stared at him now, with that sweet mouth opening into a wide, precocious smile.

"My, but you have...grown up," was the best he could manage, once he'd begun again to breathe.

Elizabeth laughed—*how musical it is, like angelic bells*, he thought—and she closed the hidden door behind her. "I should hope I have, Captain. Or perhaps, it is best I call you Charles now. Would that be all right? Not impertinent, I hope."

He took a deep breath and actually had to will his heart to slow. "I'd be pleased if you would, Your Grace," he managed to say with feigned ease.

She took a step toward him. He could smell her scent now, a mixture of vanilla and raspberries; simple, natural, and refreshingly delightful. "And it would please me if you would call me Beth, as you once did," she told him.

That beating again—a rush inside his ears. *This is madness!* he reminded his heart. *Stop it now! She is a duchess, and you are but a common policeman!*

"Beth, it is then," he replied evenly.

She smiled again, and his heart urged surrender.

"Please, sit down, Charles. We've much to catch up on, but more to the point, I've much to tell you."

He followed her to a matched set of overstuffed, embroidered sofas, installed by Elizabeth's grandfather, Duke George, for the reading comfort of his daughter Patricia. Though the seating was plush and the room filled with fresh air from a quartet of large, open windows that overlooked the west and north gardens, St. Clair had never felt so ill at ease. He had come here expecting to rekindle a friendship, and he feared now that something far more intimate was igniting in his soul.

Not far from Queen Anne House, in a private smoking room on Pall Mall Street, Paul Stuart held his own secret meeting. The earl sat in a red, tufted-leather, wingback chair, thoughtfully sipping a glass of brandy as he received his companion's report.

"We believe, Lord Aubrey, that the man left Russia on the sixth of July, but that is not certain. There is scant evidence that he departed St. Petersburg much earlier, but we cannot verify it. However, my operatives have firmly put him in Belgium in August, so beginning with that, we may track his movements."

Paul gazed into the fire, his thoughts fixed on something—or someone unseen. "And those are?"

The man thumbed through a collection of reports, reading out a series of notations he'd made on each. "Third of August, Brussels: seen in a rooming house going by the name of Prosser. An odd choice for Trent, don't you think?"

Paul thought now of Elizabeth, of protecting her, and the mental picture of her mother's mutilated corpse was ever in his mind. "I expect the unexpected when it comes to Sir William, if that is even that foul man's true name. Go on, Thomas."

The man pushed his spectacles up higher on his thick nose and nodded. "Yes. Yes, I know and share your concerns, Lord Aubrey. Next, on the seventh of August, he met with two men, both American. They exchanged envelopes, which we believe contained bearer bonds, for Trent met the following morning with a financial agent—one Reginald Anders, someone known to us already."

Paul had a bad feeling. This dark foreboding had settled into his heart long before, only it now grew stronger with each passing moment. "Anders is another member—low level, but still not without influence. He is toady to Lord Hemsfield, I believe. The man the Italian branch calls 'the banker'."

"So he is, sir," the man agreed. "I'll see to it that Sir Percy meets with his agents to keep track of the Roman branch. Hemsfield has since left Ireland for sunnier climes, I'm told."

Paul set down his brandy and leaned forward, his chair creaking, and the fire crackled as if in response. "Left Ireland? When?"

Sir Thomas Galton, Paul's childhood friend and closest ally, flipped back several pages and read out, "The eighth of August as near as we can pinpoint, when his name appears on a passenger list for the SS *Chelsey* that departed Dublin, bound for Morocco—Casablanca to be precise. Met with two men, identities unknown, but we are having them followed, and I expect a report within the week. Hemsfield departed Casablanca after seven days, sailed in a private yacht which we believe is owned by our known personage from Spain, Don Miguel de Cortez. Arrived in Rome eight days later, staying at home of Roberto Almardo, arms dealer and exporter of certain women; seen meeting with three known men from Berlin in private salon behind the opera house—I believe you can guess their names, sir—and then sailed to France, residing in Paris at a villa owned by de Cortez. Hemsfield and Sir William met up in Calais, ten days ago."

Paul's perfect memory stored each location and detail, sifting through other such mental files for connexions, clues. "Did anyone report a meeting with Sandoval?"

Galton's eyes rounded behind his reading lenses, growing larger each second. "Good Heavens! I hadn't even... Wait, let me see," he stammered, flipping back to a telegram he'd received from their Paris office. "Deniau says he heard someone mention a tall man with a limp and wearing a bright waistcoat. Could be him. No one locally could confirm his identity, but André is convinced this man was following him."

Paul wanted to smash the snifter into the wall, but instead he choked down the negative emotions, mastering his natural tendency toward rage when unpleasant surprises popped up. Spying often brought him disturbing news, and he knew anger would only cloud his reason. Elizabeth's continued safety required him to keep his wits at all times.

"I want André to give us all he knows about this man," he told Galton. "No matter how small the detail, how insignificant it may seem. How he spends his money, whom he sees, what he's wearing—everything! Also, tell me if he is observed taking notes in a book."

"Yes, sir. I understand."

"And, Thomas, I want a report in three days. So, now, let us get back to Trent. Did he leave Calais? Did he land in England?"

Sir Thomas bit his lower lip, a sign Paul knew meant the answer would not please him. "We lost him after Calais, sir," he said softly, his head lowering. "But, before you despair, let me tell you that our people saw Trent board the *Louisa Maria* in Calais, a mail steamer which docks in Gravesend, but also continues up the Thames and delivers to London. She has not yet arrived, and Lloyds believes the ship lost in the storm that ravaged the channel last week."

Paul took a moment to process this, his mind weighing all possibilities. "Are you certain he boarded the steamer?"

Galton nodded. "My man is convinced of it. William Trent is a singular looking man. He is hard to miss, even in a dense crowd of hauliers and stevedores."

The earl rose, adjusted his waistcoat, and then glanced at his pocket watch, inherited from his father and decorated with the Aubrey crest. "Have your men keep watch at every dock and train station in London and Kent. I want to know immediately if he is seen within a day's ride of Branham Hall or Queen Anne House. Understood?"

"We will not fail you, my friend," he promised, clutching the earl's forearm. "We've been together since Eton, you and I, and I'll not permit any harm to befall the woman you love. She is dear to us all now—each of us who has taken an oath to protect her and the secret. Redwing will fail! With the Good Lord's strength, we shall make it so!"

Paul smiled at last, a weary, hesitant smile, but a smile nonetheless. "You are a true friend, Thomas. Forgive my impatience. These murders in Whitechapel trouble me, and they trouble our dear one to the extent that she has returned to England six months early."

"The duchess is at Branham?" Sir Thomas asked, concern written across his face.

"She is in London, Thomas, so you and I must do all we may to keep her safe. She's asked me to tea tomorrow, and I hope she will accompany me to the theatre this Friday. I've some minor business to conduct at the Lyceum, and I'm sure Elizabeth will enjoy seeing an English play after enduring so many French atrocities."

"I'm sure she will, my friend. Shall I put men to watch Queen Anne?"

"I've already taken care of that, Thomas. Now, I must meet with Lord Pembroke. Thank you for all you do on Beth's behalf. And on mine."

The two friends parted, each going out a separate exit, one bound for the east end, the other Whitehall.

On the far side of London, in Whitechapel, a tall man wearing a moth-eaten seaman's coat and cap penciled names onto the back of a map and marked the front with many tiny, bird-shaped symbols. He walked with a slight limp, his eyes as black as coal, but flickering in a strange, electric manner. Children who encountered the shadowy figure found their memories wiped clean, left only with a strange impression of a tall man with a book. The strange apparition appeared and disappeared at will, moving from one point to the next with lightning speed.

He marked thirty-three locations on the intricate map. One was a humble rooming house, entered only by way of a narrow passage betwixt 26 and 27 Dorset, a modestly finished brick courtyard built by John Miller thirty years earlier. By mid-November, this ill-fated flat, little more than a bedroom with a weathered door and two grimy windows, one of them broken, would be known to all in London as the place of the most horrific Ripper murder yet: 13 Miller's Court.

Charles St. Clair sipped Darjeeling tea from a gold-embossed china cup, which he imagined would cost more than a week's salary for most policemen. Across from him sat the most beautiful woman he'd ever seen, skillfully pouring tea from the matching teapot.

"Won't you take a sandwich?" she asked. "I'm sure you've missed your luncheon, and my cook baked the bread this morning. It's quite good."

He shook his head. "No, thank you, Beth. This tea is delicious. I don't think I've ever had it prepared this way."

"I'm glad you like it. It's an old family recipe," she answered. "My father enjoyed his tea with citrus and cinnamon. Charles, do I make you uncomfortable? Forgive me, if I've done anything to make you feel, oh, I don't know..."

"Out of my depth?" he suggested. He'd done his best to relax, but St. Clair wondered why she had asked him to drop by—surely not to exchange tea recipes. "No, Elizabeth, you've only been gracious. As always. Or at least, as I remember you. It has been four years since we last met."

"Four years, three months, two weeks, and a few odd days. I last saw you at Aubrey House, in June of '84."

"I remember," he admitted. Charles recalled every second of that brief encounter, but he dared not reveal that to her. Not yet.

"Truthfully, I would sit here all day, if you wished it, but your letter made it sound as though your mother's murder somehow intersects with crimes now haunting the east end."

She set the teapot to one side, and he noticed that she'd turned slightly pale, perhaps caused by the mention of her mother.

"I am sorry if that dark memory brings you distress," he said, leaning toward her as he set his own cup on the table. "And I do not intend to rush you. Please, forgive me, Beth, if it sounded as if I... What I mean is that you should take all the time you need."

"Charles, you have nothing to apologise for. Yes, I have much to tell you, but it is not an easy truth to tell."

"Then, tell it in your own time," he said gently.

"Thank you, Captain. Forgive me, I know that I promised to call you Charles, but..."

"I rather like Captain," he admitted, "and I've missed hearing you call me that. Please, Elizabeth, whatever this truth is, you may trust me with it."

"I know," she whispered. "All right. To begin with, I had not planned to return to England until next spring, but all the Paris newspapers have been filled with reports of the horrors you and your men now encounter, not that far from where my mother and I were left. They began December last, did they not?"

"Perhaps," he answered, wondering where this was heading. "Much depends on whose theory is being presented. Not all the murdered women suffered the same injuries, but it is possible the killer alters his method in order to obscure his crimes."

She thought about this for a moment, and he could see genuine fear cross her face. "Yes, I imagine he might wish to do that. Last year in Paris, the dismembered body parts of several women began washing up along the Seine. Were you aware of that?"

He nodded. "Yes. A colleague visited last month from the Sûreté, asking if the Ripper's crimes might not be connected, but there is no evidence to indicate that." *She is terrified. Is this why she returned?* "Elizabeth, why do you ask?"

The telltale tremble of her lower lip again caught his eye, and she turned away for a moment, perhaps perceiving his intuitive gaze. "I believe them to be connected, Charles. No, do not ask me to explain the reason. It is—well, it is something you'd probably find impossible to credit."

"I would credit anything you tell me, Beth. Will you not trust me?"

"Oh, Charles, I want to tell you everything, but I cannot. Not yet. Will you allow me to proceed with that which I may reveal?" she asked. "I promise to be more forthcoming later."

"Forgive me. Yes, of course. Go on."

She paused again, gazing out the nearest window at the north gardens, and he noticed a tear slide down her cheek. "After I read the reports of the murders here in August and September, I made plans to leave for Kent. You see, I believe your victims are but a continuation of a long history of atrocities, and, as I say, not all the victims lived in London. Some were in Paris. Others in Rome. Three in America, that I know of, and a few more in St. Petersburg."

"Elizabeth, how can you know this?" he asked, certain that she would again demur.

She rose from the settee, crossing past several armchairs to stand near the large window. "I know. Let that suffice for now," she whispered, her back to him.

St. Clair followed her to the window, putting his hand on her forearm and turning her to face him. "Beth, won't you, please, trust me?"

She shook her head, unable to look him in the eye. He kissed her hand, and she began to weep. "I do trust you. It's just that...you will think me mad. Oh, why can't I just live my own life? I hate all of this! Why must these men hound me?!"

What does she mean by 'men'? Plural, Charles wondered.

He put an arm around her, and she buried her face in his chest, clinging to him like that same, small girl from long ago. He knew she was lost in harsh memories. He had seen her mother's savaged body—decapitated, torn and shredded. And only now, to his regret, did Charles connect a murder ten years past with those currently terrorising the east end parishes.

"I am so sorry, Elizabeth," he said, stroking her hair. "You're afraid, and I'm doing nothing to help. Is it Ripper who worries you? Beth, I know the press reports must tear open that old wound for you, but I can see no clear connexion to your mother—or to you. Why do think he might harm you?"

She looked up at him, bright tears tracking her cheeks, and she took a deep breath to steel her courage. She kissed his hand and then returned to the settee. He followed, sitting once more opposite her.

"Because, he already has."

"What?" he whispered.

"He already has. Many times, and the connexion is an ancient one, Captain," she began, her face pale and her eyes lost in old memories. "I may not tell you all, for it is a closely held and well-guarded family secret that perhaps one day you may hear, but not today. I fear that it is not my decision to make. Suffice it to say that there exists an international group of well-heeled but black-hearted men who have performed unspeakable rituals like those seen in the murders of the poor women of Whitechapel, over and over for many hundreds of years. It is a collective known only to those outside it as Redwing."

He sat forward, his brow furrowed. St. Clair had heard this name before, whispered inside shadowy meeting halls and rumoured within Trinity College's dormitories, but he had never heard it spoken in a manor house before—and by so pretty and genteel a mouth. "Yes, I've heard of Redwing, but they are myth, Elizabeth. Pure ghost story to terrify college freshmen or frighten school boys on All Hallows' Eve! Such bloodthirsty men as these night terrors portray cannot possibly exist—not in a civilised world. Not here. Not in England."

"Yet they do exist, Charles. They do. I have seen them. I have witnessed their black deeds on the grounds of my very own home! I watched whilst their ceremonies of blood extinguished more than one life, including my mother's, and I nearly paid for it with my own!"

He was stunned into silence. He knew her to be sincere, yet her claims sounded like those told by a drawing room mystic, meant to frighten foolish women and spook children. A rational man could not deem such superstitious infamy to exist.

"I am quite sane," she said evenly, reading his expression. "Sane but terrified, if I am truthful. Absolutely terrified."

Her hands, neatly folded into the lap of her dress, were visibly shaking. He thought of those small hands, tightly gripping his own almost ten years before, and he recalled the trust in her large eyes— the same trust he saw there now. Somehow, instantly, he knew it all to be true. And if this shadowy group lay behind her mother's murder, then it was altogether logical that Elizabeth might be their next target.

No wonder she is terrified!

"Forgive me. How can I help?" he asked at last, seeing her body posture relax at his simple offer. "Tell me what you need of me, Elizabeth, and I shall do it, without question. I promised long ago to protect you, and I do not intend to break that promise. Not ever."

Tears welled up in her eyes, and her chin quivered. For a second, he saw the little girl's face return. "No, you must forgive me, Charles. I've thought about this conversation—this confession—for so long, and I've dreaded how you might react. I cannot tell you how relieved I am to know that you believe me."

She began to weep silently, and he nearly went to her, but something restrained him. He paused, his heart stopping again, and he listened to her breathing, her efforts to regain composure; to be a duchess in the presence of a commoner. Or perhaps something more: to summon up courage in the presence of overwhelming fear. Whichever, Charles vowed inwardly to help her no matter what the cost to him, personally or professionally.

After a moment, her head lifted, and she had found her inner strength. "Aunt Victoria would call me a silly woman for that!" she joked with a forced laugh. "Paul can tell you all about Redwing, far more than ever I could. He has been following their deeds across the globe, but most lie within the boundaries of Europe. I believe that they have branches in North Africa and Palestine, and also across the Atlantic into America—in particular Chicago and Washington. I'm told that some of the players operate in the American west as well, but these, I believe, are but ancillary operations. London is their heart, and it is here they wish to erect their new government—a central base of operations from which to rule and reshape the entire world. And they will accomplish it, if we do not stop them soon."

"Beth, I believe all, and I shall speak with Lord Aubrey about this Redwing group as soon as possible, but what connects this shadowy conspiracy of men to murders in Whitechapel?" he asked.

"For that, my dear friend, you will only believe me if I show you. And the setting is not in London but in Kent. In the caverns and tunnels that connect Branham Hall to an old abbey and from there to Hampton-on-Sea beyond. It is a truth that will rob you of your sleep from here on out, dear Captain, as it oft robs me of my own. However, if you trust in God, and you believe that our Saviour died for our sins and rose again on the third day, then you have trusted in worlds and events unseen and unseeable by our natural eyes. It is a matter of faith. And it is only that faith which can destroy this evil. And evil it is, Charles, for Redwing receives its power not from financial wealth—though they use wealth to gain human power and control—but from spiritual wickedness and unholy rites. You will understand my meaning fully once you have seen their meeting place and beheld the evidence of their deeds. Will you come to Branham with me and discover my proof?"

St. Clair wondered if time had stopped. Not a sound, not a breath, not a crackle from the fire, not an insect wing beating time in the garden air, not even the autumn breeze could be heard, only a thick cloud of silence that nearly stole his thoughts existed now. It was as if this moment, this decision would forever alter the direction of his life—and perhaps hers as well.

Suddenly, he stood, lifted her into his arms and held her close. "I will die for you, Beth, if that is what it takes. Yes, tell me when and where, and I shall go with you to Branham and learn your truths."

She broke down completely now, melting into his strong embrace, her tears staining his shirt as she wept without remorse. She refused to allow her mind to think beyond this moment, to entertain any possibilities beyond his friendship, for Charles was her knight errant, who had saved her as a child, and who now, had vowed to protect her as a woman. She could not tell him more, although her heart longed to do so. She had other obligations. Old obligations and an old 'secret' that meant she could never marry anyone but Paul Stuart. Thinking of this and wishing these moments in St. Clair's embrace would last forever, Elizabeth's tears flowed freely, and she buried her face in his shoulder.

She remained in his arms for many moments, but the chimes of Westminster reminded them both that the afternoon continued unabated, and a soft knock on the library door caught Beth's ears. "It is my butler, letting me know that it is three o'clock," she said, wiping at her eyes, and she left his embrace as the door opened. "I've kept you too long, Superintendent. Thank you for coming."

He was being dismissed, and it puzzled him. Had he done something wrong? "Yes, and I intrude upon your afternoon, Duchess. I do hope you will share the rest of your information about these men. Redwing, I mean."

The butler had entered, and St. Clair feared that he had completely mishandled the entire visit. She needed him, but it seemed he'd failed her, somehow. The butler bowed to the duchess, and she took the detective's hand, shaking it—and her hand trembled as if fear had suddenly gripped her heart. "Yes, I did promise," she replied, scarcely able to look directly into his eyes. "Charles, I hope you know that it's not that I do not trust you. It's just...well, rather complicated. If I may, I would continue this later and tell you more. Once, I've gained permission to do so."

This last made no sense at all, but the butler had brought his hat and overcoat, so St. Clair took them and bowed, feeling dismayed and a trifle embarrassed. "I look forward to it, Duchess."

Within a few moments, the detective found himself standing outside the magnificent mansion, the October breeze blowing through his dark hair. *What did I do wrong? Perhaps, she regretted the embrace. Did I misread her emotions?*

"No," he said to himself suddenly, his mind made up. "I did not."

Turning on his heel, St. Clair ran back up the high portico steps and rang the bell. It took several minutes for the tall butler to answer, but he did not appear the least bit surprised to find the detective standing outside. "Hello again, Superintendent," Miles said with a slight smile. "Did you perhaps forget something?"

St. Clair walked inside, handing his hat and coat to the butler. "Yes, I did, Mr. Miles. Is the duchess still in the library?"

"She is, sir, but she has asked not to be disturbed. She has a headache."

"Too bad," he said. "No need to announce me, Miles. I can do that myself."

St. Clair walked briskly past the butler toward the far northwest corner of the house, and then turned left to the main doors of the library. Pushing through, he found the petite duchess gazing out the window that overlooked Queen Anne Park, and she turned at the sound of his footsteps. "Superintendent, is there something we forgot?" she asked, her face filled with a combination of surprise and hope.

"Yes, Duchess, there is. This," he said, pulling her into an embrace and kissing her lips. She did not resist, but rose up on tiptoe as his arms encircled her waist, and suddenly time, appointments, Ripper, fear—nothing else mattered to either of them.

He held her that way for many seconds, their lips joined as one, and as the electric kiss ended, he stroked her hair, and whispered into her ear. "Shall I go?"

She shook her head. "No, Captain. Not just yet."

He smiled and kissed her once more.

CHAPTER SIX

That Friday evening, at the Lyceum Theatre, Paul Stuart knew the woman on his arm was the most beautiful in all England. October had arrived on the heels of a violent series of storms, but warmer weather had followed, and the stalls and boxes of the Westminster playhouse teemed with wealthy patrons, some few with titles known to all, but most from industrial lines of work; those men who now reshaped London with *nouveau riche* capital. One such was a builder named Sir Clive Urquhart.

Knighted in the most recent honours list for his contributions to improving the warehouses and docksides of east London, Sir Clive often attended social engagements on the arm of a mistress named Susanna Morgan, a singer from Chicago. Though the beautiful chanteuse's résumé included no stage experience, she loved attending any and all performances at Covent Garden or the Lyceum as often as Urquhart's money would indulge her. She and her lover sat now in Lord Aubrey's private box at his invitation, for Sir Clive had information for the earl, or so he had promised in a note delivered by messenger earlier that week.

"The duchess is particularly lovely this evening, Lord Aubrey," Sir Clive whispered as the theatre's manager took the stage to introduce the evening's play, *Macbeth*, starring renowned Irish actor Henry Irving as the eponymous Scottish lord. "I hear that Irving's MacBeth is superb, and Ellen Terry is always a treat. The play teaches a moral lesson, I believe. One must be careful what spirits entice you, eh—what voices you follow? My father was, as you know, a true Scotsman, though he preferred France for many reasons. This Scottish play must recall your own histories, in a way, Lord Aubrey. And perhaps that of the beautiful duchess. She, too, bears a Scottish heritage, does she not? Blood speaks more clearly than human vows, or so I have read. Is it true that blood always marries blood in the old lines? No dabblings in the dark? No secret trysts with the common woman—or even the *common man?*"

Paul detested the builder, mostly for his questionable business methods, but now for his thinly veiled insinuations. And this coming from a man who strutted about London with a woman who was not his wife! Still, if he had information of worth, then the earl would endure even such insults—for now. "I cannot imagine what you mean, my friend," he said with an easy, deliberate laugh. "I say, where is Lady Margaret this evening, Clive? I hope she is not unwell."

The earl knew that Margaret Urquhart detested her husband nearly as much as did he, but her storehouse of diamonds and satins more than made up for Sir Clive's other shortcomings. No doubt, Margaret even now lay in the arms of her own paramour. However, had the monarch planned to attend tonight's performance, the ambitious lady would have ejected her husband's mistress in favour of herself. Queen Victoria resided in Edinburgh this night, a fact known to all in government.

Sir Clive's oily glance danced across Elizabeth's bare shoulders, and he bowed as she re-entered the box after speaking with Lady Ashdown in the box next to their own. "We have missed your radiant presence, Duchess," he said with a sideways grin. "Susanna, my dear, does not the duchess outshine even the chandeliers tonight? How her face glows! One might think she had shared a gentle kiss before returning, but clearly that is not so, for you, my dear Aubrey, sit here with me—the humble of the moneyed men of England—so how could she do such, eh? My dear Duchess, you blush. How becoming it is!"

Paul wanted to slap the man. He helped Elizabeth with her chair and took her hand in his, leaning in to whisper softly, "I love you, Princess. Always and forever."

She lowered her eyes, squeezing Paul's hand with her own, her rings pinching into her gloved fingers. He knew what sadness broke her heart right now, and he hated it, but he also believed all would work out well. First protect her body—then protect her heart, if he could.

"Clive, will you join me in a smoke?" Aubrey asked the builder, revealing a gold case containing five, fat Dutch blend cigars.

"Oh, but of course! Ladies, if you will excuse us clumsy men. We leave you to gossip about dresses and Scottish plays. Lord Aubrey, why don't you choose a salon for our, uh, smoke? We shall return soon, my dear," he said to Susanna, kissing her hand. His rough fingers managed to brush Elizabeth's bare shoulders as he passed behind her, and she shuddered at the touch. Paul did not miss the gesture, and he vowed to make it up to her once they returned to Queen Anne House.

Susanna Morgan rarely spoke, but as her escort departed, she surprised Elizabeth by mentioning, of all things, the Ripper murders. "It's a darn shame about all those women," she said in her Chicago accent. "So much blood!"

Beth turned toward Morgan. "Do you mean the east end murders?"

Morgan nodded as she removed a pair of opera glasses from her velvet handbag. "Yeah. How many is it now? Six? Seven?"

"I've no idea," Beth whispered. "Are you interested in crime, Miss Morgan?"

"Oh, sure, I am. My pop loves reading all about grisly killings in the newspapers back in Chicago, and I guess it sort o' rubbed off on me. These Ripper murders are splashed across every paper back home from New York to San Francisco. He's famous."

"I find murder less thrilling, I suppose," the duchess replied. "Even in a play, it somehow seems ghastly to me."

Morgan held the opera glasses to her face, however the singer's attentions were not focused upon the stage, but rather someone sitting in the stalls below. "Say, isn't that Lady Whatshername down there, Duchess? Oh, you know, the one who had that big party in June that got raided by the police. Made headlines for weeks afterward. All sorts of titles got arrested, and a lot of them wearing very little at the time. I'll wager most of Scotland Yard was involved in the cleanup."

Beth took a moment to reply, wondering just why this ordinarily quiet woman suddenly wished to talk—but more importantly, why her topic involved the Ripper and Scotland Yard. "I've no idea, Miss Morgan. I was in Paris in June. Do you mean the tall woman in the third row behind the orchestra? That is Mrs. Bayer, I believe. Though, she does not appear to be here with Mr. Bayer."

"No, not her. The other one. Behind that row, in the middle. Flaming red hair—can't be natural—wearing an enormous brooch."

Elizabeth had very good vision ordinarily, but a shadow fell across her line of sight for a moment, as if someone had passed in front of her. "What?" she exclaimed involuntarily.

"A big emerald brooch," the American continued, apparently unaware of any shadow. "It must have cost a fortune, if it's real, that is."

Beth wiped at her eyes, her entire body suddenly freezing cold. "I don't know," she said automatically, trying not to appear rude. "Excuse me for a moment," she said at last, standing to leave the box. "I've something in my eye, I think. Forgive me for leaving you, Miss Morgan, but I must find a powder room."

"Oh, sure. They're on the main level, I think. Oh, but there might be one up here somewhere."

"I know where it is," the duchess replied kindly. "Thank you, Miss Morgan. If my cousin returns, please, let him know where I've gone. I shan't be long."

Elizabeth passed through the curtains and walked toward the staircase that led to the main level. She needed air suddenly, and a strange sense of panic threatened to overwhelm her reason. As she neared the last few stair steps, she felt a hand grip her right forearm, pulling her backward, causing her to stumble.

"I say, Duchess, are you all right?" she heard a man's voice ask. The portly gentleman stood on the floor of the lobby, a wine glass in his hand. "Here now, let me," he said, passing the glass to his friend and taking Elizabeth's hand to help her. "There now. You looked a bit unsteady for a moment."

Beth appeared disoriented, blinking as she struggled to regain her bearings. "Oh, yes, Sir Andrew. Thank you. No, I—well, someone was behind me, you see, and..."

"Behind you?" the man asked. "On the stairs, you mean?"
She nodded.

"My dear Duchess, I saw no one behind you. Perhaps, you lost your footing. Irving really must secure these stair carpets better. Shall I fetch you some water?"

"No, no. Thank you, Andrew. But wait, you say you saw no one? How is that possible?" she asked, turning to look up the long staircase. She could see nothing and no one anywhere along the case. "Perhaps, he returned to his own box before you saw him. I'm sure I felt someone pull my arm."

"The mind plays tricks on us sometimes, my dear. Here now, allow me to escort you back to your box. You're with Aubrey, right? Nice chap. I imagine you'll be announcing a wedding date soon, now that you've returned to England."

She let the baronet take her arm, and Beth accompanied him back up the staircase, her mind elsewhere. "What? Wedding? I don't know. Oh, you mean with Lord Aubrey. Are you sure you saw no one?"

"No one at all, my dear. Perhaps, you've just grown too accustomed to Parisian weather. London will soon set you to rights. Now, here we are. Box two, is it not? Last one. Oh, good evening, Miss Morgan. How are you?" he said as he held back the curtains.

Morgan seemed surprised to see the older gentleman with the duchess. "Nice to see you again, Andy. Duchess, you look like you've had a real scare! Are you okay?"

"She's a bit distressed, I believe, Susanna," the man said. "Now, Duchess, shall I fetch Lord Aubrey for you? I take it he popped out for a smoke with Clive. I saw the pair of them heading down to the salons, you know."

"You needn't do that, Sir Andrew," the duchess replied, still trying to reconcile what had happened. "I shall be fine in a moment. Please, don't worry yourself. Give my best to Lady Penelope, won't you?"

"Perhaps, I should remain here 'til Aubrey returns, Duchess. I'm not sure you should be left unattended. You look a bit flushed to me."

"No, really," she insisted. "I'm quite all right. You've been most kind. Thank you."

"Very well. If I see Aubrey, though, I'll let him know. Goodnight, Duchess. Susanna, a pleasure, as always."

He bowed and left the box, and the singer reached over and put a hand on Beth's left wrist. "Oh, your heart is racing! I'll go ask one of the attendants to get you some water."

"No, no!" Beth objected. "I just need a moment. I know it sounds silly, but I'm sure someone..." she started to explain, stopping as she struggled to recall exactly what had happened.

"Someone what?" Morgan pried.

"Never mind. It's been a long day. Did you ever determine the name of the woman with the brooch?" she asked, wishing to change the subject.

"Nope. She's since moved to a different seat, though. I think her husband came back. Funny things these theatres. I love parties because you can do all sorts of things there that you'd never do in public, but these London theatres are like a big party, you know? Men and women sneakin' off to do who knows what with anybody and everybody. It's like that game. Musical chairs. You ever play that?"

Beth had a headache all of a sudden, and she barely followed the woman's strange banter. "Musical what?"

"Chairs. It's a new game that's all the rage back home. A friend o' mine learned it when he worked in Palestine. It's Russian, I think. Anyway, you have so many seats, and while the music plays, everybody moves around. When the music stops, you have to find a chair."

"How is that a game?" Beth asked. "Is it cold in here?"

"No, it's real warm, I think. You see, there aren't enough chairs. Gee, you look real pale. I should find one o' the porters, or footmen, or whatever they are, and..."

"No, I'm all right." Elizabeth reached for her evening wrap and pulled it around her shoulders. "You said there aren't enough chairs. Wait, what did you mean about people in the theatre acting like they are at a party?"

Morgan smiled as she used a small compact mirror to check her makeup. "Oh, nothing. I'm sure the earl's not doin' anything like that! Now, Clivey would. You can't trust him. He's always lookin' for a little side action, but I can't picture Lord Aubrey doin' anything like that. He's sure good lookin', though."

"Yes, he is," Beth agreed. Onstage, the three witches had just appeared upon the battlefield scene, hailing Macbeth as 'Thane of Cawdor'.

"Clivey thinks you and the earl are getting married, Duchess. Is that true?"

"I'm sorry, Miss Morgan. Would you mind if I sit here quietly for a moment? I have a terrible migraine coming on."

The singer smiled. "No. Not at all."

Using her opera glasses once more, the American looked at a tall man who sat in a box across the way. She lifted the glasses twice to signal. In response, the man who sat in shadows lit a match.

"Sometimes, it's best to just relax and let the world move around you," she said. "And wait for the music to stop. You never know who might be sitting beside you next time it does."

Downstairs, inside a smoke-filled parlour, Paul Stuart led Sir Clive to a quiet corner where two mahogany and leather club chairs stood empty. "Sit down, Urquhart," he said producing a cigar. Aubrey clipped the end and lit it with an engraved, gold lighter. Handing a second smoke to the builder, the earl sat into a chair and crossed his long legs.

"Does Susanna enjoy the theatre?" he began casually. It was never good to rush into secret meetings. There was a method to gaining information of value, something that Paul had learnt from his Uncle James, a former espionage agent, who had spent many years in such work, before and after the Crimean War.

Sir Clive puffed on the cigar, his eyes rolling toward the painted ceiling of the salon. "These murals, my good Lord Aubrey, they are of operatic scenes, I think—a holdover perhaps from the early days of the playhouse. Rather risqué, no? Yes, Susanna loves the theatre, the opera, and even the music halls, though her own voice is more suited to private venues, if you get my meaning. She has a lovely mezzo, sweet and husky at times, but she could never fill a hall such as this, and certainly not Covent Garden. She often entertains at my humble soirées. One day, perhaps, you will attend a party at my home in Grosvenor Square, yes?"

Sir Clive loved including his exclusive address when referring to his three-storey mansion—built to his own specifications as a monument to greed, decorated with grotesque statuary and lewd fountains. Paul found the place detestable and vulgar, but if attending such parties kept Clive talking, then he would do so.

"Perhaps. That would be lovely—as is the lady Susanna. I look forward to hearing her sing. Thank you."

Urquhart, born to a Scottish father and a French mother, had been raised in Paris, and his pattern of speech and accent often wandered from one nationality to the other. "Excellent! No doubt my small house is but a speck to one such as your Duchess Elizabeth, but I would hope to see her visit as well. She is so lovely! Such a divine form! So tiny a waist—and all natural at that. You are a lucky man, my friend Aubrey. Is your wedding date set?"

Paul refused to let this small man bait him, though his rude reference to Elizabeth's *all natural* figure deserved eventual satisfaction. "We have not yet announced our engagement, as I am sure you know, Clive. It is an arrangement that goes back to our much younger days, but we are now adults, she and I. We shall announce when the time is right."

The builder puffed out a long stream of smoke, which rose above his balding pate like a hazy halo. *A curious picture*, the earl thought. *If an angel, then a fallen one, surely.*

"Announce it soon, my friend. Now that the duchess has returned to England, she will draw men to her like flies to honey, and perhaps one lucky little fly will catch her eye, and you find your childhood arrangements have disappeared like so much smoke, eh?"

"Elizabeth is a beautiful woman. It is understandable that men are drawn to her," the earl countered, hoping to derail the builder's insinuations, but the little man had no intention of being so diverted from his point.

"Indeed. Many men's eyes follow her, do they not? But you need not worry, Lord Aubrey. Marriage is but a contract, and such legal annoyances are meant to be broken, so no matter. Infidelity is a bulwark of peerage life, is it not?"

"Is it? If so, then you travel in different peerage circles than do I," Stuart answered, gall rising at the back of his throat. "If you've something to say, then, perhaps, you'd best say it; otherwise, I shall return to Elizabeth."

"She is safe, my friend. No need to worry—not here. Ah, but, I have much to tell you, so we leave behind our talk of women and weddings for another day, no? For now, I have this."

He reached into the inner pocket of his tailcoat and withdrew a small, velvet bag. Leaning toward the earl, he held the bag in the air—dangling it, as if contemplating a change of mind, his beady eyes on the drawstrings of gold.

"Inside this little bag is a humble offering, so many would claim, but they would be wrong. These baubles, this shiny bit of stuff, comes from a source that is unimpeachable. Its contents are items which I know, my good Aubrey, you have seen before. You will recognise them. I expect you to have them thoroughly investigated, studied, and verified. And if this bag is all that I claim it to be, then perhaps my bank account will be reimbursed for what I have already paid for this shining bit of history. Is that not fair?"

Urquhart held the bag aloft, teasing it as a gift, testing Paul's patience. The earl sat perfectly still, his cool blue eyes fixed on those of his adversary. Not once did he even *glance* at the bag. "If, Sir Clive, these baubles as you call them have any value to me, then speak plainly. Otherwise, enjoy your cigar," he finished, starting to rise.

Urquhart's black eyes narrowed, and he pondered his foe's demeanor, his will. Laughing as if it had all been a great joke, he tossed the bag to Paul and spread his hands. "See? Am I not trusting? Examine the rings, and then, after you have satisfied yourself that all is genuine, send me a note by our mutual messenger. I am in no hurry. Your honour is well known in England, Lord Aubrey. And so is your lady's."

Paul wanted to bash the man's skull open, but he remained calm and still, refusing to open the bag. He placed it inside the breast pocket of his dress coat, next to a small keepsake he kept always with him—a locket photograph of Elizabeth taken on her eighteenth birthday whilst in Paris. He cherished her, and he would love her until his last breath, but her honour must wait if Paul were to obtain all the proofs he needed to forever erase the dangers to her *life*.

"You will not be disappointed, Lord Aubrey. Not at all. I obtained the beautiful, jeweled rings from a companion whose close connexions tell me all that happens in the high offices of our fair city. When you have verified the gems, let me know, and I shall tell you how this pouch and its expensive contents came into his hands, and so into mine."

Without one word further, Paul rose, leaving the builder to enjoy the cigar alone. Passing through the thick crowd of merchant men, bankers, and nobles, half-hearing their raucous jokes and brags of bedroom prowess, Paul left the salon behind and climbed the gold embellished staircase that led to his family's private box. As he neared the velvet curtains that draped the entrance to the elegant interior, he noticed a strangely shaped, black shadow lingering near the door to a short wooden staircase, and thence to the back-stage area.

It is but a shadow, cast by one of the large, fly-space lamps, surely, he thought. The dense shadow seemed to flicker, but then stood perfectly still, bent as if listening...and then he *saw its red eyes*—certainly no shadow then.

Paul advanced toward the monstrous shape, but as he neared the apparition, it completely disappeared! Stunned, the earl searched the area, even opening the backstage door to assure himself that his eyes had not misled him. No one was there, save a fly man, far on the opposite side of the gallery, working a series of ropes and pulleys that controlled scenery below.

The man must also have seen the earl, for his florid face jerked toward the door, and in a rather inebriated voice, he called out softly, "You're not a'posed to be here, guv! Nobody backstage durin' a show!"

Paul walked around the outer edges of the fly space, his tailcoat gathering dust as he worked his way along the slender walkway to the man's position. Producing a sovereign, he asked plainly, "Who else has been here that didn't belong, my good man?" A gin bottle peeked out from the old man's belt, and Paul added a second sovereign to the first. "These two, golden brothers are yours, my friend. I only want a true answer. Who else was back here—just moments ago?"

The man's face grew long and white. "Tweren't no *man*," he whispered tightly. "No man, but—but sumfing. Sumfing what never ought to be, guv. I tell you by the 'eavens, it never ought to be!"

Paul gazed into the man's pockmarked face, realising he had spoken truly, and he handed him the coins. "If ever you see it again, you are to tell me. Send word to Aubrey House and ask for me. I am Lord Aubrey."

The man gulped and nodded. "I will, yer lordship. I rightly will."

Returning to the hallway behind the boxes, Paul suddenly remembered the velvet bag. Removing it from his pocket, he untied the top and opened it in view of the dimly lit gas lamp. Upturning its contents into his left hand, three jeweled pieces fell into his palm. Two rings in a set: one a diamond band, whilst the other contained a flawless central diamond, flanked by a smaller pair of diamonds and two sapphires, set into a ring of fine gold. The last was a jeweled cross on a chain. All were known to him, just as the scoundrel Urquhart had promised; they had been worn by Patricia Stuart every day of her married life to her first husband, Elizabeth's father, Connor Stuart. How had Sir Clive gained access to items surely collected by H-Division more than nine years earlier? Paul replaced the items into the bag and hid them once again within his pocket.

Deciding to say nothing to Elizabeth, Paul brushed the dust from his coat with his hands, hoping her observant mind would not notice or ask for an explanation. The less she knew, the better she would sleep. Better that he lose sleep than she. Parting the curtains, he found both women quiet.

"Sorry to be gone so long," he whispered as he sat beside the duchess. "Sir Clive remained behind, Miss Morgan," he said to Susanna. "Beth, you are pale. My fault, I fear. I should not have left you."

"No, I'm just enjoying the play," she lied. "May we leave soon, though? I've caught a chill, I think."

"We may go now, darling, if you wish it. Miss Morgan, I shouldn't like to leave you unattended. We shall wait until Sir Clive returns."

Susanna laughed and tapped the earl's upper arm. "My, you are muscular!" she said with a wink. "Oh, I'm just fine here on my own. In fact, I might even wander about, have a look to see who's here."

Aubrey kissed the American's hand politely, noticing her seductive glance as he did so. "Then I shall say goodnight, Miss Morgan. Tell Clive that I shall contact him soon."

He left with the duchess, and Susanna waved to the man in the opposite box. In a few moments, the tall man had joined her, and the pair entered an intense conversation.

Once at home, the earl and duchess sat quietly in the red room, a favourite drawing room for after dinner conversation at Queen Anne House. Miles served tea and brandy along with several light desserts, retreating once he'd made sure both his charges were comfortable.

"Thank you for bringing me home early, Paul. I was surprised that you spent so much time with Sir Clive, but I imagine it was business. He is quite rude, though. Don't you think?"

"He's a bounder, but yes, we had business to discuss. His manner toward you is beyond rude, darling, and I will have none of it. I as much as told him so."

Elizabeth sat next to him, using her small hand to brush his long chestnut hair back from his soft blue eyes. "Yours is a great heart," she said, kissing his cheek. "And I cherish it. I would not risk that heart for the world."

He leaned into her embrace, letting his head fall against her shoulder, his hand in hers. "You are my world, Beth. My sole reason for being. I've loved you since you were born. Loved you at first with the innocence of a cousin, loved you later with the faltering devotion of a restless school boy, and now with the ardent passion of a man. I would walk through fire and back again if you asked it. And I would—I would..."

She kissed his forehead. "Do not think on it, my darling. Let us live for now. Forget any fears, any dangers, any secret lives from the past that rise up to haunt us. May we do that, Paul? Live only for this moment?"

"This moment, Beth?" He sat up, his blue eyes smoking into a deep grey hue as he drew her into his arms with a fire in his mind and body he could no longer hide. His lips touched hers for the first time in their adult lives, not with the sweet affection of a cousin, but as a lover. His muscular body wrapped around hers in a way she had never before experienced, and it was like disappearing into a raging inferno.

Elizabeth allowed him to take her this way, to make her his own—if only for that moment, but as his kisses grew hotter, she suddenly felt emotions stirring she'd never felt before, and it startled her. "Paul, no, please! Not like this," she whispered huskily, pushing him away.

"I am sorry! I forget myself, Beth—forgive me! Please!" He looked like a wounded child now, pain and regret etched across his brow like a brand. "Oh, my darling Cousin, please, forgive me."

She kissed his hands, her small mouth crimson with the rush of blood still pulsing in her ears. "Always, my dearest," she assured him. "Always."

"Marry me, Elizabeth. Now, tonight. Marry me! Let me protect you from all that awaits in the shadows of our lives. Please, let me be there night as well as day, to love you and keep you safe."

She wanted to say yes. She knew she would eventually say yes, but somehow tonight she could not—the memory of St. Clair's embrace and *his kisses* were still too fresh.

"I truly do love you, Paul. Love you now and will always love you. You are the Scottish knight of whom I dreamt as a child, and

I long to know you as husband, too…but not now. Not yet. Please, may I have until Christmas? Then, I will accept your proposal. I promise. And we shall marry in the spring."

He knew she meant it, but a great gathering shadow had taken root in his heart, and he wondered if the thing he'd seen at the theatre might not be some omen of dark days to come. He longed to run away with her—to whisk her away to some safe ground, to lock her up where he alone could reach her, but he knew she would never permit it. Yes, she feared what Trent and his cabal might try, but her brave heart would never allow him to risk all for her. He loved her even more for knowing it.

"I shall content my heart with that promise," he told her, "but until that official day, when you publically proclaim your heart joined with mine, until that announcement at Christmas, will you not wear this?"

He withdrew a small, blue velvet box from his pocket. He'd carried it for weeks, hoping for the right moment to ask her, to see it fitted onto her slender finger. Now, he prayed, was the time.

He opened the box, revealing a brilliant blue diamond set into a band of platinum and gold. On either side of the flawless ten-carat blue, two companion diamonds of clearest white served as sentries to the magnificent centre stone. The duchess gasped at the ring's remarkable beauty. Looking up, her eyes brimming with tears, her sweet mouth open as if to speak; she appeared suddenly struck mute. She bit her lip, her eyes dropping great tears onto her dress.

"Paul, oh, my precious Paul. How long have you been planning this?"

He hoped this meant that she accepted—even if only for their own private moment. "A month. Perhaps longer. I don't know. I only know I saw this stone last time I was in Antwerp, and I knew it must be on your hand, and yours alone. You needn't make any promises, Princess. Just wear it as a gift from your Scottish cousin."

She sighed, knowing what accepting really meant, but she loved him so—and had for so very long—that she gave him her hand. "Perhaps, we should make certain that it fits," she said, noting the look of hope in his handsome eyes.

He removed the ring from the box and slipped it easily onto her left hand, kissing her fingertips as he did so. "A perfect fit."

She nodded. "A perfect fit, but then I would expect no less from you, Lord Aubrey. Kiss me now, and let us seal our private arrangement. I promise you, Paul; we will let the world know at Christmas."

He kissed her, whispering into her ear. "At Christmas."

But that day would never come—not as they hoped. Shadows had already set sights on the pair, and a tall man had just stepped onto the sands of Hampton-on-Sea, his grey eyes riveted on the great manor house a few miles from the seaside village, beyond the dark woods.

CHAPTER SEVEN
6, October

Leman Street, even on a quiet day, could be a raucous and very dangerous avenue on which to travel, but this day—two days after the first phase of the Catherine Eddowes inquest, one day after the sudden adjournment of the Liz Stride inquest (postponed now until the 23rd) and the very day of Stride's burial—the citizenry of Whitechapel were enraged by what they perceived as deliberate mishandling by the police. In response, some men formed committees whilst others merged organically into murderous mobs, as if driven by an unseen spiritual leader, and the east end parishes rose up into a maddened riot with revenge and blood on their minds, and some even called for revolution and anarchy.

Street women who plied their trade in alleyways and crosscut rookeries had all but shut up shop, excepting those who dared not for want of bed and breakfast, and many of those terrified women now hurled accusations if not actual stones at the men in blue. The dusty sidewalk and muck-stained cobbles in front of the doors of H-Division teemed with overworked police constables holding back a mob of strumpets, ironworkers, hauliers, bakers, beggars, costermongers, and honest merchants from across the east end. But amongst their number circulated a political patchwork of university-educated anarchists, Bohemian protesters, militant suffragettes, writers, artists, news reporters, and opportunistic trade union rioters; a melee of humanity, choosing sides and vowing vengeance for the women whose names most had never even heard spoken before the Ripper began his dark work in the impoverished east end streets.

Inspector Edmund John James Reid was a short, stout man with an iron face and close-set eyes. Beside him, and several inches the taller man, stood a gruff individual who looked more like a banker than a police detective. Inspector 1st Class Frederick George Abberline, Edmund Reid's superior within CID, had been assigned to oversee the Ripper investigation, and as the colourful inspector often phrased it, was currently appointed as 'head zookeeper' at the Leman Street police station. Since the murders began, both men had racked their brains to decipher any clues left behind, only to be stymied by decisions 'up top' at the Yard by Police Commissioner Sir Charles Warren, or worse by Parliamentary muckabouts using the murders to advance their own political ambitions.

Neither man had slept well in recent weeks, but both stood now alongside their men, billy clubs in hand. The club was a one-foot-long wooden truncheon able to inflict severe pain to a shin, a shoulder, or a back in the practised hands of the division's well-trained men, and Abberline and Reid had many years of such practise between them.

It was nearing noon, and the sun stood directly overhead, illuminating the crowd and overheating the rabble who often wore an entire wardrobe upon their scrawny backs for lack of any permanent place to live. Michael O'Brien, a noisome reporter for *The Star*, took copious notes of the protest whilst his co-worker, American-born Harry Dam, snapped photographs using an expensive Kodak No. 1 box camera.

Reid shouted for both men to move. "O'Brien, you and Mr. Dam will withdraw your fancy boots from this sidewalk, or I shall find myself in possession of a very fine camera, and the two of you will spend a night in my cells!"

O'Brien, a slender man of thirty with sandy hair, stepped backward several steps until his feet touched the cobbles. "I stand upon public property, Inspector Reid. Shall I mention your threats in my article alongside one of my colleague's fine photographs?"

Reid sighed, advancing slightly toward the reporter. "Shall I introduce your wrists to a set of iron bracelets, Michael? Or do you prefer to rephrase that?"

O'Brien smiled and waved to two other detectives who now watched from within the police station facility. "Good day to you as well, Superintendent St. Clair!" he called. "Have you a quote for *The Star*? A comment on your recent investigations? Your trips to a certain fashionable address in Westminster, perhaps?"

Charles St. Clair turned his back to the glass and continued to sip his coffee. "France, tell me when that hellish man is gone. Else I shall have to kill him."

Inspector Arthur France, who had served with H-Division since before the 'duchess murder', as the Scotland Yard insiders called it, stood beside his superior, just inside the doorway by a large mullioned window. "Do you think he followed you to her house, sir?"

"I think T.P. O'Connor's minions would do anything to uncover a salacious story and sell newspapers. And when they lack for evidence, they merely manufacture it."

Charles feared his visit to Queen Anne House had been observed, but if not already known, it would only be a matter of time. He'd shared some of the visit's details with his friend Arthur France, but certainly not all. With Ripper madness providing the public with a steady diet of sensationalism, hints and accusations against anyone from Scotland Yard—particularly one connected with peerage houses—could add thousands of new subscribers to *The Star's* ledgers, and St. Clair had no wish to involve the duchess in such libelous muckraking.

"I imagine O'Brien's American friend has already photographed me," St. Clair remarked.

"Many times, sir. Those cameras cost half a year's wages, I'm told. Oh, but look, sir. Isn't that Ida Ross? The one who used to work across from your house?"

St. Clair turned back toward the window, his blue eyes narrowing. "It is. Don't tell me she's been beaten again. France, could you ask one of your men to help her inside? If Lusk's crowd sees her, they're sure to bring her even more harm. That man may claim to be a champion of the downtrodden, but he'd happily trod upon her, if it suited his ambitions."

France tapped a police constable on the arm. "Rickets, see to it that Miss Ross makes it through our doors safely."

The young police constable nodded and left to escort the prostitute indoors. In a moment, the thin woman stood near the sergeant's booking desk, trembling with fear. "Mr. France, sir. Thank you, sir, for your help. I wonder, is Superintendent St. Clair here today? I stopped by his house, and Mrs. Wilsham told me he might be here, on account o' the protest an' all."

The superintendent left his lookout spot near the window and gently took the young woman's emaciated arm, leading her away from the desk. "Miss Ross, you need a doctor."

She shook her head. "Nah, sir. I ain' got no money for such. I'll be all right. I just come in to tell ya that there's been a man at your 'ouse, sir. Funny lookin' gent, an' he's been writin' stuff in a book. Reporter, I reckon. Oh, and...and..." she started to say, but her eyes rolled up in her head, and she fell forward into the detective's arms.

"France! A little help!" he cried, lifting the frail woman up and carrying her into the main parlour of the station house lobby as France held open the door. "Fetch Dr. Sunders, if he's here."

France sent Rickets to bring the physician from his work in the morgue, and Charles poured cool water on a linen towel, using it to wipe her forehead and cheeks. The woman's face was gaunt—thinner than the last time he had seen her, and her eyes were rimmed in dark circles and ugly bruises.

Sunders arrived in shirtsleeves, and he knelt beside the unconscious prostitute. "She's in bad shape," he said bluntly. "He may have killed her this time. Poor girl."

"She told me she'd left him," St. Clair said softly. "Sunders, can we get her to the Eastern Dispensary?"

"Perhaps. I can take her over, Superintendent. Why on earth do these girls keep returning to the men who knock them about?"

"I cannot say," Charles replied as France joined him.

"Sir, it's Lusk. He's making threats again—saying he'll start arresting any and all the Jews of the city who even look at a woman."

"Will he now?" St. Clair said, rising from the chair. "I imagine Reid and Abberline can handle it, but let's go see if they require our help. Some days, France, it doesn't pay to leave Whitehall."

"I suppose that's the price one pays for being overseer for the east end, sir," Arthur France replied, as the pair walked back to the large window, where they could see a thick group of outraged citizens standing toe to toe with the two overworked police detectives. "Shall we stop it, sir? Lusk and his crew, I mean. He's about to give Mr. Abberline a clattering, it looks like. Lusk thinks he's right smart."

"Yes, well, it looks like Abberline's not lost his persuasive ways," St. Clair noted proudly. A fracas had broken out near the sidewalk between Michael O'Brien and several rough looking men from the Vigilance Committee, but Fred Abberline's mutton-chop face spat orders at the builder, making it clear that his interference was neither wanted nor needed.

George Aken Lusk and his rabble-rousing vigilantes had gained ground and support the past few weeks, and it seemed to France that they had also gained financial backing, for many of the men had foresworn their day labour jobs in favour of protesting—most working on the new, construction projects near the river basin under the banner of Sir Clive Urquhart's fashionable company, Urquhart Investment Group. France had mentioned this to Superintendent St. Clair two days past, and he now said as much again in conversation.

"I just wonder who's paying Lusk's bills," the young man said to the superintendent. "Must be nice to spend an entire week off the job and still have a bob or two in your pocket. And he's wearing a new hat, or my name's Plum."

"You know, I think you're right, Arthur. It's worth looking into," St. Clair replied. "See what you can discover along those lines and get back to me. If Lusk is in the pay of someone who benefits by the fomenting of violence in Whitechapel, then I want to know that man's name. I'd certainly like to find just cause to arrest Lusk, wouldn't you, France?"

"I pray for it each morning, sir," the younger man said.

St. Clair stepped closer to the glass and watched Reid and Abberline with a certain pride. "I'll wager those two would love it if Lusk and his lot did try to penetrate the station house. Reid especially. He's a scrapper for a runt."

France sipped Turkish coffee from a stoneware mug. "He is at that, sir. I'll fetch two clubs from the armament cabinet, just as a precaution."

"Good idea, but once done I may need to leave for an hour. Miss Ross mentioned seeing a man near my house. She thought him a reporter. I want to make sure Mary's all right. I'd hate to think some of this riff-raff have moved up to Columbia Road."

"I could go, sir, if you prefer to remain here. I assume it's why you joined us today."

"It is, Arthur. No, I can go there on my own. It shouldn't take long, and I can have luncheon whilst there. Mary Wilsham's dear to me, and I'll not see anyone molest her."

"Me neither, sir. Blimey, there's another one!" the young inspector exclaimed. "Toff slummer from the west end most likely here to join the parade. What is it about Jack that brings out these people, sir?"

"I wish I knew, Arthur. Fetch those batons, will you? I want to check on Miss Ross again, and then you and I shall join Reid and Abberline for a little exercise."

The superintendent made his way through the thick knot of uniformed officers from J and K Divisions who had been brought in to help maintain order. The surrounding cells were filled with drunks and prostitutes, and the station house sounded like a cacophonous representation of Babel.

"Sunders, how does our lady fare?" he asked as he sat into a chair near the narrow couch.

"She's in very poor condition. I found some medicinal cream in her purse, Mr. St. Clair. A mercury preparation."

His face fell. "She has syphilis?"

Sunders nodded. "Most likely. It is the bane of such an occupation, is it not, sir?"

"It is. Keep watch on her, will you, Thomas? It looks as if Inspector France and I may need to lend a hand outside, and then afterward, I've an errand to run."

In the lobby behind him, through the connecting door, St. Clair could hear the already riotous station house lobby explode suddenly into auditory anarchy. "What now?" he muttered, recognising O'Brien's voice amongst the mayhem, apparently shouting questions to someone who had just entered.

"Sounds like trouble," Sunders said with a wink. "If this continues, you might have need of that pistol you keep disguised under your coat."

Charles smiled, patting the shoulder holster beneath his jacket. "Now, Sunders, you know that firearms for inspectors and higher are now permitted. I carry it merely as a precaution." St. Clair rose and headed toward the knot of people who had gathered near the booking sergeant's desk. O'Brien and Dam hovered at the centre of a dense cluster of reporters and rioters, and betwixt them stood a woman—one who had no business being in Whitechapel.

"Good Lord!" St. Clair cried out, pushing past France into the chattering field of humanity. The woman appeared to be doing her best to answer the reporter's questions whilst the American photographer snapped photo after photo from a variety of angles.

"And is it true that you returned to England because of these rumours surrounding the murders, Your Grace? Or might there be a more, uh, how shall I say it, *personal* reason for leaving the pleasant occupations of life in the Parisian countryside?"

Charles reached Elizabeth before she could answer, deftly taking her by the elbow. "Beth, what are you doing here—alone, without an escort?" he whispered.

O'Brien scribbled quickly into the pages of his notebook, and Harry Dam snapped several photographs of the superintendent and the imprudent duchess.

"Superintendent St. Clair, sir," O'Brien interrupted. "Did we hear you address the duchess by her Christian name? My, but that is quite unusual for a police detective, is it not, sir? Speaking so intimately to a high peeress of the realm. Is the duchess here on business or pleasure, Mr. St. Clair? Would you mind offering a quote for our readers to go along with this touching photograph?"

The detective started to reply, but it was Elizabeth who turned toward the reporter, her dark eyes wide. "Who are you?" she asked plainly, surprising both the reporter and the detective. "Wait, I believe I know. I have seen you before, only yesterday, in fact, skulking about my gardens. A police station may prove a dangerous place for you now, sir, as I imagine that many here would happily remove you and your American friend to a quiet cell, where you may reconsider the propriety of your insinuation."

"Your Grace, I only meant that..." O'Brien muttered, but Beth stepped toward him, her gloved forefinger denting the reporter's waistcoat as she spoke.

"You only meant to spark a fire in hopes of igniting a conflagration of new subscribers for your rag of a newspaper, did you not, Mr. O'Brien? Oh, yes, I know your name, and I imagine most of my family also know it. Lord Aubrey, for instance," she said, her voice lowering to a whisper. "Shall I send for my cousin? I believe his is an acquaintance you have made already, or am I mistaken in that, Mr. O'Brien? He gave you a marvelous quote for your paper last summer, written intractably upon your back, did he not? Or would you rather deal with me? A helpless female peeress, you imagine. I may appear physically helpless, but I wield a mighty club, nonetheless. Shall I prove it by reminding your superior, T.P. O'Connor, that his political ambitions require a constant source of funding?"

Charles had released her elbow, surprised to find Elizabeth so ready and able to defend herself against the merciless hack, but he also knew that the press was but one danger this day, and already several unsavoury types had managed to work their way through to the perimeter of the melee, and St. Clair feared the duchess might be in physical peril.

"Your Grace, will you come with me, please?" he said, once again taking her arm. "Please."

She turned toward him. "What?" she asked, for the room's noise level was deafening and the irritating reporter continued to ask questions, his pencil scratching out copious notes in shorthand.

St. Clair shouted to be heard. "You should not here, Duchess! Where is Lord Aubrey? Why is he not with you?"

She shook her head, pointing to her ears, and he wondered if she truly did not understand, or did not wish to.

Harry Dam had maneuvered closer and was clicking his box camera's shutter over and over, and St. Clair's frustration level rose higher and higher until, at last, it snapped.

"Enough!" he shouted, jerking the camera from the reporter's hands. "If you want this back, Dam, then you will remove yourself from this station house now! No more questions. Not even one. Everyone out! Else, I shall have you all arrested!" he shouted.

"On what charge, Superintendent?" Dam asked.

"Vagrancy, assault, annoying an officer of the law, I care not. Just get out before my good humour wears thin!" St. Clair shouted.

As the throng broke apart, Elizabeth's gaze fell upon the woman in the parlour, and she gasped. "Oh! I know her!" she cried, pushing through the crowd toward Ross.

St. Clair worried that someone might try to rob Elizabeth, or worse harm her, so he waded through the mob and grasped her arm once more. "Beth, please," he said, but she paid him no heed. "Elizabeth!" he shouted, and suddenly you could hear a pin drop.

She spun toward him, her eyes wide.

"What are you thinking? You cannot just come here as if it's a pleasant day in St. James's park!" he shouted so loudly that all within the station house turned to gape at the couple.

France came to his aid, gently touching the enraged superintendent on the arm as if to snap him back to the present. "Sir, she is fine, thanks to your quick intervention. Would it not be wise to remove the good lady to Mr. Reid's office?"

Seeing Beth amongst such a hive of potentially dangerous men, St. Clair had imagined the worst, and suddenly he began to realise the true depths of his affections for the beautiful peeress. Briefly, he considered sending for Aubrey to escort her to safer ground, but he thought better of it after seeing her eyes. They had grown round with fear—not fear of the crowd, but *fear of him.*

"Elizabeth, forgive me. France is correct. Please, allow me to take you upstairs to a quiet place. Then you may tell me why it is you have risked your person, if not your life, to come here on a day when Whitechapel is an armed camp."

She pondered his words for a moment, and it seemed that she felt torn by warring thoughts. "Very well, but Charles, I know that woman."

"You couldn't know her, Elizabeth. Now come with me, please."

"I'm sure I do," she insisted. "I met her...where was it now?" she began, but suddenly her face paled. "Oh! I remember now! She talked to me that day at your..." All colour drained from her face, and the duchess put her hand on St. Clair's arm. She leaned forward to whisper. "Ten years ago, at your house," she said tightly, and she seemed to grow unsteady on her feet.

"That's it," St. Clair said, putting an arm around her waist. "In here, quickly." He pulled her into the parlour, shutting the door and closing all the blinds, so that no one in the crowd might see them.

"Elizabeth, sit down. Now."

She obeyed, and in a moment France had joined them.

"Sir? Is she all right?"

"I don't know. Sunders?"

The physician left his current patient and felt the duchess's pulse. "It races. Madame? Miss? Superintendent, do you know her?"

"Yes, but I prefer this crowd not realise it, though it's clear that the hacks from *The Star* already do. Elizabeth, look at me."

She glanced up, her pupils large. "Charles? I—I felt rather strange for a moment. Have you any water?"

"France?" he asked, and the young inspector fetched a carafe and glass from a small desk in the corner, pouring a large serving and handing it to his superior. Charles held the glass to her lips. "Drink this now, darling," he said gently. "Not too quickly. There. Is that any better?"

She nodded, fanning herself with her hand. "I grew warm, I imagine."

Sunders checked her eyes. "Are you prone to spells, Miss?"

"Sometimes," she replied. "Forgive me. I am better now. Thank you. That woman, though," she continued, pointing to Ross, who still lay unconscious. "I do remember her, Charles. I saw her..."

"Not here, Elizabeth. I'd prefer we speak of this elsewhere. Do you feel well enough to climb the stairs?"

"Yes, I imagine so."

He helped her to stand, and she seemed somewhat unsteady still. "Lean on me. We'll have to traverse the crowd once again, but only for a moment. We can take the back flight to the next floor. You are sure you're able?"

"If you are there, yes. I can do it." She looked toward the physician. "Are you the police surgeon?"

Sunders nodded. "I work at J-Division most days, but I was called over to help out on a case. Have you been ill, Miss?"

"No, not of late." She reached into her handbag and withdrew a small gold case. Opening it, she took out a calling card and handed it to the doctor, who read it and whistled.

"You are the Duchess of Branham?" he mouthed, instantly realising why St. Clair wished to remove her from the crowd. "Forgive me, Your Grace. It isn't often I meet a duchess, particularly whilst in a police station."

She smiled. "You are very kind to say so. Would you do all you can for this woman, please, Doctor? And if there is need for payment—of any amount—have the bills sent to me."

Sunders looked at the superintendent. "Sir?"

"It's all right, Sunders. If she desires it, then do it. Beth, that is not necessary."

"It is, Charles. It is. Now, I shall follow as you lead."

They returned to the lobby, where St. Clair handed the box camera to the desk sergeant. "Put this somewhere safe, and do not return it to Dam without first removing the film roll."

As they climbed the back staircase, Elizabeth thought of Paul Stuart, recalling his face when she'd accepted his ring and his trust in her promise. Why did she insist on caring for this policeman?

"In here, Miss," France said, deliberately avoiding all reference to her station in life, even though he had immediately recognised the child's face in that of the woman. Once the door had shut, the young officer looked to his superior and pointed toward the lower level.

"Best no one else down there realises who she is, I think, sir; though it's still likely to be all over this afternoon's front pages. Course, now they'll have no photographs to prove it," he said to St. Clair. Then to the duchess, he bowed. "Your Grace, if you will forgive any familiarity. I knew you as a child, when sad circumstances, which I shall not repeat, brought you to our station house. It is an honour and a great pleasure to see you again."

Elizabeth's worried expression vanished in light of this simple speech, and she put out her gloved hand to shake his. "It is I who must ask your forgiveness, Inspector France. It is Detective Inspector now, I'm told. You were but a Police Constable ten years ago, and you did much to ease my heart and make me feel safe. You have done well. No, gentlemen, I did not think. I merely acted without considering what strains your station house must now be under. Charles, please, forgive me," she continued, her eyes downcast as she remembered his passionate kisses. "I have frightened and worried you both. It is only that I have received something that I thought I ought to bring to you at once. It is a letter. And it is signed by someone you and this quarter know all too well."

St. Clair had noticed her demure glance, and he wondered if she now regretted their intimate moments four days previously. Wishing they had more privacy now, he took the white envelope she offered. "You handled yourself rather well downstairs, Duchess. I believe O'Brien and Dam will be tending their wounded pride for many days, but France is right. The story is likely to make today's press, which will then bring a flurry of reporters to your door."

"So long as you are there to help shoo them away," she said, smiling at last. "Charles, this letter. Please, look at it. It is important."

St. Clair turned his attention to the envelope. It was addressed on the outside in a flourished hand using crimson ink that sent a chill down his spine. The address read, 'To the Duchess, Queen Anne House, London – for her Eyes only'.

"Does this strike as familiar, France?" he asked.

The young inspector nodded. "It does, and it is with no great happiness that I say it, sir. This came to you, Your Grace?"

"Yes, it did, Inspector. Read it, Charles. Please."

St. Clair opened the envelope.

Inside, a single sheet of cream notepaper bled with the same red ink. The hastily scrawled words read:

Dear Duchess,

Think you've escaped old Jack's long arms? Not yet, my sweet girl. My knife may have missed you ten years ago, but it bit into your pretty mother's white flesh over and over again. I am saving something special for your tender body. Something tasty. And I shall get 'round to it—very soon.

Your crimson knight,
Saucy Jack

"That damnable devil! How dare he do this?!" St. Clair shouted, and he slammed the note down onto the desk with such fury that the blow knocked several pens and a bottle of ink off their mounting, spilling the ink like so much black blood across Edmund Reid's blotter. Elizabeth jumped at the sound, her dark eyes rounding in surprise.

France hastily daubed at the spill with his handkerchief, staining his hands and trying not to stain his clothing. "I'll fetch some ink remover from the sergeant's desk, shall I, sir?" he offered, realising St. Clair would probably prefer a moment alone to calm the duchess—and himself. Softly closing the door behind him, France made his way down the steps, but he could still hear St. Clair's outrage even on the ground floor.

"This beast dares to use such words—such threats! How dare he send these horrid lines to you? To you! And to invoke your mother, when he had nothing to do with it is maddening! How can he even begin to think that…wait. Wait a moment. How can he…?"

His stream of words slowed as his mind digested the implied truth concealed within the taunting message. At last, he grasped what the duchess had already surmised, noticing only then that she had gripped his arm tightly. "Beth, how does this man know that your mother was murdered in Whitechapel?" he finished.

"Precisely," she whispered tensely. "How *does* he know? If this Ripper madman is nothing more than one or even a group of vile men who hate women, then how does he know about a case that, to my knowledge, has been all but erased from the official police record? Yes, I know about your secret activities on my behalf with Lord Aubrey. He confessed as much to me last summer. Charles, I know that you and Paul removed the evidence regarding my mother's death so that I might be free from it and would never find her broken body on display in the exhibits of some tawdry wax museum or splashed in ink across the pages of *The Star*, but clearly this fiend knows all! But here is what is worse, my dear friend, and it is why I so impulsively rushed here today when I learnt you were in Whitechapel. This letter did not arrive in the post, as you can see, for it bears no stamp. Yet, it was found in our post bag this morning."

St. Clair felt a massive wave of dread creep into his stomach, as if something far more sinister loomed on the horizon. "He had access to the postman's bag before it arrived?" he suggested.

Elizabeth shook her head. "No. I sent to the post office and asked our postman to come by again, and he did so at ten this morning. He said no such letter was in the bag he left with us."

He smiled for a moment, remembering the girl who had investigated the publican on her own. "So you have already begun to inquire about the envelope, have you? Shall I issue you a warrant card, Duchess?"

She returned his smile, and it helped to ease the tension. "Not just yet. Perhaps another time."

"And your postman is reliable? Do you know him well?"

"Yes, Mr. Hampton is a very trustworthy gentleman whom I've known for many years, and he was kind enough to circle back on his route and submit to my questions—even though I lack a warrant card," she added, smiling once more. "I imagine you think me foolish, but I merely wished to know more before... Well, before imposing on you and your office."

"I would never think you foolish, Beth, but you could have sent one of your footmen to A-Division," he suggested. "Though, since this is H-Division's case, I imagine that is why you brought it here."

"You tease me now," she complained, and he feared he had hurt her.

"No, no, Beth, truly, that was not my intent. Forgive me. Of course, I am glad you brought it to me. It is just that today—well, no matter. So, this Hampton fellow, did he recall seeing the letter?"

She shook her head. "No. He had filled the bag himself, and he would have remembered such an unusual envelope. Our house is the first stop on his morning route, and he met no one along the way, therefore it was not surreptitiously slipped into the bag. I was quite clear about asking him this. It can only have been placed into the bag *after* Mr. Hampton left it with my butler, which must mean that someone had access to the house."

Panic again seized him as he realised what this implied. "Which also means he has access to you. No, this will not happen. I shall shoot this Saucy Jack person myself, if it comes to that, no matter what the law might say. Elizabeth, I'm sending for Lord Aubrey. I want him to take you to Scotland right away."

"No, Charles," she replied stubbornly. "Please, don't. I will not leave—not yet. I need to make you see how far this plan goes, so that you realise the deep history of it, the true evil of it. Ripper and his crimes are but one aspect to this madness. I must show you the tunnels beneath Branham."

"Paul can show them to me after he leaves you at your grandfather's estate."

She shook her head. "That would not work. Paul has seen parts of the tunnel system, but I have never shared these areas with him."

St. Clair sighed, for he could see no other option. "Very well, but we will go together to Branham, the three of us, as soon as we may. But for now, today, I want you in Aubrey's protection. I will not have you remain at a house where a madman lies in wait. France! Come up here at once!" he called into the stairwell. "I'll send Inspector France with a message to Whitehall. I take it the earl is there today?"

"I believe he is," she replied, resigned to her fate. "Forgive me for worrying you, Charles. Had I known the pressures you are under today, I would not have come, but instead gone to Superintendent Dunlap at A-Division as you said I should. But I thought you would wish to see the letter. Forgive me, please. It's clear that I've upset you for no reason."

He pulled her into his arms, not caring if anyone else in the station saw. "Forgive you for what? For coming to me when you feared? For asking me to share your danger? For seeking my aid? I would be upset and angry had you *not* done so, Elizabeth."

"Charles," she began, but he put two fingers on her lips to quieten her.

"Listen to me for a moment, my darling, beautiful duchess. I know you cannot tell me all that now worries and haunts you, but if you will allow it, I shall take that worry upon myself and remove all that makes you afraid. All that terrifies you. Will you allow it, my dearest heart? Will you let me be your protector...if not...more?"

She thought about Paul's proposal, of the ring now upon her left hand, beneath her glove. How could she hurt him?

"I want to...I do, Charles, for it seems that my fears vanish whenever you are near." She clung to him, her mind racing to all possibilities and how each would affect her family, but her heart won out at last, and she looked into his eyes, her own filled with trust. "Oh, my noble knight, yes. Yes, I will, Captain," she said, knowing she risked forever damaging her relationship with her wonderful cousin, but her heart needed to look to Charles, though she wished it did not.

St. Clair kissed her cheek and then her hands, longing to do more. "Good, then it is settled. Once Aubrey arrives, we shall make plans to go to Branham."

"If you say that is how it must proceed, then I accept it," she whispered, sitting on the sofa. "Charles, why did you not wish for me to speak with that woman downstairs? I am not mistaken. I did recognise her."

He'd wanted to avoid this conversation, but it appeared inevitable. "I'd rather hoped you wouldn't recognise her. I saw how it affected you, Elizabeth. Those old memories came flooding back along with that recognition, did they not?"

She looked away, suddenly realising where they now sat. "It was this office, wasn't it?" she asked. "Here, where I was brought that night. Where..."

"Please, don't think on it, darling," he whispered, sitting beside her. "Let the past remain buried."

She leaned into his embrace. "If only it would, Charles. I fear that the old memories do not remain buried for long. But that woman. She talked to me. That day at your house. She knocked on the door."

St. Clair blinked. "Beth, I think you misremember. She worked in the house across the street from my home, but she did not knock."

"No, Charles—I mean, yes, she did work there, I suppose. However, I not mistaken. Whilst you slept and Mary Wilsham was out, I heard a knock. I had been looking out the window at the time, and I saw her knock upon your door. I answered, and she asked if my name was Elizabeth."

"What?" he gasped. "She? The woman downstairs? You are certain of this?" he asked, standing and opening the door. "France! Now!" he called again.

"I am absolutely certain of it. Of course, I could not recall my name then, and even upon hearing it, I did not know if it was true or not. I told her that I was unsure, and she said it did not matter. That she had a message for me—for the little girl inside the policeman's house."

The younger officer arrived at the door and knocked. "Sorry to be so long, Superintendent, it took some time to locate the ink remover. Do you need me, sir?"

"A moment, Arthur." A very dark intuition nudged at St. Clair's brain. "Do you recall that message, Beth?"

"I do. She told me that a man had asked about me. She described a very tall person with a foreign accent. She told me that he would hurt me if he found me, and that I must remain with you. She seemed quite sincere. It was then that the publican walked past, and I feared he might be this very man. I tried to waken you, but you slept soundly. By the time I returned to the door, the woman had disappeared, and as I feared losing sight of the man, I decided to follow him. Charles, I had no idea then just how dangerous it was. I only thought I was helping you."

He took her hands and kissed them. "You are too brave for your own good," he said with a smile. "Arthur, I want you to do two things for me. First of all, please, stop by my house and check to see that Mrs. Wilsham is all right. And once you've made certain of that, take a hansom to Whitehall and deliver a message to Lord Aubrey in the Foreign Office." Charles quickly wrote a short note and folded it before handing it to France. "Tell him that Elizabeth is here for now, but that she must not return to her house. Do you have that?"

"Yes, sir. Right away, sir. Oh, Dr. Sunders says that he cannot yet remove Miss Ross to the dispensary. Apparently, the lady is quite upset and insists on speaking to the duchess."

"Beth?" St. Clair asked. "Do you wish to speak to her?"

"Yes, Charles, I do. May I?"

"All right," he said, helping her to stand. "Careful as we go down these steps, though, Elizabeth. You still look pale to me."

He walked beside her, making sure that she suffered no further strange spells, but he paused before leading her back into the main lobby. "Let me first make certain that O'Brien and Dam have not returned. Stay here a moment."

St. Clair walked into the large lobby, noting Sergeant Williams's curious look. "Sergeant, the reporters have left?"

"They have, sir, and it's calmed considerably outside, now that Mr. Lusk's crew have dispersed. Your threat to start arresting people put a right good scare into them, sir. Thank you for that."

"My pleasure, Alfred. Did you remove the film roll from that camera?"

"I did, sir. And Mr. Dam seemed quite angered by it, but I explained that it was in his best interest to make no fuss, else he could make application to you from the other side of iron bars."

"Well said, Alfred. Thank you." Charles returned to the hallway and took Beth's arm. "Darling, are you sure you wish to speak to Miss Ross?"

"She asked for me, Charles, and besides, I wish to know more of her connexion to—well, to this man."

"I still believe your memory is flawed, but...no, do not glare at me so!" he added, smiling. "Come. Let us see what Miss Ross recalls of that day."

As the pair entered the lounge, Sunders stood. "She's very weak, sir. My lady, it is kind of you to come down. Miss Ross? The duchess is here."

Elizabeth sat into a wooden chair near the couch and touched the woman's hand. "Miss Ross? Do you remember me? It's been a long time since last we spoke, but I remember you."

Ida Ross opened her eyes. "Oh, you was a little girl then, my lady. So pretty, an' you wore Mr. St. Clair's shirt, I think."

Elizabeth smiled. "That's right, I did. I'd forgotten that."

"An' you was kind enough to ask if I needed a coat, you was. Such a pretty thing. An' real sweet." She coughed once, her eyes growing unfocused. Then, she sat up suddenly. "Wolf! The wolf!" she shouted, her face pinching into a mask of fear.

Elizabeth's face grew white, and she reached out instinctively for St. Clair's hand. "Why would you say that? What of the wolf?" she asked.

Ross reached out for the duchess, gripping her forearm. "That man," the woman explained, her eyes wild. "He told me to say it. To tell you that the wolf had his eye upon you! He come to the house, and he told me to knock on Mr. St. Clair's door. He said your name was Elizabeth. That I should tell you that you was in danger."

"Who told you this, Miss Ross?" St. Clair asked. "Did you knock on my door?"

She began to weep uncontrollably, and her hands shook. "I don't know! I canno' remember right. It was dark, and oh he was a right frightenin' man, he was. Told me he'd slit me and then toss me into the river, if I didn't do as he said. But no one else saw him. Irene said no one was there, but I did see 'im, sir, I did! I reckon he just disappeared in a puff o' smoke or like some great shadow when the light's gone out." She began to weep, her eyes shut tight.

Elizabeth's entire body trembled, and Charles put an arm around her shoulders. "You're safe, Beth. No one will harm you here."

The duchess took a deep breath as if to steel her nerves. "Miss Ross, you say this man—that he disappeared. Did you hear him speak?" she asked. "Was it English?"

The woman shut her eyes tightly, her voice trancelike. "Not English, no. But somethin' ancient that spoke inside my head. Like he was whisperin' into my ears, though I could see no one, and... and...he said he was comin' for you, and..." Ida opened her eyes, rimmed with red and pain, but her expression slack. "What? Oh, Mr. St. Clair. I didn't know you was there."

"Her mind is unstable," Sunders said sadly. "She'll make little sense, I'm afraid."

Elizabeth touched her hand. "Miss Ross, do you recognise me?"

The woman appeared confused. "Should I?"

"Beth, we must leave her to rest," St. Clair said, touching the duchess's hand, but she would not move.

"Miss Ross. I am the little girl. You talked to me ten years ago. The man who talked to you. This thing you call the shadow. He was not really a man at all, was he? He not only talked about the wolf. He *was* the wolf," she said calmly.

Both men showed surprise, but the sick woman nodded, a moment of clarity driving her. "Yes! Oh, yes! A wolf! Like a great animal, he were, but I could hear him talkin' inside my head! He said he was comin' for you, Elizabeth. Said he was... That he was gonna kill you. Don't go near the tunnels, please! He said he would kill you there! Stay in London. Do not go to Branham!"

"What did you say?" Elizabeth asked, suddenly terrified. "Why would you speak of tunnels? How do you know about my home?"

The woman's eyes closed, and she began to sing softly to herself.

Sunders sighed. "It's advanced syphilis, my lady. She makes no sense. Forgive me, Superintendent. I should not have sent that message upstairs. It was kind of you to come down, however, Your Grace."

"Come, Beth. Let's return to Reid's office." She seemed not to hear him, but Charles took her by the arm and gently coaxed the duchess to her feet. "Darling, please. She is deranged. We must allow Dr. Sunders to care for Miss Ross. Our presence will only upset her."

"But why would she mention tunnels, unless...?" she asked, her eyes filled with dread. "How could she know anything about them? How could she know I planned to show you the tunnels beneath Branham?"

"A strange coincidence," he replied, though he found the answer unconvincing. They climbed back to the upstairs office, and St. Clair brought her a glass of water. "Drink this. Do you still feel unsteady, darling?"

She drank the water, and he watched as she regained her sense of calm, her composure. After a moment, she smiled at him, touching his hand. "My wonderful Captain, forgive me for worrying you. I'm all right. Do you truly think Miss Ross merely said those things because her mind is...deranged?"

"I do, but try to help me understand what happened ten years past. Can you do that for me?"

"Yes. I think so."

He sat beside her and kissed her cheek. "All right, then, tell me all that you remember of that day. If Ida Ross knocked upon my door, then surely she saw you chase after the publican. Why did she not follow you—go after you? Beth, you were just a child!"

"I'm not sure. As I said, she had left your doorway. At the time, I assumed that her warning meant that the man from the park had somehow found me. But how could he? And why would she speak of the wolf?" She paused, fighting rising panic. She glanced up, tears staining her cheeks. "Forgive me, I know you must wonder at my sanity now, but the wolf..." she began, her voice trailing off. She tried to appear calm, but he could see that she was, in truth, terrified.

St. Clair took her into his arms, stroking her hair. "I will not allow anyone or anything to harm you, Beth. Nothing reaches you that does not go through me first. Do you believe me?"

She nodded, but she still trembled. "Yes, I believe you. Just give me a moment. What was it you asked?"

Wondering if he should let this drop, the detective waited until she'd begun to calm. "You are sure you wish to continue?" he asked. "Long ago, the late Lord Aubrey warned me not to push you to remember things you've forgotten. Beth, I worry that I'm doing that very thing now."

"Uncle Robert," she whispered. "How I miss him. But there are times when I *need to remember,* Charles. Please, what did you ask me?"

"Did Miss Ross follow you?"

"No, she did not, and I did not know where she'd gone, but at the time I thought little of it, for my mind was fixed upon pursuing the tall man, who turned out to be the landlord. Later, as you and I returned, I stopped to talk to her again, and she whispered to me. Do you remember?"

He'd not noticed, for then all he could think of was the deadline his late wife had set for Beth's removal from their home. "No, darling, I do not. Other matters weighed upon me, I'm afraid. What did she say to you?"

Elizabeth turned pale. "She told me that the wolf was coming for me. It is why I asked her to explain it just now, but perhaps she does not remember fully. The disease has altered her memories, I imagine."

St. Clair stared, for this made no sense—unless it related to her childhood fears of an animal. "Elizabeth, this happened almost ten years ago, yet you recall this conversation as if it only just occurred, and yet—forgive me, darling—but you have told me that your memory is unreliable."

"It is at times. I've no idea why, but Paul seems to think it normal. Ordinarily, my mind is quite sharp, and I can recall fine details that many others miss. Entire conversations for one thing and faces I've seen but once. Charles, Miss Ross did tell me that. And only after I regained the memory of who I was did it make any sense."

"Do you think she meant William Trent? How can he be this wolf, Beth? Though he is a detestable person, and I would love to see him hang, I fail to understand how he could be this animal."

"No one wants him to pay for his crimes more than I, Charles, but that is not what I surmised," she told him. "Trent is demonic, but he is not the wolf. I'm sure of it. I would ask Miss Ross more, but she has—what did the doctor say—advanced syphilis? I'm so sorry. It is an illness that is transmitted through, well, through intimacy, is it not?"

"It is. Prostitutes often contract it, and then it spreads to her customers, and thence to the next poor woman. A vicious circle of death. We see far too much of that disease here, but had it been caught early, there may have been hope for her. Now, I fear, there is none."

The duchess grew pensive. "Are you saying she will die? There is nothing to be done? Oh, I would help her if I can. Would a hospital offer treatment?"

"Sunders would be the one to answer that, darling, but I doubt that any medicine could help her now. Look, let's not speak of this more. It's well past luncheon, and you look pale. Allow me to send a constable for sandwiches and lemonade. I dare not take you out, Beth. Lusk and his rabble may have left, but with the protestors still in the streets, it is too dangerous. I am sorry."

She actually laughed, and it made his heart much lighter. "How very strange, Captain. Do you recall our conversation when you stopped by to see me on Tuesday?"

Charles smiled. "Before or after I returned to your library, Duchess?"

She blushed slightly. "After, Captain. And I am so very glad you did return. I am sorry if it seemed that I was dismissing you. I worried what my butler might think, you see. It is complicated, but I preferred he not..."

"That he not make assumptions about our, uh, friendship?" he suggested, kissing her hand.

"Something like that. But you asked if we might meet again soon. And you said you'd like me to join you for supper this evening. Do you recall?"

"Of course, I do. However, I'd planned to take you somewhere a bit nicer than the Brown Bear Pub."

Again, she laughed, and he wanted to embrace her—kiss her once more. "I would have been happy no matter where you took me, Captain."

"Really? Even if I brought a packed lunch and asked you to share it with me on a blanket with a bottle of wine?"

"Especially then, for such a simple repast would have allowed me to get to know you better, would it not? Oh, my darling Charles, you are quite wonderful, but I fear our time slips away from us. When Paul arrives, it's very likely that all our plans will have to change. I know my cousin, and he will have some great plan of his own devised. I only hope it includes you, for it is important that you see the tunnels at Branham. And I always feel safer whenever you are nearby."

"If Paul constructs a plan that allows me to do that, then I shall follow wherever you lead, Duchess. And together, we will find a way to keep you safe from this Saucy Jack fellow and anyone else who might seek to cause you harm."

Four tense hours passed before Paul Stuart arrived. He came in an unmarked clarence drawn by a matched pair of chestnut mares, but the coach's driver was in fact Sir Thomas Galton, Paul's right-hand man at Whitehall, and the person he trusted most outside his own family. Arthur France and a dozen, fellow officers formed a protective phalanx through the Leman Street mob to the coach, where the earl and St. Clair helped Elizabeth inside and then joined her, Charles sitting opposite whilst the earl sat next to his cousin.

"Paul, you must take her out of London as soon as possible. Beth cannot return to Queen Anne House," St. Clair began as the carriage rolled into motion.

The earl smiled. "I've done better than that, my friend. It is what delayed my arrival; details take some time to work out. We three are on our way to board a train."

"A train? What? We three? Paul, I cannot simply leave London without contacting Scotland Yard," he answered as they moved along Leman Street toward Whitechapel Road. "Paul, perhaps..."

Aubrey smiled. "Relax, my friend. It is all arranged. I have left word with Sir Charles Warren that you are with me for the next few days. Trust me. Warren will not object. He knows from experience to steer clear of my path whenever possible. Now, I have also sent word ahead to a skilled and reliable tailor to meet us at Victoria Station, and he will take your measurements to be fitted for any items you may require whilst at Branham—or wherever it is we must travel from there. Kepelheim is a swift and gifted artisan, and he can provide your attire within forty-eight hours or less. In the meantime, should you have need of anything, I keep a small wardrobe at Branham Hall, and since we are of similar height and build, that should do for now."

He then turned to the duchess. "Darling, you know me well enough to trust I am thorough, and since it is possible that Branham will not provide safe haven for you, I have asked your lady's maid to pack your trunk. It is on the luggage rack of this carriage even now. I've also arranged for a special to take us into Branham Village rather than trust to rail schedules, and once there, a close friend awaits to convey us to the hall. Also, a special train means only we and our tailor friend will be aboard as passengers. And before you ask about the crew, St. Clair, I can tell you that this special is a one-of-a-kind. It is owned by my family, and we vouch for everyone aboard her."

St. Clair's face brightened. "You are indeed a thorough man," he said, much relieved. "How long is the journey to Branham Village?"

"An hour, perhaps ninety minutes, depending on the tracks and routing," Aubrey replied. "Branham is in northeastern Kent, and pastureland lies twixt here and there, which sometimes means sheep or cattle upon the tracks."

"Good," Charles answered. "That will give Beth plenty of time to explain just how the tunnels beneath Branham connect to murders in Whitechapel."

CHAPTER EIGHT

It was nearly five o'clock by the time the trio boarded the special train for Branham, and once they had settled into their compartment and commenced the journey, Elizabeth began to tell her reasons for asking both men to view the great maze of passageways beneath the Branham grounds.

"You ask how the tunnels connect to Whitechapel, Charles. To understand it, you must better understand me. When I was a little girl, and particularly whenever alone in the house—Branham Hall, I mean, and most usually at night—I had a recurring dream. A nightmare actually. Though some form of this nightmare has plagued me for as long as I can remember, two months before my father died, the dream crossed from my sleeping life and appeared to my waking eyes."

She paused as if struggling against the cruel memory, her eyes downcast, her hands clenched. Charles watched her breathing, her strain to regain composure, and he marveled at her inner strength.

Elizabeth took a deep breath and continued. "We'd been planning a trip to Glasgow, my mother and I. My father served as governor-general to India for a time, and then afterward, he was assigned a diplomatic post in Vienna. He'd been there only a few weeks when he wrote that he would be meeting us at Drummond Castle for a short holiday. Truthfully, I was always closer to my father than my mother—though, I'm not sure why. I suppose my father had a gentler spirit. My mother, though she loved me, often seemed distant. Charles, in truth, I loved my father dearly and believed he could do no wrong. Each time he left, each time he sailed away, I felt as if he took all my happiness with him."

She paused again to regain her calm, and then looked to her cousin. "Paul, I've never told you this story, but I have told Grandfather. If he told you, then it is more than I know. As I said, we were preparing for our train trip, when I heard a man's voice in our garden. It was the fall of the year, and the Branham gardeners had been working countless hours switching out plantings and modifying soils. I knew these men well, for I used to play around them, and they'd often instruct me as to the plants and seasons, so that I might better appreciate their labours, although as a little girl, I didn't realise that was their purpose, at least in part. They were very kind men, and they told me stories whilst keeping me company. Because my father was so often posted abroad, I spent much of my time alone."

St. Clair could picture her as a small child, younger and even more vulnerable than the adolescent he'd met in '79. Imagining her as a lonely little girl only made him love her more deeply and want to protect her all the more.

Elizabeth continued, her eyes taking on a faraway look, as she recalled painful memories. "The voice in the garden was unfamiliar to me, so I looked out my window to see if someone new had been hired. I think my nurse was calling me, but if so, I ignored her because I could see a very strange person standing in the garden, staring up at me. Now, I know you will both think me imaginative, and well, I suppose like all children I was, but this man spoke to me—not with words, but with his *thoughts*."

"Thoughts? Beth, surely not!" Paul interrupted, shaking his head. "You were most likely dreaming," he said, but his own experience had proven otherwise. During the earl's years in pursuit of Redwing, he, too, had heard thoughts—voices inside his mind from outside forces—but Paul hoped to keep that truth from Elizabeth, to shield her from it, lest her fears grow stronger. Charles, however, recalled Elizabeth's previous story of an animal that talked to her, an animal that terrified her so much that she had suffered from a strange physical episode as a child in his house back in '79. He wondered if there might be some connexion 'twixt the two.

"Beth, did this person..." he began, but Aubrey interrupted.

"There was no real person, Superintendent. Elizabeth dreamt it all."

The duchess grew angry. "Nonsense! Don't you think I know a dream from a real event?" Paul's eyebrows arched in a way that she recognised, and she backed down—but only partly. "Very well, Cousin, think me mistaken, but you will not change my mind!"

St. Clair wanted to know more, so he leaned forward and touched her hand, hoping not to appear too forward to the earl. "Please, go on, Beth. I'm interested in hearing, if you would tell it."

"Thank you, Charles," she said, clearly uncomfortable. "Very well. This man, he was tall—very tall. Taller than either of you. Yes, I know what you are thinking, Cousin; I can see it in your eyes. You would tell me that everyone looks tall to a child, but this man stood next to a statue in our north garden that I know to be six feet high, and he was easily *a head higher*. He stood there, his monstrous thoughts entering my mind, and he smiled and waved as if I should have recognised him, yet not even one of the gardeners appeared to notice his presence!"

Charles considered her words, her body posture, her eyes and mouth. He'd interviewed and interrogated a thousand or more witnesses and prisoners over the years, and he could instinctively tell when someone lied—even one most accomplished in doing so. Elizabeth was telling the truth. The animal she'd feared as a child might, indeed, be connected to this strange man in the garden.

"Beth, do you believe this person meant to harm you?" he asked. St. Clair could see her shoulders relax, knowing that she was believed.

"Yes! Though I cannot tell you why precisely. His smile appeared more malicious than friendly, and his eyes…oh, those *eyes!* They burnt like two red lamps!"

"What did he say to you? What words did you hear in your mind?" Charles continued, taking note of Paul's sudden silence.

"He bade me come down to him, saying he only wished to protect me. He said I was in danger, and that he'd been watching me since my birth. But… But, he also told me that... Charles, he told me that my father was going to die."

She turned toward their compartment window, staring at the passing countryside, her face reflecting the little girl Charles had carried, had cared for, had come to love. He could picture her now, standing before a high window and hearing this demonic speech in her mind.

Paul, too, looked out the window, and his thoughts seemed far away. "Connor died two months later," the earl said softly, his eyes fixed on the woods beyond the rail line. "A hunting accident. And that is all it was, Elizabeth. A tragic accident. There was no prediction of that sad day. It was nothing more than your imagination. You must drop this."

She started to reply, but seeing the harsh reproof in her cousin's eyes, she suddenly stopped and drew a deep, laboured breath before replying. "Yes, I suppose, you are right," she whispered tightly. "It was, as you say, an accident."

Charles leaned toward her, his hand on hers. "Beth, is that what you truly believe?"

"It is what happened, Superintendent," Paul insisted sternly.

St. Clair glared at the earl, unable to comprehend his sudden coldness, but before he could speak further, the train slowed to a stop. Paul opened the exterior door, and both men stepped out to look down each direction of the line, making certain that no one had forced the special to halt.

As they returned to their seats, the interior compartment door slid open, and a short man with a moon face appeared. "Just a water stop," he said, sitting next to Elizabeth for a moment. "So good to see you again, Your Grace," he said with a tip of his Bowler hat, which he then set to one side. "You are Superintendent St. Clair? I'm Martin Kepelheim, and now would be an opportune time to take your measurements; that is, if that is still our plan, Lord Aubrey. Is it? You look as if something has happened. Did I miss something whilst I spoke with our engineer?"

Paul's face was grim. "No. Nothing has happened, Martin. Forgive me. We have been speaking of dark matters, and I suppose my mood has darkened as a consequence. We three are in need of your smiles and excellent storytelling. Forgive me, Charles, my mind has been elsewhere. Beth, dearest, you remember Mr. Kepelheim, don't you?"

She put out her hand and offered her best smile, the kind she had been taught to wear whenever circumstances required polite conversation, but when your heart and soul have no means to produce a genuine smile. "Mr. Kepelheim, of course. I hope you will pardon me. I've not been myself today."

The tailor bowed and kissed her hand. "No need, dear lady. These times try all our souls, do they not? Mr. St. Clair, if you will step this way, I shall endeavour to take your vitals, for I have a fabric with me that will certainly bring out your remarkable eye colour. This way, sir."

Elizabeth made use of their privacy to speak to Paul whilst St. Clair met with Mr. Kepelheim, the reliable tailor, who not only fashioned the earl's clothing but also served in his network of London spies.

"You are angry with me," she said simply.

"Why, Beth? Why did you not bring that letter to me first?" he asked.

She had expected this, and she knew he had every right to ask it. "I can only say this, Paul. The murders in Whitechapel *are* connected, just as I have been telling you, so I thought it best to deliver the evidence into the hands of the police as soon as possible."

"Into the hands of one particular policeman, you mean," he answered, hoping to keep his voice gentle but failing miserably. "I can see the affection you hold for Charles, Elizabeth. I am not a blind man, but I had hoped to be the first you turn to whenever you have any fear. It is my pride that is hurt, and only that."

She knew she had stung him, but she could not un-do it. Yes, she could have taken the letter to him first, but she had not. That fact alone worried her. What hold did St. Clair have over her heart? She dared not think about it.

"Forgive me, my darling cousin," she said, kissing his cheek. "I am, as always, in your hands."

"If only that were true," he whispered, kissing her in return. "Elizabeth, why was St. Clair at your home on Tuesday afternoon? I happen to know that you had no chaperone there at the time, and..."

Her face went white. "What? Paul, how can you know that? You have someone watching my house, don't you? Paul, that is completely out of bounds!"

"No, my darling, it is not. You know that it is my task to keep you safe. No, Beth, do not interrupt me," he warned her. "This is no secret—not between us at least. Elizabeth, I want only to protect you, and I cannot do that unless I know what it is—and *who* it is that enters your life."

Her face passed from pale to tinged in pink, and he noticed that she clenched her hands as if trying to maintain her temper. "You spy upon me, and I am supposed to be reassured by that?" she whispered tightly. "And that nonsense about a chaperone does not seem to apply to you, Lord Aubrey. Shall I tell my grandfather how you behaved with me last night?"

Paul sat back, taking a moment to measure his response. It was true that he had pushed the bounds of propriety with her, but it had always been assumed that she would become his wife. He now feared that her desire no longer lay in that direction.

"Do you love him?" he asked her bluntly.

She turned away, her lower lip trembling. "Please, do not ask me that."

He took her hands, kissing them. "Darling, forgive me if it sounds as if I do not trust you. I do. Completely. It is only fear that drives me. Fear of losing you to someone else."

She wore his ring even now, and she'd wondered if St. Clair had noticed it when she'd removed her gloves earlier. The bright blue diamond caught the light that filtered through the trees along the line, sparkling like a secret sun as the train slowly began to move again toward Kent.

"But you and Charles have been friends for nearly a decade. Would you imagine him behaving any way that is inappropriate?"

"No. He is a gentleman, but I also think he cares for you, Beth."

"Perhaps. But it is your present that I wear, Cousin," she reminded him. "It has not left my hand since you placed it there; nor will it."

"Christmas seems so very far away," he said mournfully, instantly regretting the petulant response. "Elizabeth, do you really see us together as husband and wife, or is my hope in vain? No, wait, forgive me, that was unfair. I know you love me—truly I do—but I fear your heart now strays toward another, and it worries me. For many reasons, but most of all because I cannot imagine life without you. I love you so very much."

"We have been through many trials together, you and I," she whispered. "Paul, I wish I could say all the words you long to hear, but would you have me lie?"

"Are you saying that speaking love to me is a lie?" he asked, instantly regretting it.

She touched his face, stroking the afternoon stubble that shadowed his chin. "I have hurt you, haven't I?" she asked, and he heard agony in those words. "Paul, my darling cousin, for most of my life, you have been my solitary friend. I do love you, but sometimes, I worry that perhaps it is not the kind of love you deserve."

"Beth, I..."

"No, please, let me finish. I want only the best for you, and the woman you marry should love only you. You are that special. That wonderful. Paul, my mind is muddled, my heart divided. I know these past four years in Paris were intended to clear it, but..."

Paul reached out impulsively and pulled her into a tight embrace, kissing her passionately as if desperately trying to keep her as his own. She felt the same thrill she'd experienced the previous night at Queen Anne House, and the same sweet temptation to give in to this overwhelming feeling, but a soft knock on their compartment reminded her they were not alone.

Aubrey sat back from her, his hands still on her own. She was trembling, and he longed to take back his harsh words and rash actions. "Come in."

Kepelheim's large head popped into view, a tape measure draped around his ample neck. "Lord Aubrey, the man is almost exactly your measurements! I have never seen such a thing; you could be brothers! In fact, it's a funny thing, now that I think about it. Were your hair darker and short instead of dashingly long, and perhaps a slight change in the eye colour and nose, a small tweak to the brows—why you might even be twins."

Elizabeth smiled, her heart lightened by the tailor's gentle manner, glad for a reason to smile. "I have chosen twin sentinels, have I? Thank you, Mr. Kepelheim, that is quite delicious! And I shall use every opportunity to remind both men of this fact!"

Even the earl began to laugh, and all three were enjoying a moment of welcome merriment when Charles returned to the compartment.

"What did I miss?" he asked, as he sat down opposite Elizabeth.

Paul and Beth exchanged glances, and then burst into a fresh round of laughter. "Superintendent, have you ever considered wearing your hair a bit longer?" he asked St. Clair, leaning toward Elizabeth in a conspiratorial manner.

The policeman's dark brows knit together in a puzzled frown. "No. Hardly. Why?"

"Just curious," Paul replied. "Charles, you did tell me that your family is from London, correct?"

St. Clair pulled his shirt sleeves down and reached for his suit coat. "Liverpool and London, yes. Yet, my ancestry is Scottish, I believe. The St. Clair family there has some distant connexion to mine, or so my late wife told me, claiming that some spelt it differently—Sinclair, I think. I'm not sure there's any evidence to back it up, but she insisted upon it."

Paul blinked, his face breaking into a wide grin. "Really? Good heavens! We might be cousins. My aunt married a Sinclair."

"Does he jest?" Charles asked, looking to Elizabeth with all seriousness written across his face.

Kepelheim tapped the detective on the shoulder and nodded. "Even I know this to be true, Superintendent. Angela Stuart Sinclair, isn't that right, Lord Aubrey? She was your mother's sister, I believe."

Paul nodded, leaning toward Charles. "You see, if you'd studied your own family history, then you'd know the name St. Clair originated—or so my mother said—in a village in France, *Saint-Clair–sur-Epte*, and that it has deep connexions to the founding of Normandy. It is sometimes spelt out fully, S-a-i-n-t, but over the years it was often shortened to St. Clair and then Sinclair, of course, based on the original French. I've cousins that spell it both ways, and a few that use the abbreviation as you do. Have you ever visited the Castle Sinclair in Caithness? It's a complete ruin now, of course, but it once stood proud. It came tumbling down when a war broke out over inheritance. George Sinclair of Keiss claimed the right to the castle and the title in 1679, but not everyone agreed. A nasty business it was, so says Uncle James. He's our family historian. We'll have to see just how your St. Clair family weaves into ours. As I said, Charles, we might just be cousins, which may explain our physical resemblance, but might also mean you and Elizabeth are related as well."

Charles forced a smile, but something about it unsettled him. Not that he'd mind being related to either Paul or Elizabeth, but his policeman's senses were tingling, and he began to wish he could see more clearly just what forces were at work to bring him into the lives of these two titled cousins.

"You said they fought over a title? What would that have been?" he asked.

"Earl of Caithness, if memory serves," the tailor said with a wink to Aubrey. "And I believe it is currently in abeyance. The duke would have much to say about it, I think. As would your wonderful father, Lord Aubrey, may he rest in peace. Some say you, in fact, could lay claim to that title as well."

"I've enough titles to last a lifetime," Paul said wearily. "The only title I now desire is to be called Elizabeth's husband."

Immediately, he wished he could unsay it, for he saw the strain it placed on her in the sudden paleness of her fair face. He took her hand and kissed it. "But that will wait until she agrees to it. I've much to prove in the meantime, Mr. Kepelheim. For now, I should walk the length of the train to make certain we were not boarded at that water stop." Then leaning toward Elizabeth's ear, he whispered, "Forgive me, darling. I had no right to say it."

She smiled, a weary, sad smile, and he knew he could say nothing more to ease the moment. "Charles, will you keep our duchess safe whilst I take a stroll along the cars? Kepelheim, come with me, won't you? I've an idea for that new shop you mentioned to me last week."

The two men departed, closing the compartment door and leaving Charles and Elizabeth alone.

"That is the earl's ring, is it not?" he asked, wishing simply to hear the bad news quickly. "I do not recall its being there when we kissed in your library, or had you hidden it away knowing I would be visiting?"

"Why would I do that?" she asked angrily. "If I intended to marry the earl, then I would not have *permitted* you to kiss me!" She held up her left hand, determined not to be ashamed of such a pretty ring from so gallant and loving a heart. The centre diamond dazzled in blue white sparks against her face. "It is a beautiful ring, and I would not hide it. Paul asked me to marry him only last night—three days *after* you and I met."

"Then I wish you both all the best," he said curtly.

"You misunderstand me, Charles. I accepted his ring only—for now, as a promise to him that I shall accept his proposal of marriage at Christmas. And only then."

St. Clair felt little reassurance at this, so he began to stare out the window at the passing woodlands, hoping she would not see the great despair etched upon his face. "What have I misunderstood?"

he asked, knowing instantly that the anger in his voice betrayed his feigned composure. He suddenly hated Paul, though he knew it was unfair and unmanly to bear the kind earl any grudge. "If you plan to accept him at Christmas, how is that any different?"

"One might say it gives me a little time to consider...other options," she said, her voice lowering to a whisper.

He looked at her, seeing the strain the conversation had placed upon her heart and regretting his anger. He opened his mouth to speak, but she put up her hand to stop him.

"Before you say anything more, Charles, please hear me for a moment. Do you think Paul your enemy? Good heavens! He has left us alone for this very reason, so that we might talk. My cousin knows me better than I know myself, and he has admitted to me that he has reason to doubt my affections. No, do not speak yet! Not yet. I do not know my heart, Charles. I cannot, and in some ways I fear to examine it closely. Paul and I have been—well, you might say promised to each other since the day of my birth. I have loved him with all my heart for as long as I can remember."

"Yes, I know that very well," he said somewhat petulantly, the anger returning. "It was the earl's name you called over and over that terrible night, ten years past. But you were a child then, Beth—that I can understand, but now..."

"No! Let me speak," she insisted, once again putting her hand to his lips. "Please, Charles, please listen. There is so much more to me—to all of this dark nightmare—than you can even begin to guess. Though Paul wishes it were otherwise, the story of the man in the garden *is true*. It all happened, just as I have said. I'm sure that Paul knows it to be true, but he pretends it is not. I think he does this to help me, but sometimes I wish he would trust my courage. I pray the truths you'll soon discover will not alter your affections, Charles, but if so, then I shall understand. For once you know all, you may no longer wish to be—well, to be more than a friend to me."

"That would never happen," he assured her, taking her hands into his and kissing them. "Dare I hope, Elizabeth? Were you another woman, I might have said that you have bewitched me, but truly it is your gentle spirit and pure intentions that have won my heart. Your beauty and grace are beyond measure, but even that might prove less to me without your beautiful soul to complete it. As a mere commoner, a lowly policeman, society would deem me foolish for speaking to a duchess this way, but in truth, I am yours, entirely. Yours to command. Yours to toss away like so much dust, if you choose. I would wish it to be no other way. Dare I hope, Beth? Dare I imagine a future for us?"

She nodded, her eyes staring at his hands. "Yes, Charles, you do."

In answer, he pulled her to him, kissing her mouth, her cheeks, her hair, unable to constrain the fierce emotion overwhelming his heart. "I love you so very much, Elizabeth," he whispered, and she started to reply—but without warning, the train lurched, and then screeched to a dead stop, the cool autumn air split by the high-pitched scream of iron wheels upon iron rails.

Still holding her in his arms, the detective glanced out the window. "Why are we stopping? Surely, we cannot need water again so soon," Charles said, suspiciously. Alert to all possibilities, he opened the exterior door and looked along the tracks toward the forward part of the train but saw no sign of danger.

"This could be nothing, but it may be a trick," he said to her as he climbed back inside the compartment. "If we have been stopped intentionally, then it is likely a ruse to lure your protectors aside. I don't dare leave you alone, Beth. You'll have to come with me."

He helped her to her feet, and then cautiously slid open the inner compartment door. The interior of the train had gone quiet, but Charles could hear voices outside—on the other side of the tracks, arguing and shouting.

Then, suddenly, rapid gunfire!

Whilst being measured by Kepelheim, Charles had removed his shoulder holster, and he suddenly realised it was still inside the rearmost compartment of their car. "Beth, do not move," he told her, and then St. Clair briefly returned to the tailor's 'fitting room' and withdrew his Webley revolver from the leather holster. Returning to her, he put Elizabeth behind him so his body might shield her. "Keep close to me," he said tensely.

They moved forward, one step at a time, inching their way toward the engineer's compartment. As they entered the next car, four more shots rang out, and then a fifth and sixth, in quick succession, followed by chaotic shouting. Then, as if out of nowhere, Paul Stuart appeared from the side steps, blood staining his left shoulder. Kepelheim, too, bobbed up the stair, his grizzled hair in disarray, his face florid and sweating, a revolver in his hand.

"It was William's team, I'm sure of it!" Paul shouted, bending to catch his breath.

"You're hurt!" Elizabeth cried out, rushing past Charles to reach the earl. "Charles! Mr. Kepelheim! Please, help him to sit!"

Paul gasped for air as they eased him into the foremost compartment. His face was pale, beaded with sweat. "It's just the shoulder," he assured her. "A scratch. I've had far worse."

Kepelheim removed the earl's coat and waistcoat. Beneath it, the white silk shirt had already become soaked with crimson. "That's good," the tailor said, ripping open the pearl button closures to expose the wound. "Dark blood is good. Bright is bad." He pulled the earl forward slightly to get a better look at the backside of the shoulder. "Also good. The bullet has passed through cleanly. I imagine it hurts a great deal. Let me dress this now, and then whisky, I think. Mr. St. Clair, my new Scottish friend, would you be so kind as to ask the engineer, a nice chap named Lester, if he could give you my medical bag? It has a bottle of Scotch whisky in it."

Charles glanced at Elizabeth for a second, wishing he could take back all his angry thoughts and selfish words, and then dashed forward to fetch the bag.

Paul's breathing was laboured, but his face bore a wan smile as he gazed at his cousin. "Never fear, Princess. It's nothing."

She kissed his hand, regretting their previous conversation, placing his right palm against her cheek. "You are always so brave, my wonderful knight. My darling, what can I do to help? Do you want water? Shall I fetch anything for you? Paul, my love, tell me how to help."

He grew quiet for a moment, his eyelids squeezed together as intense pain flooded through his shoulder beneath the tailor's probing fingers. Beth swiped at his long hair, finding a small stain of blood beneath. "Is this another injury?" she asked Kepelheim.

The tailor checked the linear wound, which formed near the earl's right temple. "It's nothing," he lied, for he recognised the track of another bullet, clearly meant to penetrate the skull and end the earl's life. "A branch scratched him, I think. There were wild bushes by the tracks. Only that, my lady." He smiled at the duchess, but he could tell by her expression that she doubted his explanation.

St. Clair returned with the bag and a message. Sitting next to Kepelheim, he looked at the earl, recognising the deadly nature of the wound at once. "Mr. Lester tells me he wants to make sure no one unexpected awaits at the village station, so he has signaled ahead. He said that if the earl's man is not there, or if his reply is not according to the code you have arranged, then we will not stop at Branham, but instead proceed southward on a new track."

The tailor nodded. "Yes, the earl's man will send a reply signal, if he can."

Charles looked perplexed. "I'm confused, Mr. Kepelheim. What signal can be sent twixt the village and a moving train?"

Kepelheim smiled. "The earl has equipped this train and Branham station and even the hall's gate house with a remarkable device based on Heinrich Hertz's experiments with radiated waves. With this, he is able to send and receive messages through the air."

"Really? No wires? That is remarkable!" he said, noticing that Paul's eyes had opened again. "The Yard would be envious of such advances, my lord."

"If they knew about them," Aubrey whispered, his eyes rimmed in red. "We often test out such inventions."

The tailor nodded as he looked through the bag. "One day soon, even your police station will use wireless telegraphy, but for now it is limited only to the earl's experimental employment."

"It would seem, Lord Aubrey, that you have left little to chance," Charles said, relieved to see the earl breathing more easily.

"I failed to foresee an assault from the woods," he replied, gritting his teeth as Kepelheim cleaned the wound with the whisky. "Charles, we shall need your experience and sharp eyes when we reach Branham station—if we reach it. Ah! Martin, that's flesh not fabric!"

The tailor shook his head and continued probing. "Such protest. I'm making certain of the path and that nothing remains. There! You are a blessed man, Lord Aubrey. I think that man aimed for your heart. Another inch or two lower, and who knows? But here, let me stitch it up. This part will hurt, so drink this down. All of it." He handed a large tumbler filled with the amber liquid to the earl, who downed it in one gulp.

"I hope this isn't expected to put me to sleep," he joked with a wince of pain. "This is Drummond whisky. I've been drinking this since I was fifteen."

The tailor shrugged and threaded a needle he'd sterilized with a match. "So I know, but it's all I have. I did not imagine we would be heading into the lion's maw so soon. I'd hoped to visit the chemist in Branham for supplies. Now, sit still. This will take a little time if I'm to keep your scarring to a minimum. We don't wish to mar your pretty self too badly, now do we?"

He began to stitch the wound closed, and Elizabeth held the earl's hand, her eyes watching the tailor's movements. "Would you teach me to do this, Mr. Kepelheim?" she asked.

All three men showed surprise, and Paul smiled broadly. "Most women would faint at the sight of so much blood, Beth. You do our clan proud, lassie. But I wouldn't want your pretty hands consigned to men's work."

"Men's work?" she asked, her pride clearly wounded. "Are men alone the world's healers? We race toward a new age, gentlemen, where mere women will bear much of the workload whilst our men once again rush to war. Is that not so, Paul?"

He nodded wearily.

"Well, then," she continued, "should not women learn such practical skills? I am able to sew and embroider and play the piano as all ladies are expected, but I would learn more useful arts. Yes, yes, I know; even Aunt Victoria would not have me doing manual labour, as she would call it, but I can make better use of the means to which I was born, can I not?"

St. Clair watched her face, flushed with a fire he'd not yet seen in her, and he wished to applaud her courage. "There is much that is needed, which only wealth and generosity may achieve, my lady. The east end is in great need of better hospitals—one for the poor in particular. The London deals primarily with industrial accidents, and even those who are admitted must first meet the approval of the board of governors, and many are turned away and die."

"People like Miss Ross?" she asked, genuine concern in her eyes.

Charles nodded. "Yes, people just like Miss Ross."

"Then, it is settled," she answered. "When we have time to relax our attentions from worry and distress, then I shall make that my goal. A hospital, and perhaps a place where those with aptitude but no funds to pay for education may learn the skills that you apply so readily, Mr. Kepelheim."

"I like it very much, Your Grace," the tailor said, clipping the thread with a small pair of scissors. "There! Almost like new."

Paul took a deep breath and glanced at his shoulder. "Not bad for a tailor," he said. "Now, we must be nearing Branham. Kepelheim, if you would ask Mr. Lester what word he received back from the station."

Nodding, the little tailor bobbed off toward the engine. Paul looked up at Charles. "If all is well, then we must make for Branham Hall with all speed. I expect to remain there two days, no more, and then we must travel to a safer location. I shall send word to the Yard if you like, Charles, explaining that your services have been seconded by the Foreign Office until further notice. It is not the first time we have employed the investigative abilities of the CID in service of our cause."

St. Clair helped Paul on with his coat and then lifted him to a more comfortable position in the compartment seat. "Thank you, Charles," the earl said with genuine affection. "Beth, darling, would you mind fetching my overcoat from our compartment? It's cold suddenly."

She kissed his cheek and nodded, turning back toward the other end of the special train. Once she'd left the front compartment, the earl spoke swiftly. "Charles, if for any reason, I do not survive this, you must promise me that you'll keep her safe."

The detective's brow furrowed. "Don't speak of such," he whispered, but Aubrey clutched at St. Clair's forearm, intense pain etched upon his lean features. He coughed, and his breathing came with difficulty.

"Promise me!" he implored. "Beth trusts you, and I believe she would follow whatever you asked her to do. And make sure you send word to the duke. Beth's grandfather. He knows our current plans, and he expects to hear something from me by end of day."

Before Charles could answer, Kepelheim returned with a slip of paper, written in a strange series of numbers and letters.

"This makes no sense to me," the tailor said, handing the note to Aubrey. "I imagine you have changed your cipher since last I served."

"We have. Just a week ago, so I pray this is the new one. The fact that it is gibberish to you, old friend, cheers me, but I know with your head for ciphers, you would translate it easily in time. I'll give you a guide to the new one, when we reach the hall."

Stuart took the paper, mentally translating the strange symbols. "Thank the good Lord! We are safe for now. My man in Branham Village says that no enemy ranks have been spotted."

Beth returned with the overcoat, placing it across the earl's chest and shoulders. "Here you are, darling."

Just then, the train began to slow, and a clanging of bells signaled the approaching station.

"We're at Branham," she said. "I can see the platform up ahead."

"And just in time," Charles answered, looking to the earl. "Your man awaits with a coach?"

"He does," Paul said, wincing again. "I'll need your help with the trunk and baggage. We must be on the road to the hall as quickly as possible. It grows dark soon, and I've no wish to be on that wooded road after sunset."

CHAPTER NINE

It was nearly seven o'clock by the time the three men, the engineer, and George Cummins, Paul's Branham contact, had transferred all the luggage and weaponry (Paul had brought a small arsenal) to the carriage. Cummins, a gnarled but well-dressed man of mid-fifties, bore a harsh red scar on the left side of his face, but he smiled readily and honestly, taking care to assist the duchess in keeping her feet on the uneven, gravel path. Kepelheim and St. Clair helped the earl into the interior of the spacious landau, covering up both him and Elizabeth with two of four blankets that Cummins had thoughtfully placed inside.

"Fret not, Princess," Paul assured her as he settled into the richly upholstered seat. "Mr. Cummins and I have been through many scrapes. He can hit a fox at half a mile in pitch black. I've seen him do it. I trust George with my life, and now I am trusting him with yours, which I prize more highly than any other."

St. Clair felt concern, but he tried to keep his manner positive for her sake. Recalling Paul's warning, the detective's eyes scanned the woods for signs of danger as they passed. "You keep strange company for a diplomat, Lord Aubrey. Your group of men grows more intriguing by the minute, but perhaps they are better called agents," he said with an impish grin.

Paul laughed, cringing as the small movement brought deep pain to his shoulder. "Yes, well, you will no doubt be meeting more of those agents in the coming days, Cousin. And now, you are one of our company as well. This coach bears no Branham crest, but some may still recognise it. We must keep our eyes on the trees to either side of the road, but, it is my hope that a decoy I dispatched earlier will have drawn off any local mischief."

Elizabeth looked at him sharply. "Decoy? What can you mean by that? Surely, you have not endangered my maid!"

Paul shook his head, his long hair wet with sweat, his words beginning to slur now and then. "Of course not. I would do nothing to put Alicia at risk. I sent her in a special that left two hours before our own. George has told me that she arrived at the station without incident, and that she is doubtless waiting for you now. I imagine she's roused the entire household. Poor Baxter!" he finished, wincing with pain.

"Do not speak, but rest now," she told him. "I expect Mr. Baxter will have the household ready and prepared, if not all armed with whatever weapons they may muster," Elizabeth said proudly, her eyes on the detective. "Baxter is my butler, Charles, and he has spent his entire life in service to the Branham family. I daresay he would defend even you, Paul, should the need arise."

Aubrey smiled, his mind easing as they neared their destination, though his eyes looked less clear. Flinching as he moved, he kissed Elizabeth's hand. "He tolerates me, my dear. I have not been a favourite to your man Baxter since I put a snake in his pantry. Mind you, Charles, I was but a lad of fourteen at the time, but knowing his fear of the creatures, I simply could not resist. Poor Elizabeth," he continued, his face growing pale. "She was—what, dear, perhaps a year old?—and Baxter had just brought—had just, uh, brought her into his pantry to show her 'round."

The earl sat up slightly to look out the window, and severe pain shot across his features for a moment. "No, no, I'm fine. Really, Beth, I'm fine. What was I saying? Oh, yes, the snake," he muttered, his thoughts appearing to wander. "Baxter would often play horse and rider with—with uh, with—with Elizabeth, Charles. He'd carry her on his broad shoulders and bounce about, ah…but that is when my ill-chosen gift decided to—to appear, you see. *Ah!*" he cried out as the carriage passed over a series of deep ruts left by heavy rains in late September, and Kepelheim's thick brows knit into a worried line.

Paul's eyes had lost focus, but he continued his story. "I am ashamed to admit it, but Baxter very nearly dropped my dear cousin from that lofty perch, as he hopped about, trying to kill the creature with—uh, what was it again?— his, uh, boot heel, that's right."

Elizabeth's face became a mask of worry, but rather than alarm the earl, she took up the story to help him whilst Kepelheim opened Aubrey's shirt to re-examine the wound. "That's right, darling," she said. "He stamped at it with his boot. Charles, the entire household was in an uproar. My mother later told me that I was actually laughing, for the housekeeper, Mrs. Larson, who has now departed this life for a heavenly ring of keys, had rushed in to see what had caused our ordinarily composed butler to begin dancing about in a room filled with delicate china. Paul believes Baxter has never forgiven him, you see," Elizabeth said as she stroked the earl's damp hair. "In truth, Baxter has grown quite fond of you in his old age. Paul?"

The earl had gone quiet.

"Paul?" she asked again, but Kepelheim shook his head.

"He is unconscious, I think," the tailor said. "Probably best. The pain must be unbearable, and I've no morphine in my bag."

Charles kept his eyes on the woods as Paul had asked him. Burnt orange and crimson hues painted the autumnal hills, and the setting sun scattered rosy fingers amongst the shadowy pines that covered them like a regal crown. "It's beautiful here," he said to Elizabeth, hoping to take her mind off the earl's grave condition.

He could see tears tracing the curve of her cheeks as she looked up, and Charles wanted to take her hand, but he dared not. Instead, he continued speaking. "How far is the manor house from the sea?"

Beth glanced up again, wiping at the tears. "Not far. Fifteen miles or so. Perhaps twenty. I've never actually measured it, of course, but there is a marker stone on the riding path near the old abbey that says eleven miles. I used to walk there as a girl."

The memory seemed to disturb her, so Charles changed the subject. "I've never been much of a sea lover. These beautiful trees, however. How their colours sparkle in the sunset! You know, I think autumn is my favourite time of year."

"And mine," she answered, smiling. "Our house is surrounded by magnificent gardens, but the old woods have a simple beauty that the even most elegant garden cannot match. There you'll find carpets of bluebells and stitchwort, and there are great, rolling meadows where sheep and cattle graze. To the south of the hall, you'll find field after field of lavender and wild poppies, and their innocent beauty always reminds me of a painting by Monet or Van Gogh. I hope you like Branham, Charles. In many ways, this place grounds me, though it also holds much that frightens."

Her eyes took on a faraway look.

"Beth, these tunnels," he began, "I worry that seeing them again might…well, that it might cause you pain. Emotional pain, I mean."

She took his hand, clutching at it, and he longed to hold her, but he dared not, not with Paul so close to death. "Charles, I believe I can face anything if you—and Paul—are with me. Do you think Miss Ross knew something about the tunnels?"

"I don't see how she could," he assured her, though he had been wondering the same thing. Charles had said nothing to Elizabeth, but he had come to know Ida Ross well in the past ten years, and he had been mentally replaying many of his conversations with her over and over, realising that much of what she'd said to him during those years might have deeper meaning. "I imagine her illness causes her to speak random words, and it is but coincidence that she mentioned tunnels. Do not let it alarm you."

"I'm sure you're right," she whispered, but it was clear that she found no real comfort in his assurances. "I might write to Dr. Sunders and ask about her. If I send the letter to H-Division, will he receive it?"

"Yes, but I can send him a wire, if you wish, Beth. You're very kind to offer to pay for Miss Ross's medical needs. Does the hall receive the London papers?"

"Yes. Why? Oh, I see. You hope to discover whether or not those reporters wrote about me. I've no doubt they did. Whilst I lived in France, I often found myself mentioned in the press, though I'm not sure what the public found so fascinating about my life."

"I find you fascinating," he admitted. "In fact, I wish I could read French as well as you do. I'd have subscribed to every Paris newspaper had I known you were mentioned even once."

She laughed, shaking her head. "And you would have found my life rather dull, Captain. I only attend parties when required. Most of my life has been spent quietly. Most of it," she added, dark thoughts shadowing her face. "But I believe my life is about to take a turn, though I'm not sure of the direction. Oh, I can see Branham!" she cried out suddenly. "Paul, darling, it's Branham. We're home!"

St. Clair looked out the north facing window just as the coach turned left at a great bend that followed Henry's Creek, named for

King Henry II when he'd built the original castle that later grew into Branham Village. As the four horses galloped northward, the narrow roadway passed through a wide iron gate, flanked by massive crouching lions of carved stone, and then broadened into a grand avenue of fine gravel, lined on either side by regal chestnuts and graceful elms. Yellow roses, burgundy smoke-tree, pale pink viburnum, purple-leaved forsythia, and a chorus of fall colours cheered their passage toward the sprawling mansion beyond as if welcoming their duchess home.

Containing over two-hundred rooms, including the largest private library in England and a glass-domed solarium, the family seat for the Dukes and Duchesses of Branham had stood for over four hundred years. Despite its age, the family had managed to maintain it well, adding modern amenities in Elizabeth's grandfather George Henry Linnhe's time as duke, and more recently the young duchess had added electric lighting to the ground floor and kitchens.

"This is a *hall?*" Charles asked, dumbfounded. "I'd expected something a bit more, well, sedate and cosy."

"It is, in fact, considered a palace though not officially, of course," Kepelheim said, cryptically. "I've been here many times before, and each visit brings new things to experience. The gardens! Oh, I hope you will have time to see the gardens, Superintendent. Even in October, they put on a glorious show. And there is a hedge maze that kept me lost in its embrace for half a day last summer!"

"It is simply my home," Elizabeth said softly, as they drew ever nearer. "When I was younger, I remember reading *Pride and Prejudice* and realising that, as ordinary as I believed my own life to be, our home would have surpassed that of Mr. D'Arcy's Pemberley in that wonderful book. I suppose because the main character shared my own name that surely she was myself, but I soon realised that most readers—and Miss Austen as well, no doubt—would consider my home intimidating. I hope, Charles, you will not think so. We are, at heart, just plain folk. As my grandfather told you all those years ago at Drummond House, we do not stand on ceremony. Or at least, we try not to do so."

Charles wanted to embrace her, to remove all fear from her beautiful eyes, to hold her to his heart so that his might beat in time with her own; and he wanted her to be his and his alone forever. But he dared not think it. Dared not express it. Yet he felt certain that his face held no ability to hide that fact.

She gazed at him and then at Paul, who now slept. Soon, she must make a choice. But not now. Not yet. No one could have foreseen that the choice would soon be made for her.

Back in London, Sir Thomas Galton met with three men in a tavern near the western edge of Whitechapel. The group sipped dark ale and shared opinions as they pored over a strange map of the east end borough.

"You got this where again?" asked a tow-headed youth who wore an eye patch. "From Swanson?"

Galton nodded, wiping ale from his mouth. "Not directly. Swanson had it, but passed it along to Billy Ankerman and now through Reid here, it comes to us. You remember Ankerman from Eton, lads. A rascally boy, stood taller than even our Aubrey. Thin as a rail. Flaming red hair that never stayed combed. Lord Montagu's nephew."

The youth nodded. "My brother knew him. I didn't, of course, though I heard the tales from him. Some, to be honest, are hard to credit."

Galton glanced anxiously toward another man, who sat opposite him at the table. He and Edmund Reid had known each other for ten years, both men sharing a love of aeronautics and sleight-of-hand. The Whitechapel inspector had served as a member of Paul Stuart's shadow army of operatives since the 'duchess murder' of '79. "Yes, well, much what we face is difficult to fathom. As to this map, why don't you explain its curious route, Edmund," Sir Thomas said.

"According to the encoded letter connected to this map, Swanson found it in the pocket of a man who'd been knifed to death outside the London four nights past—he then delivered it to Ankerman," Reid explained. "Ankerman, so the letter says, delivered it to the Foreign Office the next morning. This puzzles me, my friends. If true, then why did this map never find its way into the earl's hands directly?"

Sir Thomas leaned back in his chair. "The earl's mind has been elsewhere this week, and he's not kept regular hours at Whitehall. So, who from the Foreign Office delivered it to you?"

"A chap named Richards. I have never seen him before, Thomas, and though I asked him to remain whilst I sent a wire of inquiry to Whitehall, he was nowhere to be seen when I returned to my office. We've no idea why, but both Swanson's name and Ankerman's are penciled to the back of this map. Neither man has been seen since Wednesday, or I would ask them myself. With Aubrey engaged in protecting our dear one, it's up to us to decide how to proceed. Look closely at the map, lads. It's marked and numbered in what I'm told is blood, possibly human."

"How did you determine that?" Thomas asked. "The duke's laboratory?"

Reid smiled. "His secret laboratory, yes. I'd love to have access to Drummond's scientists to solve our backlog of crimes. There's a German chemist named Freiburg working there now who's been using something he calls an 'antigen' to identify human blood. Amazing science, but it's not been proven a hundred percent reliable yet, so I'm to say that it's 'possibly' human. Now, I must give credit to a fellow inspector at Leman Street for this next part. Arthur France—a clever copper that our St. Clair's been grooming for the Yard. France is blessed with a talent for recognising patterns, and he suggested that these marks might correspond to crimes. I had France look into it, and sure enough at least some of them correspond to unsolved murders in the east end. That one there on Commercial," Reid said, pointing to the map, "marked in pencil with the number '1' beside Christ Church is precisely where Morehouse and St. Clair found Duchess Patricia in '79."

Galton examined the map with a hand lens. "Are they all numbered?"

Reid nodded. "They are, and the murders we uncovered are in sequential order. Some of the pencil scratchings are faint, and the map's so stained and creased, it's hard to discern all, but there look to be thirty-three in total. A number we've all seen before."

"Thirty-three? The number of rebirth to them, is it not? Some aspect of their sadistic, ritualistic code."

"Code?" the youth with the eye patch asked.

"Did your brother tell you nothing?" Sir Thomas asked, adjusting his spectacles. "Redwing reveres a system of numbers. They believe these numbers have power in the spiritual realm. Thirty-three is a favourite, and…wait, a moment. Edmund, was not Duchess Patricia's body discovered in March?"

"It was. The third of March…oh, I see what you mean. Another thirty-three. Third day of the third month."

Galton leaned back, wiping at his eyes. "I grow too old for this. Edmund, I've no idea how much this map helps us, but it's clearly meant as a message—if not a warning. Then, according to the list your man France put together, Duchess Patricia's murder was the first in this long ritual."

"Ritual?" the one-eyed man asked. "Pertaining to this number thirty-three, then?"

Galton nodded. "So it would seem. Redwing often practises extensive rituals. Some reach across time, others across space, you might say. I know of one that was enacted in five separate places at once." He continued, "So then, the one the press calls Fairy Fay is number eight, and Eddowes is sixteen. Edmund, could it be the duchess is right? That Jack is indeed a member of Redwing? Is William Trent behind all of this?"

Reid gulped the last of his pint. "Aubrey's thought that for weeks now. He denies it to our duchess to keep her mind at ease, but she is stubborn."

Galton laughed. "So she is. But your Charles St. Clair is also resolute and insightful. Those three together form an interesting combination."

"Indeed they do." The detective inspector glanced at the face of the younger man at their table. "How'd you lose your eye again?" he asked casually, lifting his hand to signal the landlord for a second round. "You're buying this time, Galton."

The youth leaned back into the chair, and his crooked smile widened. "I told my girl that it was in an affray over her honour, 'course, but to you gents, I'll give the same truth my brother would've had, God rest his soul. I had nodded off whilst on the night train out of King's Cross, bound for Yorkshire to attend my brother's funeral. I was alone in my compartment when I was roused from my slumber by an unseen hand."

"Unseen?" Reid marveled. "Were both eyes shut then? This was a dream my friend."

"Nay," he argued, "no dream, but a nightmare nonetheless. After being shaken so violently, my eyes had opened wide like a baby bird's beak. This *thing*, which I shall call it, for I know not what it was, well, it yanked me clean out of my seat, threw me to the floor, and then pulled my head up to its—well, I'll say its mouth, but it had no such a thing. Yet, I heard words in my head, as clear as a church bell. *She will bear the reborn son, and that son shall lead us. His shall the world become, and his blood our freedom purchase.*"

Galton nearly laughed, but in truth, he had heard these words before—or at least he had seen their like. "You know this from where, boy?" he asked, pointedly, noting that Reid's face, too, showed recognition.

"From only that moment," he continued. "My brother, the late Sir Harold Malmsby, a man you and yours knew well, had once warned me about Shadows that speak. I'd thought him mad or jesting, yet here it was, and here was the voice, speaking in riddles. What does it mean?"

Galton took a breath and then forced a laugh. "Nothing! Tis but a riddle we've seen left here and there. Nathan, you and your brother spent too much time wandering the moors near Malmsby House. Your good father, may he rest in peace, may have died penniless, but he certainly left a legacy as a storyteller. Seriously, boy, how did you lose that eye?"

Sir Nathan Malmsby shook his head and set his mug down heavily. "It is all true! This shadowy thing whispered the words I've just said, and then—well, as best I can explain it, this Thing put its ghostly finger through my left eye, and it's not healed since, and that's been six months past. My eye is there, but it bears a red mark, like something clawed it, and I can see through it no longer."

Reid leaned forward and lifted up the black eye patch. Beneath was a bloodied eye with a cloudy lens, along with what appeared to be fresh, crimson slashes that ran diagonally from the inner eyebrow to the outer corner of the eye.

"It is as you say," the Leman Street detective said flatly. "Well, join the ranks, lad. Many of us have such rakes and scars upon our persons. This is not a flesh and bone army we fight, but one made of sinister smoke, as from the pit of hell. This map troubles me, gentlemen. The next number after Eddowes is number seventeen—here, Galton. See? Yet, I can find no crime in any police archive since Catherine Eddowes's death that matches a house on Goulston. If this is a roadmap for murder, then we may have sixteen more ahead of us. Should I start posting men at all these other locations? Our ranks are thin as it is."

Galton took the fresh mug of ale brought by the barmaid and gulped it down all at once, surprising everyone. "Perhaps. In truth, I cannot say, my friend," he continued, wiping his mouth of foam, "but I must report this to our inner circle. You've done well to bring it to us, Reid. As always, your loyalty to the cause shows the truth of your soul. Malmsby, since you're filling your late brother's shoes, I want you to take a message to our contact in Kent," he said, handing the young man a small envelope. "Go to your brother's old territory near Gravesend and give this to a baker named Switham. He is a rotund man with a jolly laugh and thick spectacles. He and his wife Meg will put you up for the night, but be back here in two days with the baker's reply. If you find any sign that Trent has been seen at the docks, if there is anything amiss, send word the usual way."

"Usual way?" the boy asked eagerly.

"You know. The code. Telegraph it to me at Whitehall."

Clapping on a wool cap and downing the last of his beer, the youth nodded and pulled on his overcoat. "I'll not let you down, Thomas."

"You'd best not, lad. You might be a baronet now, but you're amongst many with far grander titles who know less and receive little due, so think not that you have privilege here. Even the duke considers himself just a foot soldier. Off with you now!"

The lad turned and headed toward the door, scuttling off into the night toward Whitechapel Station. After a few minutes, Sir Thomas lowered his voice and whispered to his two companions, Reid and another, a man named Malcolm Risling, the second son of Lord Pemsbury. He'd said little during their conversation, having learnt long ago that social rank held no part in their dealings. Risling was thirty-one and unmarried, and he had an innate ability to sense truth in any situation. He now spoke in whispers.

"Thomas, I've been watching a man in that corner over there. No, don't turn. His is a face known to me, although I cannot say from where. He kept his eyes upon us as we spoke, and his gaze also followed the lad as he left just now. I've a bad feeling about that young man, but more to the point, I have no great trust in his claim to be Malmsby's younger brother, but if he is, then we must question his loyalty. I have looked into it, as you suggested. Our dead comrade did have two younger brothers, but one died in North Africa, and the other—well, his location is unknown. He left home at fifteen over a quarrel with their father. The last known location I have been able to ascertain was near Brussels in the company of a widowed countess. I think she found him amusing, or so my contacts tell me. But this countess also has ties to the other side, and possibly to William Trent."

Galton's face blanched. "Can we have made such a mistake at so perilous a time? May heaven prove you right soon, if this is true, Risling! And may that same wonderful heaven intercede where we may have failed. I must send word to Aubrey at once. They may be riding into danger!"

CHAPTER TEN

The staff at Branham met the duchess and her knights at the front entry, Cornelius Baxter, the butler, at the head.

"Welcome home, my lady," he said warmly, his thick eyebrows arching in unison with each word. "Lord Aubrey, what has happened? Gracious heavens! Come in quickly. In this room, gentlemen. Bring the earl to the fire. Shall I send for Doctor Price, my lady?"

The group followed the butler through the expansive, tiled foyer and into a quiet drawing room to their right. There, a bluestone fireplace rose to the coffered ceiling, flanked by large portraits of Elizabeth's mother on the left and her father on the right. Several overstuffed sofas dotted with comfortable pillows sat about the carpeted salon, and a black Labrador retriever, who had been sleeping by the pleasant fire, jumped to her feet at the approach of her mistress. The dog nuzzled the earl's hand, recognising an old friend.

"Hello, Bella, my girl," Paul said sleepily as the men laid him upon the sofa nearest the blaze. The dog's thick tail fanned the air, and she licked at his fingers. "Good girl," the earl said thickly, closing his eyes.

"He's lost a great deal of blood," the tailor explained to the butler. "Baxter, my old friend, we must send for Doctor Price, for my field dressing skills can only go so far. The bullet passed through, but it must have nicked a vessel. I had thought not, but he continues to bleed despite all attempts to stop it."

Baxter's distressed face revealed a deep affection for the earl, regardless of earlier stories, and he nodded before disappearing into the foyer once again. Mrs. Alcorn, the housekeeper who had taken over for Mrs. Larson three years earlier, brought in tea and hot water.

"I can fetch our medicine chest, if that helps, Mr. Kepelheim."

"Yes, that would help. Thank you, dear lady. You are a blessing as always. And perhaps brandy? I believe the earl keeps a cask or two in the cellar, is that not so?"

"Quite so," the buxom lady replied with a glance toward Elizabeth's other companion. "And you, sir? May I bring you something stronger than tea as well?"

"Mrs. Alcorn, this is my Captain Nemo," the duchess explained, "but you may call him Superintendent St. Clair. We would never have made it here without his aid."

"A pleasure to meet another friend to our young duchess, Superintendent. Will a brandy do, or would you prefer something else?"

After the tense journey, Charles longed for a drink, and he nodded. "Thank you, Mrs. Alcorn. Brandy will suffice nicely. You will do me a great service, I assure you."

"Mrs. Alcorn," the duchess said, "there used to be a small supply of Aunt Victoria's favourite cognacs. Do we still have any? If so, bring one of those."

"The *Danflou* or the *Le Burguet*, my lady?" Alcorn asked from the doorway.

"Either. The *Danflou* is quite nice, if we have enough. I imagine it will require decanting, though."

Baxter had returned just in time to overhear the last of this exchange, and he answered. "I have taken care of that already, my lady. This afternoon, when the earl wired that you would be arriving, I took the liberty of preparing a number of his favourite spirits, the *Danflou* amongst them. Mrs. Alcorn, you will find four decanters on my desk; each is marked."

The housekeeper curtseyed and left the drawing room, shutting the doors behind her. Kepelheim opened the earl's shirt once again, which was stained to the waist with fresh blood. "If the bleeding does not stop soon, he will need a transfusion," he said, glancing up at St. Clair.

"He may take my blood," Elizabeth offered, ignoring Charles's vigourous, objective shake of the head.

"No! I will not allow that, Beth, nor would Paul."

She sat into a chair next to Aubrey, her head against his, tears mingling with the blood still seeping from the stitched bullet hole. "He gave his blood to me when I was a little girl. I fell down a great cliff and suffered a deep wound to my leg. It bled as this does, and

Dr. Lemuel insisted that I would die without blood. Paul had just turned twenty-one, and he had come down to Glasgow to visit with us—my parents and myself. He gave me three transfusions over the course of two days. I only survived because Paul was there for me. The doctor told us then that his blood is compatible with mine, because had it not been, I would have died. I owe him my life!"

Charles pulled up a side chair, covered in blue silk, and gently put his hand on Elizabeth's forearm as he sat. "Let us try mine first. Paul would himself refuse your blood if were he conscious, dear heart. And if he and I are truly cousins in some way, perhaps then, mine will suffice. And there is far more blood in my veins than in your slender body."

She began to weep, leaning into Charles for strength as she gazed at the earl's pale face. "He did all this for me! For me! If he dies, my heart shall die a thousand times over, Charles!"

"I will not let that happen," he promised, kissing her hair softly. "Not so long as I have breath."

Mrs. Alcorn returned, carrying a large, brown leather medical bag. She set the bag onto the table nearest the earl and opened its brass buckles. Inside, she had placed a large bottle of 1857 Glenlivet single malt.

"A footman is bringing up the decanters Mr. Baxter prepared, but in the meantime, I hope this medicine meets with the doctor's approval," she said with a wink. "There are four glasses as well, should my lady require a stiffener."

"Mrs. Alcorn, you are an angel," St. Clair said, rising and kissing the housekeeper's hand.

"Oh, go on!" she giggled, her entire body jiggling. "Now then, Mr. Baxter has sent our first footman Mr. Milton to the village for Dr. Price. I cannot imagine he'll be back here before an hour from now, given the distance and the time, but I know that you, Mr. Kepelheim, possess certain skills, and I've trained as a nurse, so how may we proceed for Lord Aubrey? If you believe a transfusion is in order, well, I've assisted at those also, and I know the procedure. Mr. St. Clair, if you're to be the donor, then you'll want to find a sofa. This can take a lot out of a person; even a grand, great man such as you."

Charles liked her, and he praised Almighty God that such wonderful people served here. "I am in your hands, Mrs. Alcorn."

"All right then. I can fetch syringes, or would you prefer to use the tube method, Mr. Kepelheim?"

"Tube is more efficient. Let us transfer a small amount first and see how Lord Aubrey responds. He is not in danger of death yet, but I do not wish to push him closer."

Charles and Kepelheim moved a second, long sofa close to the fire, and set it parallel to the one where Paul now lay. Searching the large medical bag, the tailor found several needles within a long black leather case marked with a large gold 'B' for Branham, and along with it three flexible rubber tubes.

"I see you have had need of these before," he remarked to the housekeeper.

"Yes, one of our grooms was kicked by a horse last summer, and Dr. Price left this transfusion kit for the hall's use. It saved our groom, that is certain. His son gave the blood, and it worked well. That same groom stands outside even now, his shotgun loaded, keeping watch along with thirty other men from the estate."

"You are a woman after my own heart," the tailor said with a wink. "And these have been boiled?"

"I did so before I stored them, but perhaps I should do so again. We've a pot of boiling water on in the kitchen right now for whatever purpose you require. Our cook, Mrs. Stephens, is keeping an eye on it."

"That would be best," Kepelheim said, handing the entire kit to Alcorn. "Boil the needles as well. I have seen what sepsis can do to a man, and I've no wish to see it again."

"So have I," she replied soberly, bustling off into the main hallway toward the back staircase.

The tailor felt for the earl's pulse, counting as he checked his pocket watch. "It's still strong enough, but it grows weak and rapid. His heart struggles to keep up its good deeds."

"Beth, perhaps, you should wait in another room," Charles suggested, wondering how she might react were the earl to lapse into a coma, or worse—to die.

"I will not leave him," she insisted. "Nor would I leave if you were lying upon that couch, Charles. And I know Paul would understand. I also know that he would share his blood with you. I pray it is a match, but if not, I am prepared to give all I have, Mr. Kepelheim."

"That will not be necessary, dear lady," he said softly. "But he will need some from our good friend St. Clair, and soon, I think."

The minutes ticked by at a snail's pace. Elizabeth remained by Paul's side, watching his chest rise and fall, rise and fall. St. Clair paced back and forth, wishing he'd been the one who'd taken the bullet; wishing he'd paid more attention to the earl's warnings. Only fifteen minutes had passed by the time Mrs. Alcorn returned, but it felt like an eternity to those awaiting.

"All clean," she said. "And we've had a telegram from the station in the village. Mr. Milton found the doctor eating his supper, and they left for Branham five minutes ago. They will be here in thirty minutes or less, I should think."

"God be praised for that news," Kepelheim said, lifting his clasped hands to the heavens. "You may have noticed the telegraph lines coming into the gatehouse, Superintendent. The Duke of Drummond had those strung whilst our beautiful duchess learnt the latest dances in Paris."

Beth smiled, knowing the tailor was trying to keep her calm. "My grandfather is prudent, is he not, Charles? And I shall show you all my new dance steps once we reach Scotland, Mr. Kepelheim."

The tailor nodded. "I look forward to it, my lady. Now, we must begin. Mr. St. Clair, if you will lie down here on the second couch, your head even with the earl's, and roll up your right sleeve, please. I cannot promise that this will be comfortable, but it will not be unbearable to a man of your disposition, I should think. Mrs. Alcorn, do you have anything with sugar in it? Lemonade perhaps? Punch or very sweet tea? Biscuits? We shall need them to quickly restore Mr. St. Clair's vigour. Energy is lost when blood is lost."

Elizabeth rose, taking the blue chair now, her face a mask of ash. The Labrador nosed the earl once, and then moved to her mistress's side, sitting as if waiting for the procedure to begin.

Kepelheim wound a small rubber tube around the policeman's upper right arm and then inserted a sharp needle which was attached to another thin rubber tube that ended in a large glass reservoir, held now by Mrs. Alcorn. As the blood flowed downward into the tube, the reservoir slowly filled, until a pint of dark red blood stood ready for use.

"Now, I'm going to stop the flow, and I want you to rest, Mr. St. Clair. I will try but half this at first. Then we shall wait to see how the earl fairs with a strong policeman's bold blood in his veins."

Mrs. Alcorn used picture wire to attach the reservoir to a tall candle stand.

"Very clever, my good Mrs. Alcorn," the tailor said with a wink.

She smiled. "We had to make do in the war. Few supplies and far too many soldiers to bind up."

"Quite so," he replied solemnly. The tailor now turned his attention to the earl, who had slipped past sleep into a deeper, dreamless state. "He is very weak now," he said to Elizabeth. "But he is a strong man, and I have seen him in worse states than this."

Elizabeth gazed at this tailor with new eyes, and she wondered what secrets he and her cousin had shared—what adventures, many she suspected on her behalf. "You are a kind man," she told him. "If ever there is anything I might have within my power to do for you, Mr. Kepelheim, you have but to name it."

He blushed, his eyes glowing from the praise. "Seeing you safe and happy is my reward, dear lady," he said honestly. "Now, let us see if this blood can make a difference for such a good man as this."

He released a clamp on the tube that descended from the reservoir, and St. Clair's blood began slowly flowing downward into the earl's pale arm. "This part of the procedure will take longer," he explained. "His veins cannot accept so quickly what Mr. St. Clair so bravely gave. In ten minutes or so, we shall know more."

Ten minutes passed, and the tailor checked the earl's skin and pulse. "No rash, which is good. Good. So far, it is good."

Another ten minutes passed, and whilst the tailor listened to Paul's heart using a binaural stethoscope, the great doors to the foyer opened, and Baxter could be heard talking with the doctor and giving orders to the first footman. The butler opened the drawing room doors, ushering in a tall, thin man with white whiskers, wearing a slate grey Inverness cloak over a black frock coat. The medical man removed his hat and cloak and headed straight for his patient.

"Good evening, Mr. Kepelheim. I see your ministrations have been put to good use. I'm delighted you proceeded with the transfusion," he said, examining the earl's eyes. "He is in a coma, I think. Or nearly so. Such does not occur in a man so vital as the earl unless much blood has been lost. Yet I see you found another strong gentleman to provide what Lord Aubrey needs most. No, no, my friend. Do not move," he said to St. Clair. "Your part may not yet be over, and you must recover, so lie still."

Charles obeyed, keeping his sea blue eyes focused on Elizabeth, who sat as still and pale as a statue.

Baxter entered the room again, whispering something to the housekeeper, who nodded and left the room. "Mrs. Alcorn will bring you all a cold supper, my lady. In the meantime, if I may speak to the superintendent? No, sir. I shall come to you."

The large butler swept gently past the tailor and the doctor, who were both hovering over the earl's prostrate form now, and he moved to the policeman's left side so as not to be in the way of the instruments. "Sir," he whispered. "We've had a message from London. Our footman can make neither head nor tail of it, for it is in a cipher. I do not pretend to know all that Lord Aubrey engages in, but I know enough to recognise this as a message for him. What shall we do?"

St. Clair sat up slightly and tapped the tailor's arm. "Mr. Kepelheim. A word."

The makeshift doctor whispered something to Dr. Price, who nodded, and then the tailor moved next to Baxter. "I am all attention," he whispered to the detective.

"Can you read the note Mr. Baxter received from the footman?"

The butler handed the tailor a cream-coloured slip of paper bearing a string of nonsensical words and numbers scrawled hastily across it in three lines. Putting on a pair of spectacles, he appeared to be working out the message based on the changes he'd seen in Paul's note on the train. "The letters and their arrangement have altered somewhat, but it is similar to our former code. Let me think a moment. I may be able to determine, based on positions of—yes! I think it says, 'Danger. Traitor in London. Leave at once.' And it is signed Galton. I know this man. Sir Thomas Galton. He is a worthy and honest companion to the earl and a central figure in our work. If he says we are in danger, then you can believe we are."

St. Clair considered their options, which seemed few. "Is it possible that this refers to the ambush along the rail?"

Kepelheim thought this over. "Perhaps, but I do not think so. The time on this indicates it arrived after we left the station for the hall. No, I think this means fresh danger. Mr. Baxter, you said that you have men guarding the house and grounds. We must warn them to be alert all the night, for we cannot possibly move the earl for a day at least."

The tall butler nodded, his face filled with concern for the earl. "I shall see to it, sir. And I shall join them, too, if it comes to that."

St. Clair admired the aging butler. He could just picture this massive gentleman bouncing Elizabeth on his shoulders, stamping out a garden snake in his pantry. "Mr. Baxter," he said, "if you require additional armaments, I believe you will find quite a selection in the earl's luggage."

Baxter grinned, his greying brows rising high. "I have already taken the liberty of availing myself of one or two items from that prolific bag, sir. Now, my lady," he said, turning to the duchess, "if neither you nor the doctor require anything more, I shall take a turn around the park outside. It is a beautiful night."

Beth nodded as Kepelheim rose, his hands bracing his aging knees as he did so. "And I shall take in the night air with you, Mr. Baxter. The stars this time of year are breathtaking."

Dr. Price shared a quick word with the tailor before nodding once again as agreeing upon an action, and then returned to his patient. "I've asked Mr. Kepelheim to shorten his stroll should we send for him. If the earl requires a second transfusion, another pair of hands will be very helpful."

Kepelheim and Baxter stood near the doors, and the tailor looked back just before they closed. "Mrs. Alcorn's nursing has given her experience in this procedure as well, Dr. Price. Should I not be available, you may call upon her skills in my stead."

The doors shut, and the room grew quiet. Price continued checking the earl's skin colour and vitals. His lined face was one that Elizabeth knew well, and she recognised concern when she saw it.

"Doctor, will he die?" she asked him bluntly.

The doctor looked back at her, taking a moment to reach for her hand as a father might. "My dear, the earl is a strong man with a strong heart. He would not leave you, and he shall not. The transfusion appears to be compatible, for I see no indication of fever or flushing of the skin. His pulse has grown stronger since my arrival, which is a very good sign. Put your mind at ease, my lady. You've this other kind gentleman to thank for his part. Without his blood, I fear we might not be so hopeful as we are now. In fact, the earl would most certainly have died."

She broke down, weeping joyful tears mixed with the release of strain, held within her body for two hours. Charles sat up, but he was restrained by Dr. Price. "No, no, my generous friend. You, too, must recover. You will do her no good if you remain weak. An hour more, and you may get up and comfort her. For now, be still and rest."

Mrs. Alcorn entered just then pushing a tea cart, laden with cold meats, cheeses, fresh bread, and a bottle of red wine. "I would have taken this to the dining hall, but that seemed a bit posh for our purposes, my lady. Our men must recline, so better to bring the supper to them. Our footmen and grooms and Mr. Kay, the new underbutler, have all joined the others outside—for a stroll. My lady, your maid awaits in your apartment whenever you are ready to retire. I think she's napping, to be perfectly honest."

"No need to waken her, Mrs. Alcorn. I shan't be retiring anytime soon. If I must sleep, I may do so here."

They ate their supper quietly. Elizabeth made a cheese and beef sandwich, cut it into four small triangles, and handed one to Charles. "Do you need help?" she asked him seriously.

He smiled and pushed himself up a bit higher against the cushions. "I think I can manage a small sandwich on my own." *How selfless she is*, he thought, *how beautiful*. Yet, his detective's mind was filled now with questions that only the earl could answer. Just what was the secret that so many were protecting, and how did it connect with Whitechapel?

"You will show me the tunnels tomorrow?" he asked, trying to keep her talking.

"Yes, if we are able. I've not been there in many years, but I doubt their layout has altered. I once knew them as well as I know the maze outside."

"Kepelheim said he was lost in that maze for half a day!" he laughed, glad to see her smile at last.

She wiped a crumb from her mouth and swallowed. "So he was. However, I memorised every turn and twist as a girl. I used to race to the centre with my father, and whenever I beat him there, he would always make me feel as if I had performed a mighty feat, lifting me high over his head and telling me what a bright lassie I was. He allowed me to win, of course. Oh, how I miss him, Charles! If he had lived, my life would have been so different. That is my father

159

there, to the right of the fireplace," she said proudly. "Was he not a handsome man?"

St. Clair gazed at the large portrait, which showed a tall man with muscular build, dark hair and eyes, wearing full Scottish dress in Stuart tartan red. "He looks like a younger version of your grandfather," Charles said. "A very handsome man indeed. Is the portrait life-size? If so, he was indeed tall."

"It is. I'm told he stood six feet, five inches. He was athletic and quite strong, but also a gentle man. And a kind one," she replied wistfully. "I could never understand why my mother married again, but if she felt lonely, then why marry such a horrid man as William Trent?"

St. Clair recalled the brutish man who had tried to forcibly remove Elizabeth from Leman Street in '79. Not before nor since had Charles come across a man who exuded evil more than Sir William Trent. "How did your mother even meet a man like that, Beth? What circles in your world could possibly have intersected with Trent's? And, though I never had the joy of meeting your mother in this life, I cannot imagine any situation where she might have found that man pleasant!"

"I was too young to have any say in the matter, but I remember my grandfather expressing himself in rather colourful language. You know Drummond. He is not shy when it comes to voicing his feelings on a matter."

"No, he is not," St. Clair laughed. Then he remembered what the earl had asked: that he contact the duke and report their situation. He made a mental note to say as much to Baxter, who would surely know how best to send a telegram.

Elizabeth did not notice the concern that crossed the detective's face for a moment, as she continued gazing at Duchess Patricia's portrait. "My mother met Sir William at the seaside, actually. On the shores of Hampton-on-Sea. The tunnels beneath our property connect to a system of caves that lead to a cove near there. She suffered terribly after my father died. He died that autumn, the very autumn I spoke to you of on board the train in... In a shooting accident in Scotland," she finished, looking at the earl.

She paused, and St. Clair knew she was thinking of the Shadow Man she'd seen as a child, the one who had warned her that her father would die, but he said nothing. Perhaps Paul had good reason for discouraging such memories in his cousin.

She continued, "We spent several months with my grandfather and Lord Aubrey's family after burying my father. You recall I mentioned a fall I took when Paul gave his blood to save me, well it was about that time that my father died. It is strange. I have only dim memories of it. I suppose my father's sudden death caused me to lose track of time—perhaps I was in a state of shock."

Again, her eyes took on a pained expression, as if she struggled to recall memories long ago lost. "After convalescing for several months in Scotland, my leg had begun to improve, and my mother decided to leave, though I begged her to remain another month. Mother insisted that spring had arrived, and we had lingered longer in Scotland than we should. It was unusual for us to be away from Branham during Christmas, for it is a special time each year spent with many of our dear servants' families. I have always loved holidays, but somehow even the return to my home for resurrection services did not cheer me. No matter. Mother thought it best, so she and I took a special train south, which brought us back to Branham just as the new lambs were being born. I suppose it was early March. The weather that spring was unusually warm, and Mother thought it would be a nice distraction for us to have a picnic by the sea. She loved the sea as a girl, and I imagine she thought I had inherited that same love of the water, but in truth it is the land that calls to me—the hills, and the meadows, and the woodlands. But I keep many of her prized sea shells in a large window box upstairs. I'll show them to you tomorrow."

Charles gazed at the portrait, glad to see the beautiful woman before she became the savaged and mutilated corpse left on Commercial Street in '79. "I imagine she made a pretty sight when she was a girl, playing on the sands with her golden curls shining."

Elizabeth smiled, and St. Clair was happy to help distract her from Paul's situation—if even for a moment. "Oh, she was, Charles! She was! Hers is the portrait on the left, of course, but that was painted after my father died, so you see a woman in mourning. When she was happy, when she was young, she was a vision! There is a painting of her in the west gallery that would break your heart, she is so beautiful. Her large blue eyes, lithe and graceful form. Mother was far taller than I, and her golden hair brought her admirers from all across Europe. But she married Connor Stuart, and he loved her as she deserved. William—well, she met him that March. It was a Saturday. I remember, because it was the day before Palm Sunday. Many of the local families were out enjoying the unusually warm sea air. A few brave souls even ventured into the cold water, though only a few.

"My mother had misplaced her gloves, and we looked and looked for them. I had seen her pack them, but she searched in vain. Then a tall man in a cream suit appeared, her gloves in his hand. He asked if she had lost them, and she said yes, of course. It never occurred to her that perhaps he had stolen them—but it did occur to me. I did not like him, not for even one moment. She walked along the beach with him all that afternoon, pouring out her grief to him. My governess and nurse remained with me, but Mother turned all her attentions to him. Do not mistake me; I was not jealous. But I felt an evil from his foul speech that chilled me to my marrow! I told Paul as much when next he visited."

She kissed the earl's damp hair, her eyes growing misty.

"Paul had wanted to come back to Branham with us, but he had government business in France, as I recall. He did come down that May, and he and my mother had some terrible arguments—something very unlike them both, for they had always been such good friends. Paul felt she had chosen unwisely, and he feared that this man—whom no one knew—might cause my mother, but also me, harm. How right his prophecies were! By June, despite everyone's warnings, Mother had secretly married William, and he moved his things and several dishonourable friends and servants into Branham. It is not that we lack space. Certainly, we have room here for many, but Trent's behaviour soon revealed him to be a man with dark secrets. That is why I started following him, whenever he would disappear into the tunnels."

"How did William know about the tunnels? Are they well known to locals?" Charles asked.

She shook her head. "No. Though some of the old sailors tell tales of the caverns and of pirates, most have no knowledge of the tunnels. I believe Henry the Second dug many of them, when he built the original castle that lies at the centre of the village. King Richard built the first hall east of here, but it has since fallen into disrepair, along with parts of the tunnel system. King Henry the Fifth, ordered the current hall be built so he could expand his reach into Calais, but he did not live to see it completed."

"Wait—the Plantagenets built this house? I thought it was built by the first duke."

She fixed her eyes on Paul's pale face, anxiously hoping he might open his eyes. "I have said too much already, but I will answer this one question. The rest you must hear from Paul. Were he awake, he would most certainly be angry with me for sharing what I already have. The first duke was more than I can explain. It is—complicated. Suffice it now to say that our home dates back to the Plantagenets."

His mind sifted through her veiled hints. Paul referred to a secret that he and his trusted men kept. Elizabeth referred to a secret, which it was not her decision to share; in fact, she feared telling it. What did it all mean? And how did it connect to Whitechapel? Why would William leave Patricia's brutally beaten and savaged body there?

"He awakens, I think," Dr. Price said, dabbing a bit of brandy to the earl's pale lips.

Elizabeth leapt to her feet and fell down on the carpet beside the earl. "Darling, can you hear me?"

His lips moved, and his dark lashes blinked. She touched his hand, and he squeezed her fingers in return.

"Oh, my Paul!" she wept, wiping at his hair and brow. "Open your eyes. Look at me, Cousin."

The eyelids twitched, and then slowly opened. The blue eyes were bloodshot and filled with pain, but he smiled wanly despite it. "Hello, Princess. Miss me?" Her head dropped to his chest, and he drew his good hand over to touch her hair, stroking it like he might a child's. "I would not leave you, Princess. Of that—of that, you can be certain. Is that Charles over there? Was he injured also?"

St. Clair sat up, leaning toward his friend. "So you've at last finished with your little nap, Cousin," he said amiably to hide his concern. "No, I've taken no bullet, but I've given you some red policeman's blood to mingle with your Scottish blue."

Paul looked at Price, who nodded. "This brave man has given you much blood this night. Your wound was far more serious than Mr. Kepelheim first surmised. It is only this gift which has saved you."

"Then I owe you my life, Cousin. And fine Scottish blood it is, too, I'll wager. Surely, we are related if we can share such intimate gifts."

Price touched the detective's arm. "The earl must rest now, but so should you, Mr. St. Clair."

Paul tried to sit up, but pain shot through his shoulder, and he fell back onto the cushions, his face white. "I'm sorry, Beth! Tell me, Charles, what is our situation? Do you think us safe here for the night?"

St. Clair did not believe them safe anywhere currently, but he answered as honestly as he dared. "It is nearly ten, so it would prove difficult to move even if you were well, Lord Aubrey. I would spare you the truth, but you would only find it out eventually, so here is where we now stand. Your man Galton sent a coded message by wire shortly after we arrived here, which was then conveyed to myself and Mr. Kepelheim by way of your childhood 'enemy', good Mr. Baxter. I do not think that gentle giant bears you any ill will, Lord Aubrey. He did in fact seem quite distressed at your condition. He is, even now, outside with every man who can shoulder a weapon, watching out for you and us. A brave man that."

"Outside? Watching out—wait!" Paul repeated, his blue eyes darkening. "What did the note say?"

"That there is fresh danger coming our way. Galton told us to flee, but in your condition that is impossible, and before you insist we go, I can tell you that Elizabeth will not leave without you."

The earl's face exhibited a range of emotions but fell at last into resignation. "You're right. I know this stubborn woman, St. Clair. My dearest love, I know you," he told her gently. "But if I died now, I would do so, content that you are by my side."

"You will not die, Lord Aubrey," Price said, standing up at last. "You have passed the danger point, and I am glad to see it. Now, I shall partake of a little supper, and you, my lord, must also have a few morsels. Your Grace, perhaps you would bring a small cup of broth to him? I perceive a soup tureen on the tray, which our good Mrs. Alcorn has delivered without a word. A lovely and sensible woman, is she not?"

Elizabeth ladled a cup of the beef broth into a china cup and helped Paul to sip some. "Careful," she warned him. "A few sips and then you must sleep."

He obeyed, and once Paul had fallen into a deep slumber, Elizabeth gave a cup of the hearty broth to St. Clair. "You, too, must gain nourishment. Your part in this is larger than you may know. I cannot thank you enough, my Captain. Once again, you have come to my rescue."

"And your Captain is glad of it, my lady," he said, taking the soup. "It looks like he'll sleep now, Beth. Perhaps, you should also try to rest. Go to your apartment. I can keep an eye on him."

"I won't leave him—or you," she said. "If I am to sleep, then I may do so on that settee in the corner. I don't take up much space, and I want to be here, if Paul—or you should have need of me."

He longed to hold her, but he feared appearing callous, so the detective satisfied himself by touching her hand. "I'm sure the earl will rest better, knowing you're nearby."

She looked at him now, her dark eyes brimming with tears, her hand trembling beneath his own. "Thank you, Charles. For everything. For believing me. Yes, I should try to sleep. I shall see if Mrs. Alcorn will bring us some blankets, and I'll make certain the fireplace is stocked with wood."

"I can do that, Beth."

She smiled. "I didn't mean I would literally bring in the wood, Captain," she replied, tilting her head toward the bell rope by the mantelpiece. She pulled the long velvet rope, and in a moment Mrs. Alcorn appeared.

"Would you ask one of the footmen to stock the wood box with plenty of kindling and logs, Mrs. Alcorn? And, if you have some blankets that I might place on the earl—and offer to our guest, also?"

Alcorn called to a young man who had just passed by her, a shotgun in his hand. "Mr. Priest, would you fill the drawing room wood box with fuel before you join the others? My lady, I shall fetch those blankets. If there's anything else you need, just ring."

She closed the doors, and Beth turned back to the detective. "Do you think me lazy for doing that?" she asked, and he could see that she meant the question seriously.

"I think you employ a great many people who might otherwise have no job at all, Elizabeth. And they clearly love and admire you. As do I."

She kissed his forehead and removed the empty broth cup, placing it on the tray nearby. "My father always said that, too. That our estates employ many people. I try to be a fair and understanding employer; though, it's rather hard to think of myself that way. As an employer, I mean. I always feel more that they take care of me, not the reverse."

"They do so because they love you. Now, your eyes grow tired, as do mine. Let's see if we might not sleep for a few hours."

She kissed his forehead once more, her lips lingering for a moment, and then walked to the earl's sofa and kissed his cheek before curling up on the settee. By the time Mrs. Alcorn returned with several quilts, the young duchess had already fallen asleep. Alcorn draped a red and yellow quilt across the earl and then a smaller blue one across Elizabeth. She brought two green ones to St. Clair. "You look as if you could sleep for days, sir."

He took one of the quilts and smiled at the housekeeper. "I believe I could, Mrs. Alcorn, but I'm not sure it's wise. I have worked as a policeman for over thirteen years, so it's not easy to allow other men to stand guard whilst I rest."

"I understand, sir, but if you're to be ready for any battle that may come, should you not avail yourself of sleep before it does come?"

"Yes. You're right, of course. You are a wise woman, Mrs. Alcorn. Very well. I shall see if my eyes are as weary as you perceive them to be. Goodnight, Mrs. Alcorn. And thank you."

She tucked the quilt about his shoulders. "Goodnight, Superintendent."

She left quietly, and in less than five minutes, St. Clair had fallen into a deep sleep.

CHAPTER ELEVEN

Hours passed, and Beth slept peacefully on the small settee near the earl. Only once, did Aubrey stir during the night, calling out softly for her, and she quieted him as moonlight bathed the room in silver, returning to her own couch once he'd fallen back into dreaming.

From his own makeshift bed, St. Clair watched Elizabeth, wondering how their lives would change now. How his would move with hers. He tried to return to sleep, but it was a fitful effort, for his thoughts were consumed by questions, and his right arm ached each time he turned. From time to time, he could discern footsteps and hushed voices as the men who watched the grounds exchanged information, a bit of food, a joke, or simple words of encouragement. As a policeman, Charles found it difficult to let a troop of civilians stand watch over his welfare, and he prayed the Lord would keep them all safe until they could escape to Scotland.

But it was her safety that concerned him most. Though Elizabeth knew it not, Charles had slowly been falling in love with her for many years. The last time he had met with the young duchess had been four years earlier at the earl's London house, a chance meeting for only a few moments, but those moments had forever altered her image in his mind and heart. He remembered how lovely she'd already become at sixteen years of age. At that time, he was estranged from Amelia but still legally married, so he had said nothing, though he'd longed to do so. Now, as a widower, the law no longer stood in his way, but did he dare to imagine becoming her husband? He was but a common detective, and she walked with peers and princes.

Finally, falling back into a restless sleep, St. Clair dreamt of Whitechapel; of chasing Jack the Ripper, the demonic slayer of trusting women. But each time he came close to catching the elusive killer, he found himself investigating yet another murder—more and more, with each successive victim more horribly mutilated than the one before until the streets ran red with blood and gore. But worst of all, the final woman's body was that of Elizabeth—torn into thirteen pieces, her beautiful body ripped open—her dark eyes dead and dull.

He awoke, drenched in sweat, the room still as the grave with only the sound of the mantel clock and the steady snoring of the Labrador near Paul's couch. Unable to sleep now, he checked Elizabeth, and found her sleeping peacefully. Glancing outside, Charles could see the waxing moon shining high in the trees, so he decided to walk.

The house was eerily quiet, making the sharp echo of his boot clicks on the enormous foyer's black and white tiles seem that much louder. He stepped outside and found Baxter and Kay standing guard alongside Kepelheim and several other men. The butler tapped Kepelheim on the shoulder as Charles approached.

"Shouldn't you be asleep, Superintendent?" the tailor asked. "It is two hours yet 'til dawn."

"I've slept enough," he said, his hands in his pockets. "Chilly out here though. You're a fine one to talk of sleep, Kepelheim. How long since you had some?"

"I'm an old man. I don't sleep much any longer. Isn't that so, Mr. Baxter? Sleep is for the young."

The butler nodded. "I've not enjoyed many nights with deep sleep since turning sixty, so I suppose that's true. As we age, we men begin to think of our mortality, do we not? One day, I shall sleep in Christ, but for now, there's too much work to be done."

Standing on the edge of the wide, marble-pillared portico, Charles could see the west gardens and some of the north, where he could just make out the tall shadows of what must be the western edge of the hedge maze. "Is that where you spent an entire afternoon last summer, Mr. Kepelheim?"

The tailor laughed. "Indeed. When it is light, perhaps, we might wander through it, Superintendent. There is a beautiful reflecting pool at the centre along with a circular bench and an impressive knot garden. It is worth seeing, if you can find it."

"The duchess tells me that she can almost run it blindfolded."

Baxter smiled—a rare thing for him. "She can at that, Mr. St. Clair. Ah, you should have seen her as a little girl. Such a love for life! We've missed her these past four years, though the duchess came home each May for the fete and every Christmas, of course. My lady has always made all who work at Branham feel like this is *our* home, too. She is a rare flower."

St. Clair smiled, thinking of Beth as a little girl, but then he recalled her strange tale of the 'Shadow Man' who spoke to her with thoughts. "Baxter, do you know which window belonged to Beth when she was, oh, seven or so? She told me a story about something that she saw out that window, and I'm curious to examine a statue she mentioned."

Baxter took up his rifle and turned to Mr. Kay, the underbutler. "Kay, I shall be a few moments. See to it that Priest keeps watch in my place. Mr. St. Clair, if you'll follow me, sir, I can show you that very statue."

The west garden featured hundreds of spectacular roses, edged by annual plantings, many of which had already faded, and there were brick paths that led through a variety of perennial beds, alive with spectacular grasses, ornamental trees, and bed after bed of asters, daisies, delphiniums, coneflowers, penstemon, monk's hood, salvia, dahlias, and phlox. Even in the moonlight, Charles could see how beautiful the gardens were—*no wonder Kepelheim longed to see them.*

Baxter led on, passing through an arched wicket gate covered in white star clematis, which filled the air with a sweet honeysuckle fragrance. "The north garden is this way, sir. My lady's childhood rooms overlooked the northwest statuary park that leads into the maze."

They walked on, St. Clair marveling at the size and majesty of the grounds. "How large is the estate, Mr. Baxter?"

The butler thought for a moment. "Well, I suppose it depends on how one defines that term. Officially, the village of Branham is part of the property, though the family long ago signed an agreement with the townsfolk to permit a locally elected council to govern. Most of the farmers in the area are tenants. I imagine that if one included all the original land, then it would amount to a quarter of the county."

"Good heavens! I shudder to think what the annual upkeep is on all that property."

"It is sizeable," the butler said simply. "You understand that I am not privy to the final figures, of course, but it most likely runs into the neighbourhood of fifty to sixty thousand pounds a year—but that includes the salaries of all the staff as well as maintenance of all the Branham properties, some of which are in France, and I am only guessing, of course. Those expenditures also include a small school and infirmary on each property. There are six in all, I believe, if one includes the homes in New York and Dublin, both of which are shuttered now."

"New York? Really?"

"Oh, yes, it has been part of the family since Duke George married Countess Carlotta, the only child of Count René de Oradour. Duke George was my lady's grandfather, of course. He made a successful match with the countess, for the two of them seemed to love each other, despite the many troubles—but then that is a tale for another time."

"That's an interesting way to leave it," the policeman answered with a smile. Charles tried to process such an enormous annual budget with so many employees and houses in France, Scotland, Ireland, England, and even America to maintain. He'd considered his own salary of five hundred pounds a year a tremendous sum compared to other policemen and professional men, but to imagine that the Branham estate paid a hundred times that amount every year truly shocked him.

"How does she manage it? I mean, is the estate self-sustaining? Forgive my prying, Baxter, but it is just such a large amount!"

The older man laughed softly. "So it is. I can say this much, for I know it to be fact, the estate is self-sustaining because of several wise alterations made by my first employer, Duke George. The duke combined a number of the vegetable farms into large, livestock enterprises, and he updated the old family herb farm, where many of our own medicines and some for the army are now made. We also have a vineyard that produces several prize-winning wines, and a small brewery that sells to the county and even to many London taverns. Duke George made similar alterations in the other properties, and he sold off two that he felt were beyond improving. But the old duke also invested in a diverse portfolio of stocks, which he was kind enough to open to all in service who wished to contribute. Each month, a small sum is withheld from my pay packet, and over the four and a half decades since, I've managed to accumulate a nice retirement account. I believe the earl could tell you more. Ah, here is the statuary park."

The pair had wound around to the north face of the mansion to find themselves in a grand garden lined with life-sized statues of the dukes and duchesses who had reigned over the centuries. The pathway turned to the left, and pale marble likenesses lined either side of a long, brick walk that fed into one of four entrances to the enormous hedge maze. Baxter turned to face the house and pointed up toward the second storey.

"There, just above us, sir. If you count up to the third window, you will be looking into my lady's childhood rooms. Three windows overlook this spot from that apartment, the two directly above us and the third to the right of them—our right, of course. Was there a particular reason you wished to see it, sir?"

St. Clair counted up, and he could see two, large oval windows and one rectangular. The oval to the far left showed a light burning. "That is her bedroom? There, to the left where we see a light?"

"It is. I wonder why a light burns there? We've only gas lamps and candles for the upper storeys currently, though my lady has promised to electrify the entire house next year. I shall send one of the footmen up to look into it."

"Actually, I'd like to do that, if you don't mind, Baxter. If someone would guide me, that is. I fear this huge house is as much a challenge to me as the maze is to Mr. Kepelheim. So, if I were standing in front of that window, overlooking these statues, I would see which one?"

"Both of them, sir."

St. Clair turned, making calculations in his head. The first two statues, one of a duke on the left and the other his duchess, stood on shallow bases, and the duchess statue could stand no taller than five and a half feet.

"Baxter, how tall are you?"

"Well, sir, the last time Dr. Price had cause to measure me was last year, and he made my height at six feet and two inches."

"I thought as much. That's close to my own height. Would you mind standing beside the statue of the duke there?"

"Not at all, sir. This is Duke Henry, sir, the first Duke of Branham. Do you need to know how tall it is?"

"You are quick, Baxter, yes. That would be very helpful."

"It is six feet precisely, sir. We had cause to measure it many years ago, when it required repair."

That must be the statue Beth referred to. Now to see if it is visible from her window.

"Thank you, Mr. Baxter. If you have no objection, then, I shall find Mr. Priest or another footman and investigate why a light burns in the nursery."

"Very good, sir."

"Baxter, would you mind remaining here until I arrive there? I may have further questions that relate to that statue."

The impressive butler smiled and planted his feet in the gravel. "I shall await your signal from above, sir."

St. Clair turned back toward the front of the house, recalling all Elizabeth had told them on the train regarding the Shadow and the statue. The moonlight threw long dark fingers across the path, cast by tall cedars and the hedge maze, and now and then a fountain or statue. He could hear peacocks screaming, probably startled at his presence, and overhead the hooting of an owl. Turning to the left, he gained the main entry and found Kepelheim speaking to a young man with sandy-coloured hair inside the foyer.

"All is well to the north?" the tailor asked, his hand on a small pistol.

"Quiet so far, which is a blessing. Mr. Priest?" St. Clair asked the young man, who nodded. "Would you show me to the duchess's childhood nursery?"

The young man again nodded, but Kepelheim interrupted. "I, too, know where these rooms are located, Mr. St. Clair. If you would permit me, perhaps we could discuss your wardrobe whilst we walk."

Stephen Priest remained at his post, and the tailor and the detective walked to the back portion of the cavernous foyer, their boot heels clicking on the tiles eerily. "Beth's right. This house puts D'Arcy's Pemberley to shame," St. Clair said as the tailor led him to a hallway, turning right. "Wait. Isn't the main staircase back there?"

"Yes, it is," Kepelheim replied, "but there is a faster way to the nursery. And it is easier on my old legs."

They walked down a short corridor lined with small portraits and lit by four electric lamps. "The duchess brings progress to her little corner of England," the tailor said, stopping in front of a set of polished white doors. "Open the door on the right. It will slide into a recess within the wall," he told St. Clair.

The detective obeyed, and to his surprise, found himself looking at the metal cage of an electric lift! "I've only seen two others like this," he marveled. "Do you know how to operate it?"

"I do. Mr. Baxter showed me last summer after my excursion into the maze, which left me more than winded, I am ashamed to admit, but then I am old. So, in we step, and then we close the grating. This lift may go down to the kitchens below, or rise all the way to the attics. It has been used to transport goods, luggage, and furnishings, saving much wear and tear on the staff's backs and an old tailor's knees. If this is progress, then I am all for it. The operation is simple, Superintendent. You see we are on the ground floor, which is shown by the lever resting on the letter 'G'. If we wanted to visit the kitchens and wine cellar, we would move the lever down to 'K', but if we wish to rise, we move it up. Since our destination is the second floor, we slide the lever past number one to the number two, and up we go!"

The lift jerked into motion, rising slowly above the main floor, past the first, and then stopping on the second. St. Clair and Kepelheim pushed the grating to one side, opened a wooden door identical to the one on the main floor, and stepped into a dark hallway.

"We turn right," the older man said, and St. Clair followed. Kepelheim paused for a moment, feeling his way along the wall. "The main staircase landing is just up here, I believe. You can see the gas lamps burning and make out the turning of the next flight. I think there is a candle table just here."

Sure enough, a low table and several chairs decorated the beautiful landing, and Charles could see the waxing moon and stars through a large round window beyond. The tailor followed the corridor and turned right, leading St. Clair through a set of large doors and into a second hallway, which either continued or turned to the right.

"This way," he said, ignoring the passage to the right. "That hallway leads into the ballroom, an enormous space, but without our duchess, who thinks of dancing, eh, Superintendent?"

"Indeed," the detective muttered, wondering if the day would ever come when he might dance with the beautiful duchess. Somehow, he doubted it.

Kepelheim led him along the passage toward another set of doors. Once through, the way forced them to turn right, where they climbed a short staircase. "It is a bit like a maze, is it not, Superintendent?"

"It is. It reminds me of some of the great hotels in London. Kepelheim, how is this house electrified? Most in London still use gas for illumination—even many of the government buildings."

"Tomorrow, when it is light, I shall show you the power house. A brilliant young friend to the Duke of Drummond designed it. It runs on coal, and it supplies electricity to the hall, as well as many of the surrounding farms, the winery, and the village, including the small hospital that the family owns. You will soon discover that the duke keeps his eyes open for inventors and scientists who have sound ideas but little financial backing. Both Drummond House in London and Queen Anne House use electricity powered by the same invention. And the duke sells the excess to Whitehall."

St. Clair laughed. "The next time I switch on the power in my office, I'll remember that! Is that the north side of the house?" he asked, pointing to the left side of their corridor.

"It is." The tailor placed two candles into holders and after lighting one, handed it to St. Clair. "The nursery is up here, on the left. I'm not sure anyone resides on this floor right now."

"Yet, there is a light shining in the nursery," St. Clair replied. "Is there a gas lamp there that might be lit for some reason?"

"I doubt it. Yes, I mean it is piped for gas, or so I would think, but no one should be in there. Is the duchess asleep?"

"Yes. She is in the drawing room with the earl. Perhaps Alicia is in there."

"We shall see," the tailor said, his hand touching the grip of his pistol. "I do not like this, Superintendent."

"Neither do I," he admitted. "Is that it?"

Kepelheim walked forward, his right hand on a polished brass doorknob. The door was painted glossy white, as were all the interior doors and trim work of this wing. He turned the knob and pushed the door open.

A rush of stale air brushed against their faces, and Charles felt the hair on his neck stand up. "This room feels foul," he said as they entered. Keeping their candles high, both men moved forward slowly.

The small apartment consisted of a parlour, where they now stood, a large bed chamber, bath, and play room to the right and a second, smaller bed chamber to the left, where the nurse had once slept. Ahead, St. Clair could see one of the two oval windows. Stepping forward, he unlatched the hinged window and pulled it open. Below, he could see the statues, but both lay to his right, not straight ahead.

"I'm going into these rooms," Charles said, passing through a small bath, the play area, and then into the main sleeping chamber, where Beth had dreamt as a girl. All around the walls St. Clair found bookshelves, each one filled with volume after volume, and in the centre of the far wall, opposite the fireplace, stood a beautifully carved desk of inlaid wood. Atop the broad desk sat a miniature of the hedge maze. Walking to this desk, Charles discovered several filled diaries, a bottle of ink, a blotter, and a child's drawing of a strange creature that resembled a tall man with wings and large eyes.

"Martin, what do you make of this?" he asked, showing the charcoal sketch to the tailor. "It is signed by Elizabeth, dated September 1876, which is about the time she saw—well, she saw something out this window."

"This is not a nice image," the tailor said simply, his brows knit together in worry. "You will soon discover why such a drawing is troublesome, Mr. St. Clair."

Charles crossed the room to the window seat, where Elizabeth must have stood as she gazed out the window. He unlatched it and pulled it open. Below, he could see Baxter, who was looking up; the butler waved.

"I see the light has gone out!" Baxter shouted up.

St. Clair had forgotten all about the mysterious light, and he turned back toward the room. From below, the light had appeared to be coming from the area closest to the small bed. *Dear God, please tell me that there isn't something sinister in this room—near to where she once slept!*

St. Clair gazed down again at the statue of the first duke, known now to be six feet tall. Baxter looked very much like he stood even with that figure.

"Beth told me that she saw a shadowy man who spoke to her from the place where Mr. Baxter now stands," he told Kepelheim. "She said this Shadow stood a head taller than that statue on the left.

If so, then the Shadow Man must have been nearly seven feet tall! Is that possible?"

The tailor called down to the butler. "Can you move closer to the statue of Duke Henry, my friend?" Baxter waved again and moved to his right. "Very good! Now, if you would stand there for just a moment more."

Charles imagined Elizabeth as a small child, leaning out this same window and hearing the Shadow Man speak. "I think, assuming Beth did not dream this creature—and for my part, Martin, I believe her—then this Shadow thing was indeed very tall. It worries me, to be honest."

Just then, St. Clair heard a faint panting sound, and he turned to find Bella the Labrador standing at his side. She jumped onto the window seat and barked twice at Baxter. Then, suddenly, the dog turned back toward the room, a ridge of hair rising up along her black back, and she began to howl, her head up, and her thick tail straight.

The sound sent a chill down St. Clair's spine, and he moved his candle all about to see if anything had entered the room—perhaps a mouse or even a bat. He could see nothing, and still the dog howled.

"This is most alarming," Kepelheim said, his gun raised. "First you see a light which should not be there, and now our faithful retriever sees that which we cannot. Charles, I think we would do well to go back downstairs and make sure all is as it should be."

St. Clair agreed, and he took the dog by the collar and led her back into the hallway. Then, remembering Baxter, he returned to the small bedroom, where to his shock, he found a tiny light, glimmering just above the small bed. Having followed the detective back inside, the dog began to growl, her hackles high, and she slowly approached the ethereal light.

Charles felt a rush of irrational terror rise up in his mind—as if he *recognised it*. He stepped toward it, forcing himself to do so, for he imagined the light could, in fact, *see him*, and inside his mind, he heard strange whispers in an unintelligible language.

Handing the dog to Kepelheim, Charles reached out to see if the light might be merely a reflexion of moonlight, but as he did so, the strange ball of light darted up to the ceiling and danced above him wildly. Bella leapt onto the bed, standing on her hind legs and scratching at the flowered wallpaper, barking furiously.

Martin drew his weapon. "Do not try to engage it!" he warned the detective. "Do not touch it!"

St. Clair stepped onto the bed beside the animal, bending to reach her collar. "Good girl," he whispered, keeping his eyes ever on the light. "Martin, can you hear anything?"

The tailor glowered as he leveled the pistol at the apparition. "No, nothing. Do you?"

"I'm not sure…perhaps…" he whispered. "It's moving down now. Over top of Beth's desk."

Charles's heart hammered in his chest, but he advanced once more toward the light. The colour had shifted now, and the once yellowish light flashed with hues of red and green, pulsing as if sending a coded message. "I think it's trying to…communicate," he said.

"Charles, do not engage it!" the tailor shouted.

St. Clair returned to the floor. "Come down, Bella," he said, his hand on her collar as the animal jumped to stand beside him. "It's as if it is looking at me."

He started to walk toward the desk, but the blinking light hovered over the miniature maze, growing brighter and brighter until, with a loud pop and a rush of wind, it vanished into nothingness—as if a door to another realm had slammed shut.

St. Clair stared, unable to move. The dog lunged toward the desk, but Kepelheim put his hand on its collar. "Superintendent?" he asked. "Charles? Are you all right?"

Nothing. No answer.

The tailor stepped forward and placed his hand on the detective's shoulder. "Charles. Superintendent, are you all right?"

St. Clair spun around, his face pale, eyes wide. "What just happened, Martin?"

"I think we should go back downstairs, my friend. Come."

His heart pounding, Charles ran to the window and shouted to Baxter. "Did you see that light?"

The butler's large head bobbed up and down vigourously. "I did, sir! It flashed like lightning!"

"Yes! Thank you, Mr. Baxter, that will do. We're going back to check on the duchess and the earl!" He shut the window, looking one more time at the strange drawing Elizabeth had made as a child, at last deciding to take it with him to show Paul.

Back downstairs, Bella settled down near Elizabeth, who still slept peacefully, oblivious to the supernatural display which had just occurred in her childhood rooms. Aubrey also slept deeply, unaware of the strange visitation St. Clair had witnessed. With an hour until first light, Charles drew a chair beside his duchess, pistol at the ready, and waited—just in case.

At dawn, the household shifted into a bustle of activity. The male servants, led by Mr. Baxter, devised a rotation strategy for keeping watch whilst taking sleep in turns. Elizabeth asked them not to worry about ordinary chores, but to concentrate on standing guard, for she knew that was what Paul would want.

Neither Charles nor Kepelheim spoke a word to the duchess about the mysterious phenomenon in the nursery overnight, but they did speak of it with Baxter, who said he'd experienced many unusual events during his time at the estate, which had begun when he was only nine.

Sinclair and the tailor sat in the larger of two kitchens where Mrs. Stephens kept water boiling for Dr. Price and busily made up sandwiches and a large roast pig to serve to the men. Esther Alcorn poured tea for the guests. "Here you are, Superintendent. Mr. Kepelheim, would you like some biscuits? We have the chocolate ones you like. Mrs. Stephens baked them only yesterday."

The tailor's eyes opened wide. "With the almond flavoring?" The housekeeper nodded, and Mrs. Stephens turned to also nod. "Then, yes, oh yes! Mr. St. Clair, you will want some of these, if you are inclined toward chocolate. They are as tender as your gentle soul, my friend, and in your mouth, they melt into a whisper of delight!"

Charles held up his hand. "None for me, Mrs. Alcorn, though I would usually indulge. I prefer to save my appetite for that bacon I smell in Mrs. Stephens's skillet, but I promise to try them later. Tell us, Mr. Baxter, what do you mean by unusual events?"

The butler took three of the biscuits and began to dunk one into his teacup. "I was born on the estate, you know. My father managed the brewery for many years, and my mother served in the house in a variety of positions. The brewery is located to the southeast of the house, about four miles from here, beyond Parker's Clearing, and our family of six was permitted to reside in a large cottage nearby.

The events to which I refer began the year I turned nine. I recall it because I had recently entered service here in the hall as a page to the old duke. George Linnhe was a grand man, similar in height to you, Superintendent, but stouter, if you get my meaning. Great height has been a hallmark in the generations of dukes and duchesses through the years, and it is most interesting that the little duchess inherited neither her mother's height nor her father's, who stood even taller than you, sir. But she could not be more perfect in my eyes, and she has strength of heart surpassing many a tall man, so there it is.

"As I said, I had turned nine, and the butler, Mr. Fordham, asked me to fetch a large, silver coffee server from the east wing attic. I'd never been up to the attics before, but I took the ring of keys and climbed the winding stairs up to that dusty realm. Those are strange stairs, sir. Like a wooden maze in some ways. I'd been up them several times before, so I knew how to navigate them, but they are most strange stairs. Mr. Fordham insisted I use them, as the regular servants' case was then being refinished, and of course we had no lift at that time. Along the way, I had to pass by the entrance to the second floor, and I heard music playing.

"Now, there used to be a nursery in that wing, but it's not been used regularly for many generations. In fact, the duke had not yet married, so there were no children living in the hall at the time. The music sounded like a violin, and I thought it my duty to investigate, since old mansions like this—with unused apartments—may house intruders for weeks with no one the wiser. So, summoning up my courage, I followed that long hallway toward one of the empty suites. It was the third door from the far end where I discerned the source of that music, so I knocked."

Kepelheim whispered. "Did anyone answer?"

"Yes," the enigmatic butler replied evenly. "A ghost."

The tailor's brows shot up. "A ghost! You saw it?"

"I not only saw it, Mr. Kepelheim, I conversed with it. Superintendent, you might now be thinking that it was a living person to whom I spoke, but I tell you that it was not, for I knew this gentleman to be dead."

Sinclair thought of Beth's stories of shadows and secrets and of the mysterious light in the nursery the previous night. Was this apparition another such supernatural visitor? "Who was it then?" he asked.

"It was the duke's father, Richard Henry Linnhe. He had died three years earlier, and he was known throughout the county as a great violinist. In fact, he was carrying his violin when he answered the door that day."

St. Clair listened patiently, trying to discern truth from fiction. "Mr. Baxter, as you have noted, I am a detective, so I must ask you this. Is it possible this person was a vagrant who bore a striking resemblance to the late duke?"

Baxter took a bite of his softened biscuit. "No, sir. For Duke Richard had been killed in a duel, and he bore that large bullet wound still, upon the pale aspect of his ghostly brow."

Kepelheim took three more biscuits from the plate. "Yours is not the first account of seeing that ghost, Mr. Baxter. I myself have heard it from others—a few of them guests—who have described seeing this wounded apparition and also hearing his haunting violin, usually those who stay in or near the east wing. So, did you ever make it to the attic?"

"I did, sir. And when Mr. Fordham asked what had detained me, I told him of my experience. That good gentleman advised me to remain silent about it to Duke George, but Fordham confessed to having seen the ghost as well. Many times."

St. Clair glanced up as Mrs. Stephens brought him a plate of crisp bacon. "For you, Superintendent. If you don't mind my sayin', sir, you look like a man who enjoys a full English when he can get it."

The detective laughed. "Do I?" he asked, taking a small bite of a thick slice. "Oh, my! This is amazing! You know, my housekeeper is a wonderful cook, Mrs. Stephens, but I'm not sure even her bacon is as delicious as this."

"I add brown sugar to the skillet, sir," the Scottish cook said proudly. "And the meat's cured right here on the estate. You'll not find better anywhere in the kingdom."

"I'm sure," he said, finishing the slice and wiping his hands on a linen serviette. "Mr. Baxter, you said you'd experienced numerous, strange encounters. Did any of these occur near the duchess's nursery?"

The butler's head tilted to one side, and his left brow arched high. "None that I experienced, sir, but two of the nurses said as much. They reported hearing strange voices and seeing—well, I suppose one might call them multicoloured *illuminations*—that danced upon the ceiling. The first, a Miss Bellringer, became so rattled by the peculiarities of those rooms that she tendered her resignation and moved to Bournemouth. The second, a Miss Taylor, I believe. Is that right, Mrs. Alcorn?"

The housekeeper had been refilling teacups and she paused a moment. "Miss Tyler, sir. A bit too young to be a nursemaid, I thought, but Mrs. Larson wanted to give her a try, for she was an only child and needed the work. You understand, Superintendent, that these girls weren't wet nurses but rather served as companions to my lady. The little duchess was two years old by then and these girls weren't much more than children's maids, who kept watch on her, supervised play time, helped her to dress, and were trained in basic nursing care by Dr. Price."

"But both saw something inside the nursery?" he asked.

Baxter added two sugar cubes to his fresh brew. "So they said, sir. Miss Taylor—I mean Miss Tyler, of course—once reported seeing a very strange man at the window."

"Standing outside, in the garden?" St. Clair asked.

"No, sir. She said that he was inside the room. Standing beside the little duchess's bed, though of course at that time, my lady was the little marchioness."

"Of course," St. Clair muttered, his mind fixed on solving the riddle. "But this person stood *inside* the room?" the detective persisted. "An intruder, perhaps?" he asked, though he felt certain after his own experience within the strange apartment that what the maid had seen was far more mysterious if not malevolent.

"I do not believe so. Now, as to your earlier question, my own experiences generally occurred within the east wing. The apartment I've mentioned was most often the locale, but the winding stairs are most dangerous and, shall we say...active? Do not ever attempt them without a candle or lantern, sir. The faces, for one thing, not only watch you, but they have been known to speak."

"Faces?" St. Clair asked. "What faces are those, Mr. Baxter?"

"The ghosts' faces," he answered evenly. "Not Duke Richard, sir, but other ghosts. One might even call them... Demonic. If one believes in such things. I, for my part, do, sir."

"As do I," St. Clair heard himself say. "Or I begin to believe." Charles munched on a slice of bacon quietly, pondering something

Elizabeth had told him the previous evening about Trent and the tunnels—that he had accessed them from the east wing. Finally, he leaned toward the butler to ask, "Mr. Baxter, has anyone else ever stayed in that east wing apartment, or has it remained shuttered?"

Martin Kepelheim set down his teacup and nodded to the butler. "Tell him."

Baxter took a deep breath. "Yes, sir. Someone did. In fact, he insisted upon that apartment being his own. Sir William Trent."

"I'd thought as much," the detective replied. He looked at the clock that hung over the kitchen's large fireplace. "Well, my friends, the morning moves ever forward, and I fear I must leave this very interesting conversation. I promised the duchess that I would tour parts of the estate with her today, and I mustn't disappoint. Mr. Baxter, thank you for your company and your revelations. Martin, I imagine I shall see you again soon."

"At breakfast, in fact, which will be at ten?" the tailor asked Baxter.

The butler stood and looked to the cook. "It appears we are near to that time, sirs. I hope you understand that our customary hospitality would be more punctual than today's. If you would be so kind as to wait another half hour or so, I shall recruit several of the maids to help set the table. It is highly inappropriate for ladies to serve in a great house, but as our footmen are all engaged, I hope you will not mind."

St. Clair rose and clapped the tailor on the shoulder. "I think we can find something to occupy us until then, Baxter. For now, we shall get out of your way."

As they reached the servants' staircase, Charles tapped Kepelheim on the back. "Shall we take a look at that east wing?"

The tailor nodded. "I thought that might be the real reason you wanted to leave the kitchen, but we can take only a few minutes. And say nothing to the duchess. She has her own tales about that wing, and they are far worse than Baxter's. She strikes me as vulnerable just now, so it is best she not be reminded of them—for as you will soon discover, our Elizabeth has an unreliable memory, which may not be entirely organic in nature."

"What do you mean by that?" the detective asked.

"I mean that her dear mind may have been tampered with."

"By Trent?" he asked as he followed the tailor through a narrow hallway off the kitchen and toward a closed door that resembled a closet.

"Yes, quite possibly by Trent, but I think even earlier than that by...well, by entities not entirely human."

"What?" St. Clair gasped.

"Yes, I'm sure you're curious to know what I mean by that, but consider what we saw in the nursery last night. Would you call that flickering light material or spiritual?"

"I'm not sure," the detective answered honestly. "Neither and both."

"A fair assessment. Ah, here we are. Welcome to the winding stair, Superintendent. Light your candle, won't you?" he said as he opened the 'closet' door. The interior looked like a large open rectangle of inky blackness, but as they stepped through, light seeping from beneath the door at the landing above combined with St. Clair's small flame to reveal the outline of a narrow flight of stairs, which ended at a large door painted in black enamel.

"It is rather intimidating, is it not?" the tailor noted as he led them up the steps. "Let me see," he continued as he stopped before the closed door. "This leads into the ground floor of the east wing, I believe."

St. Clair stood behind the tailor, holding an unlit candle. "Really? Why would the staircase end here? I see no other flights."

Martin wiped his brow with a white kerchief. "It does not end, but you will understand in a moment. This is part of a bizarre case that the family refers to as 'the winding stair'. I would have led you to the main staircase or even the lift, but we cannot access the east floors from there. More on this later, but for now let me see if I can recall the way. You heard Mr. Baxter refer to this case as a 'wooden maze'; well, that is an apt description. I have traversed this case only thrice before, and each time left me winded and disoriented, so beware. Also, it helps if you do not look at the walls."

"Mr. Baxter's ghostly faces?" the detective asked.

"Oh yes, but also a nauseating sense of movement. Just keep your eyes ahead as you walk, but be sure to glance at your feet from time to time, for the steps are tricky."

Charles watched the tailor, who, rather than walk through the door to the main floor, turned toward the wall to his right and pulled a long bell rope in the corner of the landing. Instantly, a hinged door sprang inward, and a foul odour filled the air.

"We go in here. I'm glad you thought to keep that candle, my friend. Now remember, do not look at the walls."

They passed through the hidden door into pitch blackness. "Shine your candle on our feet for a moment, Superintendent, whilst I get my bearings," Kepelheim said. "Yes, there. Do you see them? Those steps ahead move in a circular pattern, but they lead nowhere. I know this, for I used them once. There is another set over there. Keep to the left. There is a nasty drop beyond the false stairs."

"Who would have built such a death trap?" the detective asked.

"Perhaps a better question is, *what* would have built it? This house has been owned and used by ten dukes and duchesses since Duke Henry, eleven if you count our dear one, and not all have served Christ. All right, this is the end to the first flight, I think," he said, turning a wall-mounted, silver candlestick toward the left. "Yes, this is it."

Another hidden doorway opened, and they passed through it. This case wound around like a spiral, and each step seemed to Charles more shallow than the one before it.

"I fear my large feet are not designed for these small steps."

"Ah, but our dear duchess's tiny feet have passed along these treads more than once. That blessed woman braved this maddening passage many times as a little girl."

"You will tell me all about this eventually, I hope," St. Clair said as the tailor paused before another black-painted door.

"I will, yes. I imagine you will soon hear all the many truths about this strange house and its residents." He touched the black door, his ear to the wood. "Yes, this is the second floor. Let us hope the door is not locked."

Kepelheim turned the knob, which yielded easily, and he pushed the door open. "Ugh! This hideous wing holds more than secrets. It is the same foul stench that hung about the nursery last night."

Charles followed the tailor through the door and to the right. "Third door from the far end?" he asked, and the smaller man nodded.

The hallway's many painted doors lined the sides, and St. Clair counted them to himself. "I count seven doors on this side, so logically it would be the fourth from this end, correct?"

"I believe so," Kepelheim replied, moving forward, "if indeed we may rely upon logic in such an illogical design."

Charles kept the candle high as they walked. The first three apartment doors stood open, as if inviting the men inside, each one revealing sumptuous but somewhat dusty suites with shuttered windows and cold fireplaces. They stopped at the fourth door, which was shut. Kepelheim tried to turn the knob, but it would not budge.

"Perhaps, it was locked after Trent disappeared," Charles suggested. "I suppose we should go back down."

The tailor touched the door. "It feels wrong," he muttered. "It may have been locked in '79, but I suspect there is more to it. Something is wrong about this entire wing, I think. If we have some time this evening, perhaps Mrs. Alcorn will lend us her keys, and we can return, eh?"

"You would make a fine detective, Mr. Kepelheim."

Martin smiled. "Who says I am not one already? But if so, I am a hungry one, so let us find our way back to the main floor and discover what else Mrs. Stephens has prepared. Now that you have walked through that manic staircase, do you feel brave enough to return through it to the kitchen? I fear that the far entrance to the east wing is sealed. It is what I hinted at earlier."

"Sealed? By whom?"

"The Duke of Drummond ordered it done to keep his granddaughter from returning here after her mother's death, though I seriously doubt that it impeded her."

St. Clair smiled. "She is determined, is she not?"

"Yes, but our dear one's courage of heart has been known to take her into danger. I shall show you the doors later, but for now, we must pass back through that wooden maze."

Whilst Charles and the tailor listened to Baxter's ghostly tales in the kitchen, Elizabeth had finally gone to her own apartment on the first floor, finding Alicia sleeping soundly on a velvet sofa in the luxuriously decorated parlour. Tiptoeing past the sleeper, the duchess passed through her bedchamber and entered the large, private bath where she turned the tap to start hot water flowing into a blue and white, hand-painted porcelain tub.

"Oh, my lady!" the maid exclaimed sleepily as she leapt up from the couch. "Do forgive me. I would have done that for you, if

I'd known you had come up, my lady. I fell asleep awaiting news about the earl. I'd have slept in my own room if…"

"Nonsense, Alicia. I'm glad you slept. We've far too many people with bleary eyes already this morning. Whilst I bathe, though, would you set out something new for me to wear? I have just noticed that my clothing is stained with Lord Aubrey's blood."

"Of course, my lady. The earl is better, I hope."

"He is. Much better, thanks to our good friends and many prayers. He now sleeps soundly, and the stitches in his wound are holding."

The maid opened a large cedar-lined closet and withdrew a blue silk, day dress. Elizabeth had started to unbutton her blouse and glanced up. "No, not another dress. Some trousers, I think. And no corset, please. How I detest that tortuous device! A simple chemise will do. We shall be rummaging through the tunnels this afternoon, and I'll need to climb, so sturdy footwear. My riding boots will suffice, if you cannot find my gardening shoes. I don't care, really. Whatever you think will work, Alicia, so long as it is practical."

It was nearing eleven by the time the duchess joined St. Clair and Kepelheim in the breakfast room. Her thick, dark hair was still damp and braided down her back, and she wore woolen trousers in a dark blue gabardine twill along with a white silk blouse and dark brown waistcoat. The trousers were tucked into brown riding boots, which rose to her knees.

St. Clair stood, a broad smile upon his handsome features as she entered the room. "My, my, Duchess. You make a charming groom."

Elizabeth laughed and sat opposite him at the sumptuously laid table. "I shall make you pay for that remark, Captain, but I am famished now, so it will have to wait. How is the earl this morning, Mr. Kepelheim?"

The tailor was enjoying a bowl of oatmeal but had also risen when the duchess had joined them. Sitting now, he returned to his feast, spooning in some brown sugar as he answered. "He is much improved, I think. Dr. Price is with him now, but the earl seems more alert, which is good. He will need at least another day before we may safely move him, however. The good doctor has cleaned and redressed the wound to make sure all bleeding has stopped, which praise our wonderful Saviour, it has, but someone as restless as Lord Aubrey is likely to reinjure himself if not restrained by a soft hand."

"I shall do my best, Mr. Kepelheim," Beth said with a smile. "Charles, should we postpone our walk until tomorrow?"

"Whatever you wish," St. Clair answered. "If you prefer to remain with the earl, I can try to find the tunnels on my own."

"You would never manage it, I fear. Even were I to draw you a map, those turnings are disorienting. Perhaps, we could leave around two. Of course, if Paul is worse, then…"

"I think Lord Aubrey will only grow stronger, dear lady, so long as he follows instructions," the tailor interrupted. "He must rest one more night, at least, and afterward, the doctor says we may all take the train or a boat or whatever the earl thinks is best. For my part, I have beautiful fabrics with me, so I shall make use of Mrs. Alcorn's sewing machine, I think, whilst we wait."

"She will be happy to show it off, Mr. Kepelheim," Beth said. "It is the latest model. Charles, are you well this morning? Your face is rosier by far, I might add. I am very glad of it. Your contribution to the earl's recovery can never be valued. In truth, you saved his life."

Charles had more of the bacon and eggs, advised by Kepelheim and Price to eat plenty of iron, which both would provide. They had also recommended he take a packet of raisins with him on his field trip to the tunnels later. "I am very glad of it, Duchess. And I am much recovered, thank you, and ready to explore these caverns. You've but to say the word. I shall, however, bring my revolver."

"I hope you will," she answered, taking a bite of toast. "All right. I'll check in with Paul and Dr. Price, and then we shall decide when you and I may commence our journey into the labyrinth beneath our feet."

St. Clair looked to Kepelheim, and the men exchanged worried glances. Both knew that the tunnels would be the perfect place to stage an ambush.

CHAPTER TWELVE
7, October, 1888

Sir Robert Morehouse shuffled through the mound of paperwork his secretary had left on his desk. Since retiring from active police work as a chief superintendent, Morehouse had joined the Home Office as a specialist in domestic crime, working directly with the Police Commissioner, Sir Charles Warren. This day found him trying to locate a memo he'd received a day earlier from Inspector Edmund Reid regarding a new theory on the Ripper.

"Carson! Where is that memorandum from Reid?" he called into the small office just outside his own. "I say, Carson!"

Jim Carson, a bright law student working his way toward acceptance at Gray's Inn, popped into view. "Found it, sir! Here it is. Just as it arrived yesterday morning, still in its pouch."

Morehouse chewed his pipe as he unwound the heavy string that fastened the top of the leather packet, fumbling inside for the memo. He found a small white square of paper, bearing seven sentences:

> Sir, the investigation into suspect John Langan requires Home Office approval. Not sure why we've hit political roadblock. Also, G. Lusk wants pardon for Ripper accomplices. Has written to H.O. May flush out news, but I doubt it. Abberline suggests bringing in bloodhounds, but Sir Charles refuses.
>
> Request your help.
> —Reid

"Bloodhounds?" he said aloud. "Carson, fetch me that Ripper box file from the Yard, will you? And send a message to Sir Charles asking him to join me for luncheon at one. Café Royal. Got that?"

The young man's cheerful if somewhat harried face appeared again, his arms filled with official governmental, red boxes. "Yes, sir. At once, sir, though I'm not sure Sir Charles is working today. It is Sunday, sir."

Morehouse blinked, his mind rolling through this phrase as if it had been spoken in a foreign tongue. "Sunday? Ah, yes, I see what you mean. Crime does not take a break, even on Sunday, so I've no idea why Warren would do so, but I imagine you're right. Make a note then that I wish to speak to him first thing tomorrow."

The young man's mouth dropped open as if to speak, but he waited a moment, praying his superior would realise that he, too, had been asked to work on a day ordinarily reserved as a day of rest. "Very good, sir," he said at last, grateful that he had a job at all. "I believe the Royal opens today at two, so I'll dispatch a commissionaire to make the reservation in your name for tomorrow afternoon at one. Would you like your boxes now or later, sir?"

"Later. It is Sunday after all," Morehouse said with a wink. "Forgive my calling you into work today, Carson. Yes, I'd simply lost track of the days. Each seems the same to me with my wife out of town. I'll pop home and then be back this afternoon, so I'll go through the boxes then. You should go home, as well."

"I could stay, sir."

"No, no. Go see your new bride, and ask her to indulge an old man for his absentmindedness. Tell you what, take her some flowers. On me. There's a fiver in my pocketbook, inside my overcoat. Right side. No right as you look at it. I guess that's my left then."

"That isn't necessary, sir. Katy understands that my job sometimes..."

"The job must never take a backseat to our wives, Carson. That is a lesson I learnt too late in life. My dear wife spent far too many nights all alone, and were she home today, I'd be there with her now. She's at her sister's, you see. Millie's been ill. Now, take that fiver, lad. I insist."

"Thank you, sir. That's very kind of you." Carson fished in all the pockets of the coat, but found no wallet. He did locate the five-pound note, though, inside the lining's hidden pocket. "I've found the banknote, sir. Your pocketbook is missing though. Shall I begin a search?"

Morehouse was now engaged in opening a thick stack of mail, and he waved automatically for the secretary to proceed with his instructions. Donning his own overcoat and grabbing an umbrella against the threat of rain, Carson pocketed the five-pound note and headed toward a small flower stand near the end of Downing Street. Katy liked tulips and daylilies, but they usually sold out quickly, so he ran to the flowerseller, a smile already crossing his wide face as he thought of his bride of two weeks, waiting patiently with Sunday dinner at home.

Alone now, Sir Robert, who'd been knighted that year for his service to the Yard, had just opened an envelope with no postmark, but with his name emblazoned on the exterior in a flourished hand. Morehouse read through the disturbing letter, which contained dark implications if not outright threats:

7, October
9 a.m.

Sir Robert,

You do not know me, but I know you very well. I have watched as your career soared even in those early years when your choices in company were not always completely 'legal'. You needn't worry, however, my good fellow. I am reliable when it comes to keeping secrets. However, if you wish your dark liaisons in Paris, Vienna, Brussels, and Rome to remain *sub rosa* and not dismay your lovely wife, nor cause your superiors to regret your meteoric rise to so high a position, then you will meet with me in your office this evening at six.

Be there, Sir Robert, or I shall be forced to mention the name of a certain contessa to your faithful and lonely wife, Lady Martha.

I shall be there at the stroke of six. Do not disappoint me.

A.

Morehouse re-read the letter several times, thinking back to rash acts of his youth that commenced whilst studying in Brussels. She had been older, experienced, and exquisitely beautiful, and her tastes in men had run a strange gamut from young and virile to almost childlike and feminine. Foolishly, the naive Morehouse had allowed her dark demands to steer him into waters far deeper than any twenty-year-old British male dared try to navigate, but in he had gone, nearly drowning for his foolishness.

Morehouse had, at last, escaped the woman's control one year later, his mind and body spent, and his faith nearly shaken. *The things he had seen! The depravities!*

Upon returning to his trusting father, Morehouse had given his heart to brighter faith and even considered entering the clergy, but his father had turned him instead toward keeping order and upholding the law. So, he had joined the police force at twenty-two, never regretting it, leaving his raucous past behind and buried.

Until now.

Someone knew. *They knew!*

Who is this A? he wondered.

The clock struck eleven, and Morehouse lowered his head onto his desk and began to pray.

The bright sunshine of morning soon lengthened into afternoon, and Charles St. Clair found himself with time on his hands. Though the earl's condition had improved, Price had asked the duchess to sit with her cousin to help restrain the earl's rash inclinations to rise and risk tearing open the wound. Kepelheim had decided to use the hours to work on a pair of trousers in St. Clair's size, borrowing Mrs. Alcorn's shiny, new Warwick sewing machine and experimenting with its four different stitches. Left to his own devices, the detective chose to explore the expansive grounds.

As he strolled past a line of armed men, Charles paused here and there to ask directions or talk weaponry, and eventually his feet had taken him to one of the four entrances to the hedge maze. This one stood on the western edge of the maze, and at first, St. Clair hadn't noticed it. He'd passed along a collection of intricate knot gardens and colourful rose beds, walked through an ironwork gate, and at last discovered himself standing before the tall entry.

Unlike the entrance from the north side of the house, which rose up at the end of the statuary park, this one emerged unexpectedly at the end of a verdant hallway of ancient yews. Turning back to look, St. Clair blinked, for behind him also stood an entrance, as if the evergreen hallway ended in mirrored archways.

He looked again at the first entrance, making sure that he had not mistaken his position, but indeed there it was, and the great oaken door stood open, as if enticing him to enter.

Then he heard the voice.

"Charles!"

St. Clair's breath caught in his throat, and his heartbeat began to quicken. He turned once more, and behind him, near the other, mirrored entrance stood a very tall man with dark hair, his back to the detective.

"Charles!" the man called, cupping his hands to his mouth. "Charles! Where are you, lad?"

"I'm here!" St. Clair answered. The man paid him no heed, but kept calling the name over and over as if frantic.

Behind him, he could hear movement, so the detective turned once more, and to his surprise, discovered a small boy, not more than four or five perhaps, standing near the entrance at that end of the strange, reflected hallway.

"Are you Charles?" he asked the youth, who stared at him curiously. The lad had jet black hair and light blue eyes, and he appeared frightened. "It's all right. I'm a policeman."

"I'm lost," the boy said, his voice hinting of Scotland. "Where did everybody go?"

"I'm not sure," St. Clair said, walking toward the child. "There's a man calling for you. Don't you hear him?"

"The earl?" the boy asked.

Assuming the boy meant Lord Aubrey, he shook his head. "No. Come with me. I'll help you to find the house."

The boy started to walk toward Charles, but before their hands could touch, a great wind rushed through the yew corridor, and the sky overhead turned to pitch as thousands of ravens blotted out the sun.

"A storm is coming," the boy said, backing away, terror filling his eyes. "*He* is coming!" The lad then turned and ran back toward the other entrance.

St. Clair raced toward the boy, intent on protecting him from the sudden storm, but as he reached the other side, the child had disappeared. Instantly, the sky lightened as the ravens also vanished, and Charles now stood in the centre of the maze. Before him, he could see a tall man with long black hair that spilled across his broad shoulders in waves, his eyes red as flame.

"He is coming," the man told him. "Death awaits if you do not protect her."

St. Clair's pulse raced now, and his ears filled with the sound of screaming winds and deep-throated laughter. He sensed the presence of hundreds, perhaps thousands of entities, and he knew them to be evil spirits; and it seemed as if the hedge maze itself were alive with malevolent thoughts. A violin played upon the howling winds, and he heard the cries of many wolves, circling 'round him.

St. Clair awoke, his eyes snapping open, as one of the gardeners tapped him on the shoulder.

"It's time to wake up, Charles."

The detective blinked. He sat in a willow chair, not far from the yew trees. "I'm sorry. I must have fallen asleep," he muttered.

The man was tall and beautiful in form and face with long white hair, and he touched St. Clair's hand kindly. "You must keep watch, Charles. Do not fall asleep again. The enemy comes, and only you can save her."

The man then turned to walk away, his image slowly thinning into a mist.

St. Clair rubbed his eyes, wondering if he still slept, for all around him the gardeners and footmen patrolled as if no one had noticed the vanishing man. He glanced at his watch. Just after one.

He stood up, pinching himself to make certain he was truly awake, wincing at the pain. Several men were patrolling the garden, and they waved. The detective returned their greeting as he walked toward the group. "Did any of you see a tall man with long white hair a moment ago?" he asked them. "He wore a uniform not unlike your own."

The three men strode toward the detective, the eldest of the trio carrying a rifle. "No, sir. No one like that, anyways, sir. I'm Powers, the Chief Gardener. Are you Mr. St. Clair?"

"I am, Mr. Powers. I thought I saw someone else, though. Also quite tall. And a boy—though, that probably was a dream."

Powers nodded. "It's easy to fall into a dream near them yews, sir. Like they cast some spell on a man. They's more 'n a thousand years old, them yews. Been 'ere since afore the first hall, afore even the old abbey. Afore the town, ya know. There's old legends 'bout them yews an' that maze."

"The hedge maze, you mean? Surely, it is not as old as that, Mr. Powers."

"No, sir, it ain't, bu' the maze what was here afore it must've been standin' for, oh, I reckon over a thousand; two maybe."

"Wait a moment, Mr. Powers, are you saying this maze was planted on top of another?"

"It were, sir. But it weren't no hedge maze but an old tunnel maze, what sat just under a green labyrinth. An old hill, ya know. It were used by the Druids, they say. Or some such."

"Powers, is the duchess aware of any of this?"

"No, sir. The duke—her ladyship's grandfather up in Scotland, ya know—he made us all promise never to tell 'er. It were Mr. Paul, Lord Aubrey, I mean, what found it out. When 'e were in France. Is the earl better, sir?"

"He is, Mr. Powers. Yes. I shall ask him to tell me more about this maze when he is stronger. Thank you, Powers. Thank you very much."

Charles set off for the house, finding his feet moving more swiftly as he neared the south garden's main entrance. Catching his breath and praying to God to help slow his heart and ease his mind, Charles walked back toward the house, hoping to find Martin Kepelheim.

Once inside, the tailor met the detective near the staircase, his short arms laden with fabrics and threads. "Superintendent, you arrive just in time. I've a pair of trousers for you to try on, and then perhaps...oh, but wait, Mr. St. Clair, are you unwell? What has happened, my friend? Your face is white!"

St. Clair passed by the tailor, and the latter followed him down the smaller hallway and into the lift closet. "Let's talk upstairs," he said to Kepelheim. "I have to make sure I'm not mad."

"You saw something," Martin whispered as St. Clair threw the level toward the number '2' and the cage began to rise.

"I did. And now, I would return to our little duchess's childhood rooms. Martin, this house has far too many secrets, and before I follow her into those tunnels, I want to make sure no one—human—lingers in these halls."

"Human? As in someone with Redwing, you mean. You worry that the fresh danger Sir Thomas warned us of is already here?" the tailor babbled as he followed the long-legged detective down the turning hallways. Kepelheim placed the trousers and other items on a chair near the landing and checked his pistol. "Humans may think themselves powerful, but even Redwing's operatives fall when shot. Spirits do not. Did you bring a weapon with you, Mr. St. Clair?"

"I did. Although, it's in the drawing room just now. How's your aim?"

"Passable. How is yours?"

"I've won the Queen's prize at Wimbledon each year since turning twenty-five. Does that tell you?"

The tailor passed the revolver to his friend. "It does. Now, let us see what this room holds today. And whilst there, I hope you will explain why you are so insistent upon coming back here."

St. Clair held the weapon in his right hand as he pushed open the door with his left. As before, the rooms had a foul smell about them, beyond anything musty, but a dark odour that spoke of evil things. "The light is back," he said as they moved into the playroom. "It's hovering over the miniature of the maze."

"I doubt that any bullet would extinguish that light," Kepelheim observed. "Be careful."

Charles stepped forward slowly, his eyes fixed on the strange light. As before, it shifted from one colour to another, and the detective imagined hearing voices—as before.

"What do you want from me?" he asked. "I know that you are more than just a reflexion. What are you?"

The light floated above the centre of the model, growing ever more brilliant.

"What are you?" he repeated, but as before, the light suddenly began to dance about the ceiling, darting here and there as if grown manic. "Who is coming?"

The light stopped.

Kepelheim stood just behind Charles, and he spoke in a whisper. "I think you have its attention."

Charles stepped forward. "Who is coming? You told me that it is Death. That I must protect her. What do you mean by that?"

The light grew larger, and Charles perceived a voice, like a whisper. *"They are coming."*

"They?" he repeated, and Martin looked at the detective oddly, for he had heard nothing.

"Ride. Ride swiftly, or she will die. When you see the horse, ride!"

"Who? What do you mean?" he asked, but the light zoomed back into the miniature maze and vanished in a flash of light.

Charles turned around, and he seemed unsteady on his feet. "Martin, I think I need to sit."

"Lean upon me, my friend," Kepelheim said as they left the nursery. The tailor helped the detective to a small parlour near the turning toward the west wing. Kepelheim then sat into one of the chairs, wiping at his brow.

"What happened back there?" the tailor asked. "Charles, did you hear something I did not?"

St. Clair suddenly felt very tired, and he let his head fall against the back of the chair. "I'm not sure," he said. "Perhaps. Martin, I may have dreamt something—or perhaps experienced something near the maze. Did Paul ever talk to you about an ancient labyrinth that used to exist where the maze now stands?"

The tailor's old eyes blinked, and he appeared to be weighing his response. "Why do you ask?"

"Mr. Powers, Beth's Chief Gardener, told me that there used to be an old hill with a labyrinth on it, and that beneath it lay tunnels. A maze of tunnels. He said Paul learnt about that history whilst in France recently."

Again the tailor grew pensive for a moment. Finally, he leaned forward, his hands on his knees. "Yes, last year whilst in France, the earl uncovered a hidden history about Branham, as it existed before the hall was built. He uncovered this during his travels in Normandy, in fact. Say nothing of this to Elizabeth. She has enough to give her nightmares without learning about the ancient pagan rituals that once took place here."

"Pagan? Powers said something about the Druids. Is that what you mean?"

"Worse than that. Older than that. If Redwing is the current, human face of an ancient and very evil band of rebel angels, then imagine if you will, Superintendent, what types of rituals Redwing's forebears engaged in, when paganism ruled our land. I tell you that no sane man could summon up the images without blinding his own eyes! No, the earl will never tell her, and you must follow that wisdom. Our little duchess may possess great courage, but the dark powers that surround her would love to use her in ways so foul that the Ripper's deeds would seem a lark!"

Charles suddenly felt great despair, but also fear. "I'm tired," he said at last. "I may go sleep for an hour."

"Yes, yes, I think that is wise. I'll lead you to one of the readied apartments. Mrs. Alcorn showed them to me. And I will tell our duchess that you require rest. Shall I send a footman to wake you?"

"Yes, I think that's a good idea. Tell Beth to send for me whenever she wishes to leave."

"Very good. Sleep, my friend. Later, you can try on these wonderful new clothes, but for now, rest and put all our strange experiences out of your thoughts."

Charles selected a large apartment not far from the main staircase and lay upon the bed, and in minutes, he'd fallen into a deep sleep.

Two hours later, a footman knocked upon the detective's door, and Charles hastily washed his face and straightened his shirt and waistcoat. He pulled on his suitcoat and climbed down the main stairs. Though still weary, the sight of Elizabeth at the foot of the case, cheered him as no tonic could, and he kissed her hand. "I take it our plans are in place?"

"They are, Captain, if you are ready. I'm told you grew weary earlier. You gave the earl two transfusions last night, Charles. If you require additional rest, then..."

"Not necessary," he assured her. "Truly, Beth, I'm fine, and I am as prepared as ever. However, I'd like to stop by the drawing room before we go. My revolver is still there."

The Labrador met St. Clair at the entry to the large parlour, her eyes bright, tail wagging rhythmically. "Hello, Bella. Good girl," the detective said, patting the dog's head. "Ah," he told the duchess. "I see the pistol on that small table. This won't take long."

Elizabeth took a moment to kiss the earl's face whilst the detective secured the leather holster around his back and shoulders, re-buttoned his waistcoat, and then donned his suitcoat once again. As they left the room, she showed him a large willow basket, sitting near the main doors. "I have prepared a lantern, and Mrs. Stephens has made us a picnic," she said, as St. Clair picked up the basket.

"It seems you've thought of everything," he said, smiling.

They left the hall, turning eastward once outside. It was nearly half past three when they set out. The day was bright and sunny, and Elizabeth suggested to Charles that they walk to the tunnel entrance. "We could take a coach or even ride, but it's a lovely day."

"Aren't the tunnels connected to some of the rooms inside the hall?" he asked, holding the basket in one hand as they walked. "Wouldn't it be simpler to enter from there?"

"Yes, but the section we're heading for is accessed more quickly from above ground. You'll understand when we get there. I hope you don't mind the walk, Captain. I can use the exercise, and it gives us time to talk."

She led Charles into the woods northeast of Branham Hall, where they passed a dozen sentries, each waving and tipping their hats, weapons ready should the need arise. It did him good to see the small army of workmen, farmers, and servants rallied 'round their duchess.

"You certainly seem in your proper setting here," the detective said. "Though Paul and I kept in touch over the years, you and I weren't able to spend much time together before you left for Paris. Well, no time at all, really. I saw you just the once at Aubrey House—and then, you were gone. Did you enjoy your life there?"

"I suppose I did. If music lessons, language studies, and drawing classes are enjoyable. Don't misunderstand me, Charles, I do like all those things, but I sometimes wonder what it is I'm meant to do with my life. That's why I asked Mr. Kepelheim to teach me something truly useful."

"Many people who toil and scrape for their next meals might love to trade places with you, even for a day," he said. "I hope that doesn't make me sound critical, Duchess. It's just that this life— *your life*—is so vastly different from the lives of the citizens of Whitechapel."

"I am all too keenly aware of that," she said, and he realised he may have hurt her.

"Beth, really, I meant no offence," he said, stopping so he could look into her eyes.

"I took none, Charles. Truly, I didn't. It's just that, well, I want to help people like those in your Whitechapel. People like Miss Ross. I can still remember the faces of those living near your house and close to the police station. They treated me very kindly, and I should like to return that kindness. Do you think a hospital would make a difference to them, or is there a better way to help?"

"I think the hospital is a marvelous idea. Might that mean you would spend more time there? It's a very rough borough, or parts of it are, Beth."

She had picked up a fallen branch and begun tapping it on some of the shrubs alongside the path. "Mr. Powers must be letting some of this path go to seed. He generally trims back these flowering shrubs by now."

He walked beside her, slowing to allow her to keep pace. "Have I said something wrong?" he asked her, certain he'd hurt her in some way. Her thoughts seemed faraway now, and he noticed tears glistening on her soft cheeks. "Beth? Please, Elizabeth, I have hurt you, haven't I?"

She stopped, her head down as she tapped the branch against the hard packed earth. "Do you think me—do you think me vain, Charles?"

"You? Vain? Beth, you are not—never. I have known many women who spend their entire morning in front of mirrors, primping and selecting clothing and arranging their hair into just the right form, but they have no substance. They are vain. Not you, dear. Never you. You have a natural beauty that—that would make any man want you."

"Any man? Oh, Charles, if only it were that simple."

He took her hand. "Elizabeth, you know I'm in love with you, do you not? I tried to make that clear on the train, and if you'd have me, I'd live the rest of my life with you."

She looked away. "Really?" she whispered, and he heard deep emotion in her simple question.

"Isn't it obvious?" he asked, for he believed all the world must surely see it on his face.

"I, well—look, it's nothing. I'd wondered if your feelings were those of a friend only, especially as you and Paul have grown close."

He touched her face, and it was like electric fire passed between them. She felt it, too, and tried to pull away. "Charles, we dare not—dare not risk…"

"Dare not risk what, Beth? I realise that you have obligations to the earl, and I certainly have nothing to offer you, save my undying love, but if you *could* choose, then…"

She closed her eyes, squeezing his hand. "But I cannot," she whispered.

"Cannot or will not?" he asked.

"It is complicated," she replied, her attention fixed on the path rather than look into his eyes.

"Why must it be? Elizabeth, I love you, and if you feel the same about me, then why is it so difficult? Even if you have obligations, can those not be altered? Changed?"

"I… Charles, I'm not sure. Perhaps. Oh, it's not my choice. It isn't. It never has been."

"You mean your grandfather? He doesn't strike me as the kind of man to harbour prejudice against me simply because of my status in life."

"Of course, he is not," she answered. "Grandfather likes you, and he pays no heed to class distinctions."

"Then what is it? Beth, darling…" he began, but she shook her head, her voice low and filled with anguish.

"May we pretend—for now—that such choice lies within my power? I want to enjoy every moment with you that I can. That is why I asked if we might walk. I cannot say more, but I hope you know it has nothing to do with any perceived difference betwixt your social status and my own. It is…"

"Complicated, yes, you keep saying that, but, Beth," he continued, taking her hand and turning her to face him. "If you *could* choose, then…?"

"Oh, my darling Charles," she whispered, and her eyes filled with tears as she rose up to kiss him on the cheek, but he gave her his lips instead. It was a moment when time stopped, and for that infinite moment, she pretended she really could choose her Captain, and for Charles it was enough. She needn't say it. He knew her heart. She loved him, and that was all he needed to keep on believing. Even if it could only be pretend.

He took her hand as they walked, and the entire world took on a brighter hue. The sun warmed their path, dancing upon the fallen, autumn leaves and shimmering upon her dark hair. After a few moments, they passed by the power house and soon a small farm, and then came to the ruins of the original hall, which served now as a home to bats and mice.

"This was built by King Richard," she explained, "and it was much used in its day, but it came under attack many times, finally falling into disuse by the time of Edward, the Black Prince."

"It's such a ruin, wouldn't it be safer to raze it?" he asked.

"My grandfather, Duke George, nearly did so, but he changed his mind, telling my mother it was always to stand. It's historic, apparently. I've thought of having a contractor look into restoring it, but I'm not sure the bats would appreciate being dishoused."

They both laughed, and she leaned in closer to him as they walked. Charles felt in no rush to enter the tunnels, for he knew Beth's mood would surely darken then, so he slowed his pace, relishing every moment at her side. They stopped along the way to eat the picnic lunch Mrs. Stephens had packed. Sandwiches, lemonade, apples, and raisins for Charles.

"Your cook is determined to build up my iron supply. Your staff loves you very much, Beth. And so do I."

She let him kiss her again, and they lingered on the blanket for as long as they dared, finally packing the container and leaving it on a bench to collect on their way back.

It was well past five by the time they reached the old abbey. Without knowing it was here, St. Clair would easily have missed it, so covered by vegetation and massive trees was it. "It's certainly a gloomy place," he said as they walked up what had once been a long, gravel drive lined with gnarled yew trees. "Are you sure there's still a building in there?"

"It has been five years or more since last I walked here, but yes, I am certain of it. Henry the Second built this abbey as penance for St. Thomas a' Becket's murder, I believe. My history is a bit muddled, not because my memory fails, although it does at times, but because history is so sketchy with regard to Branham and all that happened during its founding. Truthfully, much of it has been removed from English histories for reasons you will soon learn from the earl.

However, I can tell you that the abbot who presided over this settlement worshiped a deity quite at odds with our Lord and Saviour."

"What do you mean?" he asked, thoughts of the mysterious, dark-haired man inside the maze filling his mind.

"You will understand more once you see what lies beneath our feet," she said.

They had reached a massive, oaken door. It was thick and fastened with iron bands and square nails. A great iron bar crossed the middle of the door, and it took them both to lift it. "How did you manage this as a child?" he marveled.

"I didn't. It was only ten years ago that I learnt that the tunnels actually come up here. I've entered them from here only once, five years ago, with Mr. Powers to help me, but the first time I came through this door was that night. When William took me."

"What?" he asked, touching her shoulders and turning her toward him. "Look, before we enter this old ruin and descend into whatever hell you witnessed as a child, tell me, did he—did he *do* anything to you? Did Trent touch you in any way that was, well, improper?"

"Outside of cracking me on the head with a great cane and tossing me into the back of a market wagon, then driving me to Whitechapel? No, but—well, I think not. I know what you mean, of course, Charles. I cannot say for certain, for in all honesty, my memory is hazy regarding parts of that night. However," she continued, her eyes looking off into the distance, "I have a dark dream that recurs from time to time, and in it, William—or perhaps not he but someone else, *something else*, is standing over me—trying to, well, I'm not sure. It is only a dream, I think. I hope. But I do remember what he did to my mother. That was no dream. It was all too real, as you know, for you saw her poor body—and now you shall see where it happened."

Charles opened the door and secured it with a large rock. "To make certain we are not locked in," he told her.

He took her hand, and she led him into the abandoned abbey. The crumbling walls and staircases were covered in lichen and slime. Large bats hung from the exposed beams, and a dense flock of ravens scattered as the pair moved into the semi-darkness. St. Clair lit the lantern, and he kept it high so they could avoid any animals or obstacles. Once or twice, their progress was impeded by a fallen stone or timber. They passed through room after room, and finally into a narrow passageway that ended in an anteroom with two doors. Near the far left, behind what had once been the sacristy, Elizabeth showed him a worn set of stone stairs. He lifted the lamp, and the steps threw black shadows, curving downward into the earth.

"I see now why you chose to wear trousers. This place is not only filthy but quite dangerous."

She paused inside the small room. "Skirts and heels are hardly practical for such a place."

He shined the lamp over the steep stone staircase. "Do these lead into the tunnels?" he asked.

"Yes. But first look at the walls, Charles. The first time I saw them was when William carried me out that night. I shall never forget them."

He held the lantern higher, shining the dim yellow light along the damp, stone walls, and as his eyes adjusted he actually gasped.

"Dear God in heaven! An abbot did this?"

"He and his followers," she explained. "That is what I have learnt over the years. It is a cryptic history, and there are few copies still to be found, but according to obscure church records, the abbot and his priests were finally burnt at the stake for their heresies in March of 1579. The abbey itself was burnt shortly after."

"I should hope so!" he whispered.

The shapes were foul, and the imagery clearly anti-Christian. Demonic entities—some in gigantic proportion—were depicted in bloody rituals and sadistic poses, many with small children and even infants, which made the bile rise in St. Clair's throat.

"You saw this as a little girl?"

She nodded. "I did. When William brought me out through here, he was carrying a lantern also, and its light danced upon these scenes making them seem almost alive. I remember screaming and then crying. That is when he struck me. I did not regain consciousness until we were on the road to London. I cried out then as well, seeing my mother's torn body next to me in the wagon, and he pulled the horses to the side of the road and dragged me from the rack. He shook me mercilessly, for that man has no mercy, and then—then there was another, something else—someone else, I cannot remember clearly, but William struck me again, this time harder. I awoke only when I was being carried into your station house."

He pulled her close, kissing her hair and forehead. "May Almighty God help me to save you from this madman!" he whispered, protecting her with one arm as he held the lantern with the other. She circled her arms around his waist and let him warm her, strengthen her. "I will not permit Trent to harm you ever again, little one," he promised. "If I have to kill that man myself, he will pay for his crimes."

She kissed his hands and stepped back. "I know, Charles. I have always known it. Known that you would protect me and love me. I saw it in your eyes all those years ago, just as I see it there still. But now, my brave Captain, we must descend."

Paul Stuart awoke shortly after five o'clock, his head pounding, and his left shoulder on fire.

"No, no!" Kepelheim warned him. "You must not get up! Dr. Price was very firm on this, my impulsive friend. You must remain flat and resting until tomorrow morning."

The earl pushed himself upward, disregarding all his body told him to do. "Where are Elizabeth and St. Clair?"

"They have gone into the tunnels. They said you knew that was the plan. Had you not been injured, then you would be with them, but you saved Elizabeth's life when you took that bullet, my friend. You probably saved all our lives. Your cool nerves and keen aim took out four men, before the fifth shot you in return. I am certain that he rode swiftly to report back to his evil friends, but we have a little breathing space now, so let us enjoy it."

Paul wanted to share the tailor's positive mood, but his worries for Elizabeth and the dark news from Galton ate at his mind and heart. "Any further word from Thomas?"

"Not a whisper," the tailor said as he hand-stitched a seam on St. Clair's new waistcoat. "This is nice fabric, Lord Aubrey. You should let me make you a suit out of it. Such a nice hand."

Paul wanted to scream, to pace, shoot, act—not lie about all day like a child. "Hand! What good is fabric that feels silken to the touch when I cannot do what I must? Lord in heaven, help me to bear it!"

Then seeing his friend's remonstrative glance, the earl's face grew less flushed, and he attempted a weary smile. "Forgive me for the outburst, Martin, but it is maddening to lie here, helpless, wondering what is happening below ground. Yes, perhaps, when all this is over, my friend, we shall have time for fabrics and suits, but until then I would be content to have a rifle in my hand and the enemy in my sights. When did they leave?"

"Two hours ago, perhaps longer. Certainly not much. She said not to expect them back before late afternoon. The tunnels are long and complex."

"Two hours!" Paul sat up, trying to stand, but he fell forward, his head spinning.

The tailor jumped up and cradled the earl, gently easing him back into the soft cushions. "Paul, you are not strong enough to do this. Be sensible! Trust in St. Clair's shooting arm now. I looked into him, you know, per your uncle's instruction. A very interesting man. A man of fierce courage and conviction. He holds many prizes in shooting competitions."

"Does he?" Paul relaxed slightly, trying to put his trust in a man he knew would happily take Elizabeth's hand in marriage if she would have him. A rival. And yet—a friend. And perhaps even a relative. "What did you discover about his family? Anything?"

Returning to his sewing, the tailor adjusted his spectacles, his large head tilting to catch the best light. "Well, I can tell you that he was adopted. Did you know that? I do not think even he knows it. A couple claiming to be his aunt and uncle raised him, but they are no relation to our Mr. St. Clair. He was taken in by them when he was but seven, after his parents were killed in a railway accident, or so the story was told to him. Not quite true, though. I found his parents' records—or at least one for certain, but I am on the trail of the second."

"You are one clever old man," Paul said, his blue eyes lighting up. Even though he might not be involved in the adventure, he could use this time to learn more about their situation, and that may yet keep them alive. "Tell me more."

The old tailor's eyes were sharp, and he kept keen watch on the earl as they talked, making sure he did not make another foolish attempt to stand. "If you remain quiet as you have been told, then I shall share it. Only then."

"You may rely upon my submission," Paul said, a genuine smile creeping across his lean face. "Go on."

"Well, this is what I discovered originally, and it set me into motion to learn more. Since then, I have discovered many layers to peel back. I found a document that the Liverpool registry office claimed was a copy of a birth certificate issued for one Charles Arthur St. Clair, but there was no father listed, and this copy did not have the right look, you know? Here is the second layer of this interesting onion puzzle. It seems that the mother, a woman listed on this purported copy as Angelina McKay was actually not married, and the child never knew his true father. But something about this story did not feel right either, you know? So I did a little more digging, unpeeling more of that interesting little onion, and I uncovered an old set of letters and legal documents. It is good that the duke commissioned me with this task long ago, just after our policeman friend first entered our duchess's life, is it not? I have spent many years, traveled countless miles, and expended much money—well, the duke's money, of course—in finding out his true past."

Paul closed his eyes, trying to connect the various names in his remarkable memory. "Angelina McKay? I have cousins named McKey, sometimes spelt McKay," he said, impatient to see where this tale was headed.

"I shall get to that. Let me tell my story in my own time," the tailor continued calmly, threading the needle again. "So, last year, I traveled to Liverpool where this train accident that orphaned young Charles took place, and there I find a woman who knew the mother. An old friend, she said. She kept letters, which the mother of Charles the orphan, had given into her care. 'Do not let anyone take these unless they can prove they are from me,' she had said to her friend, and she gave this friend a symbol which would provide proof of any messenger who might come to take it. It is this."

The tailor leaned forward and wrote in pantomime on the table between them, as if tracing a shape, forming a capital P crossed by an S and bounded by a circle.

"That cannot be!" Paul insisted, sitting up once again. The tailor pushed him back into the cushions, cautioning him that he would call for Baxter if the earl did not comply. After much persuasion, Aubrey obeyed, but colour had risen to his face, and he seemed wide awake now. "But that is our symbol! Our secret sign! Did you see it with your own eyes?"

"I did, in fact, see the original, and it is the same. Also a fact: I have this box of letters and other papers in my luggage, which I shall not fetch for you now. I will agree to bring it to you only after you have rested today. Too much excitement may cause that wound to re-open, and that will do nothing for our dear one."

"The woman gave you these letters then?"

"She did, when I showed her my own symbol upon the cards we in the circle use to prove trust. Now, promise you will behave, and I shall tell you more. Otherwise, I shall finish my sewing upstairs."

"Yes, yes, I'll be good," he assured the tailor. "But, Martin, how can you ask it of me, when you know what this means?"

"It may mean nothing; it may mean everything. How can we know until we pursue it?"

The earl could not stop thinking. "The mother—St. Clair's mother. Where was her home? Did you learn anything more about the father?"

The tailor calmly clipped at a small black thread with a tiny pair of scissors. "Yes. But more of that in a moment. I had reason to suspect that the mother arrived in Liverpool on a ship. That much the woman was sure of, but the origin of that ship and its name, she was not so sure of. She did think it had a Scottish sounding name, though. So, I did what you would have done; I traveled to the docks and asked for the names of all ships that had docked there during the three years before this alleged 'train accident'. I will tell you all about that later, but for now, the ship is more important. There were many, and I wrote down all that had Scottish sounding names. I took her that list, which contained nearly fifty names. She is a woman of good character, I think, but her eyes are not so good, so I read them out to her, and she stopped me when I said *The MacAlister*. Well, back I went to the docks and asked to see the ship's registry for all passengers who may have sailed on her from any ports in Scotland to Liverpool. It took many hours of tedious work and the odd financial inducement, but do you know I found the name of a woman very close to the one listed on the birth certificate? A female passenger with a young son. Not Angelina McKay at all, but Angela Sinclair. And her name in full was listed as Angela Marie Stuart Sinclair."

Paul nearly leapt to his feet, but a warning glare from the tailor kept him still. "She was my mother's sister! Aunt Angela! Is it possible—could Charles be my cousin in truth?"

"We must not jump to any answers before we know all the questions, my friend. You taught me that many years ago, as did your wonderful father, may he rest in peace. So, because I knew you would make that connexion—and that you would be so quick to jump to those conclusions, I traveled to Glasgow and found a small fishing village called Crovie. I believe you know it."

"I should. It's only thirty miles from Castle Drummond. Angela sailed from there?"

"Yes, she did, according to the ship's records. She may have altered her name in an attempt to hide, or perhaps someone else altered it to obscure our detective's true past. I tried to trace anyone named Angelina McKay—to find family or friends in the village, but I found doors slammed in my face, if you can believe it. Me! I'm such a nice fellow."

"You are that, but those villagers won't talk to outsiders. My uncle could get the story. We'll go there once we leave here."

"I'd thought as much, which is why I packed my best woolens. And if you've found my information helpful, then perhaps your lordship might find a few extra pounds to supply more of those fine Scottish tartans once we're there?"

Paul suddenly felt energized. "My friend, I shall buy you a trainload of tartan wools if you want them! Finally, a plan…but, wait a minute. Wait. Kepelheim, if we have learnt this, then who else might have done so?"

"Now that is the right question, my lord earl. The right one at last, which tells me your head is clearing. Good! And is it mere coincidence that our paths have so crossed with St. Clair, if all is as we think it may be? Divine assistance is not too much to believe in, but there is also the possibility that our enemy has unseen friends, who have been manipulating events for a very long time."

Paul slapped his forehead suddenly, the sharp crack echoing along the walls and windows of the large room. "That is why!" he cried out. "The one thing I could never reason out was why Trent drove Patricia's body all the way into East London, when he could have just left her in the tunnels where Elizabeth has always insisted the murder took place. Oh, when I think of the questions the police and even *we* put to her over and over again about that night, and how she stalwartly insisted that Trent had killed her mother beneath the grounds of Branham, and then taken them both in a wagon, all the way into London. That never made sense to me until now!"

"I do not follow," Kepelheim complained.

"No? Consider this. William left Patricia in the H-Division district with a singular purpose. Think about it, Martin. How better to enlist an unknown policeman into the battle than to lay a beautiful and mysterious murder victim on a well-lit street like Commercial? But more to the point, it may explain why the fiend left Elizabeth there, too. And why Trent appeared in such a merciless attitude the following day. What gallant police officer would not champion a crying child—especially an officer who has recently lost his own child and is known to have a soft and pliant heart? We've looked at this all wrong from the beginning. We should—*I* should have believed Elizabeth, and perhaps then we might have uncovered the truth sooner. St. Clair must be told all, Martin. As soon as he returns."

"I agree," the tailor said just as the doors opened to reveal Baxter's looming presence.

"You have a message, Lord Aubrey. I have asked the gentleman who delivered it to wait, as he claims to be known to you. Shall I send him in whilst you read?"

Paul took the message. It was another coded telegram; this one from his uncle. "Yes!" Aubrey said, realising the contents. "Tell him to come in at once!"

The butler retreated for a few moments and then returned, accompanied by a squat man with mutton chop sideburns and a dark blue overcoat. "Detective Inspector Reid of Scotland Yard, sir," the butler announced and left the trio alone.

"Mr. Reid, sir! Edmund! Welcome, and please come in. My uncle has sent you? Please, do sit, my friend. Sit!" The earl pushed himself up against the cushions as much as he dared now, allowing Kepelheim to prop up his head.

"Lord Aubrey, I am honoured to be on errand from your esteemed uncle. Last night, he received disturbing news of your rail journey by way of an urgent telegram sent by my colleague Charles St. Clair, and the duke bade me ascertain that you and your company were safe, and that you, sir, are well. He had been told you were injured, and I see it is so. Is there any way I may assist you? I have brought a certain item in my wagon that may provide an exit in an emergency."

Paul glanced at the tailor, clearly not following this last. "Unless you can fly us out of here on the wings of a hawk, I cannot think of any help you might bring us, save your marksmanship, Mr. Reid."

Reid smiled. "That sir, is just what I have brought you. Wings."

CHAPTER THIRTEEN

As they descended slowly and carefully into darkness, Charles kept Elizabeth close to his side, the lantern held high. Torches had once lined the ancient stone steps, though most of their mountings had long since given way as the mortar crumbled. He could still make out the black smoke stains that they'd caused, after many years of use.

"Watch out for rats," he warned her, but she made no sound, for the underground passages were familiar territory to Elizabeth, and she knew just where she was headed.

"To the left once we reach the bottom. The ceiling lowers, so mind your head. I know that William sometimes had to stoop, as did his friends."

"His friends?" he asked, crouching down to clear his tall head as they passed beneath an arched doorway.

Once through, she spread her hands and said, "Here it is."

The archway opened onto an enormous cavern that soared high overhead. They had descended in darkness, down over two hundred, treacherously worn, carved steps in a winding pattern, so it was likely that the abbey, which had been built on an earthen mound stood directly over them.

"How is this possible?" he marveled. "It must be fifty feet high!"

"At least," she said. "If we turn to the right, past that large carved column, we would reach Branham, going beneath the old hall, but that route is dangerous and many passageways are low or collapsing. I learnt later—on that awful night—that there is another way, discovered by William, but I only traveled it once, so I would not attempt to retrace it now. As a child, I had no trouble clearing the lower areas, but Paul nearly got stuck once when I took him through after my mother married William."

"He's been through them then?"

"Only parts. Only once. Paul had come to visit at Easter, the year after Mother married William. He'd asked permission to take me with him to Scotland, but William refused. So Paul remained here for three weeks—no doubt a torment to Trent!—and he spent all that time with me, a silly little girl who wanted to ride ponies and play at tea. But whenever I knew no one overheard us, I told him all I had discovered whilst following William—well, all I'd discovered up to that time. I found this place only after Paul left. There, in the centre of this main room, you see evidence of many large fires. Three times, I watched through a tiny crack beyond that wall there, and what I saw terrified and sickened me."

He held her close as they moved forward, his mind suddenly remembering the Webley Bulldog nestled inside the holster. "Would you hold the lantern for a moment?" he asked her, removing the weapon and making certain the double-action revolver's cylinder was filled. "I'll not let anyone harm you, Beth," he vowed as he snapped the gleaming chamber back into its housing.

"I have no fear when you are near me, Charles. I know that nothing can reach me if it does not get past you. Somehow, I've known it since first we met. From that moment when I first saw your wonderful eyes, my Captain."

She moved forward, the lamp held as high as she could manage it, her steps echoing sharply on the cool stone floor and high rock walls as she walked. "But look now, Superintendent. Use your great detective skills and imagine this place ten years ago. See what lies beneath our feet. There, in the space near those old coals, you will see *her blood* mixed with that of many others. It is still there, like a great, crimson lake of grief!"

She moved toward the centre, holding the lamp close to the ground so he could see, and he gasped. The entire cavern floor looked as if it had been painted red with blood!

"William murdered your mother—here?"

She nodded. "They had been arguing much of the evening, and he actually began it. It was as if he wanted an excuse to do it—to bring her here—to hurt her; kill her. It was after supper. I had gone up to bed, and my nanny had just begun laying out my bed clothes, when I heard them shouting. She sounded terrified, and it was not the first time. Mother threatened to leave him, to divorce him, but he laughed. Nanny thought somehow that I could not discern the words' true meaning, but I did.

"I waited until she began running my bath, and then I fled, rushing down the steps toward my mother's apartment, but not finding them there, I ran back again to his. As I told you last night, Trent had chosen his rooms because there is a passage to the tunnels that connects there. I had seen him use it many times, though he knew it not. As I opened the door to Trent's drawing room, I could see him wrenching my mother's arms so hard that she fell at his feet. I nearly rushed in to stop it, and I wish I had, but I'm not sure it would have ended any differently. William's apartment not only connected to the tunnels, it was also far from any servant's rooms. Only my nursery, which was directly overhead, lay near enough for anyone to hear, and he clearly wanted *me* to hear it."

"Wait, Beth. I'm confused. Mr. Baxter told me that your stepfather's apartment was in the east wing, but your nursery is in the north wing. How could you possibly have overheard an argument so far from there?" he asked, but she grew pale, clearly upset.

"You're right. Oh, Charles, you're right! My nursery is—was in the north wing, but..." She paused, her eyes searching the ground as if somehow the truth might be found there. "Yet, I know my memory is correct. That is what happened. I know it is. You do believe me, don't you?"

He kissed her hand. "Yes, darling, I believe you, but perhaps the horror of it somehow mixed up some of the details. Forgive me."

"Yes, I suppose that's possible. It's taken me some years to remember much of it, perhaps I'll eventually recall more that explains the discrepancy, but I am sure what I've told you is right."

She was upset, and he regretted bringing it up at all. "Don't think on it now, Beth. You say William intentionally created this raucous argument for you to overhear it. Why? Why would he do that?" he asked. "I don't understand his madness."

She took a moment to reply, and he noticed her hands had begun to shake, so he took the lantern from her. "Thank you," she whispered, her voice cracking. "I think I begin to understand why he wanted me to witness his deed—why he involved me at all," she confessed. "Again, I cannot tell you more—and I am sorry to keep saying that, but I will tell you what happened as best I can recall it. I watched from the doorway, fearing he would see me, and wondering if I should go fetch Baxter or someone else to help. I knew, though, that the servants had been warned by Trent—many times—never to interfere or they would lose their place, so I kept my silence for fear of incurring William's wrath upon them. Then he opened the great fireplace in his sitting room; it is designed to turn. I'll show it to you when we get back to Branham."

He hesitated to speak, but cleared his throat and confessed. "I hadn't said anything to you, Beth, but Kepelheim and I explored that floor of the east wing this morning, and Trent's apartment is locked. All the other doors opened, but not his. Might your grandfather have rekeyed it?"

"I'm not sure," she whispered. "Why would you go into that awful wing?"

"It's not germane to this, darling. I shall tell you later, but I would like to see the rooms, if we can find some way to unlock it."

"Did you ask Mrs. Alcorn?"

He shook his head. "I didn't have the chance to, but I will when we return. Do you think Drummond may have had it shuttered?"

She sighed. "Yes, it's entirely possible. Grandfather hated Trent, and after Mother's death, he sealed off the entire wing from the other parts of the house. Now, the only access is either through the winding case or through his friend's apartment next door."

"His friend? Baxter said nothing of that."

"He wouldn't, because I doubt that Baxter knew about it. He was a horrid, disfigured man named—oh, what was it?—Minster, or Manster—no, it was Monstero! Appropriate, too, for the man looked as if he'd been pieced together by Mary Shelley's Dr. Frankenstein! I'm not sure if that was the man's true name or not, but it's what Trent always called him. He wasn't always there, though. Strangely, enough, he often visited when the moon was new, as if he hated moonlight."

"What?" he asked, unable to follow her reasoning. "Why would he..."

"Never mind. It was a childhood game of mine to try to fathom why the creature fascinated Trent so much. The monstrous man was nearly eight feet tall. He towered over Trent, and I always wondered why he obeyed him. There is a passage into Trent's rooms from that apartment, and the apartment itself communicates with the east attics by way of a narrow staircase, hidden inside a linen cupboard."

He stared at her. Elizabeth Stuart was the most beautiful woman he'd ever seen—more beautiful than any woman he could even imagine seeing—and yet there was an ever-widening sphere of intricacy to her that fascinated him. "How did you discover that?" he asked.

"Merely by exploring," she replied enigmatically. "I'll tell you more about my childhood curiosity at a later date, Captain. For now, believe me when I tell you that Trent's fireplace swings open, and if we're able to get in, I shall prove it to you."

He touched her hand once more, ducking as a bat flew overhead. "Bats! A reminder that we're out of man's domain, I suppose," he said hoping to see her smile, but she did not. "Beth, I've made you think that I doubt you, and I assure you that I do not. Darling, I want only to understand." She began to shiver, and he took her into his arms. "You're cold. Would you like my coat?"

"No, I'm all right. Forgive me, Charles. It's just that Paul has so often doubted me that I'd feared perhaps you..."

"I believe you, Beth. I believe everything you tell me. If there is any discrepancy, then I'm sure there's an explanation, but I have no doubt whatsoever about your claims. If you say it happened; then it happened." She began to weep softly, and he kissed her forehead lovingly. "Darling, are you sure you want to continue?"

"Yes, please, let me finish, Charles. It's important."

"Very well. You followed him into the fireplace?"

She nodded, tears tracking down her cheeks. "Yes. It leads into the tunnel system, and that night, he... He..." She paused for a moment, her entire face pinching into a mask of regret and pain—and he saw that small tremble of her lower lip that he had come to recognise as a sign of great inner distress. She took a deep breath as if to steady her mind. "Charles, he dragged my poor mother inside and said that, if she screamed, he would kill *me!*"

Elizabeth paused again, her entire body shaking. "I knew I had to help her somehow, so I crept after him. He had shut the fireplace, but I had seen the location of the switch plate beneath a small carpet, so I activated it again, stepping onto it with all the weight in body, and it opened. And then, after waiting a few eternal moments to make certain he did not perceive me, I followed them down the passageway and eventually into the tunnels below."

"And he did not know you were there?"

"At first, I thought I'd eluded his ears and eyes, for I crept quietly behind him, careful to keep away from his lantern. Following his lamp was simpler than it may sound, for I had done it before. And the things I had seen made me fear all the more for my mother."

"What do you mean?" he asked her. "Darling, I saw your mother's poor body. What could be worse than that?"

She shivered again, for the cavern was damp and cold, but the memory colder. "Oh, Charles, you cannot imagine it. You asked me earlier what I meant by William's friends. Well, you see, he met—*other* men down here. Those images etched and painted upon the walls in the abbey above? They were acted out by real men—*prominent* men, using real animals and even *other prey* down here."

He gasped, nearly cried out. "No! Dear Lord, can such men exist? I might believe that three hundred years ago pagans may have practised such unthinkable rituals, but civilised men living in England? Now? Beth, I met your stepfather, and though he is a craven and cowardly blackguard, I would never imagine *even him* in such heathen rites as those walls bespeak!"

She touched his arm. "But William did do those things, Charles, and he probably still does. You would be shocked to learn the identities of some of his fellow heathens. I recognised the faces of some of those mad revelers once—recognised them as men who'd visited our home, who'd dined with Trent and my mother. It was the second time I followed him here, when these wretched men shared in their devilish rites, but that time most had not yet donned their masks."

"Masks?"

"Yes," she said. "You saw those imps and demons drawn above? Well, these men wore costumes and masks to *act out* their roles, and it shames me to tell the things they did to each other and to their terrified victims. The first time I saw them here, they raised up foul chants to Satan and other infernal deities whose hideous names I cannot recall, whilst they slit the throat of a lamb, drinking its blood and defiling its remains in unimaginable ways—oh, but the second time!—the time when I saw some of their faces? Then, it was not a hapless lamb they sacrificed, Charles, but a small *boy* with whom they engaged their knives and deviant desires."

"Oh, my sweet Beth!" he cried out, trying to hold her, but she pushed him back.

"No, please, let me finish! Charles, I truly wanted to help that boy, to tear him from their murderous grasp, but I could not. I dared not! I had neither strength of voice nor of body to attempt such a feat. And so I watched, horrified. I felt frozen, unable to move. I have lived with the memory since that night. Lived with my failure to help him. Lived with my guilt. Oh, I can still hear his screams!" she cried out, covering her ears with both hands.

"Darling, it isn't your fault," he assured her, taking her into his arms. "You were but a child yourself. Oh, my dear sweet Beth, how I wish I could tear these memories from your mind. Remove them forever so you might have peace."

She clutched at his waist, weeping into his shoulder, her entire body jerking with great sobs and spasms of regret. "A boy, Charles! Just a small boy! Those men. How could they? I tried to tell Mother about it, but she said I'd dreamt it all."

He stroked her hair, whispering love to her, calming her, and she slowly regained her strength, through his. With her face pressed against his chest, she continued. "I learnt, years later from Dr. Price, that a local boy of that description had been found in a rail yard, dead and drained of all blood, and that this sad event was not uncommon in our county. The boy's viscera had been cut out and displayed upon his poor corpse, and his most...private members removed and taken. Does that sound familiar to you?" she finished, looking up.

"Ripper," he whispered, the puzzle pieces at last clicking into place. "I finally see why you connect those crimes to this place. No wonder you feared for your mother's life!"

"I did. I feared what he might do to her. Feared that those other men might also be here, masked and ready with their knives. And so I followed until he brought her here, and then and only then...did I scream."

Charles could picture the moment, and it terrified him. "And so he found you."

She shut her eyes, and he knew the dark memories were over-whelming. The little girl he'd met, carried, protected, later fallen in love with, and now longed to marry, had seen more blood and torture than most grown men.

"He did find me," she continued, her voice trembling. "William tore me from my hiding place and showed me to my mother, saying he would kill me then and there, abuse my body, slit my throat, and drink my blood, if she not obey his every command."

"I shall kill that man with my bare hands," St. Clair vowed.

Elizabeth began to weep again, crying out as she fell to her knees. "She pleaded for my life, Charles; she begged! It was here! Right here, where he made her watch as he dragged me to the centre of this cauldron of blood. She promised to do anything he asked if William would but spare me, and for a moment, he seemed to relent. He—he set me aside, telling me that he would return to me in time, and then he went to my beautiful, terrified mother and dragged her to her feet. He then looked at me, those cold eyes burning with hell's own flame, and he ordered me to beg for *her* life now."

She wept bitterly, her voice cracking. "His hands closed 'round her slender throat, and she was choking, dying, and I begged, I pleaded with him to spare her! I fell to my knees, and I promised him I'd be good, that I would do all he asked from then on—and then, suddenly realising the spiritual darkness at work in him, I looked to heaven instead, and I began to pray. It was all I could think to do, and I spoke our Lord's prayer out loud.

"Hearing the words of our Saviour drove William into madness, and he tossed my mother to the ground as if she were nothing but a ragdoll. She cried out, one tiny whimper, and I think that may be when she died, for she moved no more. He then snatched me from my knees and carried me up those winding steps, through the abbey, and to the outside, where a wagon and two horses stood waiting. It had all been planned, Charles! That man, Monstero the Monster, stood by, ready to drive the team. Ready to obey his master's every command. I kicked and screamed, and it was then I felt the first crack of his cane upon my neck. I collapsed into a deep sleep, waking later in the wagon as I have told you."

He helped her to her feet, wiping the tears from her eyes. "You're safe now," he whispered. Exhausted by the dark memories, Elizabeth began to cry again, and he held her close, kissing her hair and forehead, making plans how he might remove the threat of William Trent from her world forever.

CHAPTER FOURTEEN

The sun had set below the woodline, though Charles and Elizabeth had no way of knowing it. Ominous clouds of ravens had begun to gather above Branham Hall, and below them, a small army of brave men patrolled the grounds, their weapons ready should any enemy dare to breach the line.

Paul Stuart had begun to rally, his hopes raised by the man from Scotland Yard, and he perceived that his uncle had launched a plan of action that just might rescue his beloved duchess from what was proving to be a deadly trap.

"They are not yet returned?" he asked Baxter, who had brought tea and sandwiches.

"They are not, sir," the butler replied.

"What can be keeping them? Edmund, I fear your device may have arrived too late."

"You must eat, my lord," Baxter urged, placing a plate near the earl. "Mrs. Stephens has made your favourite. It is pork roast with that spicy sauce you brought her from Spain. And there's a fine port wine as well a lemon chiffon cake."

The earl had little patience now and even less of an appetite, but he knew his body required nourishment, so he did as the old butler had asked. As Aubrey nibbled at the sandwich, Dr. Price recorded observations and wrote instructions to whatever physician would attend his charge at their next hiding place.

"You must keep still, sir!" the doctor insisted, struggling to obtain a reliable blood pressure. "Mr. Baxter, can you not hold him down?"

The butler's thick brows rose in concert. "I shall endeavour to do so, but it has been my experience that only my lady's stern command may alter Lord Aubrey's mind when once it is set upon a task. Still…" He reached around Paul's broad shoulders and set one large hand on either side of the earl's head. "Will this do, Doctor?"

"Nicely," Price remarked, squeezing the ball that forced water into the von Basch sphygmomanometer cuff now around Paul's right wrist. "Mr. Kepelheim, I have made a list of the earl's vitals for reference, and I am also giving you a list of all medicines I have administered, though few in number, to deliver to the next doctor—should you find one ready for your aid—wherever it is you are going."

Reid had been huddled with the tailor, and the two pored over maps of England and Scotland, drawing pencil lines and whispering. Kepelheim looked up from the maps, nodding. "Yes, yes, that is much needed, thank you! And perhaps I should have these medicines with me in case there is no doctor, eh?"

Price agreed. "I shall send my own medical kit with you, Mr. Kepelheim."

Paul put his hand on the doctor's wrist. "That is most generous, Doctor. Allow me to reimburse you for all your time and sacrifices. As soon as you have finished here, perhaps Mr. Kepelheim will fetch my wallet and bring it to me. It is in my overcoat pocket, Martin."

Kepelheim pushed himself to his feet, wincing as his aging knees complained. "Oh, to be young again! Here. Here is your coat, Lord Aubrey. Which pocket? Inside? Oh, yes, let me see. This small bag perhaps?" he asked, holding the velvet bag Paul had received from Sir Clive the night of the play. Had that been only two nights past? How time had lingered in their lives since, pulling them into dangers that threatened all their plans—if not their lives.

"Give me that," the earl said, reaching out with his good arm. "I had forgotten this strange gift. Do you know Sir Clive Urquhart?"

Kepelheim and Reid both nodded as did Baxter. The butler spoke first. "That, uh, *gentleman* visited here last May, sir. Just after the Branham fete."

Paul's eyes rounded. "What? He called here? Did Elizabeth receive him?"

"She did, and once he left, my lady's demeanor became, shall we say, less positive. She did, in fact, throw a Georgian vase into the fire."

"Well, that's not good," Paul laughed. "Beth seldom loses her temper, but once lost, the safest position is to stand out of reach of her throwing arm! Baxter, did anyone perchance to overhear the conversation twixt the duchess and Sir Clive?"

Mrs. Alcorn, who had been busying herself in nursing duties, glanced up at the butler, who nodded an approval.

"Well, Lord Aubrey," she began, "I happened to pass by this very room as my lady and this Sir Clive—a devious person, if I may be so bold…"

"You certainly may!" Baxter agreed, gathering up several empty wine glasses onto a tray.

"Thank you, Mr. Baxter. Well, as I said, this Sir Clive person spoke words that led me to believe he had come here to solicit funds from my lady."

Kepelheim glanced up from the map to which he had now returned. "Funds? Dare I ask for what he needed funds? The man boasts of his wealth with every rotten breath!"

Baxter merely cleared his throat in approval.

Paul opened the bag and withdrew the contents, holding them in his right hand, for his left arm was now enclosed within a sling and fresh bandage. "I believe this begins to make sense," he told the company. "Mrs. Alcorn, do you and our esteemed Mr. Baxter recognise these?" He handed the rings and cross to the housekeeper, who gasped in shock.

"My word! Are these…good heavens, where did that wretch of a man get these? My lady, Duchess Patricia, Lord rest her soul, had these rings still upon her finger when last she breathed!"

Baxter took the set and his gentle eyes grew dark with an inner rage, a rare display of emotion, indicative of his great love for the late duchess. "Foul fiend!" he bellowed, touching the gold to his heart. "These are the rings given that gracious lady by her true husband, the duke's son and your most kind and remarkable cousin, Lord Aubrey. That foul usurper, Trent, insisted she continue to use them as her new wedding set, for he was too mean a man to buy her jewels. He took only—never gave! Inspector Reid, would not these have been upon her hand and heart still when you policemen found her in that east end street?"

Reid left the table and placed a pair of spectacles upon his nose, examining the jewelry. "Yes, I remember seeing these a few days after the murder. I was assigned to the Yard back then, just promoted to Detective Sergeant. Sir Robert Morehouse served as division head at Leman Street. He showed them to me and several others who had been brought in to consult on the case. Yes, and St. Clair was there as well. He confirmed that it was these pretty items found upon the duchess's body that night. It was their value and beauty that first astonished us, for it would have been highly unusual for anyone living in Whitechapel to afford so high a price."

Paul nodded. "Sir Clive gave me these in secret on Friday evening. He never said why, but he told me that when I had viewed the bag's contents, I would one day reimburse him for their price. I shall happily repay that man as soon as I am able, though not as he expects!"

Kepelheim withdrew a loupe from his coat pocket, a miraculous space that often seemed bottomless, for the little tailor always happened to have most any item at need. "These are expensive cuts," he said, turning the ring. "The sapphires are first quality, and the diamonds are flawless. The wedding band alone would buy my house!"

"So, Urquhart procured these from someone, but who in Scotland Yard, or at H-Division would have stolen them from evidence storage?" the earl asked.

Reid answered for his part. "Evidence is kept as long as it is possible to maintain it in proper condition, and space grows rare these days. Also, Lord Aubrey, did not Duke James press Whitehall to remove all of the paperwork regarding the duchess's murder? I remember myself, being asked to secrete certain documents via messenger to him at Drummond House. Perhaps, the jewels took a similar route."

"I suppose that is possible," Paul answered, "but that merely raises more disturbing questions. If someone within our inner circle conveyed the evidentiary items, then how came these to Urquhart? Edmund, I fear your police force may have servants to our enemy's cause within its ranks."

Reid removed his eyeglasses and nodded. "So, it does appear, Lord Aubrey. I hear the clock chiming six. Should not her ladyship and St. Clair have returned by now?"

Paul tried to rise, losing his balance and catching himself before he fell by reaching out for Price's arm.

"Steady," the doctor warned. "Do not tear your stitches again!"

Ignoring the advice, Paul remained sitting for a moment, and then tried once more to stand. "Reid, prepare your conveyance at once. We cannot delay longer. I'm driving over to the abbey to fetch them both." He slowly rose to his feet, swaying slightly, but Baxter and Price caught him as he fell.

"You go nowhere, my lord," the old butler said with a heavy heart, for he dearly loved the man like a son, though he would never tell him. "I shall send a horse with Mr. Clark, our Chief Groom, a man who can shoot down a flea in the dark with his eyes blindfolded. He will give our fastest stallion to my lady and the superintendent, and Mr. Clark will ride alongside to defend their path as they make for, uh, Mr. Reid's conveyance."

Paul didn't like it, but he knew the butler's plan might be their best chance, so he nodded to Baxter, who bowed and left to put the plan into action.

Charles had heard enough, and though they had brought no timepiece with them (he cursed himself for leaving his pocketwatch at his bedside), the detective knew it must be growing dark, for tiny shafts of light which had been filtering down from openings in the ground above their heads had ceased to shine.

"Beth, we have to go!"

She had fallen to her knees, her trousers picking up gravel and blood stains, as she searched the cavern floor with her bare hands. "But they must be here!" she cried, her voice trembling. She moved the lantern to a spot nearer the great patch of crimson, feeling along the uneven altar of death with both hands.

"What do you search for, darling? Please, allow me to help, for we cannot remain here, Beth, we cannot!" he said.

"My mother's rings and necklace. I sent to H-Division last year asking for them and was told that no one had recovered such items. She wore them that night—she always wore them. They are all I have left to remind me of what she sacrificed for me, Charles! I need to see them! Sir Clive Urquhart, that awful man, came here claiming he had them, but that is impossible. No, I think he is in William's pay, and was sent here to see what I remembered from that night. Oh, where are they!?"

Charles picked her up gently and brushed dirt from her face and hands. "Stop, dear. Stop! Your mother still wore them when she arrived at Leman Street. I myself saw the rings and necklace, taken from her poor form."

223

"You have them?" she asked, her face open and amazed. "But you never said. Oh, but I suppose you wouldn't have. I was only a girl, and they would have been part of the evidence. Are they still there, Charles? Is Sir Clive lying, as I suspected?"

"Truly, Beth, I do not know, but… Wait! Hush, hush…*listen*, oh merciful heaven, I think…!"

He turned down the lamp and held her close, straining his ears for sound. From far down the length of the great cavern, toward the sea, St. Clair could hear the faint echo of footsteps and hushed voices, speaking to one another. His heart froze.

"Beth, we must go now! I fear that men, whose only intent is to cause you harm, are coming up from that direction."

"That would be the pirate cove," she said, her eyes glowing in the low light. "Charles, we cannot go back up through the tunnels that connect to Branham. I do not trust my memory to find the way William used that night, and the other passageways are blocked. We must return up the abbey steps."

"Then we pray to our Lord that He protects us, and that the abbey is not already filled with gunmen!"

Morehouse struck a match and lit the gas lamp just inside his office. It was nearly six, and most of the lonely Sunday workers within Whitehall had long since left for the day, their arms loaded down with red wooden boxes containing secret government papers, leaving only a few, faceless men and women to mop floors and empty dust bins.

As he entered the now familiar space, Sir Robert headed straight for his desk drawer, top right, unlocked it and then removed his revolver, making certain it held a full complement of ammunition. He'd told no one of the mysterious letter, but he had sent a package to his solicitor with instructions that, should he be reported dead or missing, the contents of three sealed envelopes should be delivered personally to the addressees on each.

The first was to his dear wife, who had patiently loved him despite his many shortcomings, for thirty years of marriage. The second to his lifelong friend and colleague Fred Abberline, with a confession regarding the duel now facing Sir Robert and a copy of A's note attached. The third was to be sent to Charles St. Clair, again with a copy of the note and a complete confession of not only the indiscretions with the contessa but also Morehouse's secretive investigation into St. Clair's background, an assignment he had received shortly after the young policeman was posted to H-Division as a detective constable.

Sitting in his desk chair, the investigator thought through all he'd accomplished, his eyes proudly scanning a wall filled with framed citations, awards, and photographs—two with Mr. Gladstone and one with Queen Victoria herself as she made him a Knight of the Garter on the 23rd of April, 1888.

His office sat in the corner of the second floor of No. 6 Whitehall Place, and it contained a marble fireplace, six large bookcases, a settee and tea table, smoking chair and stand, a magnificent world globe set into a figural brass holder, and a curio of curved glass where all his Crimean War ribbons and medals gleamed from within their velvet boxes alongside a St. George's Cross and a solitary carved figure, given to him by the contessa. This last, small item rarely garnered any notice from visitors, but as his eyes paused upon the figurine—that of a white bird with upraised wings and bowed head and a single ruby set into its left wing—the aging detective realised what he must do.

Taking the pistol and setting it into his lap, he turned his sharp eyes toward the doorway, praying as he waited.

Finding their way back up the stone steps to the old and defiled sacristy proved even more difficult than descending. Charles led the way, keeping the lantern high and close to the wall, but its candle had begun to sputter as it burnt down.

"We are nearly there, I think," he said, hoping to keep his voice reassuring. "Keep watch on your feet, Beth. The rise on these steps varies, and they are sometimes slippery."

She followed, ever holding his strong hand, trusting in his leadership, in his capacity and courage to defend them both. As his boots met the sacristy floor, Charles quietly thanked God, and then turned to help Elizabeth ascend the last and rather high step.

"I wish to remain no time in this foul room," he said, moving swiftly toward the door that he remembered led to the hallway, and once through, to a series of doorways and rooms he prayed would take them to the entrance. He had trusted in Elizabeth's remarkable memory for turnings when following her through the maze of stone and timber, but now as they entered the darkened chambers, devoid even of moonlight on so cloudy a night, he pulled her close, praying he could guide them to safety.

"Never fear, my love," he whispered. "We shall reach the end soon, and then we will run to Branham if we must!"

"I am in your hands," she told him. "The path, Charles, is left, left, right, left, right, then left again into the main room."

He praised the Lord and quickly kissed her on the forehead. "You read my mind. Well done! Now, in a few moments, prepare yourself to run."

"You have a pistol, I see," spoke the man in shadow.

Sir Robert's right hand gripped his revolver, kept hidden beneath the desk. How could the visitor know?

"You make assumptions," Morehouse replied coolly. "Come closer and show your face. I take it you are A."

"I am called that for now. My face is not material to our purpose. Suffice it to say that my knowledge is. And that knowledge is vast and very old."

"And this knowledge is used for blackmail?"

The Shadow's head tilted to one side, and Morehouse thought he perceived a faint smile, though it was difficult to tell. "Such a human complaint. Blackmail would not be required, if you understood what it is I offer you."

"And that is?"

"Life, Sir Robert. Merely life. Embellished with both wealth and power. Is that not why you pursued your shady endeavours with the contessa? Did she not open your eyes to truths beyond mere, mortal imaginings?"

Morehouse's mouth went dry as he recalled the debauched nights spent with the bloodthirsty woman with the unwholesome appetites. "How...how can you know about that? I told no one of those...experiences."

"I know all, Sir Robert, but your dear wife need never hear of your dark deeds. She need never hear of the ceremonies in which you participated. The nights of wild abandon, the illicit drugs and fetishes, the animal lusts foisted upon innocent..."

"Stop! Stop! You have made your point! What is it you want from me?"

"Not much. Adoration. Alliance. Amour. Who knows?"

Morehouse's hands grew sweaty, and he swallowed hard as his forefinger tapped the revolver's trigger. "And if I give you these things?"

"Then, you may have whatever your heart desires—within reason, of course. Ultimate ends are not necessarily within my control, you understand, but I might be able to postpone that end," the voice spoke. "Do I detect shame lurking within your heart, old friend?"

"I am no friend to you, nor to your kind, if indeed you are Redwing!" Morehouse shouted, his heart hammering in his chest from fear.

The Shadow remained still, merely indicating annoyance by the tiniest movement of a shoulder. "Is that the limit of your imagination, Mr. Morehouse? Pity. One wonders how it is you were nominated and accepted for so prestigious an honour as Knight of the Garter. But then, perhaps, someone unseen whispered into Her Majesty's ear one night."

"I suppose you claim to be that whisperer?" Morehouse asked, his throat a desert.

"I've been known to make suggestions. Dreamers dream, and fools follow. Both live life with eyes willfully shut. Are you blind, Sir Robert? Do you sleep?"

"If by that, you mean my eyes are closed to the realities of the world, then you are the fool."

"And you begin to test my patience," the Shadow replied.

"You test mine, sir. Flesh and blood bleeds, no matter how vast a man's knowledge. If you intend me harm, then come forward and test my mettle!"

"Flesh and blood?" the man shape laughed, and the booming sound nearly broke the detective's eardrums, though he knew at once that it came not from a mouth, but rang instead within his own head. "Flesh and blood. How deliciously biblical! I truly enjoy such futile, human jibes. I am so much more—eternally more than puny man will ever hope to be. I stride across continents with a mere thought! I fly through the heavens with the sun upon my magnificent scales! Your attempts to slow my progress will ever fail, and your material weapons will never find purchase in a body as glorious as mine. I am beyond your measure, Sir Robert. Beyond your ability to perceive as a whole. A being as far above you, as you stand above the punctuation on a page."

Morehouse trembled now, his hand shaking. "What—what are you?"

"I am your oldest nightmare," the Thing replied, stepping forward into the light. His face was unfamiliar yet strangely known. He was tall, nearly seven feet in height. His hair was shoulder length and fell in dark waves about his broad shoulders. His attire appeared old-fashioned, yet vastly expensive. But it was his eyes that most troubled Morehouse, for they shone like fiery lamps!

"You are a man!" Morehouse shouted, jumping to his feet and firing all six rounds into the being's midsection. The room filled with acrid smoke, and the weapon grew warm in Sir Robert's hand, but as the smoke cleared, the shadowy figure had not moved.

It stood.

And it smiled.

"No! Impossible! You should be dead! How—how can…?"

"How can this be?" the creature asked, revealing six bullets within the palm of his left hand, pristine and shining upon a leathery glove. "Because I control all you see and experience. Including your weapon. And now, my dear Sir Robert, you will either agree to worship me, or you shall die in your secret sins."

Morehouse thought of his wife, knowing she would never understand. He thought of his iniquities, his many mistakes, but rather than worship this devil, he fell to his knees, and lifted his eyes toward heaven. "God help me! Christ Jesus, forgive me, please, and save me now, I beg you!" he cried out just as the pistol, which had emptied into a Shadow, turned in his hand and fired six impossible bullets into his brain.

A dozen men and women, having heard the shots, raced toward the second floor office, and the demon knelt beside the human's dead form. "Pity," the Shadow said. "I'd have enjoyed torturing you in hell, Sir Robert. Last minute repentance is so unfair."

He left the gun next to the dead policeman, former sinner, now a citizen of heaven, and rose to a great height, lifted up on three sets of wings, and then disappeared through the open window like black smoke from a chimney.

Sir Robert would be named a suicide by some, though his case and his last confessions, would soon be read by those members whom Paul Stuart called 'the inner circle', and this penitent sinner's legacy would give those who fought the Dragon ammunition to fight on.

Edwin Clark, the Chief Groom for Branham, had saddled two horses, a magnificent, white Arabian-Lipizzan cross stallion named Paladin, and a rare brindle Thoroughbred mare named Sadie. It was Sadie he rode now, for he knew her to be the second fastest horse in their stable. She was fearless and could turn on a dime at midnight. Paladin, though temperamental to most, became a lamb when carrying the duchess, and Clark knew she had wisely worn clothes that would allow her to ride with daring. St. Clair would have to ride with her, for that is what Aubrey had commanded, and Clark had learnt in many skirmishes during his thirty years of service that the earl and his family always gave sound advice. He considered them his generals, and so he, the cavalry soldier, would obey to the letter.

He carried two rifles on his back, both loaded, plus extra ammunition and another rifle in a saddle pack, and in his belt a pistol. He had also brought a small Bible and a cross, for the faithful believer may have followed earthly generals, but his utmost ruler was a king!

On he rode, the stallion tethered beside, and the galloping pair of steeds sped through the dense Branham Woods, leaping over fallen limbs and dodging beneath hanging boughs, racing toward the ruins so swiftly that their hooves scarcely touched the ground.

Elizabeth and Charles had just made the final turn, when voices rose up from behind them. Trent's men had gained the cavern and many torches made their progress up the stairs faster. Charles paused as he searched for the doorway in the pitch blackness.

"Where is it?" he asked, his heart pounding in his ears. Her arms were around his waist as they walked, but then suddenly he perceived the duchess fall, and he turned to help her.

"My foot," she whispered. "I've twisted it, I think. Oh, Charles, I am sorry! But look there! The moon shines for a moment, and the doorway is in sight!"

Picking her up, Charles threw the lamp away, for it had all but died, and he dashed toward the doorway, which he thanked God they had left open, praying they might know what to do once on the other side. Holding her tightly, remembering how he had first held her this way, nearly ten years before when she had been but a frightened child, his long, muscular legs made the forty-foot distance in just nine strides, miraculously missing every fallen stone, rat, and timber that lay across the darkened path.

Once through the door, he paused for a moment, catching his breath, still holding her in his arms, and he realised with dismay that it had taken them nearly two hours to walk here from Branham. Even if both could run, they could never outpace the pack of murderous men that now were but moments behind.

"Beth, darling, I don't think we can make it back through the woods. Is there another way?"

"I can try to run," she offered, but he would not set her down.

"I love you," he confessed, kissing her mouth, cheeks, and eyes as if this might be his last chance to tell her. "You are my heart, Beth, my life. I shall always thank God for allowing me to know you, my darling. Now, I'm going to take you into that covered wood over there. I want you to find your way back to Branham as quickly as you can. I'll keep these men occupied whilst you…"

"No! I will not leave you! Either we die together, or we live together!"

Just then, a miracle appeared, breaking from beneath the canopy of black oak and Scots pine and galloping through the phalanx of ancient yews. Two horses and a rider stopped within three feet of the desperate couple.

Seeing the pair of magnificent animals, the stranger's words suddenly flashed through St. Clair's mind: *"Ride. Ride swiftly, or she will die. When you see the horse, ride!"*

"Get on the stallion!" Clark shouted, jumping down to take Elizabeth from St. Clair's arms. "Once you are mounted, I will hand her up to you, and then you must make for Parker's Clearing. It is to the southeast of the house, on the far edge of the woods near the brewery. Can you find that?"

Elizabeth nodded. "I shall guide him," she said, kissing the groom's cheek. "Mr. Clark, you have saved us! But there are evil men behind, and they will emerge any moment from that door!"

St. Clair had taken his seat on Paladin, who calmly bore his new rider as if he knew the stakes. Charles reached down and helped

Elizabeth to find her place in front of his, and with the stranger's prophetic words still echoing in his mind, he took but a second to thank the man. "God keep you!" he said, spurring the horse forward.

"But what of him?" she asked as the wind whipped their faces, his arms around her whilst holding the reins.

"He is well armed, and I expect he came for a fight. We must pray we see Clark again, but now he is keeping our pursuers occupied, and my only job is to see you safely to Parker's Clearing!"

"What then?" she asked.

"Then, we rely upon the plans of my new cousin, I should think. What is this horse's name?"

"Paladin."

"Fly, Paladin! Fly as if the devil himself follows, for by our Saviour's blood, I know that to be true!"

They rode through a gauntlet of brush and boughs, but despite the darkness, Paladin managed to keep his riders from suffering even one scratch. The horse's hooves flew across the packed dirt path, his mind fixed on one singular purpose: to keep them safe and deliver them to their destination or die trying. No horse could catch him, no stone impede him. It was as if he wore the wings of Pegasus, and neither the lady nor the brave gentleman in his care felt the slightest bump, so smooth was his progress.

Beth leaned forward against the horse's long mane, keeping her eyes on the path but trying to stay clear of St. Clair's line of sight. They rode for what seemed like an eternity, and Charles held her tightly, praying as they raced through the dense woods.

"There!" she cried out as the path curved to the left. "Just beyond that rise is the clearing!"

Charles did not need to signal the horse, for the animal seemed to know their goal, and he tore 'round the corner, his hooves digging into the earth as he leaned into the maneuver. Nor did Charles have need to coax the horse to go faster, for Paladin could see their prize ahead and he doubled his speed when no other animal could have; despite his heart near to bursting, Paladin flew!

"What is that?" Elizabeth called out as they neared the clearing. In the centre of the grass-covered area stood Edmund Reid, and next to the stalwart detective his greatest surprise. Wings indeed!

"It's a hot air balloon!" Charles cried out, recognising his H-Division friend as the horse slowed and stopped. "Reid, can it be you?"

The detective reached up and helped Elizabeth as Charles climbed down from the saddle. "No time for reunions, St. Clair. The earl is already inside with our luggage. We must get you and the duchess into the basket, and then fly!"

Charles needed no further instructions. He picked Elizabeth up and handed her to Reid, who had already leapt into the square basket. Above them, several hundred feet into the air, soared a great oilcloth balloon of white and green, emblazoned with 'Queen of the Meadow' on her mighty sides.

Elizabeth dropped into the basket's interior, falling to her knees at seeing Paul's pale face and bandaged arm. "My Paul," she whispered, holding him tightly.

The earl's eyes brimmed with bright tears, "You are both safe! God be praised!"

St. Clair jumped inside, and he glanced back toward their path, and so far it was empty, but he knew the band of William's men could not be far behind, for he had seen a knot of mounted riders far to the east, riding up to join their comrades from the cavern. "What of Kepelheim?" he asked, finding only the four of them inside the balloon.

"With the weight of the luggage, she cannot lift more than four at a time," Reid explained, untying mooring lines as several footmen and groundskeepers aided his work. "Mr. Baxter and Mr. Kepelheim have armed themselves and will cover our escape should your pursuers reach the grounds 'ere we reach altitude and those lovely clouds above."

Beth turned to the aeronaut. "But can we not take Mr. Kepelheim at least? I am but a little thing. I barely count as one."

Reid shook his head. "I made that very case, my lady, but Kepelheim refused to leave Baxter's side. They have formed a friendship, I think. But with God's mercies, we shall see our tailor friend again. That man is made of stern stuff!"

Paul drew her close and held her fast. "Keep down here, all of you! As we ascend, we are still prey to rifle fire. St. Clair, keep down! Elizabeth, stay near me now." His eyes rolled, and he appeared close to fainting. Blood seeped from the bandage.

"He is bleeding again!" the duchess cried out. "We shall need to tend his wound."

As the great balloon lifted into the night air, St. Clair searched the luggage and found there the medical bag Price had given to the tailor. Pinned to the strap was a short note. *"Instructions inside. A doctor awaits at your destination. My prayers go with you all. – K."*

Looking inside the kit, Charles found it well stocked with medicines, bandages, tubes, needles, and even brandy. "That blessed tailor's thought of everything!"

Edmund Reid lowered a thick rope to the duchess and asked her to hold it. "Keep this line taut, my lady, as the superintendent and I practice our craft. St. Clair, you will find a rifle to your right, fully loaded. Use your keen eyes, and if anyone aims at this balloon, shoot!"

And so they rose, higher and higher into the clouds and the night. A bullet sang past once or twice, but Reid and St. Clair made short work of those taking aim. From their height, they could see Clark astride Sadie, her mane flying in the wind as she galloped. Clark, turned backward in his saddle, fired shot after shot into the mounted men who thundered behind.

Others were on foot, and Charles could see them split into two parties, one moving into the east gardens toward the hall, and the other racing southward toward the clearing. Charles blessed the plans that left most of their enemies without horses, for speed of foot was no match for speed of hoof, and Clark reached the main entry long before the raiders. The last thing the detective could see were Clark, Baxter, and Kepelheim standing shoulder to shoulder, guns at the ready, to guard their lady's passage to freedom, though it may cost them their lives.

"What wonderful men they are!" he cried out, tears blurring his vision. And the Queen of the Meadow rose up into the clouds, out of sight, and Edmund Reid, aeronaut deluxe, set his sights on Glasgow.

CHAPTER FIFTEEN

Sir Thomas Galton knelt beside the body of Sir Robert Morehouse, taking careful note of the scene. A friend at Scotland Yard had sent word to the inner circle member, who then rushed to arrive even before CID's A-Division detectives. Galton worked quickly, removing any evidence that might connect the murder to their cause. Inside Morehouse's desk were two leather-bound notebooks which, though they probably had no bearing on their work, Galton tucked into his satchel to read later.

He looked at the honours framed on the wall, at the books, and lastly at the curio cabinet, pausing his gaze at the carved bird. Looking once more into the halls behind, Galton removed the figurine and placed that, too, in his satchel. Lord Aubrey would want to see this, he knew.

Wishing he could remove the revolver, Galton chose to leave the body and gun as he'd found them. He said a quick prayer over the fallen detective and then made for the nearest exit.

Three hours after Galton ran into the night, a coach and four pulled up to the grand entry of a garish new home in Grosvenor Square. The eclectic attempt at neo-classical style had been designed and constructed by the home's outrageous but very rich owner, Sir Clive Urquhart. And it was the very same builder who now alighted from the carriage in the company of his mistress, Susanna Morgan, and a tall gentleman of imposing appearance, both in formal dress.

"We have much to discuss, my dear Sir William," the builder said, leaning into the carriage and handing the driver a five-pound note.

"You will see Miss Susanna safely to her townhome, yes? Very good, my man. Goodnight, my dear. Give your man a kiss now. So sweet, is she not, Sir William? And a pretty singer, too. Go now, my man! Go!"

He stepped back from the carriage, waving with his cane as he walked toward the front entry. An impressively dressed butler opened the door, and both men entered the marble and gold foyer.

"You see the lovely, big-bosomed woman in that painting—the one depicting Venus?" he asked Trent. "Miss Susanna posed for that, though do not tell my wife. She is an understanding and most accommodating woman, but to know such comparisons, for that painting is very accurate I can tell you, would give the good Lady Margaret too much heartburn, eh? Come now into my private salon, it is back here on the right past the Pan fountain. He pipes us to our pleasures, no?"

Trent found the statuary and paintings vulgar and pretentious, but he needed Sir Clive's assistance, at least for the present, so he indulged the *nouveau riche* bounder by admiring every gauche colour and ridiculous pose. "Marvelous!" he gushed. "Simply marvelous! Of course, these styles reach back to antiquity. Ah, the world then was quite different, was it not, Sir Clive?"

"Decidedly, so. Yes, it is decidedly so. Please, sit here, Sir William. By the fire. My butler and new maid—another lovely lady, by the way—they will serve us in a moment, but before we indulge in cigars and cognac, let us discuss the little problem in Kent."

William sat into a massive leather wingback and leaned into its sumptuous embrace, his face aglow. "What of Kent?" he asked, his eyes closed, long fingers drumming the chair's right arm.

"My men, they have telegraphed me that your raiders failed at Branham. It seems that our little bird escaped with her gallant men in a hot air balloon."

"A hot air balloon!" Trent laughed. "How delightfully unexpected. You must give credit to the duke and his wretched little band for creativity. We needn't worry, though, Clive. Despite what the Stuarts might believe, their plans to escape merely offer us a new and far better opportunity. Blood lies behind all, my greedy friend. Blood is the life."

"Blood? Whose blood? I do not understand. Perhaps, it is my builder's brain, which cannot compare to your magnificent mind, but I had thought our goal was to ensure the marriage of the duchess to the earl. Has that changed?"

Trent swung one long, muscular leg over another, as he tapped at the arm of the chair with an enameled ring. "Plans must always shift with the enemy's attempts to foil the original. My friend has been plotting a much better blood match, and he shared it with me ten years ago. I think it unlikely to succeed, but I may be wrong. It seldom happens that I am mistaken, but my friend is never wrong—so he tells me. It is but a new strategy, and you have no need to know the endgame."

"Endgame? A game of chess, yes. I see! Your queen is taken, then you must change your tack, no?"

"Queen is a very nice way to put it, but I think that waiting just a short while longer will provide us an even more powerful blood with which to perform our rituals. And I do love those wonderfully erotic rituals. They provide pleasure and practicality, as we raise up the new king."

"You lose me sometimes when you speak of blood and rituals, my friend. I am the thinker always, but this I do not understand. Is not the duchess the blood?"

"She is, but hers is only half the source. We need both to achieve our ends."

"The other—that is the earl, no?"

"Perhaps," he said, smiling widely as the young maid entered the salon, "perhaps not. It may be that Aubrey's blood is no longer required, which would much please me. The earl is too smug, and I would love to put a bullet into his brain. My friend will let us know." Trent untied his tie. "Over here, my dear," he told the maid, admiring her snug uniform. "I have such a craving tonight. I wonder if you have a remedy."

Sir Clive grinned, happy to have pleased his new and powerful friend. Snapping his fingers, he called to the butler. "Gerome! We will be wanting my special cart, I think. And bring the absinthe. Libation for our benefactor and music to soothe the darkest heart."

The butler set a wax cylinder into the mechanism of the Victrola and cranked the handle several times. In a moment, Act II of Tchaikovsky's *Swan Lake* streamed from the beautifully etched horn just as Trent began unbuttoning his waistcoat.

The Queen of the Meadow landed as planned in the south garden of Drummond Castle on the evening of the eighth. The voyagers had fared well for the most part, and along the way, all four passengers had indulged in a picnic meal provided by Mrs. Alcorn. Reid had been particularly happy to find a box of chocolates and other confections included by the thoughtful housekeeper, whom the detective had found to be a bright woman with a loving heart. Had he not been happily married, Reid mused to his companions, he might consider retiring one day by the sea with the gentle housekeeper.

The long journey had not been without its perils. Several times, the threat of men watching them from the ground alerted St. Clair and Reid to arm themselves, but each time the groups proved to be nothing more than curious onlookers. Still, St. Clair had made a note of their locations as best Reid's navigational skills could provide, and he kept these to share with Paul, who had spent most of the journey asleep, as well as with the duke upon their arrival. The entire trip from start to finish took nearly twenty-four hours, with one stop for their picnic and the second in a field to tend the earl's wound and wrap Elizabeth's foot, which by then had become swollen and painful from sitting in one position for so long.

St. Clair and Reid took the rigging in turns, the younger man eager to learn a new skill from the experienced aeronaut, and the pair of policemen spent the long hours sharing case histories and more to the point, theories on the Ripper murders whilst the duchess slept beside the earl. Both detectives agreed that every theory but one fell short, and that was the one which commenced with the discovery of Patricia, Duchess of Branham on Commercial Street.

As they touched ground—all four weary to the bone, the earl still in a fitful sleep—a team of young men ran toward the balloon to tie it down.

"The duke's an avid aeronaut," Reid told a surprised St. Clair, "and he's actually quite good at it. He'll no doubt want to take this for a spin over the coastline before I return it to Covent Garden."

"This isn't your own then?"

"It would take my entire year's wages to buy even a small one," he confessed, stroking one of the main ropes and running a calloused hand across the edge of the varnished basket. "This is a beauty, and I've had the honour of sailing her many a time, but it's the duke that arranged for it. And here he comes! What a lion that man is!"

Sure enough, James Stuart raced ahead of his footmen, his arms outstretched toward his guests. "Reid, you old son of a sailor! I knew if any man could get them here, it would be you. Here, Princess," he said to Elizabeth, "put your arms 'round your old grandpa. There's a lass. You dressed just right for adventure. No boots? St. Clair, it's a pleasure to see you again, son!"

Charles was reaching down to help the earl, but he shook Drummond's hand first. "Thank you, sir. I am indebted to you, as is the earl. He needs tending as soon as a doctor can come. He's been bleeding now and then. Oh, and Beth's boots are inside here, sir. We removed them to examine her foot. She turned it in our escape."

James kissed his granddaughter's face as he held her tight. "Did you now?" he asked Beth. "Well, we'll soon fix that. My bonnie lass, you are such a sight! Come now, we'll put you all into this coach and let the horses do the work back to the house. Reid, can you and St. Clair get Paul out all right? I can hop in if you need my help."

Reid laughed. "And let you sail away in her? Not likely! We can manage, Your Grace. Here, if one of your lads can take this baggage, it will leave more space for us to reach our arms 'round the earl. He's been in and out of consciousness since just after we sailed over Carlisle."

Several men took the luggage, medical kit, and lunch basket and loaded all onto a small wagon. The passengers were carefully helped into an open carriage, the sleeping earl next to Elizabeth on one side, and the duke and St. Clair on the other. Reid stayed behind to secure all the rigging and tether lines. He performed a final check before deflating the huge balloon and instructing the duke's men as to how best to load it into a large wagon drawn by a team of Clydesdales.

As they drove, James reached over to the detective and offered a warm handshake and smile. "Once again, St. Clair, you have kept her safe and brought her home. I've much to tell you, lad. I know you're all exhausted, so tonight we shall do nothing but let you recover whilst Dr. Lemuel practises his medical arts on Paul. Lemuel cared for my dear wife and son in their last days. Princess? Does your foot pain you?"

She shook her head, barely able to keep her eyes open. She'd slept only a few hours, for fear of missing Paul should he awaken, and now she let herself relax at last, her head nodding against Aubrey's right shoulder.

"I can see soft beds are needed," the duke said cheerfully. "Not to worry, Charles. You and I shall have a fireside chat, I think, whilst these two see the good doctor. Mrs. Calhoun has a fine supper ready for us all, which is catch-as-can style, meaning no sit down, which suits me to the ground. Ho there, Laurence!" he called to the driver. "Take us to the side doors on the southwest side. It's a much shorter walk to Paul's room."

Then to St. Clair, he explained. "I've put a Bath chair next to that door. My wife was unable to walk toward the end, so we had the chair built for her. It's a bit small for my nephew, but it will get him 'round if he needs it, though I expect he'll try to walk even when ordered not to. But having it will make it easier for the doctor as well."

"You've thought of everything, sir," St. Clair remarked. "I cannot tell you how beautiful Reid's balloon looked as Elizabeth and I galloped into that clearing, Trent's men at our backs."

The duke gazed lovingly at his beautiful granddaughter, and he placed a hand on St. Clair's forearm. "It's you I need to thank, lad. You've been her knight more than once, and you have forever won a place beside my hearth. And, from what I've heard, she would agree."

Though St. Clair wondered what the duke meant by 'what he had heard', he made no remark. Instead, he turned to watch the picturesque scenery go past, more to hide his face from the duke's perceptive gaze than to admire the beauty of the landscape. "You've a magnificent setting here, sir."

"She is a grand place, isn't she? Drummond Castle lies at the foothills of the real highlands—up where Briarcliff sits—that's Paul's estate. Aye, but we've got a beauty all our own. Castles come and go, houses rise and fall, but it's the land that remains. We're just passing through, I suppose. It's all God's land. Aye, and what a jewel He's given us in Scotland!"

As their carriage halted, Paul's eyes opened, and he appeared to be half dreaming. "Beth. Beth…" he called out, and she whispered into his ear, her hand on his heart. "Sleep now," she told him. Obediently, his eyes shut again, and he was once again dreaming.

St. Clair helped Elizabeth down from the carriage, and seeing her limp, the duke suggested the detective carry her into the castle.

"Follow Laurence there, Charles. He'll show you where Elizabeth may sleep tonight. There's no point in putting her into her usual apartment, since she clearly cannot climb. We'll make up a sitting room with a comfortable bed for her. Paul is down the hallway on the left. You can't miss it."

The duke and a footman eased the earl into the Bath chair, unlocked the brake, and wheeled it into a pleasant cornflower blue drawing room, often used by the family after dinner. There were two, beautifully crafted French doors that opened onto a colourful rose garden and the sea cliff beyond, and on the northwest wall, a white marble fireplace and cheerful fire greeted them. St. Clair carried Elizabeth into a connecting drawing room, this one with emerald green wallpaper and row after row of books on painted, white shelves. Over the fireplace, which shared a chimney with Paul's blue room, hung a painting of three beautiful young women in matching yellow dresses and white sashes, standing near the edge of the sea cliff.

Charles eased Elizabeth onto her makeshift sleeping couch, but she had nearly fallen asleep again. "Captain?" she whispered, and he stroked her hair.

"You're safe," he told her, and she nodded, falling into dreams once more. Wishing he could kiss her properly, he satisfied himself by kissing her hand. "Sleep well, little one," he said. "May you have beautiful dreams."

As he stood, St. Clair's gaze fell upon the large portrait. "Who are they?" he asked the butler in a whisper.

"Those are the Stuart ladies," Laurence replied as the two men left the drawing room and shut the door. "The duchess will sleep better, if we do not disturb her." As they walked, the butler continued, "The Stuart ladies were considered the most eligible and beautiful women in all of Scotland. If you recall the portrait, sir, the tall one in the middle is the youngest, Lady Victoria Regina, who lives in Paris. The others are the twins, both deceased now. Lady Abigail Charlotte married Lord Aubrey's father, and Lady Angela Marie married Robert Sinclair, the Marquess of Haimsbury."

"Sinclair, you say? How curious. I might be related to the Sinclairs, or so claims Lord Aubrey."

"Really, sir?" Laurence asked, with a tilt of his head. "Well, sir, after the marquess died in a duel—some say he was murdered—

Lady Angela disappeared with their only child, a son. Two years later, their bodies washed up on the shore, for she had set sail; some think to escape the man who'd murdered her husband, and the ship was destroyed in a brutal storm. I'm told that it broke the duke's heart. I would tell you more, but I'm not up on my histories, as I'd like. I've been studying with our parson on Sunday afternoons. The duke likes his gentlemen and ladies to read and learn, so since my elevation to butler, I've worked doubly hard. It's a rare place to serve, sir. The duke, I mean. He treats us all like family."

"And so you all are!" the duke's baritone rang out as he left Paul's drawing room, shutting the door behind. "How's my grand-daughter?" he asked the butler.

"Sleeping, sir." The duke tapped St. Clair on the shoulder and then tiptoed toward the green room, peeking in through the door as he opened it. "Princess?" he called in a whisper.

In the semi-darkened room, Beth turned slightly, but it was clear that she'd fallen into a deep sleep.

"She's off, and who can blame her?" he whispered and shut the door. "I imagine it was draining to spend an entire day in that cramped balloon basket, but she's here and that's all that matters. Thank you for that, Charles. Mr. Laurence, if you can do so without waking our sleepers, open the windows in both rooms. The moon's full tonight, and the skies are clear. The sea air will do our princess more good than any doctor's pills."

"I should take that as an insult were I not accustomed to it, Your Grace," a gentleman's voice replied.

Charles turned to find himself looking at an extraordinary man. His hair was black on the sides yet white in the middle, and he wore a garish, red and green checked waistcoat over a pair of peacock blue trousers. A gold monocle dangled from a silk strand encircling his thin neck, and his feet were shod in shiny red leather.

"I am Dr. Lemuel," he said to the detective. "The earl appears to be in relatively good condition, Mr. St. Clair, and I understand you and your friend are to be thanked. So, I thank you, sir. Now, if you and the duke wish to continue your conversation in another part of the house, I should very much like to examine the duchess— in private."

James and St. Clair exchanged glances and both left the hall-way. Charles walked with the duke past Paul's drawing room and out into the large corridor that led to the west entrance. Once there, the duke paused and burst into laughter. "Take no note of Lemuel, lad. He's always like that, but he's the finest doctor in the area. Now, what do you say to sharing a bottle of my best scotch?"

St. Clair was more tired than he dared mention, but the duke's clever planning and deep pockets had provided the means of their escape, so he followed the gentleman eagerly, arriving after five minutes' walk to a leather-paneled room where two large Irish Wolfhounds lounged by a massive stone fireplace.

"Sit down, lad. I've asked the staff to leave us alone for an hour whilst we talk. Reid's already gone up to bed, and he'll likely leave at first light to return the balloon. More's the pity. I'd have enjoyed taking her out over the coast."

"Yes, Edmund mentioned that you are also an avid aeronaut. I fear your granddaughter did not inherit that love of flying."

"And you, son? How about you?"

"Sir?" St. Clair asked, unsure of just how to reply. "I fear my boots seem to work best on solid footing, though Reid did teach me the basics of operating the balloon. Perhaps, I might have enjoyed it more had I not been so worried about Beth's—and your nephew's—welfare."

"Well said, son. If you're hungry, there are sandwiches on that tray over there, and we've plenty wine, if scotch is not your passion. We distill our own here, so I've been drinking this lovely spirit since I was a lad. You look all in, Charles. Relax. Take off your boots, if you like. I want to have a heart to heart with you, and you may as well be comfortable."

Taking the duke at his word, Charles selected two beef and cheddar sandwiches, set them onto a blue china plate, and joined his host near the fire. "Scotch is fine, sir, if that's what you're having. I've not been drinking it as long as you by any stretch, but my aunt and uncle served it on special occasions."

"So? Your aunt and uncle are Scottish?"

St. Clair shook his head. "No, actually they were brought up in Liverpool. They passed away some years back. We moved to London when I was twelve. My parents were killed in a train accident when I was very young, and my aunt and uncle took me in. To be frank, I remember nothing of my life before the accident. A doctor once told me that I'd sustained injuries that left me with memory gaps. I suppose that is one reason I was so concerned when I found your granddaughter had suffered a blow to the head in '79."

"Aye, that concussion. Trent is an evil man, Charles. Evil to the marrow, and he's not even a man, I'll wager, but you'll learn more about that side of things soon enough. You remember nothing about your parents then?"

"Nothing," he said, taking bites whenever he could. "As I said, my memory is gone from that period of my life."

A knock sounded, and the efficient butler entered, carrying a large, red leather box. "Is this what you wanted, sir?"

"It is, Laurence. Thank you. Set it on the table here."

The butler complied and then left the room. The duke leaned forward, his hand upon the mysterious box. "I've not yet read these, Charles, but I suggest you do. Kepelheim sent them with Reid, and he told me in a letter posted two days ago that he'd either send them or bring them. I pray that man will reach us here in the coming days. If he survived what must have happened after Reid effected your escape, then Kepelheim will join us here. If not, then we must mourn a good man and a faithful friend to our cause."

"You've not received any telegrams from them?" St. Clair asked with concern.

"Not yet, but there could be any one of a dozen explanations for that, son. I've asked members of the London team to go over there and get back to me tomorrow. This isn't the first time Branham's been through an attack, nor will it be the last. Now, relax. You've earned your rest."

Charles took a long drink of the whisky, nearly losing his breath by doing so. James slapped his guest on the back playfully. "It takes a real man to gulp down that fire! Well done, son!"

"Yes—well, yes," he coughed, his throat an inferno. "Well, uh, Kepelheim. Yes, he's far more than a simple tailor, of that I know. The cause? The London team? Is all this connected to what Lord Aubrey calls the 'inner circle'?"

"It is. And you are now a member, not just by your selfless deeds, my boy, but also because of your blood."

Charles set down his sandwich and stared at the duke. "Forgive me, sir. Did you say my blood?"

"I did. Read the contents of this box, Charles. In it, I'm told, you will find proof of what Kepelheim explained to me in this letter."

He held out a cream envelope, handing it to the detective. "Read it through and then examine the documents and photographs that Kepelheim secured for us. After, you and I shall talk more, because I want you to know just how your life intertwines with ours. Blood is at the heart of what our circle defends, and yours is an important part of that, Charles. And it answers, for me at least, a question that has nagged at us all since that night in '79, when Elizabeth first came into your keeping."

Something about the box called to him, though St. Clair could not explain it, but his brain was far too weary to comprehend much—not just now. "I promise to read the letter and examine the box, sir. However, I must forgo it until later this evening, or even the morrow, I beg you. My mind simply cannot hold it now. All I want to do is sleep."

The duke nodded, sitting forward. "Fair enough. It's a secret that's kept for a long time, so it will keep a bit longer. I'm just— well, it's selfish, I know, but I'm anxious to share it all with you, Charles. But you're right. Drink some wine and enjoy a morsel. You can sleep in the room opposite Elizabeth's if you wish. I'll have the room made up. I doubt you'll want to be far from her."

St. Clair wondered just how much the duke suspected, but he would not refuse an offer that allowed him to make sure of Elizabeth's wellbeing. "Thank you, sir. She is precious to me. To us all."

"Well said, son. I'll go have a talk with that doctor now. You rest. I'll send in Laurence. He's recently become butler since old Brannon's retirement, but he was my valet for four years, so he can be yours tonight should you require it. And, I'm told you left your home with naught but the clothes on your back. My son was close to your size, as is Paul. I'll have my man collect a wardrobe to get you through until we can see to your needs with new items. If Kepelheim shows up, he's the fastest needle in London, so we will make a Scotsman of you before you can sing Annie Laurie. And you'll need a kilt! My bootmaker can be here tomorrow if you've a need. I see yours have seen some wear."

St. Clair gazed down at his boots and saw they were stained with crimson and grey stone dust. He let his head drop against the chair's high back as he pictured that horrible scene. "Your Grace, these hellish stains are but a glimpse into the chilling altar of death Elizabeth showed me beneath that abbey. It is where she watched her mother strangled and far worse. That ground is painted red with human blood. God help me, I shall tear Trent's eyes from his head when next we meet!"

"I've no doubt you will, son," the duke said proudly. "I've not one doubt that you will."

Charles took the duke at his word and retired into the makeshift sleeping chamber across from Elizabeth and Paul. His room was part of a small suite of parlours, and when he entered, a young foot-man named Carlton had delivered hot water, towels, soap, a razor, and small mirror. He also left a nightshirt, linen, and all the clothing the detective would require to maintain his appearance for the next week. He found that Connor Stuart's clothing was slightly large for him in the waist but that Paul's coats and overcoat fit him almost as if he'd been measured for them. The shirts fit as well, though half an inch short in the arms—but overall the earl's borrowed clothing would do nicely.

Though he'd been exhausted earlier, St. Clair found his curios-ity regarding the mysterious leather box more than he could over-come, so after turning up the gas lamps near the fireplace, he settled into a soft chair and began to read Kepelheim's letter.

6, October, 1888

My Dear Friend Duke,

This will be relatively short (well, short for me at least!), for I must post it before leaving for Victoria Sta-tion, but these are the basic facts as I have uncovered them regarding our wonderful friend and knight errant, Mr. St. Clair. I have confirmed your suspicion that 'St. Clair' is indeed NOT his true name, but how he came by it is most interesting, as you will see. The official tale is this: his aunt and uncle, a very nice couple who met and married in Liverpool, were Edna and Elijah Burke. They took the seven-year-old St. Clair into their home after learning his poor parents had been killed in a train accident in that same town. Charles attended Harrow and later Cambridge, and when finished, he joined the police force. There are no family photographs of our detective's dead parents, nor of him prior to 1862. It is as if Charles Arthur St. Clair emerges fully formed out of the aether at age seven. Again, this is the official biography, and I obtained this scant information from your friend at the Yard, so using this as a starting point, I traveled to follow the trail.

You know how I love an adventure, so I took my threads and needles and rode the train north to that great maritime city, Liverpool. Once there, I went to the railway station master and asked where I might learn about a train accident there sometime around or before '62. The kind gentleman with the whistle and ledger told me to go to the *Liverpool Sun* newspaper office, and I hired a cab and found a man named Whitaker. He was a typical newsman, all questions, few answers. I told him I was researching genealogy for a legal case, and he happily sent me to their archives, where I met another fine fellow named Pratt. Simon Pratt. He thumbed through many archived papers, back to the dates I sought, and found nothing. Nothing. Nothing. I tell you nothing. Did I say nothing? The only railway accident that led to death anytime within that period was in 1859, and it was a cow they found dead. Not people. No people. Not even one.

So, I asked about the Burke family, the aunt and uncle, who once ran a green grocery in Liverpool before moving to Lambeth. I was sent again, this time to a registry office, where I learnt that in 1862, a boy child of seven years with no memory of his past was left at their doorstep. The boy was taken shortly afterward by the Burkes, but more on this in a moment. This boy had a note pinned to him that named him as Charles Arthur St. Clair and that his mother had died at a mental asylum. Do not be anxious, friend Duke. I know you, but be patient. There is much more to tell. And if you have not already surmised where this leads, you will soon understand fully by my proofs, because after all, legal proofs are what we require, are they not?

So, where did I go next? Yes. I went to this asylum. After hitting many a bureaucratic stone wall, I found an agreeable nurse named Betty Quincy, who had worked there in '62, and she remembered this female patient. The woman was supposedly rescued from a ship that ran aground near Liverpool in July of 1860—yes, I have the date correct. Mrs. Quincy told me that the dying woman gave another nurse a box filled with letters, legal papers, and photographs, and that this nurse has now retired, but this Betty Quincy she remembered her name. It is Ida Payne.

So to Ida Payne I go, and it was a challenge finding her. She now lives under a false name in a fishing village north of Liverpool. It took me three days of twice daily visits to convince her to speak with me, and it was only when I mentioned the name Angela Sinclair that she finally opened the door to me. She told me a new and very interesting tale. Now, this curious and convoluted story was told to me over the course of several visits, so I shall write a short summary now and tell you all when next we meet. Mrs. Payne is a careful woman, but she slowly began to trust me, and she revealed to me that the woman who died was her friend, and that this friend did indeed leave a box with her. I asked about the shipwreck, but this Ida Payne, she denied any wreck. She said it was lies—all lies. She told me that she first met her friend when she arrived in Liverpool on a boat with a Scottish name, and this woman was very sick when they docked, feverish and mad with worry. Ida was there to see off her brother, but noting that the sick woman had no one to help her, Payne took her to see the doctors at the asylum where she worked at the time. The doctors determined that the woman required admission and observation, but days turned to weeks, and weeks into months, and Payne watched her new friend deteriorate into despair and madness.

This beautiful but sad woman was named Angela, and she begged Ida Payne for assistance in finding her son. He should have been with her when she disembarked the ship, but he had disappeared. This son was very ill—he had lost his memory, and he was in grave danger, she told Mrs. Payne. I asked if the boy had amnesia. Yes. That is what she was told, said Payne. The sick woman showed her a photograph of the child (which is inside the box—more on this in a moment, so be patient!). Angela described the boy, asking Ida Payne's help in finding him. The boy, he was kind and tall, and blue-eyed with thick dark hair that curled. He spoke with a Scottish accent. His full name was Charles Robert Arthur Sinclair III. Not St. Clair. I asked about the boy. Was he ever found? Yes, she told me. Two years later, one week after the mother had died inside the sanitarium.

Ida Payne told me that the mother had been deemed insane because the police thought she'd made up the boy—she was diagnosed with advanced syphilis and left to linger alone. Ida Payne did not believe this diagnosis, but she remained there as a nurse to tend and aid Angela. Payne alone hunted for the boy to help her friend. Later, she learnt from a cousin that a boy just like the one Angela had described was left at the registry office. (I confirmed this with the local police, who had a record of it.)

No one knew precisely when the boy arrived, but a man took him there. A tall man with a foreign accent and a fur hat, she said. The tall man claimed that he had found the boy at the shipyard, and that he had no memory, so the man looked after him for two years. He only then remembered his name, but nothing else. There was a note pinned to the boy with a copy of a birth certificate—a false birth certificate—listing his name as Charles Arthur St. Clair. This mystery man said he would send a nice couple to the registry office to claim the boy as their nephew. They would raise him. Then, he paid the registry office five hundred pounds (an enormous sum!) and asked that they enter the false birth certificate to show that the boy was born in Liverpool in 1855, and that his parents died in a rail accident in 1862. This false record showed his name as St. Clair and his mother as Angelina McKay with no father listed.

I asked Ida Payne if she knew anything more about this strange man with so much money and influence that he could buy his way into the registry office, but she had little to offer, save this: She thought she had seen him once, and if this man was the same, then she told me he was evil, for he had vanished before her very eyes, like smoke on a mirror. She said she would likely die soon (she did cough a lot), so she was unafraid, but this man's identity was a mystery to her.

I asked if she still had the box the woman gave her. She did, but Angela told her never to give it to anyone without the sign. What sign, I asked? The secret sign, she said. I asked her if that sign looked like this—and I made a P crossed by an S enclosed within a circle. She was amazed! She could not believe I knew the sign. She thanked me, gave me a piece of cherry pie and offered me the box. I ate the pie and took the box, but I warned the woman to change her name again and move, because others who did not know the sign might find her. She laughed, and told me that they had already tried. Three times, men came, and each time she asked for the sign. One made a funny bird picture, she told me. I laughed, took the box, and I gave her the three hundred pound reward you offered for information regarding your missing nephew. She was shocked but took the reward. I thanked her, told her the pie was good, and I left.

So. Now you know. I've traced the mother's point of departure to Crovie, a sea town near the castle. When I arrive there next week, I shall make inquiries to assure that no Angelina MacKay actually lived there, but my friend duke, it is clear to me that your thoughts have been right all along. We have found our Charles at long last. – K.

Charles finished the extraordinary letter and then read it through again. His uncle and aunt had both died within the last five years, so he had no way to verify any of this information with them. Angela Sinclair? Was this woman his real mother? And what of his father?

Kepelheim makes no mention of him, and yet he traces Angela's journey back to a small village not far from this very castle.

Wishing he'd allowed the duke to share more with him earlier, Charles began to pace. How was he to reconcile this news with all he'd been told growing up? Why fabricate an accident, unless it was to throw him off track entirely? And who was this mysterious, wealthy man?

In truth, he had no recollection of a life before the Burkes, but he did remember being told to speak with an English accent as a school boy. His uncle had even hired a tutor to help him learn to speak in a polished manner, and his teachers in school had helped him to excel. Though the Burkes had little money, they had somehow managed to send him to Harrow and then to Cambridge, where he'd tied for first in the Mathematics Tripos, but a chance meeting with a police detective revealed a keen aptitude for criminal investigation, prompting Charles to apply to the Metropolitan Police rather than pursue a higher degree.

He shuffled through the papers and photographs inside the box, finding a faded Daguerreotype inside a Union Case of a handsome, dark-haired man with a small boy on his lap. The child looked to be four or five years old, and he seemed eerily familiar to Charles, though the detective could not reason why. The man's features resembled his own, particularly the shape of the eyes, nose, and forehead. The letters appeared to be correspondence from Angela Marie Sinclair to her husband, Robert Sinclair, written on stationery bearing a beautiful crest and engraved with the words 'Marchioness Haimsbury, Rose House' at the top.

What could this box mean? Was his entire life a lie? Had someone miscopied his name as St. Clair rather than Sinclair, or had it been an intentional 'error' meant to throw off investigation as Kepelheim's detective work seemed to indicate? And who was this mysterious man of wealth and influence who left him at the registry office? As he paced, Charles began to awaken, and though the hour of midnight drew near, he wondered if a stroll around the castle grounds might not refresh him more than sleep.

Dressed in Paul's borrowed clothing and hunting coat to keep warm, Charles left the room and wandered through the halls, eventually reaching the grand foyer at the front of the house. Despite the hour, the detective noticed that four men kept watch outside the main doors, rifles on their backs. The Irish Wolfhounds and a pair of terriers ran amongst the men's legs, chasing down unlucky rodents. Waving to the men as he exited the castle, Charles set out on the worn, brick walkway that led around to the steep cliff that overlooked Loch Linnhe. Carlton had mentioned that the 5th duke had built a knot garden for his bride on this side of the castle, and that it rivaled anything found in French or English gardens. Castle Drummond had replaced an ancient motte and bailey keep in the 16th century with a classic take on a French chateau, and since then, Carlton had explained, each duke or duchess had added a wing, a tower, or a garden to commemorate his or her reign. In Scotland, it seemed primogeniture was not a given, as with most titles in England (the Branham ducal title being a rare exception), but that daughters may inherit and even share inheritance.

Am I from Scotland? he mused as he wandered along the cobbled sidewalk toward the southwestern entrance they had earlier used to bring in the earl and Elizabeth. To his surprise, Charles found a small curricle and pair, parked near the door, and no sooner had he rounded within eyesight, but the carriage's driver snapped the whip, and it raced away down a side road toward the southeast. A deep, worrying alarm bell sounded in his brain, and Charles ran back through this same side door, toward Elizabeth's room. Not bothering to knock, he burst into the room.

Empty! No one! Running next to the earl's room, he snatched open the door and found Paul sleeping soundly, the room dark, and the windows shut.

He next ran into the hallways and began to shout, not caring if he woke the dead. "Carlton! Laurence! Your Grace!" he shouted, dashing from room to room like a madman. In moments, lamps and candles blazed to life, and two dozen men and women emerged from all doors to meet his calls. Amongst these was the duke himself, dressed only in a nightshirt and robe, a white cap upon his head.

"What is it?" he called, running down the main staircase, two steps at a time, and rushing up to St. Clair.

"She's gone, sir! Someone's taken her!"

"Who? Elizabeth, you mean? Why, she's just sleeping."

Charles led the duke into her sitting room, and Drummond gaped in despair at the empty couch. "Can she have gotten up? Beth! Beth!"

Shouts of Elizabeth and Beth and my lady rang through every hallway now, and soon Paul Stuart, pale, dazed but resolute, appeared at his doorway, eyes bleary, his face set.

"She is gone?" he asked, his voice but a whisper as pain shot through his arm and shoulder.

"She is. A man in a black carriage drawn by a matched pair of paints took her. Not fifteen minutes past. He headed southeast, toward the main road," Charles explained.

"I'm going after them," Paul declared, reaching for his boots, but falling instead into St. Clair's arms. "Please, Charles, you must save her! Please! I beg you!"

The duke called for a horse, one named Clever Girl, and he walked Charles to the southwest door, where five minutes later a groom rode up on a silver mare with a black mane and tail.

"Charles, take her. She is my fastest horse, and she can maintain speed for an hour without tiring. If you go now, you can still catch them, but if you are unsure of their path, take the drive out to the main road, then head south toward the north part of Glasgow. Five miles or so before you reach the city, you'll turn eastward at a white stone church with a great steeple; follow that road. It'll curve 'round a lot, but it will lead you to the house, all right. Look for a thatched roof, stone cottage with a white fence and a large red door, sitting atop a small hill. It is thirty miles or more, but you can get there if you hurry. That rig belongs to our turncoat doctor, and he's drugged her and taken her for money, I know it. No time to think, son. Just ride! And bring our girl back to us!"

Again the stranger's prophetic warning rang inside the detective's brain: *"Ride. Ride swiftly, or she will die. When you see the horse, ride!"*

Charles mounted the horse and thanked the angels who had put the thought into his mind to walk just then as he spurred Clever Girl toward the road, the full moon high overhead to light the way.

CHAPTER SIXTEEN

The horse Clever Girl was indeed quick on her feet, and Charles soon found himself within sight of the carriage. Though traveling at great speed, the driver must have noticed St. Clair in pursuit, because he cracked his whip, and the paints raced faster still. Ahead, the road—not much more than a gravel lane—turned sharply to the left, and the coach would need to slow to take it safely. Having ridden horses since age nine, the detective gripped his long legs more tightly 'round the horse, and she spurred into a mighty burst of speed, her hooves taking the road in leaps that seemed to Charles impossible.

The carriage came to the bend, but the driver did not slow, and one of the two wheels left the road briefly as the vehicle leaned precariously to the right.

Good Lord! Charles thought. *He'll turn over if he keeps this up!*

Charles rode for nearly an hour, but the horse did not slow, and once again he had nearly caught up to the carriage as a two-storey thatched roof house with a red door appeared on the hill ahead. Charles slowed Clever Girl's pace and followed the carriage as it stopped in front of the house. Without waiting for the mare to completely halt, he jumped down from the saddle and ran to the carriage, finding himself face to face with the strange-haired doctor, who now held a serious and deadly looking shotgun.

"Don't make me shoot you," the man said, but Charles did not even pause his steps. Instead, he wrenched the weapon from the thin man's hands and turned it back on the kidnapper.

"Why?" he demanded. "Why have you taken her? I swear, if you have harmed her, you will die here, where you stand."

"She is only sleeping!" the doctor assured him, his entire frame shaking. "I had no choice! They knew about my past. They knew about the charges in London. They found them, even after I had paid to hush it up! I couldn't say no. They told me only to take her and leave her here for the night. That they would contact me. That they would protect me."

"Who?" Charles asked, pointing the shotgun at the doctor's forehead. "WHO?"

"Redwing. I know, I know! They are the enemy, but they promised they would not harm her. They gave their word!"

"They lie," he replied through clenched teeth.

From the carriage, he heard Elizabeth moan, so he took the gun and turned to see that she was unharmed. "Beth?" he called softly. "Beth, darling, can you hear me?"

She moved slightly, apparently unaware of his presence, her eyes closed in dreams.

He turned the gun back onto the terrified physician. "Tell me his name," Charles demanded.

"I do not know names. They only sent a letter and documents of—of the women I had sterilized."

"Sterilized? You mean, you made them incapable of bearing children?"

"It was all for research! I swear to you! But it is illegal, so when the police in London discovered my activities, I had to flee and change my name. I was only a medical student then. I've reformed!"

"You call this reform?" he asked, pointing to the woman he loved. "Did she give permission for her abduction?"

His face fell, and he shook his head. "I am but a man. You cannot know. You do not know what they are—what they can do!"

"What drug did you give her? Tell me now!"

"It will not harm her," he claimed. "Just a mild soporific."

"Tell me the name. Now!" the detective demanded.

The doctor opened his mouth to answer, but a shot rang out from somewhere above them, a sniper on the hills. Lemuel's checkerboard hair turned to crimson, and blood dripped down his face onto the garish waistcoat. He dropped dead at St. Clair's feet.

A second bullet sang past the detective's ear, so rather than take on an unseen foe, he quickly placed the gun into the floor of the carriage, climbed onto the seat, and then turned the curricle back toward the castle as he cracked the whip. He called to Clever Girl, who seemed to understand, for she ran ahead and crossed over the lush green hills, disappearing as she headed toward home.

The round moon had disappeared behind a thick bank of clouds, and Charles prayed as the carriage lurched ahead at full speed. But to where? He'd lost track of the long road's many turnings, and now that he no longer chased behind he found himself hoping to catch sight of the castle or its towers over the next rise. The sniper might also be anywhere, perhaps following them, he realised, so seeing a small farm, he made a decision he would soon come to regret. He turned the carriage toward the farmhouse to ask directions.

Elizabeth lay inside the dark interior, and the exhausted horses panted for water, their breath clouding the crisp autumn air as Charles knocked on the farmhouse door. Though it was long past one in the morning, a muscular older man opened the door, wearing an undershirt and woolen trousers held up by braces, hastily donned from all appearances. The man spoke in a thick Scottish brogue.

"Awa' w' ye! Unless ye ha' goot razin' fer callin' nigh on to two o' the mornin'!"

Charles caught just enough to determine that the man had stated a perfectly rational fact. "Forgive me for waking you, sir. We are guests of the duke, and we've become lost on the road. I'm from London, as you can tell, I'm sure, so I've no way of knowing which way to turn."

The man's face lit up. "The duke's hoose! An' yer lost? Oh, aye. I' happens all the time," he replied, his accent thinning to a more decipherable level. "You an' yer missus are an hour away from the duke, an' no one'll be aweek nigh. Wai' 'til sunrise, an' I'll show ye the way mysel'."

A woman's voice called out from a room near the back of the house, and soon a flaxen-haired woman of similar age to the man joined him in the doorway.

"Lost," he told her. "Guests of the duke's, an' los' their wee."

She laughed and nodded. "Lost your way? Oh, aye, come in," she said, her mild accent far less strenuous on the ear, and Charles fetched Elizabeth from the carriage seat. The man left to water the horses and bed them down in his barn for the night. Charles carried Beth into the small house, gently setting her down into one of a pair of well-used wooden rocking chairs.

"My name's Maggie," the woman said cheerfully. "I'll put a kettle on to boil. I hope ye like yer tea strong. Tha's how Hamish prefers it."

"That would be wonderful," he said, checking Elizabeth's face and hands to make sure the doctor had not harmed her. Paul's ring glittered on her left hand, a stark reminder of reality. She still wore the trousers and shirt from the day before, knees stained with blood, having collapsed into sleep after arriving at the castle. *No doubt, Lemuel drugged her almost immediately, the fiend!*

"Your missus, she's powerful tired. And, merciful heavens, no shoes!"

Charles wasn't certain the couple were to be trusted. He had begun to suspect all around him, and this moment helped him to understand in small part just how heavy a burden the Stuart family had carried. "She turned her poor foot whilst we were walking... fell down a hill and scraped her knees," he lied. "And we'd already strayed far from the castle it seems. We were on one of the duke's horses," he explained, "but she bolted whilst we were walking. A horsefly bit her, I think. We had foolishly thought a midnight ride would be pleasant. I'm no country gentleman, more accustomed to London life. I fear that my darling fell down, but we discovered we were close by to Dr. Lemuel's house. He gave her medicine for the pain, and I think it's made her drowsy, poor thing. Her boots are in the carriage."

"Ach, that explains it then," the wife replied, striking a match to a large candle on the mantel. "I reckon the doctor lent ya his carriage to take the lady home. Lemuel's a quiet man, and his hair's strange for sure. Some 'round here think he was frightened by the de'il hisself. My Hamish thinks it's all tosh, bu' there's many 'round here tha' believes it."

Beth stirred slightly, and the woman noticed the large blue ring. "Lord, but you are surely kin to the duke! A pretty present from a loving husband, to be sure. How long ha' ye been wed?"

St. Clair thought for a second. Was this a test? Should he confess the entire truth or concoct yet another story to keep Beth's true identity secret? Reaching out in her sleep, her fingertips brushed his hand, and his mind was decided. She now relied upon him for protection, and he in turn could trust no one, save the inner circle.

"Two weeks," he lied again. "We're on our honeymoon."

The woman's face beamed, and she kissed Charles on the cheek and clapped her hands in delight. "Newlyweds! Ach, this is a real blessing! You'll be wanting privacy, I know. I'll have Hamish make a fire in the cottage next door. We built it for our son and his bride four years past, an' they have two children now, bless the Lord! Our Ian's moved his family to the city to find his fortune. He's studyin' you know. He's a way wi' books—oh tha' lad loves to read. So you've the place all to yerselves. You can bed down there for a few hours, and then when it's light, Hamish'll draw you a map to find yer way back to the castle. It's not a bad ride if you can cross the hills, but it's nearly an hour's drive by the road, bu' once you've the sun to guide ye, ye'll have no trouble."

Surely, he was taking a chance with all their lives by accepting the offer, but without a clear path back to Drummond, he could think of no other option. If only he'd paid more attention to the roads!

"You are very kind," he said just as the husband returned.

"Your horses were worn ou', lad. Dr. Lemuel's team, I think."

Maggie brought tea and poured two cups, handing one to Charles. "Will she be able to drink, sir?"

"Beth," he called, kissing her cheek. "Darling?"

She opened her eyes briefly, looking up at the woman. "Are we there yet, Charles?"

He kissed her again. Her skin felt cool to the touch. "Not yet, darling. Are you cold?"

She nodded, sleepily, but opened her eyes long enough to accept some of the hot tea, draining the cup in a few sips. "Where are we?"

"A farmer's cottage. You turned your foot, remember? Our horses have gone as far as they can. Hamish and Maggie have offered us a cottage for the night."

She touched his face. "My darling Captain. You are so brave. Maggie?"

The woman nodded and poured a second cup of tea, handing it to Beth. "Tha's me, Missus. Your Captain is a handsome one. An' it's clear he's over the moon about you. Drink a bit more, if you can. There now. Oh, sir, she is worn out."

Beth had managed another small sip, but her eyes refused to remain open, so Charles took the cup and handed it back to the woman. "Thank you, Maggie."

The woman set down the kettle and walked through a narrow doorway to the back of the three-room cottage. During her absence the farmer lit a pipe and began to smoke, the hazy exhales spiraling above his head. "It's a lucky thing finding Lemuel. He tended the lady's foot, I imagine. It's swollen. I can see tha' right off. Ach, tha' Lemuel's a queer bird, no doubt o' it. Some say he wears the crown o' the de'il."

"The devil?" Charles clarified, slowly making sense of the man's brogue. "Do such things happen in this day and age?"

"Aye. Tha's so, they do. The de'il nary sleeps," Hamish replied. "Leastways, no' 'round here."

St. Clair mused upon this simple statement. Despite having been a Christian since turning ten, Charles had always found the notion of a real Devil, of demons, somewhat archaic, but his own experiences the past few days began to make the detective wonder just how true the old Bible tales might be. Belief in a Saviour implied a belief in a realm beyond natural sight—in heaven and angelic messengers. In sin. So, if angels who are loyal to God exist, then how could he not believe in those who rebelled? Might they not also have 'messengers', minions who carry out their fallen master's demonic orders?

Maggie returned with a thick pile of quilts, placing one around Elizabeth's shoulders. "Now, you leave them be, Hamish Campbell. These young folks are on their honeymoon, stayin' as guests o' the duke, so we've no cause to be bringin' up such talk."

The farmer puffed, his black eyebrows moving up and down as his pipe swiped from side to side. The smoke curled in silver swirls, in and out of his white hair, but he seemed kind enough. Charles wished the sides in this battle wore badges marking their loyalties. It would make the task easier for him and safer for her.

"Is tha' so?" the old man asked, winking at his wife. "Weel, I'll lay a fire in the hearth o' our Ian's cottage. Ye can sleep 'til dawn. Bu' if you're a guest o' the duke, he'll ha' his men out lookin' fer ye a' first light. If you canno' follow the map I make, stay still, an' wait fer him. His men know every crag n' cranny o' these hills."

"Thank you," Charles said, shaking the man's calloused hand.

The farmer laughed. "Aye. Wi' soft hands like yours, it's clear you're a city man! Well, Maggie, I'm off to make Ian's cottage warm. Put a ho' water bottle in wi' them quilts. Your lady, son, looks to ha' a chill," he added, leaving and shutting the door.

Maggie took a large willow basket and set the quilts inside. "I'd already thought o' tha', but bein' on yer honeymoon, a hot water bottle might no' be so needed as wi' me an' my old man. Oh, life is all ahead o' ye, sir."

"Thanks so much," he said, meaning it. "I'm Charles, by the way.' He thought for a few seconds, and then suddenly added, "Charles Sinclair."

"A Sinclair? Well, that makes sense then. The Sinclairs are close kin to the Stuarts, or I'm not a Campbell! My old man an' me are cousins, ya see. I grew up north o' here. Up by Briarcliff. Tha's the seat for the other Stuarts. The Earls of Aubrey. I wager you're kin to them as well."

Names and places were beginning to click for Charles. Was he actually a Sinclair? Could Paul be his true cousin? Then, if that were so, would that imply that Elizabeth also might be a cousin, somewhere along that branching tree? "Yes, we're all related. I'm not much good at keeping track of family lines, though. My cousin Paul is much better than I."

"Paul? Oh, now, tha' would be the new earl, am I right? A lovely man. His elder brother died when he was but twenty, you know. A duel."

This was new! "I've not heard that family story. My branch left for London some time back."

"Such a sorry tale. Hamish doesn't care much for stories o' dukes and earls and all tha'. He's a man o' the land, an' he just wants a day's bread and a pipe to smoke. An' I love 'im for it, bu', my mother was in service to the earl's family when I was a lass. She told me many tales aboot tha' wonderful family, an' some would be though' a lie, if my mother, may she rest in peace, had no' seen 'em wi' her own two eyes! An' I saw things, too, tha' would no' be believed."

"Such as?" he asked, growing ever more curious about the family which may be his own.

"Weel, there's the *taibhse*, the ghost ya know, for starters."

His eyes grew round. "Ghost?"

"Oh, aye. The ghost appears on moonless nights up on the cliff. The castle is a great old house, an' it was built to stand agin' any army. You've seen it, I imagine."

Charles shook his head. "No, but we'd planned to go up there next with my cousin as guide. Paul said he'd show me all the family properties."

"Then you've a grand tour comin'! Briarcliff Castle o'erlooks Loch Leven, not far from Glencoe. Tha' bein' the blood site o' the massacre, ye know. *Mort Ghlinne Comhann*, we call it in Gaelic. The Murder of Glencoe. A traitorous deed foisted upon the Mac-Donald clan, and I'm ashamed ta say tha' it was a pair of Campbell cousins who stood behind it all. Nigh on ta forty honest men were slain in their beds. Men who opened their homes to soldiers, and woke to naught but blood and fire. And another forty or more women and children escaped the burnin' o' their homes, but wi' nowhere to go, they perished in the snows that February." She paused to wipe her eyes. "Your cousin's family, the Aubrey Stuarts, they tried to help, though some were in Paris at the time, appealing to their cousin, King James for guidance. It was a troublesome time, ta be sure. Those angry spirits roam aboot even today, some up by the castle on the cliff, for it's said they blame the Stuart line for not doin' enough. My ma, she used to say prayers while scrubbin' floors, washin' linen, an' all the way to do private business afore the modern niceties was put in. Oh, the castle's all modern now, bu' still full o' the *taibhsean*—ghosts. My ma saw young master Ian's spirit tha' very night. The night he died, ya know."

"Ian was the earl's firstborn son?"

"Aye. It were tha' other fella'—what were his name? Oh, it's on the tip o' me tongue—a foreign name, I think."

A foreign name? Not William Trent then. "Did your mother ever see this man?"

"No, but I did."

His dark brows shot up. "You did? Do you recall his appearance? Surely, not another ghost."

She shook her head, taking a seat on a stool near the fire. "I were ten years old. I'd been workin' to the house for a year as a cook's helper. Always could boil an' bake an' mash e'en as a wee thing, bu' Mrs. MacTavish taught me to make fancy things, she did. A lovely woman. She still serves there, I think, an' she saw 'im, too!"

"Go on."

"It must've been half eight. We'd just laid out the meals for the laird's supper, an' I was tol' to bring in more water from the well room. Bein' a fortified castle, the water was once guarded in a big stone room nex' to the kitchens. I took a bucket and went to fetch the water, but I could hear two men shoutin' words such as only my Uncle John used to use. I stepped up onto the stone seat o'er by the window—not more'n a slit, meant for shootin' arrows or muskets back in the day, ya know. I could see the young master, a sword in his hand, standin' agin' the cliff, an' another man, taller e'en than the young laird, an' him laughin'! Can you imagine it?"

"This other man with the foreign name. He was very tall then. Did you see his hair, his face?"

"You do like a good ghost story, sir. Well, so do I. And aye, I did see him, full in the face, an' forgive me for sayin' it, but he looked like old Nick hisself!"

"You mean Satan?" Charles asked.

"Aye. His eyes was red aflame, an' his long black hair caught the settin' sun like a great fiery halo 'round his head! He wore a black moustache an' beard, and his clothes looked queer strange. He could no' have been Satan, o' course, but he seemed so to me. The young master fought bravely, but this man—the devil man—he cheated, did'n' he? He said somethin' akin to this, 'I will have her, though she's not yet born! And there is naught ye kin do to stop me!' His accent were pure strange, an' I know it don' make sense, bu' tha's wha' he said. Then he thrust in his sword—an' I swear on me mother's grave it's true, it were made of *fire*—and then he pushed the young master off the cliff!"

Charles could scarcely believe his ears, yet the woman appeared sane. Why would this farmer's wife make up such a tale? How could she know that demonic men like William Trent—and perhaps a second man, a foreigner in old fashioned clothing—even now haunted the Stuart family, if not his own? Could this tall man be the same one Elizabeth had seen as a girl? The one who spoke with the strange accent? Might he even be the tall man in the fur hat who had left him at the registry office in Liverpool?

"Did you tell anyone what you saw?" he asked.

"Aye, I did. I ran an' told the earl. He rushed out to the garden, bu' the young laird lay at the bottom o' the cliff, stone dead. The strange man was nowhere to be seen, bu' the earl said he believed me. He talked wi' me for more'n an hour, an' it was while I was talkin' to the earl tha' my ma saw the young laird's ghost, walkin' out in front o' the castle. The earl's new wife, she saw it, too, an' she fainted dead away! She went into labour that very night."

Charles could picture it in his mind, and he nodded. "Really? The earl believed you, you say?"

"He did. A lovely man he were, too. Five years later, he nearly died, you know. Someone tried to murder him. Sliced him twice, right under his chin."

Sinclair recalled the linear scars beneath Robert Stuart's jawline. "It seems as if trouble has visited my cousin's family all too often. Thank you for telling me, Maggie."

The door opened, and Hamish returned, brushing his hands on his trousers and relighting his pipe. "You've a warm bed to go to now, lad. The house is down the lane to the right. Can ye carry yer missus all right?"

"Yes, thank you. You've both been very kind, and we've only been a nuisance. I should like to repay you, if you will allow it."

Hamish shook his head. "No, lad. The duke's friends are ours. Sleep well now. I'll knock a' dawn. That'd be in four hours or so."

Charles picked Elizabeth up once more, her head falling against his shoulder, and he carried her to their 'honeymoon' cottage. How he hated the lie, but keeping her safe from harm was his job now—and, perhaps, had been all along.

The duke's household was in an uproar. After Charles's hasty departure on Clever Girl, Paul had nearly collapsed. Mrs. MacAnder, the housekeeper, had used Dr. Price's medical kit to clean and bathe the wound once more and redress it. She'd insisted Aubrey take the morphine Price had provided, but he'd refused. And now, three hours later, nearly four in the morning, the earl wanted to scream.

"Where are they?" he shouted as the clock struck the hour. "Lemuel will pay for this. I shall see that traitorous man hang!"

The duke gave his nephew a glass of whisky. "Drink this. If you'll not take the morphine, then use this to stiffen your resolve. Sinclair knows what he's about. I trust him with her life."

Paul drank the liquid fire, wiping his mouth with his good hand. "And if Redwing's operatives met them on the road? He should never have gone alone."

James gulped down his own glass of scotch. "Perhaps. We can trust his nerve and his strength of will. He loves her as much as we do."

Paul's hand closed into a fist, shattering the drinking glass. "I *know that*, do I not?!"

Mrs. MacAnder jumped to the earl's side, wiping at the blood that ran from his palm.

"You'll not do yourself or Beth any good, by making both hands useless," the duke told him calmly.

Paul's head fell back against his chair. "Useless. That is all I am to her now."

James glanced up at the housekeeper, and instantly she knew his orders. Quietly, she gathered up the broken glass and left them alone, shutting the doors behind.

"Paul, you seldom lose your head, and I know it's been a struggle these past few days, but…"

"But she's in love with him, James," he said in so mournful a tone it bit into his uncle's soul.

"I know that, son," he said gently. "Have known it for a very long time. And he loves her, too. That is plain as day, but we've a vow to keep, that goes beyond our earthly pleasures. You took that vow, and when he's returned with our Beth, Charles will take it, too."

"James, I loathe myself for feeling this way about him, but I cannot help it. In truth, I also love Charles and respect him as a friend—and from what you've been telling me, as a true cousin. We'd joked that our resemblance to each other must mean we were related, but if all that Kepelheim's efforts have uncovered is true, then he is indeed a Sinclair and nephew to my mother, but he is also nephew to you—and my cousin by blood. It is always the blood, is it not?"

"Always," James echoed, gazing into the fire. "The blood. It's what Redwing has always been after. Blood to rule the world. And if they can use Elizabeth or her child to do it, they will."

"Her child? Didn't they murder Patricia to get to Beth? I had thought it was she they hoped to crown."

"They have always wanted a male, laddie. A king to rule through, a king to make the world worship the beast to come."

Paul tried to reason through this revelation. "What if she chooses Charles? How then do the lines meet?"

"I've not yet worked out all," the duke admitted. "It's my hope that Kepelheim makes it here. He's the keeper of the lines. He'll know how this would change our course."

"She wears my ring," Paul whispered. "She would not, could not say yes to my proposal of marriage, but she told me she would accept at Christmas. I wonder now if we shall ever see Christmas."

"Keep your heart fixed on our Saviour's promises, son. Christmas is always a ray of hope, for it reminds us why we fight—and whom we fight. Or perhaps, it is better said *what* we fight."

The doors opened suddenly, and Laurence came in and whispered to the duke. James shot up from his chair and called for the men to rally again in the yard in front of the house. "Saddle up the horses—now!"

Paul sat up, trying to stand. "What has happened?" he asked, fearing the reply.

"It's Clever Girl. She's returned to the stable, and there's no one on her back."

CHAPTER SEVENTEEN

Martin Kepelheim had spent the last day recuperating. Mrs. Alcorn's ministrations and medicines, alongside those of Dr. Price had been much in demand during the past twenty-four hours. After the Queen of the Meadow's dramatic ascent, the tailor had stood shoulder to shoulder and sometimes back to back with Baxter and his men against two parties of well-armed scoundrels, twenty to each party. Now, a day later, forty-three men lay dead, three from Branham and the rest from their enemy's ranks. Those bodies had been searched for letters or other information that might aid the inner circle members regarding Redwing's plans. Only one, a thick-set villain with oddly shaped ears that grew to a point, bore anything useful, but that was a prize indeed!

"Mr. Baxter, we shall need to send a telegram to the duke and to Galton at once, but we must not include our news. Have Mr. Powers's men finished restringing the telegraph wires?"

Cornelius Baxter, his right arm dressed and in a sling, nodded from a chair near the fire. Generally, he would consider such behaviour presumptuous, but today, he knew his lady would insist upon this small pleasure. "They have indeed, Mr. Kepelheim," he replied. "Those monstrous invaders cut through the entire cable, I'm told, but Powers brought in a friend who works in London as an electrician, and together they've repaired the broken line. I'm sure the duke is most anxious about our silence."

"Yes, but he is not one to panic, is he, my friend? I shall compose our communiqué right away. All messages sent must be in code, of course, but even a cipher can be broken, and we must not lose this advantage," Kepelheim told him. "How many injured all told?"

"Including the two of us, seventeen. Davis is the worst. He's the lad who rode in at the eleventh hour, guns blazing. It was rather like those western battles we saw last May during the fete, was it not, Mrs. Alcorn?"

The housekeeper was limping, but she continued with her tasks. "Those Americans," she said, rolling up a bandage. "I remember thinking how thrilling it all seemed. That is, until I saw it for real last night. I hope never to see such again!"

"You did us proud, Mrs. Alcorn," the butler said, his old eyes gleaming with delight. "Who would have pictured a refined woman such as yourself swinging into action with a fireplace poker and a pair of kitchen shears? I shall treasure that memory until my final days."

The tailor took the lady's hand and kissed her fingertips. "And so shall I, dear lady," he said with a wink. "I would not be here to tell it, were it not for your courage and quick thinking. That said, my friend Mr. Baxter, tell me how the search goes. Have your valiant men completely combed the estate and those infernal tunnels that connect to hell?"

"So I'm told, sir. Powers and his men have searched it for signs of more invaders. They worked the passages all the way to a strange cove near the coast," the butler replied. "I'm told no other intruders were found, but there is evidence that the group had camped near there for some time. It's God's mercies that our lady and Mr. St. Clair were not molested whilst below ground. Pardon me, Mr. Kepelheim, as you've informed us, it is Sinclair, of course. Or more properly, Lord Haimsbury. I'd thought he looked somewhat familiar."

Kepelheim laughed. "Yes, our Charles Sinclair wears the same handsome features as that of the child who visited here many years ago, does he not?"

"He looks rather like his father," the butler remarked, sipping a glass of sherry.

"So he does," the tailor said. "I wonder how the detective has reacted to learning he's a high-ranking peer of the realm. Of course, had Inspector Reid not brought that magnificent balloon, none of us would be here to speak of it. Which reminds me, Mrs. Alcorn. Has our courageous Chief Groom yet awakened?"

"Dr. Price tells me he still lies in a coma," the housekeeper replied. "Dear Mr. Clark is to be honoured above all. He alone brought down a dozen or more, and all whilst in flight upon a horse! It truly was like one of those western shows, wasn't it? The Indians turning to shoot at the cowboys behind them. Did I say that right, Mr. Baxter? Cowboys, or is it cowmen?"

"It was more like a skilled Englishman with a Lee-Metford repeater," the butler answered proudly, to which all nodded in agreement.

"And what of our skilled Scottish friends? We must know if the inspector's wonderful balloon arrived at Drummond Castle," Kepelheim said as he finished encoding the message. "There! I have completed the cipher, which your man, Mr. Baxter, may send to the duke. That dear gentleman must have paid a small fortune to run telegraph lines from Drummond to Glasgow, but praise be to the Lord that he did! I would not wish such a message to pass through too many hands and past too many sets of eyes."

Baxter stood and took the card, raising a brow at the odd collection of numbers and letters upon it. "I marvel that any of those eyes could read it," he said, limping slightly as he headed toward the foyer where he rang a hand bell. Within moments, young Stephen Priest, his own head bandaged, appeared in casual attire.

"Begging your pardon, Mr. Baxter. I've only now finished with the doctor, but it was my turn in the rotor for the wire room. Shall I change into livery, sir?"

"No, no. I believe our situation calls for more relaxed rules, but only for the time being, Mr. Priest. Send this right away, and make sure that the operator at Drummond Castle acknowledges receipt, and then bring any reply to us immediately. Is that clear?"

"As crystal, sir. I mean, yes, sir, Mr. Baxter."

Baxter thought a moment and then stopped the lad with a touch on the arm. "Stephen, your head? You are well enough to perform?"

"It wasn't much, sir. Just a slight wound, and Dr. Price says no real damage. Thank you, sir."

The lad hobbled away, his left leg bandaged beneath his trousers, and the aging butler saluted, a tear in his eye.

In Scotland, Charles Sinclair, for he now began to think of himself as such, made certain of the security of their cottage, checking first the latch on the door and the locks on the windows. The one-room cottage had but two windows, one on either side of the entrance, so by facing the door, he could defend their position if needed. The only bed stood in the far corner of the room, layered in half a dozen quilts, now keeping Elizabeth warm as she dreamt.

Deciding his best action would be to remain awake all night and keep watch, Sinclair took up his post in a simple wooden chair near the fire. Despite the cheerful warmth, he felt cold. Fear? If so, not for himself. He'd faced gunfire before, many times. No, this was different. Perhaps it was the ghost story the farmer's wife had told him. The man with the foreign accent. The man's appearance sounded eerily similar to the stranger he'd seen inside the maze. *But that was a dream, wasn't it?*

It seemed impossible that this could have been William Trent, however the basic description—except for the accent and strange clothing—nearly matched the man he'd met ten years earlier. Trent had been clean shaven then, but facial hair is easily altered. What was it about Trent that nagged at him so? Often times, Charles had struggled to recover his childhood memories so long ago lost, but even a visit to an alienist in his teen years had done nothing. The man, a Dr. Prüsscher, as Charles remembered, had suggested he contact a mesmerist; that a new French therapy of the mind might unlock the past.

Who am I really? he wondered as he watched her sleep. There was no denying it; he had fallen deeply in love with Elizabeth, but it was a futile love. She belonged to another man. Always had, always would. That man may be his own cousin, but Paul Stuart had certainly become a friend, and betraying him could never happen. He must stop thinking of Elizabeth in that way.

And yet, the play of light upon her soft face danced in his mind, and he feared his own heart more than any phantom. Tea would help keep him alert and watchful. He reached into the basket and withdrew the sealed glass jar that held the strong brew that Maggie Campbell had prepared. It would have gone cold by now, but its effects would not be diminished, so he unscrewed the lid and began to sip the sweet liquid.

The inner circle and all its exploits played in his thoughts, and he wondered who else might be included in this team of unsung heroes. He prayed dear Kepelheim would soon arrive, his sewing needles, experience, and delightful mannerisms helping their cause and easing their minds. He thought, too, of Lemuel and wondered how a man whom the duke trusted with the lives of his family could have fallen into the traps of their common enemy.

To keep awake, he stood and stretched, walking close to the windows as he sipped the tea. The skies had cleared now, and the full moon shone upon the rolling landscape, bathing everything in an ethereal silver. The duchess turned in her sleep, moaning slightly.

"Charles," she whispered, and he wondered if she had finally started to awaken.

"Elizabeth? Darling, are you all right? Are you cold?" She reached out, taking his hand, and he longed to pull her into his arms. "Beth? Are you awake?" he asked, but her eyes remained shut, her breathing regular.

Tears formed at the corners of his eyes, and Charles realised no matter how firm his resolve, he would never be able to stop loving her. She turned toward him, the moonlight falling upon her face, and he kissed her small hand before making certain that the quilts were tucked in securely. Returning to his sentry position by the fire, Charles finished the tea and set the empty jar back inside the basket.

Outside, on the moors and hills, wolves howled, hunting for their night's feast, and Charles thought of the cattle and sheep outside belonging to the farmer. *All we like sheep have gone astray*, he remembered suddenly. *Dear Lord and Saviour, help us now, through your ministering angels, to battle the human wolves of this world!*

Despite the tea, Charles felt his eyelids grow heavy, and he imagined that gypsy music played upon the night air. He had read that gypsies often traveled along these lowland highways, and strange tales of magic heard as a boy floated through his mind like ghosts.

Heard as a boy? he asked himself. *Did I once hear old Scottish ghost tales? If I was born and raised here, then my mother—Angela Stuart Sinclair—may have once told me such tales before a fire much like this.*

His eyelids closed, and Sinclair fancied he could see gypsies dancing around a great campfire, their women arrayed in multicoloured, ruffled skirts with tiny bells on their trim ankles and tambourines in their soft hands. One particular dancer, fair of face with long waves of raven hair, moved closer to his dreaming mind, and as he fell into slumber, Charles reached out for the seductive dancer and drew her close, his eager lips drinking in hers, as their bodies entwined to the rhythmic music. He had never felt such heat before, not with his wife, not with any woman. She melted to him, their bodies dancing together, perfectly in sync as if they had been so designed—created for each other alone—perfectly joined with the night and the song of wolves!

He lingered there in that wild dream world as if in a delightful trance, and his dreaming mind reached out for a final thought seeded before he fell asleep, asking the beautiful dancer if her skirts, her hips, her warm, seductive body had been implanted in his mind by some stage hypnotist.

He smiled in his sleep, the dream driving to erotic conclusion, the dancers and the dance. And outside, the wolves circled, and a large male, a massive grey with eyes of fire, howled at the bright, round moon.

Charles awoke suddenly, his eyes snapping open as if an electric shock ran through him. Outside, through the windows, he could still see the pale round moon and hear the wolves upon the moors. He had no idea just how long he'd slept, but he felt warm, wonderfully warm.

He moved in the bed.

The bed?

Sinclair's eyes rounded wide in shock, panic overtaking him, seizing him like a cold vice, and what he saw sent an icy chill into his heart. There she lay, *his Elizabeth*, her body nestled against his, warm and flushed. Her clothing and his lay scattered upon the cottage floorboards, and her trusting face was turned toward his bare chest, her delicate arm draped across his stomach.

"Dear God! What have I done?!" he cried out, leaping from the bed and pulling on his clothing—*Paul's clothing*. It was like a fairy tale or an old Arthurian legend of Druid wizards turning one man into another. He had worn Paul's clothing, and now—like a manic wolf—he had claimed Paul's bride!

"Elizabeth, darling, you must wake up!" he urged her, his head spinning and his eyes straining to focus. Yet, how seductive she looked still, and he nearly found his eyes drifting shut once more, his mind circling back to the dream and the dance. "The tea! Can she have tampered with it?"

He thought not. Maggie had seemed so kind, so very helpful. "Something is not right about any of this," he whispered, dreading

Beth's eyes when at last she opened them, when she realised *what he had done to her*.

"Beth, please, dearest, you must wake up!"

Slowly, her warm body turned, and her dark eyes fluttered open. "The dream," she whispered, reaching out for him. "I must return to the dream, the beautiful dream. Charles, my Charles," she whispered, her eyes round, her pupils wide as saucers.

"Beth, darling, listen to me. We have been drugged. You must arise and dress. We must leave this accursed place at once!"

She blinked slowly, languidly, and he knew she could not awaken. Perhaps, some strange admixture of the drug Lemuel had given her with this new poison affected her strangely.

Lemuel. *What if the kidnapping was merely the lure? What if this is the real trap?*

A knot grew in his stomach as he lifted the duchess from their bower, and he began dressing her as quickly as possible. "Beth, I care not what may befall us on the road now. I fear this place more. Please, dearest, you must help me. Put your arm through this sleeve, please, Beth. Help me!"

It took many minutes, and he managed it at last, but she still slept, her eyes opening now and then, her breathing slow and rhythmic, her slender arms limp. He unlatched the door and gazed out into the night. He could see no wolves, and yet he had heard them clearly.

It was but a dream.

Fearing that to leave her, even for a moment, could lead to tragedy, he took Elizabeth into his arms and carried her to the barn where the horses and carriage had been housed. After settling her into the seat and covering her with a quilt, Charles swiftly hitched the pair, and then led them and the rig out as quietly as possible toward the road, for he did not wish to alert their hosts—people who must surely be in the pay of the enemy.

Once they were far enough away, he took the reins, cracked the whip, and raced toward the smell of sea air. On they drove for an hour, and off in the distance, he could hear wolves howling, but this was no dream. Looking back, Charles could see a pack of six, mouths foaming, their eyes red, led by a seventh: a huge grey, whose fiery eyes seemed fixed upon them both.

As the horses galloped, Charles began to pray aloud, hot tears and the lingering effects of the drug blurring his vision.

"Father, Good Saviour, please, help us! We need your aid! I have failed, and I am unable to do what I must," he prayed. "Help us, please, Lord Jesus! For her sake, please!"

As if in answer, gunshots rang out in the night, the sharp reports pinging off the rocky crags, and behind the carriage, one of the pack fell in a pool of dark blood. Another shot, and a second wolf dropped dead upon the road.

Charles lifted his eyes toward heaven and sang out, "Thank you, Father!"

And then, about a mile ahead, he could just make out riders, five of them, galloping toward him like mounted avengers, rifles spitting heavenly fire, until all but the lead wolf lay dead upon the dusty road. This one ran at incredible speed, nearly catching their carriage, but just as the beast's enormous head reached Beth's side of the curricle, the entire road lit up with the dawn, and Charles heard the gigantic creature cry out—howling like a banshee—before disappearing into the silvery smoke of morning's light.

The horsemen rode up to the curricle, taking the panicked paints by their bridles and slowing their manic pace. Gradually, the horses came to a stop, and the duke's courageous butler, Matthew Laurence, removed his hat and said with a smile, "We're grateful to the Lord for His aid in finding you, sir. And not a moment too soon."

Charles felt as if his heart were about to burst. His face was pale and covered in sweat, and his pulse hammered like a blacksmith in his ears, causing him to nearly faint. His vision darkened, but he could feel Laurence and his men helping him into a large Drummond coach, setting him next to Elizabeth. And as her head fell against his shoulder, Sinclair began to weep tears of exhaustion and relief.

CHAPTER EIGHTEEN
9, October

It was nearly 7:00 a.m. by the time Charles, Elizabeth, and their escort reached the castle. Elizabeth still lay in a deep sleep, and Charles had all but collapsed, so both were helped or carried into their makeshift bedrooms in the west wing.

Paul insisted on visiting Elizabeth, despite being warned to remain off his feet, and he now sat next to her, great tears dropping from his deep blue eyes onto her blouse.

"Beth, oh my Beth! What has that wretched man done to you?"

Charles lay across the hall being examined by the housekeeper, and he jumped suddenly, his guilty mind hearing this and wondering what Paul might suspect. Was the reference to a 'wretched man' referring to the treasonous doctor, or to him? Did Paul somehow know what had happened in the cottage? But then, what had actually happened? Had anything occurred? Charles had no way of knowing…unless *she* could remember it. He only knew he had dreamt of passion in a woman's embrace and then awakened in her warm bed. Perhaps, nothing happened.

But their clothing had been scattered on the floor, he reminded himself. And he thought he recalled seeing bright blood upon the sheets—but he forced the memories down, praying the drug now played tricks with his mind.

He shut his eyes, longing to remember truly, worrying about the woman he loved more than life, but his memories remained little more than a confused garble of ghosts and guilt. "Lord help me, I cannot remember!" he cried out, weeping, and the housekeeper hushed him.

"There, now, sir. You're all a-fever. Mr. Laurence, can you hold him? He's thrashing about like a madman!"

Standing nearby, Drummond feared for his loved ones. "What happened out there?" he asked Laurence as the butler looked up from his position near Sinclair's couch.

"Wolves, sir."

Drummond's face pinched with concern and dread. "How many?" he asked, tensely.

"Six, sir, plus the leader. As usual, the pack went down easily, but the leader cannot be taken with bullets. He left off the chase though with the sunrise. Lord Haimsbury, sir, he said something about a farmer and his wife—and gypsies. He wasn't making much sense, my lord. His eyes, the pupils are so wide; they've nearly gone black. So have those of the duchess."

James kicked at the wall, his poorly aimed boot glancing off the polished woodwork. "Fool!"

"Sorry, my lord," the butler said softly. "We tried, sir."

"Not you, lad," the duke replied gently, putting a hand on the young man's shoulder. "You did well. Better than I at your age. Your father, rest his soul, would have been proud of you tonight, Matthew. No, I'm the fool. This was clearly all a ruse. I was meant to send Sinclair out after the doctor. Wait, you said there was a farmer? What farmer?"

"I don't know, sir. We can learn more when Mr. Sinclair—Lord Haimsbury, I mean—is making more sense."

The duke turned to the housekeeper. "Mrs. MacAnder, do you know what this drug might be?"

She opened the detective's eyes, prying the lids apart with her fingers. They looked like midnight pools, and his cheeks were flushed. "I canno' say for sure. He is feverish, sir. I am worried he may have been poisoned. I've seen devil's cherries do this to a man, dilate the pupils and cause nervous prostration—the old wives called it *dwale*, I believe, and it's said to be a favourite of witches."

Paul appeared at the door, leaning against the moulding of the frame, his own face flushed. "Whatever they gave Charles, they gave also to Beth. Her eyes look the same. Did I hear you say the wolves attacked?"

Laurence helped the earl to a chair, nodding. "Yes, sir. The big one was the leader—like before. We killed the six, but nothing takes down the big grey."

"With red eyes," Charles moaned. "Red eyes! God help us! Save us! What have I done?" he moaned, his body shivering.

"This is all my fault," Paul said, looking with concern to his friend. "If I'd been more careful on the train, then I would have avoided injury, and none of this would have occurred."

James kissed his nephew's head and looked into his face. "Son, we are in deep waters now. All that we know—all that we've done has been but prelude. Everything has changed, and the enemy knew it before we could realise the change had come. He is piping a new tune, but we must not dance. We may seek our Lord's guidance and protection, but He asks that we use the brains he gave us in this battle. Our fight is, as St. Paul said, against spiritual wickedness, and against powers and principalities. Not things of this world, but of an unseen realm of beings who are at war! That big grey may not flinch at a bullet, but he'll bow to the Christ, will he not? Good, then, buck up! Our Saviour is still at the head of this war, so no more despairing, nor blaming yourself. We must take our places on the battlefield in the armour we're given and trust to Him for the rest. Now, I say we all sleep if we can. It's been a restless night, and we're all exhausted.. We shall investigate more tomorrow."

The duke then turned to the young butler. "Laurence, a word."

He walked into the hallway and led the butler toward the guest library, going inside and shutting the door. "Lad, do you think you could try to find this farmer that my nephew mentioned?"

"Yes, sir. Do we have a name?"

"Ask Charles if he can remember it, but do not push him. He's been through much this night. Your loyalty and quick thinking have revealed you to be worth your weight in gold, my boy. We must discuss a new position for you soon—as one of our agents. For now, you go sleep 'til you're rested, and then tomorrow take your men to find that farm."

"Thank you, sir. I won't fail you."

"You need only be concerned with pleasing Christ," James said, tapping the man's shoulder with pride.

Laurence left and returned to Charles, who had calmed somewhat in the past few minutes. "Sir, can you tell me anything more about the farmer?"

Sinclair's face flushed again, and his fists clenched. "They did something! The tea! Or—music, wolves. I'm not sure. Farmer?"

"Yes, sir," the lad persisted patiently. "First name? Last?"

"Hamish and Maggie," Charles said suddenly, his mind miraculously clearing for a moment. "Two cottages, a barn, sheep, cows. A large windmill. Wait—wait!" he said, gripping Laurence's arm and turning to look into his face. "The barn. A great red one, but it had something painted on it. Just above the doors. A large, white bird."

Sitting nearby, Paul's face grew ashen. "A bird?" he repeated, his stomach knotting. "Did it—did it have a red spot on its wings?"

Charles nodded, his pupils like saucers. "It did. But only on one of them."

Laurence looked at the earl, and both men knew.

Redwing had infiltrated the county.

It was past four in the afternoon before Charles awoke, his head pounding, but his fever gone. He could vaguely recall the events in the cottage, remember the dream dance and awaking next to Elizabeth, but he had no clear memory of what may have truly happened between them. He prayed it was all merely a dream and decided the best course for him to pursue now was to find his courage and serve her cause by joining the inner circle.

As he rose to dress, he found a note, written in the duke's strong hand telling him a meeting had been called in his private library, and it would commence as soon as Sinclair could join them, anytime that afternoon.

Still somewhat unsteady on his feet, Charles sat next to a table where he found a pitcher filled with water. Pouring the water into a beautifully painted porcelain bowl, he glanced into the mirror Carlton had brought him. As he shaved, Sinclair wondered if his face held the secrets of his lineage, for in truth, he did bear a striking resemblance to Paul Stuart. Their foreheads were identical, high and broad. His own nose was slightly straighter and a bit wider in the bridge, and his brows and hair much darker. His chin bore a cleft like the earl's, though not as deeply chiseled. Both had almond shaped eyes, and his irises shone with a variant of Paul's blue. Even their hairlines and ears were similar. They could indeed be brothers.

Sinclair heard a gentle knock and turned to find Matthew Laurence, looking tired also, standing in the open door to the drawing room. "Sir, the duke asks if you are ready," the young butler said, his face drawn, his green eyes rimmed in red.

"Yes, thank you, Laurence. And thank you for last night. Had you and your men not arrived when you did, we would never had made it. The duchess and I owe our lives to you."

Laurence bowed. "It is my honour, sir. Now, if I may, I shall take you to the others." As they walked, Charles asked about Elizabeth and Paul. "The duchess still sleeps, sir, but she is in no danger now. Mrs. MacAnder is keeping close watch over her, and she believes the duchess will recover fully by evening. And the earl has much improved with sleep and awaits inside the library with the others."

Their journey took them along the main foyer and into the central part of the house, where a grand gallery, lined with the portraits of dukes and earls, shepherded them through a series of large meeting rooms and a small anteroom that ended at two enormous, oaken doors. Pushing one open, the butler showed Charles into the immense room beyond.

If Elizabeth's library in London had impressed the detective— had that been only a week before?—then, this room would fit a king's idea of perfection. The domed ceiling soared forty feet above their heads, decorated with gold-leafed mouldings and hand-painted murals, whilst four golden chandeliers provided sparkle and light. Along each wall, red and gold, handcrafted wallpapers peeked from between massive shelving, each vertical carved and embellished with roses and vines. Above each, in the centre of the lintel moulding, a curious symbol that looked like a circle enclosing a stylized shepherd's crook or perhaps the letter 'P' crossed by what looked like the letter 'S' stood out in relief, and every shelf was crowded with priceless volumes and many, many Bibles in all languages, as well as roll upon roll of original manuscripts contained within leather tubes.

The room smelled like leather and wisdom, and in the centre of this remarkable space, around a single, rectangular table of gilded mahogany sat the duke, Paul, two men unknown to Charles, and to his great relief, Martin Kepelheim.

The latter rose as Sinclair entered. "My dear friend!" the tailor exclaimed. "It is so good to see you, and in surroundings that suit you, I think."

Charles stepped forward eagerly and embraced the older man. "Kepelheim! It is a joy and relief to see you, my brave friend. How fares Branham?"

"Bent but unbroken," he answered, walking Charles to a chair to the duke's right. "Sit here, my friend, and we shall all hear it together. I will make my report, and then others will share theirs. You listen now. And learn."

He sat, pleased to see the earl looking much stronger, less pale. "Lord Aubrey, I am delighted you're well enough to join us—whatever 'us' means. This is a mystery to me, to be sure."

Paul smiled, his eyes brighter than they'd been in days, although his face still carried pain. "You will know very soon. And you must stop calling me Lord Aubrey. But I perhaps race ahead of the agenda. Uncle James?"

The duke sat at the head, Paul to his left, Charles to his right. "This has been a long time in coming," he said, "but here we are, at last, come to a day we have looked to for decades, nay perhaps centuries. Charles, you have joined a group of men—and women, as you will learn one day soon—who have taken vows to stand against an enemy not made of flesh and blood. Our chief historian and keeper of the lines, Mr. Kepelheim, will begin. But first, we must pray."

Charles was surprised at this, but he bowed his head along with the others, and he heard the duke's manly voice speaking in penitent tones.

"Dear Father of all that is good, thank you for keeping our circle safe, and for protecting Paul, Charles, and our darling girl Elizabeth. Thank you for the miracle taking place before my eyes—the return of one beloved and sorely missed," he continued, his voice cracking with emotion. "You have preserved Charles for your reasons, and through your power, no matter what the enemy might believe. Help him now to accept his part in your plans with courage and grace, and may he never again leave us. Now, oh Lord, help us to see with your eyes the battle that surrounds us. Help us to follow your leading when our mortal eyes are blind. Help us to fight until our strength fails, and then rally as your Spirit renews and revives us. Help us to be wise as serpents, for it is against such that we fight. Help us to recognise the serpent's path and to strike as you lead us to do so. And may all we do honour you. In our Saviour's mighty and wonderful name, we ask it. Amen."

All said 'amen' after, and Charles raised his eyes to a table filled with men of purpose. He knew not exactly what their purpose was, but he was about to find out.

Kepelheim began, standing as he spoke. "History. It is a strangely mutable topic, gentlemen. Schools teach it as if a simple list of names and dates suffices to explain a complicated tapestry that reaches from the Garden of Eden to our table here today. Without repeating much, but providing enough so that our new member may understand our core command, let me say the name we hate. Redwing. It is an ages old cabal of men and women in league with devils, and its sole purpose is to unseat Christ and usher in Satan's eternal reign upon the earth."

Charles listened, his mind slowly clearing after the night's vivid dreams and terrifying events. That same mind, similar in design to Paul Stuart's, could not help making connexions, and this very quality, which had made him a superior investigator, would now help him to understand a deep, supernatural mystery.

"Redwing," Kepelheim continued, "began officially under that name in 1420, though its roots reach back into ancient history, ultimately to Eden and perhaps earlier. But for now, we shall concern ourselves only with the Redwing face of this many-headed dragon.

"In December 1421, Henry the Sixth was born. Our official histories record that he reigned until 1461 in times of great confusion and conflict, leading to a Lancastrian civil war that put a York on the throne, whom school children memorise as Edward the Fourth, no? The War of the Roses is always on their examinations, is it not? Yet, how many historians have read the obscure diaries of the time, the banned letters, the secrets that passed from hand to hand, generation to generation, and were surreptitiously recorded and catalogued? Do they consider the burnt books and the deathbed confessions and even church documents that rarely see the light of day? Charles, my good friend, your teachers at Harrow and Cambridge did not tell you—could not tell you of the children born who have been erased from official history. Of the deals made, or of the agreements signed, but here—in this magnificent library—we have copies and in some cases originals of them all. And lest the enemy think to destroy these copies is to destroy truth, then that enemy is mistaken, for many such copies have been hidden throughout the world, and as you will see in a moment, my friend, the original of one such document has been signed by kings and queens, prime ministers, and archbishops."

The duke put a hand on Charles's arm as if to encourage him, but the detective suddenly felt lost. "Martin, are you saying that our succession of monarchs is corrupted?" Sinclair asked.

"Good, you follow. Yes, in fact, I am saying precisely that," the little tailor said plainly. "We are taught that Henry the Sixth was the only son born to the hero of Agincourt, but is that so? Our teachers say it is, our history books say it is, but can we trust it? Charles, if I told you now that even Queen Victoria and Lord Salisbury know that it is not, would that shock you?"

"Frankly, yes!" he said, his mind struggling to sift through it all, but a small part of his memory not only believed it, but even seemed *to recall it*. "Wait, wait a moment. I think—I think I remember hearing this as a boy, but that cannot be true."

"Yet it is true, Charles," Kepelheim explained. "You have simply been taught to forget it. Your childhood memories were stolen from you. Not by a train or shipping tragedy, but by design! Charles, the Burkes adopted you when you were seven, but you were separated from your dear mother on the docks of Liverpool when you were five. Someone found you there, perhaps *stole* you, and that man then spent the next two years making sure you did not remember anything about this castle, or Briarcliff, or Branham—or about your own family's estate, Rose House!"

Rose House. He had a vague memory—something tiny, small, like breath on a mirror. "Perhaps…" he said.

"Yes, perhaps," Paul told him. "Charles, I remember a little about my friendship with you when we were boys. You visited Briarcliff a few times, and I spent a Christmas at Rose House. Later, when I was only six, I remember visiting Rose House with my father and Uncle James when they went there to close it, and I saw a portrait of you. I told Father that the boy in the painting looked like he could be my brother. He said that we'd always resembled each other but that you were missing. Presumed dead. It never occurred to me that the detective I'd befriended in '79 might be my own true cousin, but something about you always felt familiar, even from the first time we met."

"It has been a long plan that we missed," the duke explained. "Charles, we've spent years protecting a secret bloodline that maintains both the Plantagenet and Stuart royal houses, but we missed your part in it, because we thought you were dead, son."

"Wait, it's too much," he said, his head aching. "My mother? Angela. She was your sister, sir. Is that right?"

The duke nodded. "Aye. Angela and Abigail were twins. Not identical, you know, but nearly so. Your mother, laddie, loved you as few mothers love a child. And you wear her eyes, son."

Charles felt as if his heart had taken on the weight of a thousand dark regrets, and he recalled the portrait of the duke's sisters. The beautiful Stuart ladies. "But, I... I cannot remember her at all. Why is that?" he asked, tears staining his cheeks.

"You will remember both her and your good father, I believe," said Kepelheim gently, "and we must be prepared for it at any time. Redwing set this plan into motion many years ago, but we kept thinking that it was Elizabeth they were after, her blood, for she is the direct descendant of King Henry the Fifth's firstborn twin sons, the ones born in France after his secret liaison with Catherine—it is the true reason he married her that June. These sons were taken at birth and kept in a remote abbey by Henry's French father-in-law, Charles the Sixth."

"Wait, that cannot be true!" Charles persisted. "There is no record of Henry having twin sons, in France or anywhere else."

"There is, but it has been expunged from the official histories," the tailor replied patiently. "The two boys, named Henry Charles and Henry Edward, were raised to age ten in an abbey in Calais. Then, the boys were separated to protect and preserve the Plantagenet bloodline, should the third son—the one we all know from school, the one who became King Henry the Sixth—die without issue. Henry's reign and the men who sought to unseat him left England bleeding, but when Edward the Prince of Wales was murdered at Tewkesbury, the throne of England had no king. It is then that the elder twin, Henry Charles was asked to take the throne by the men who had guarded his secret. This Prince Henry lived in Scotland, and he had been raised since age ten by the 1st Earl of Aubrey as his own son. The other prince, the younger twin Henry Edward, had been raised by the Marquess of Anjou in Kent. Neither brother wished to reign, for they had loved each other from their childhood, and they realised that devious men would murder the other, if one chose to reign as king. So, it was decided that neither would take the throne, and the House of Aubrey and the House of Anjou make a pact to protect the lines for a future time when the two lines might rule as one. This was done in secret, and the York and Lancaster houses, whose men were willing to murder and make war for the right to rule, did not know the pact was made. Only when Edward the Fourth, the York victor, took the throne, did our small band of predecessors, the first inner circle, speak to this new king and tell him the truth of the royal blood that flowed in the veins of twin brothers. If the secret became commonly known, the news would lead to another war, and that would leave England open to a French invasion, so the new king was willing to make a deal, which he then signed. He granted the elder brother a new title, to him and all his descendants, that of Duke of Drummond. The younger was made Duke of Branham, both with promises that whether male or female, all firstborn children from both lines would not only inherit that title but would also be deemed *rightful heir* to the throne of England so long as their lines continued."

Charles realised his breathing had accelerated, and the room grew warm. His head spun. "No, no," he protested. "This must be fiction."

Mr. Kepelheim crossed to a hand-painted cabinet and withdrew a locked box, which the duke then opened. Drummond removed an etched gold tube and opened its cap. Inside was a rolled document, which he handed to Kepelheim, and the tailor set the ancient scroll before the disbelieving guest. "Read it aloud," he told him.

Charles scanned through the contents, written in an antiquarian style with quill pen and sealed with a great royal seal, then he read it out for all to hear:

"TO ALL WHO BEAR WITNESS BELOW, it is hereby decreed that the twin sons, Henry Charles the Elder and Henry Edward the Younger, both born on the twenty-first day of September, the year of our Lord, Fourteen Hundred and Twenty, in Calais, France, by the sovereign and most holy body of our most glorious king Henry V, out of the carriage and delivery from the body of his most glorious consort queen, Catherine of Valois, are herein acknowledged to be the sole and rightful heirs to the thrones of England and France, and that through their royal bloodlines, all heirs to their bodies through direct descent, be they male or female, are also proclaimed rightful heirs and princes; to wit, should any heir so wish it, he or she shall immediately be placed upon the throne and crowned sovereign king or queen.

I sign this day, 4, March, the Year of our Lord, Fourteen Hundred and Sixty-One.

Edward IV, Rex."

Kepelheim continued. "So you see, Charles? It is all true. And you will note, my friend, that this document has also been signed by every king, queen, prime minister, and archbishop since that day. There, near the bottom, you will find Victoria's signature on 20th June, 1837, the day her reign began."

The duke looked to his nephew and again at Sinclair. "You two do indeed look like brothers," he said, "and it is due to your being true cousins, sons of twin mothers. Your mother, Paul, was my sister, but Angela was also my sister. Charles, if you're wondering how it all works out, Kepelheim has every detail, but my mother died when I was born, and my father remarried in 1835. That wonderful woman was Charlotte MacAllan, only sibling to the Earl of Granndach, and two years after, she gave birth to Angela, the elder twin, and Abigail the younger.

"My father was dying from a disease he'd caught in India, and he wanted to see his daughters married properly before he left this earth, so in January of '54, Abigail married my closest friend Robert Stuart, whose first wife had died three years earlier. Angela married Robby Sinclair, the young Marquess of Haimsbury one week later. My father died one month after. You and Paul were both born in 1855, just four months apart. That same year, I left to fight Redwing, our common enemy, privately, whilst serving publically in the Crimean War, and I spent many of the years that followed traveling back and forth: Constantinople to Cairo, to Paris, to St. Petersburg, to London, to Glasgow, but I saw you many times, lad. And you and Paul spent Christmases here in '57 and '58, though you were quite small then. I've kept a few of the drawings you made for me, son. In my scrapbook. I'll show them to you later. You were quite the budding artist!"

All laughed, and Charles noticed tears at the corners of the duke's dark eyes.

"When I returned for good in late June of 1860," Drummond continued, "Haimsbury—your father, Charles—had died in a duel, and your mother had fled, staying briefly here, but then disappearing or possibly taken by Redwing. We had little to go on, to be honest. I searched everywhere for you and your mother, Charles. Everywhere! It nearly drove me mad," he said, and he paused for a moment to wipe his face. "Two years later, we uncovered evidence that her body and yours had been recovered after a great storm destroyed several ships bound for England, and we were even shown your battered bodies—not a pretty sight, for those bodies, we were told, had washed up on a shore in Ireland more than a year after the ship was said to have gone down and had been exhumed for our identification. We now know all that so-called 'evidence' must have been fabricated to obscure the truth, but how were we to know then? We'd tried to protect Angela just as we have Elizabeth, for we knew that any son she bore would be a direct descendent of the Scottish twin, as am I, but there was more to it.

"Your father, Charles, descended from a family that we've long suspected might play some part in Redwing's plans. That foul group has been manipulating bloodlines for many centuries, and the blood of Haimsbury House and the Sinclair family stands as near the top as that of the Plantagenet twins, though we are not sure why.

"And Elizabeth, if you are beginning to make those connexions, my friend and nephew—Charles, our beloved Beth is actually a direct descendant of *both* twins. Both. That is why we felt certain Redwing would come after her, and since her birth, there have been many attacks upon her life and upon her mind. A son is one thing, but a daughter who descends, if she were to marry a son who is a direct descendant also—any child of that union would be the prize!"

Paul cleared his throat and spoke next. "Charles, my true cousin, my friend. It has always been planned for me to marry Elizabeth, for a number of reasons. Firstly, that she have constant protection by someone within the inner circle, but secondly, through my father, I am the direct descendant of James the Seventh, the last Stuart king. Also, because Uncle James and my father both felt that keeping Elizabeth in the family was the only way to protect her from within.

They put her into my arms when she was born, and I was told this beautiful girl was to one day become my wife."

The duke continued, "But Charles, you are also descended from James the Seventh. Your grandmother, Adelaide Stuart, who married your paternal grandfather, was Robert Stuart's elder sister."

"Robert Stuart? Paul's father, you mean?" Sinclair asked, trying to sort through the names.

The duke nodded. "Yes, that's right. Bobby Stuart and Adelaide were Charles Stuart's only children. So, you are second in line to inherit the Stuart royal blood, after Paul, and it might even be argued that you are first, since Adelaide was the elder child."

Charles could not help wanting to scream. "Wait! Wait!" he exclaimed, leaping to his feet. The images of the gypsy dancer and the sound of wolves clouded his mind, and he struggled to concentrate. "This is too much."

James reached over and touched his nephew's hand. "Son, it's clear that you love Elizabeth as much as any of us does. It seems to me that she also cares for you, so it may be something we should consider. Paul, I know that you love Beth, but my granddaughter is old enough to choose her husband, is she not? Should old decisions made when she was but an infant rule her life?"

Aubrey looked uncomfortable, but he nodded. "I want Beth's happiness above all else. But I also want her to be safe."

"Then, perhaps, we should consider this new path. Paul, had Charles not been lost, it's quite possible that he would have been tasked to look after Beth. And now, in a way, it's come full circle. Charles, do you understand what I mean?"

Sinclair began to understand more than they imagined. "Yes, all right. I believe all this. If true, then because Connor is dead, after you, Uncle, I am the male heir through the elder twin, is that not correct?"

All nodded.

"And as a Sinclair, my blood is also prized by Redwing. And, God forbid, if anything should ever happen to my dear cousin here, I would be the heir to the Stuart dynasty."

The duke interrupted. "But, Charles, it is possible that to Redwing, you *already are* the Stuart heir."

"All right then, for the sake of argument, let us say that I am. Fair enough?"

All nodded once again.

"Then, would it not be madness for me to even contemplate marriage to another Plantagenet heir, especially one descended from both twins?"

Again, all nodded, but the duke interjected, "However, if that means someone we know and can count on would be in a place to keep her safe, then…"

"No!" Sinclair insisted, slamming his fist on the table. "No! I've no desire to rule as king, nor I suspect, do you Paul. Why should Elizabeth not live her life as she chooses?"

"Because," Kepelheim explained, "Redwing will choose for her, if we do not. Your blood is indeed what they most desire, Charles, and wishing it away will not alter that fact. If we had any doubt, then this message removes it," he said, handing a stained piece of paper to the duke. "We found this in the pocket of the hybrid leader at Branham. All had deformations of some degree or another, but the leader was much larger, and his ears and claws more pronounced. They are wolf creatures, but more advanced than those we saw five years ago. Read the message, sir."

The duke read it through and then passed it back to the tailor.

Kepelheim explained. "This telegram was sent the *very afternoon* the Ripper letter was left in Queen Anne House—a letter that so alarmed our dear one that she fled to you, Charles. The message reads: 'They are on their way. Attack 1800 hours Sunday. No harm to her or to Sinclair. We need his blood.'"

The detective's face paled. "Ripper," he muttered. "Elizabeth hinted at this when we met at her London home. She implied that a long ritual encompassed the Ripper's deeds, but I found it hard to understand."

"Beth knows some of these truths, Charles," the duke replied, "but we've kept much from her. Despite that, she has discerned far more than even many of our members."

"I fear she may be right about Ripper," Sinclair said as pieces began to fit into place. "Uncle James, is it possible that all those murders are but moves in a long, unthinkable game? A game of blood? A ritualistic chess match meant to empower their leaders?"

"We've begun to suspect precisely that." The duke placed his hand on his nephew's. "But calm your heart, son. I know this must drive fear into your spirit, but trust in the Lord. He gave His blood to save us."

"But Redwing wants to use our blood to save themselves," Sinclair answered, his eyes filled with tears. "All those women are dead because of... Because these men want to rule the world. And they would do anything to achieve that, would they not? Even harm Elizabeth?"

"They would. Look what they did to her mother," Kepelheim observed. "It was their strategy to place poor Patricia in Whitechapel to lure you into their web. They need to match your blood to Elizabeth's, else their centuries long plans will fail. Why, we are not sure, for it is beyond your connexion to the Stuart line. Something in the Sinclair blood is important to them."

"My blood?" the detective echoed, standing up. "Mine? Why? She descends already from both twins, why must they add mine to it? Why must Beth live her life in fear of them? And Paul, my friend and true cousin, you could have been killed!" He clutched at his head, which pounded, partly from the whisky he'd been drinking, a spirit he was unaccustomed to, but also from lack of sleep and emotional strain.

The tailor touched Sinclair's shoulder compassionately. "My dear friend, I fear for you and for her. Redwing will hound you both until you give them what they desire, but I believe that infernal group has underestimated you, Charles Sinclair. And by bringing you back into your rightful family, they may have committed a grave error. I pray it is so. But no matter what you choose to do, Elizabeth will remain in danger until the day Christ calls her home."

He looked at the tailor, his eyes filled with tears. "Martin, I will gladly give my life, but not hers. Never hers. Is there nowhere she is safe?"

Paul walked around the table and touched his cousin's shoulder. "Here, Charles. Here. She is safest with us—her family. But first we must find and deal with Trent. He is the primary London leader. He has had unnatural desires for Beth for many years."

Kepelheim nodded. "Charles, I do not expect you to know this, but we gave aid to a traitor to their mad cause some six years ago, and before he died—for his injuries were extensive—he admitted to us that Sir William's original plan after murdering Patricia was to keep Elizabeth for himself. That he planned to marry her and force her to bear *his* child and place that son on the throne of England."

Charles felt all the blood drain from his face, and he suddenly fell forward, the supporting arms of the duke and his cousin Paul breaking his tumble and keeping him from striking his head on the table.

"Steady!" Aubrey said. "Don't follow my dizzy path, Cousin!"

Charles felt nauseous, like the world had begun to revolve on a new axis. And perhaps it had.

"If—if," he stammered, catching his breath, "if this man's confession is true, is it possible that Trent intended her harm, intended to, to *force* her that very night?"

He kept picturing Elizabeth, the petite girl of almost eleven years, and how he'd asked her if her stepfather had touched her in any way improper, and she'd said she could not remember, and that she didn't wish to remember. The animal she spoke of, and the attack she'd suffered when he'd pressed her. He had presumed the head injury had muddled her mind, but *what if Trent tried to rape her?*

"When," he began, taking a glass of water from the hands of Kepelheim and swallowing it all down. "When Beth was with me at the station house—whilst we waited for you, Paul—I asked her if William had, well done anything to her. I cannot recall exactly what my words were, and I tried to be gentle, but still get to the truth, for only our doctor could perform an examination to confirm whether or not she had been...forced, and I wanted more information before subjecting her to anything so traumatising as such an examination."

Paul leaned forward. "What did she say?"

Charles struggled to remember rightly. "She'd suffered a head injury, so she had only a partial memory, but she seemed to have special fear of him. I did not know the man, but I could tell Beth was terrified by her experience, not only because of her mother, but because he had—I believe he may have tried to do something to her," he continued, but then suddenly remembering the blood upon the sheets in the cottage Charles realised Trent could not have succeeded, even if he had tried—*she had been a virgin, untouched until that night. Until he had...*

Charles lowered his head, suddenly feeling very ill.

"Lord Haimsbury, perhaps you are not well enough yet for these revelations," one of the strangers said, but Charles looked up and waved away the idea.

"No, I can manage, wait...Lord Haimsbury? Who?" Charles asked. "Oh, I suppose you mean me. Yes, I am fine, thank you. Paul, I don't believe Trent completed his intent, for our police doctor would surely have noticed the, uh, evidence, but it is possible, that evil man may yet intend to fulfill this mad plan to take her as his own."

"It matters not if he succeeded, Charles. Just knowing he *intended* it is enough for me. I shall kill William with my bare hands," Aubrey vowed.

"And mine will be there with yours," Charles promised, his eyes fixed on his cousin. "We must do all we can to find this devil and bring him to account. Not only for Beth and her mother, but also for my parents. And for your brother, Paul."

"My brother?" he asked, clearly not following. "What can you mean? Charles, my brother fell off the cliff behind our home. It was an accident."

Sinclair shook his head. "No, it was not. Not if the farmer's wife spoke truly. She told me that her mother once served at Briarcliff, and that she followed her mother into service at the castle, and that she was drawing water from your well when she saw it happen. Your water is in a well tower, is it not?"

"Yes. Like many old castles, it is, but ours is one of the few still in use."

"So then, perhaps her tale is true," Charles said. "This woman, this Maggie Campbell, she said she was ten at the time, and she saw a strange man dueling with your brother in the garden near the cliff, which she could see through an opening in the well room wall—like a bowshot window."

Paul nodded, his eyes narrowing with concern. "Yes, we have such windows in the well room, originally designed for guards to use defensively. It is one of three such towers. The room is circular and connects to the kitchen. One window does overlook the rose garden and the cliff beyond it."

Charles wanted to get drunk suddenly, and he poured a large shot of scotch and downed it with one gulp, much to the surprise of all. "Then, it may be this woman's tale is true. She told me that the man with whom your elder brother dueled not only thrust him through with a blade, one she described as looking like fire, but that he then pushed your brother over the cliff."

"What?" the earl gasped. "Did she know who this man was?"

Sinclair shook his head. "She could not recall his name, but I asked her to describe this murderer, and she gave me a description that could fit Trent, though his hair was longer. He wore strange clothing and spoke with an accent, but perhaps this was Trent in another shape or disguise. What do we truly know about the man? Also, I asked Maggie if she'd told anyone at the castle, and she said that she reported it to your father."

Now Aubrey looked as if he needed a drink, for his once pale face had flushed with rage. "I cannot believe it! If my father knew this, then he never said one word to me! Can William be ageless? Ian died the day I was born, Charles. My mother, I'm told, nearly miscarried because of it, so this would make William what—sixty at least? Impossible! He looks no older than forty at most."

"Not impossible for those with occult powers," Kepelheim remarked. "I have only recently seen documents that describe a man of suspect birth who bears all the characteristics and physical traits of William Trent, and if Trent is this man, then he travels as companion to another far more devilish. Some of these documents are over three hundred years old."

"Satan's man, he is, of that there can be no doubt," spoke one of the two men unknown to Charles. "Lord Haimsbury, it is my honour to see you again, though you may not remember me. I was the rather sullen driver who conveyed you, your cousin, and our dear one from Leman Street several days past. I am Sir Thomas Galton, a London member and Eton friend to Lord Aubrey."

Connexions within Charles's brain clicked into place, and he smiled. "Sir Thomas, I thought something about you tickled a memory. May I offer my thanks to you for your aid on Elizabeth's behalf? Paul mentioned you often during that rail journey to Branham. He places great faith in your abilities, sir. And, I believe, I had seen you even before that day, had I not? In Whitechapel, at the Brown Bear."

Galton bowed slightly. "Your memory for faces is indeed accurate, my lord. I have met with our Edmund Reid there once or twice, and I'll confess to you, sir, that the duke asked that I also begin to look into your activities several years ago, though he did not tell me that the detective whose steps I dogged was in truth the Marquess of Haimsbury."

"Neither did that detective know it then, friend Galton! I assure you that this news is fresh to me. I only learnt some pieces of it last night."

"Then, it honours me to be among the first to call you such, sir. Yes, I took the train up from Euston and connected in Carstairs to arrive in Glasgow this morning just after dawn. I'm told that you and our duchess—whom Lord Aubrey and the duke often call 'Princess', far more than a nickname, which you must now realise—that she and yourself had faced one of Trent's many shapes on the moors, and that he disappeared at sunrise. That is his way. I have seen it with my own eyes. And my eyes have seen something else this circle must know. William Trent. I have seen that hellish fiend this very day. In Glasgow."

Everyone gasped, and the duke's eyes flashed angrily, but Charles showed no sign of surprise. "Indeed?" the detective remarked. "It makes sense. If Trent took the form of a wolf upon those roads last night, then perhaps he hopes to draw us into the open by returning to human shape."

Paul agreed. "Yes, Charles, that does make sense. He hopes to tempt us into leaving the castle, no doubt."

"Quite. Why else would he appear in his own human form to a man he surely knows is a circle member?" Charles asked. "You are certain it was Trent, Sir Thomas?"

"I am. And he appeared fully human as of this morning, but Trent can take many forms, so you must come to know them all, Lord Haimsbury, if you are to catch him. He has taken the form of smoke and shadow, slipping beneath windows and doors where he may, and some claim he can vanish at will. There is some truth to ancient legends of vampires and werewolves. We deal with him in flesh, but he can find us in animal or even spirit form. We must be prepared to fight them all."

"Mr. Palmer," the duke spoke to the second gentleman, who sat next to Kepelheim. "I'm told you bring ill tidings, also."

"I fear that is so, Your Grace. Lord Haimsbury, I am honoured to be here at your first meeting, and I share your shock and disbelief, for when my father first taught me our family's mission, I wondered if he had not lost all reason."

The group laughed, for each had experienced this in his early days.

"So, my friends and fellow warriors, I tell you that one whom you knew and who, too, cared for our dear duchess, has fallen at the hands of Trent. Sir Thomas was the one who first surveyed the scene, perhaps ten minutes after it occurred, but then I was called in. You see, Lord Haimsbury, I serve as Chief Investigator for the Foreign Secretary, and he tasked me to make certain no espionage was involved. There was not, but it was also not a suicide as the authorities have now ruled it to be."

"Suicide!" Galton shouted. "Are they blind? He was shot six times! How can a man shoot himself six times in the head?"

Palmer pursed his lips and looked calmly at his London friend. "Justice and the wheels that grind therein are often subject to outside control and 'greasing', shall we say, by men of means. Lord Haimsbury, I am sorry to tell you that your friend and colleague Sir Robert Morehouse is dead."

Charles felt shock. Dead? How could he be dead? Morehouse had taken him in as a detective constable, taught him to police, taught him to think. He'd proven friend during times of joy and in times of sorrow. He had wept with Charles at the graveside of his young son and again at that of his estranged wife. They had chased criminals together, traveled together, laughed together, cried together. And they had both responded to the scene over nine years before when Patricia, Duchess of Branham, had been found dead and mutilated next to her unconscious daughter in Spitalfields.

"It is like the world is falling down around me," he whispered, his head in his hands, a tear tracing his cheek. "Bob and I—we shared much heartache and triumph. He drove me mad with his demands for perfection, but in many ways he was like a father to me. You say Trent did this?" he asked, anger filling his mind and heart.

"So it seems," Palmer replied, "for several workers reported seeing a tall man with a cane, lurking in the building after hours, and others claim to have heard a man's voice speaking to Sir Robert only a few moments before the gunshots sounded."

"Then that devil must account for all his crimes," Sinclair vowed. "If it means my own life, he will pay."

Aubrey touched his cousin's shoulder. "I am sorry, Charles. Bob was a good man. He will be much missed."

"So he will be." Grief rained down the detective's face, and he poured himself a shot of scotch, and lifting the glass high, said, "To Sir Robert Morehouse, gentlemen. The best policeman ever seen in Whitechapel, and the dearest friend any man might find. May he be there to greet us when we, too, are at last called to our Saviour's side."

"To Sir Robert," they all said reverently, raising glasses high, eyes bright with tears, and as they drank, each head bowed as they pondered the truth in Sinclair's words.

James stood, and placed one hand on Paul and the other on Charles. "Let us also toast to both my dear nephews. May they live long and live well. And when I am gone, may they always remember this night, when the Lord reunited us. May their courage never fail. May their minds be ever sharp. May their weapons be not material only, but also spiritual, and may they remain ever and always friends."

Paul smiled, clasping his cousin by the shoulder and raising his glass once again. "To my heroic Cousin Charles. The 11th Marquess of Haimsbury!"

All echoed the toast, and the meeting then fell into a less formal one, the Londoners huddling with the earl whilst the duke and Charles shared a brandy near the fire.

"Well, lad, how does it feel to be rich and titled?" he asked Sinclair.

The detective laughed. "Truthfully, I do not believe it, but if you say it is so, Uncle, then I must acquiesce. I've had much to drink this night, something I'm not accustomed to, so perhaps you are all just an illusion."

"It is true, lad. All true. When my sister Angela died, I was deemed the closest heir to the Haimsbury title, so it's been in my keeping ever since. I shall have my solicitor draw up all the papers and submit the claim to the crown, but they'll not object. Kepelheim's legal proofs and your uncanny resemblance to Paul speak the truth. And I'll make the transfer to you, probably in the next few weeks, I should think. The estate has five houses, as I recall, several large manufacturing companies, oh, and a nice London mansion that is just the other side of the park behind Queen Anne House."

Paul stepped over for a moment and tapped Charles on the back. "You're a wealthy man, Cousin. I think you might even be richer than I. Perhaps, *you* should pay for Kepelheim's shopping trip for tartans!"

Kepelheim grinned, his large head bobbing into view behind Paul's. "I have a list."

CHAPTER NINETEEN

10, October, 9 a.m.

Matthew Laurence stood before a blazing fire. He and his fellow riders had arrived at the farmhouse within two hours after leaving Drummond Castle, having asked at several neighbouring farms about a large red barn with a bird painted on it. Everyone in the area knew the place, referring to it as White Bird Farm, and some claimed it had spirits that came there on full moon nights. Even before they reached the farm, the men could see the black smoke rising over the hills and smell the stench of death.

Thinking of the wolves and their supernatural leader two nights before, and how the moon had indeed been full, Laurence made every effort to enter the burning buildings, hoping to find at least one of the farm couple still alive, but he found both dead inside the front room of the main house, shot through the head.

As they watched the buildings burn, Laurence feared the news would bring comfort to no one within the circle, but he kept careful notes of all he found regardless. The duke had taught him to pay close attention to detail, and so he did. He noted the wolf tracks that ran circles around the farm, closing in on the smaller of the two cottages. He made copies of strange symbols found on the ground near the small cottage but also inside the blackened skeleton of the large barn. When the fires finally died out, nothing remained unburnt inside either house, but it was clear that something evil had lived here. Perhaps the couple knew the extent of their involvement with supernatural beings, perhaps they did not. The painting on the barn may have been made without either knowing what it stood for, but their behaviour spoke against them. Drugging their guests had been done for some dark purpose. The only question to answer now was why.

Once the examination of the farm was complete, the riders spurred their horses northeastward to the thatched roof cottage once occupied by Solomon Lemuel. As with the farm, this house, also, had been torched, but only the roof had burnt. A rainfall overnight must have extinguished the flames before destroying the stonework, which seemed to have protected some of the interior furnishings.

Near the front door, Laurence found the doctor's body, already decaying and soaked through from the rains. "Stanton, you and Gage start looking through the inside. Parker, you and Anderson check the stables. I want to know every bit of information this man concealed. Bring me all documents you find, along with any clues regarding whoever shot him."

The four riders followed their leader's commands and began the work whilst the butler searched the doctor's body for evidence. The bullet had entered the occipital region of his head cleanly but not exited. The angle of entry made it appear that the shooter had done so from high up on a nearby ridge. "Anderson!" he shouted to the younger of the two men he'd assigned to the stables. "After you finish, take a look up on that hill beyond. Look for any signs of our shooter."

"Yes, sir, Mr. Laurence," the youth replied with a nod of his head.

The butler opened the doctor's jacket and fished inside the pockets: A gold sovereign, a Waterman fountain pen, and a calling card from someone named *Hannibal Alexander, Esq.* His trouser pockets yielded only two peppermint sweets, wrapped in paper, but Laurence took these nonetheless and placed everything into a drawstring bag to deliver to the inner circle. As he stood, he noticed the faint traces of carving on the wooden door to the cottage. The morning sun's angle made it difficult to perceive the precise shape, so the butler used his hand to follow the shallow lines. "Gage, come here!" he called to a tall man with dark hair. "Bring me a bit of the charcoal left from the fire, will you? That tree took some of the heat, perhaps one of the branches will serve."

The rider broke off several bits of charred wood and delivered them to his superior. "Here you are, sir," he said in a thick Scottish accent.

The butler took the charcoal and pointed into the house. "See if there's any paper in Lemuel's desk. Get me several sheets, if you find any."

In a moment, the fellow servant returned with six sheets of cream paper. "Will this do, sir?"

Laurence smiled. "Nicely." He placed a sheet upon one of the carvings and used the charred wood to make a rubbing. After doing this with each of the carved figures, he had used up five of the six sheets. Sighing, Matthew Laurence showed them to his friend. "The duke will not be happy. Anything in the stables?"

"Just the usual, sir. Tack, hay, pitchfork, and an old saddle. Shall we examine all the furnishings?"

"Yes. Everything," Laurence replied. "Someone has tried to obliterate this house already, so this may be our only opportunity. Use the wagon and strip the place if you have to. I want nothing important to remain. Go through his papers, his personals, his dishware if you have to, but I want to know everything there is to know about this traitor!"

11 a.m.

The hybrid creature known to our company as Sir William Trent strolled as if he owned the world. He had always enjoyed his time in Scotland, particularly time spent anywhere close to the Stuarts. How he had come to loathe that noisome family over the years! Were Redwing's plans in his hands alone, he would have torn them all into shreds long ago, using his fangs and claws and reveling in their warm blood, but even he—whose life had been unnaturally extended and augmented—had to bow and scrape to the one they called Prince.

It was late morning. Glasgow's shops teemed with life, and the tall man with a wolf's head cane walked amongst them like a god. Turning to his companion, a beautiful woman with auburn hair and long legs, Trent asked if she might wish to join him in a quest for a bit of jewelry to adorn her throat. "Lorena, my dear, would you prefer emeralds or diamonds?"

The woman's coppery locks gleamed in the morning light, and her green eyes would have rivaled any emerald. Her ruby lips parted slightly as she considered the question. "I should prefer blue diamonds," she said with a tilt of her head toward a jeweler's window.

William laughed heartily, taking her arm. "How perfect! Blue diamonds, indeed! Think yourself a queen, my dear?"

"Perhaps not a queen, as some may wish for, but I am certainly better than many whose blood qualifies them as such."

"Now, now, Lorena, you must take care. Blood is something to be cultivated, to be painstakingly bred, and the eternal kind which we seek, comes only from carefully laid plans and many sacrifices. Personal and otherwise."

"True," she mused, casting her cat eyes toward his seductively. "Tell me truly, William, why do you still yearn for that untutored girl's flesh, when you could share your bed with a woman who has seen the eternal fire?"

"Watch your tongue, my dear, for that untutored girl has bold friends, and they might just tear your pretty flesh from your bones. Or put a bullet in your brain."

"Pah!" she said with a swish of her skirts and a snap of her gloved fingers. "They have no power over us—ah, but, the one she calls Paul. Now, that one, I should love to taste and tutor. His muscular form pleases me, and his mind would bring much to our Prince, would it not?"

As they stood before the window glass, Trent's eyes kept watch on a coach and four bearing the ducal crest of Drummond which had now stopped behind them. "You may get your chance, my dear. I believe that same young man will shortly alight from that carriage. Such foolish men they are to bring her right into my arms. Should I take her now?"

Lorena watched the reflexion in the window, her green eyes fixed on the four passengers who exited the black coach. Two tall men, a woman, and a third man of smaller stature.

"Of course, the other is handsome also. The one called Charles," she said, licking her lips with anticipation. "And he now has power and riches. I wager he would cover my throat with blue diamonds."

"He is not to be touched. He is the chosen one. We require his blood; you know this, Lorena. Breeding takes time, and much effort and many generations of work have gone into Sinclair. We must draw our ever-tightening noose about him by slow and subtle means. When at last the great detective realises he has been trapped, then it will, of course, be too late."

"I shall find a way to separate the chosen one from the others, then. This Paul Stuart is indeed enticing. How his soft hair gleams in the sunlight! He is godlike, is he not?"

"Careful, Lorena," Trent warned. "Keep your speech measured. We must not reveal anything that would lead them to our next move. Normal humans are so very small, are they not?"

She turned around, nearly saying something, but Trent had vanished into a cloud of light. "I must learn that wonderful trick," she said to herself as she crossed the street toward the earl and his party. Next to Paul Stuart, stood the chosen one, a muscular man of similar height and appearance with a wide, dimpled smile and azure eyes. He wore no hat, and his raven hair was cut shorter than the earl's chestnut locks, stopping just at his collar, and it blew slightly in the morning breeze, revealing a broad forehead and a regal brow.

My, but this detective does look like a prince, she thought. *He is handsome indeed and smiles with ease—yet he seldom looks at anyone other than the woman.* The duchess appeared pale and delicate, and she leaned upon the chosen one. *She is weak*, Lorena thought to herself. *Good. Now, to lure her other protector aside so that the noose might tighten further around the chosen pair.*

Setting her foot upon the cobbled street, the tall woman made toward the quartet, secretly removing her hatpin as she did so. As if on cue, a gust of wind blew, and her peacock green hat with the cream feathers and ruby adornment flew several feet away and landed precisely—as though directed—at the earl's feet.

Nicely done, she said in her mind, knowing Trent heard her thoughts. Stepping off the sidewalk, Paul picked up the hat with his unfettered right hand and walked up to her. "Such a beautiful hat would be a great loss," he said, handing it to Lorena.

Though attractive before, the mysterious woman's large green eyes seemed to grow all the more lovely, and her cheeks and lips blossomed into blushes meant to please. "You are so very gallant," she told him. "Whom may I thank for such kindness?"

He bowed slightly and kissed her hand. "I am Paul Stuart."

"Well, Mr. Stuart, you are a white knight in a field of lesser men. I am Lorena MacKey."

"I've relatives that are MacKeys. My mother's cousins in fact."

"From up north, near Glencoe?"

His face opened into a handsome smile, and his cool, blue eyes caught the light, glittering. "Why yes. Don't tell me that your MacKeys also come from there."

"They do," she said, walking back toward the jewelry shop to pull him away from the others.

Involuntarily, Paul followed her, standing soon in the very spot where Trent had stood only a moment before.

"Katherine MacKey is the cousin I knew best," he told her, "but she died during my final term at Oxford. I'm not sure if the family still lives there. So many people have left the old villages now."

"I am one, or rather my parents were," she said, her eyes brazenly fixed on his. "Katherine MacKey is a familiar name. Glencoe is a very small place, so surely she is a cousin to me as well. My parents left before I was born. I was born near London, in fact."

"What brings you to Glasgow?"

"Shopping, well today at least, I am shopping. I actually came to attend a funeral. The mother of a friend from my college days has died, and I've come to support her—but, oh! I am prattling on, and here you are injured! What a foolish doctor I am not to speak first of your condition rather than worrying about a silly hat!"

Paul's head tilted, and his grey-blue eyes rounded in surprise. "You're a doctor? A physician?"

"Guilty of both," she admitted. "I studied at the London Medical School for Women and had the honour to work with Dr. Blackwell. I learnt a great deal from that dear lady, but I find myself drawn to more homeopathic remedies, though my doctoral studies focused around chemistry. I believe the cures and treatments employed by the old wives, as we love to call them, often possess chemical properties that bring true healing. Oh, my good knight, I'm keeping you standing here, and your poor shoulder! A fall? Surely not, for you are most athletic and graceful."

Paul shook his head, then looked back at Elizabeth, who was engaged in conversation with Charles and Kepelheim.

"You're most generous," he said, actually a bit embarrassed. "No, it is a misadventure, nothing more."

She took his right arm and gazed into his face. "You must be more careful." And then looking toward the carriage and the three nearby, she feigned remorse. "Oh, sir, your friends wait upon your return. Do forgive me. I lose my head in the presence of so kind and handsome a gentleman. I must let you return to them to accomplish your shopping."

Paul's mind asked many questions, and though he had often confronted devious females in his service to the circle, he feared harming the gentle heart of this woman with the sparkling green eyes.

"We came to buy cloth for our tailor. He is a friend. May I introduce you?"

She took his right arm firmly and offered a brilliant smile. "I should be honoured, sir."

Paul walked her to the carriage, noting Elizabeth's odd expression as they approached. "Forgive me, Beth. I've been talking with this kind lady, and in so doing, I have abandoned you and my cousin. Allow me to introduce Dr. Lorena MacKey. Dr. MacKey, these are my cousins, Elizabeth, Duchess of Branham, and Charles, Marquess of Haimsbury. And this extraordinary and multi-talented gentleman is Mr. Martin Kepelheim, our tailor and good friend."

Lorena gasped and pretended to be surprised, shaking the tailor's hand but curtseying to both Charles and Elizabeth. "Paul, you did not mention your cousins are so high-born! I am honoured, Your Grace, to meet you. And Lord Haimsbury, it is a genuine pleasure."

Beth smiled, her face still rather pale, but she appeared in a good humour overall. Charles laughed, his eyes bright for the first time in two days.

"My goodness, Dr. MacKey," he said, "you've no reason for any ceremony with me, I assure you. But this gallant gentleman who took such care with your windblown hat is himself the Earl of Aubrey."

Lorena's eyes rounded as she feigned shock. "Oh my! I have made quite a gaffe, have I not? Lord Aubrey, your kindness is now multiplied many times over, and it is clear that I delay your outing. Please, accept my apologies for any impertinence."

Paul held onto her arm, for she had tried to pull away. "No, no, dear lady, we are simple friends on a quest for tartans. Will you not join us? I would put a question to you regarding matters that lie within your domain."

The tailor glanced at Charles, his face serious for a flash of time as if to send a silent warning. "Shall we visit MacCallum's establishment?" he said in a jovial tone. "I know this shop, for I have visited it often, and I'm eager to spend Lord Haimsbury's newfound coin on expensive fabrics for his many, new suits."

Sinclair laughed heartily and put his arm through Elizabeth's, his steps leading the group of now five toward MacCallum's. "I do not yet have access to my newfound wealth," he warned Kepelheim, "but if MacCallum's management will permit me, I shall open an account."

"Put it on our uncle's account, Charles," Paul suggested. "His people will sort it out later. In fact, Kepelheim, I shall put in an order for a new formal jacket."

"I am keeping it all in my enormous head," Kepelheim answered with a laugh. "And perhaps three or four new shirts and a waistcoat. Your styles could use an update."

Paul laughed easily, and he felt lighter than he had in days, yet his eyes swept constantly over the taller heads that bobbed along the busy street. William Trent had been seen, and they had come to confront him, rather than wait like so much prey. Following Galton and Palmer's departure that morning, the earl had announced his intention to go to Glasgow alone to search for Trent, whilst Elizabeth and Charles remained behind to continue their recovery. However, Charles had insisted that Paul should remain with her for the same reason. Finally, Elizabeth had settled the argument saying both should go, and since neither man would permit her to remain without accompaniment by one, she would instead go with them, for surely her presence in Glasgow would be the perfect bait to draw the wolf from his lair.

As they walked, Charles, too, scanned the faces around them, but his mind was ever on Elizabeth. What did she remember of the night in the cottage? Had she, too, experienced a dream? He must speak to her, and soon, but it would require privacy, which now they sorely lacked.

Turning into MacCallum's Emporium, Kepelheim shot toward a display of silks and tweeds, motioning to the floorwalker for service. Charles found the experience somewhat new, so he let the seasoned tailor make all the choices, exchanging small talk with Beth as they moved about the main floor of the three-storey mercantile.

"It reminds me of a smaller Harrods," he said as they passed by a display of handkerchiefs and cufflinks. "I shall miss the simplicity of being a mere policeman."

"Will you?" she asked, turning her eyes to his worried frown. "You keep a secret, Captain. Will you not share it with me, your ardent admirer?"

He paused, pretending to show interest in a long glass display case filled with fine watches and other men's jewelry. "Shall I buy a new watch, Duchess? A timepiece to wear upon a fine chain when we share an evening at Covent Garden?"

"You tease me now," she complained, a slight pout crossing her lips. "I ask a sincere question out of love and concern, and you toss it aside like it matters not. Covent Garden indeed!"

He paused, looking intently into her eyes, her hand in his. "Not here. Not now. We must talk, Beth, and soon, but not until we are safely alone. Will you allow me that?"

Her face paled. "Yes, forgive me. I had not thought. You are worried, then?"

"Desperately worried for you, my love," he whispered and kissed her forehead. "Now, help me to select a watch, and let us engrave it."

"Only if I may compose the message," she whispered in return. Then looking over at the earl and his new companion, she wondered aloud. "Tell me, Charles, what impression do you have of this lady doctor?"

"Is it her profession or her sex which most troubles you, Beth?"

She did not even so much as smile. "Neither and both, I suppose. It is my old sense of dread and all that has happened these past few days. He does seem to find her to be amusing, though, don't you think? No, I am not jealous, or at least I think I am not. Paul has shown no such dark sentiments concerning my friendship with you."

Sinclair leaned in and whispered into her ear, "Ours, my dear Princess, is far more than a friendship, and we both know it to be so."

She paused, her eyes still as she processed this in her mind. "Yes, I know."

He kissed her cheek again and laughed—a trifle strained, but a laugh nonetheless—selecting an eighteen karat gold Sir John Bennett that featured a rampant lion on the case, and he then passed it to their attendant.

Beth held up her hand. "Sir, might I write a message on a slip of paper for engraving inside that handsome watch?"

Nodding, the attendant gave her a small notepad and pencil, and she scribbled something, handing it quickly to the gentleman so that Charles could not see it. "A surprise," she said with a mysterious smile. "Thank you, sir," she added as the man took the watch and note to a back room for engraving. "Oh, and, sir," she called, causing the clerk to turn. "When finished, you may deliver it to Drummond Castle, to the attention of Lord Haimsbury."

"May I not see what is to be memorialized upon a timepiece to which I must refer hourly?" he asked with a dimpled grin.

"You may, when the memorial is forever etched upon it, but not before. Now, since our tailor is occupied, and Paul is as well, perhaps you and I may take tea and enjoy a few moments to ourselves."

Charles had not expected an opportunity so soon, but he nodded and told Kepelheim where they were headed, which was a tea room just opposite the emporium, and they walked out the door and into a conversation which would change the course of all their lives.

Paul watched as Charles left the shop with Elizabeth on his arm, knowing her to be safe in Sinclair's company, but wishing she did not care quite so much for the charming marquess. Distracted by these thoughts, he found himself hearing only half of what the lady doctor was saying.

"Forgive me," he said, realising his rudeness. "Come, let us sit over there, shall we, Dr. MacKey? Soft chairs are more suited to a gentle lady than standing too long at a shop counter."

"My dear, Lord Aubrey, I assure you that my legs have endured much standing during countless dissections and endless hours of tending to patients. I am made of stern stuff. And unlike titled ladies of leisure, I do not break easily."

"Of course, and again I beg your forgiveness," he said. "Old rules are quickly changing, and women take up new places in society. But if you would sit with me for a moment, it would allow my shoulder to rest, and my mind to seek answers which you may have."

"Oh! Of course," she answered, fluttering her eyelids and tilting her head to catch the best light. "Please, we will sit. I am the one who is rude, and my duty is to heal not harm. Please, let us rest your poor wounded shoulder. When did it happen? Are you under care?"

He helped her to settle into one of several tufted leather chairs in a small lounge, designed to allow gentlemen to try on boots or drink and smoke whilst valets filled shopping lists. "I have seen a doctor, but I am uncertain as to how well he tended me. He'd been a good friend to my family for many years, but his mind was fixed upon other things in his final hours, and now he is dead, I'm afraid."

She touched his hand, leaning in to offer comfort, confident that she had already sunk one claw into his tender heart if so careful an enemy shared news of Lemuel's betrayal with her this soon, though only to hint at it. "A family friend, too? I am very sorry, Lord Aubrey. Death is all about us, and he calls sometimes when we expect it least. Did your physician leave family to mourn?"

"No. He was a bachelor, or so I believe. Truly, I begin to wonder if I knew him at all, but isn't that the way with people sometimes? Your sympathies do you credit, Doctor, and I suspect they come more from a tender heart than from a practised mind. My question is regarding a medicine I have recently become aware of—a herb actually, one that grows wild upon the heaths."

"Do you know its name?" she asked.

"Our housekeeper called it Devil's Cherries, I think."

She wanted to smile, for Lorena knew now that she had him, but she must appear curious for merely medical reasons. "Yes, I know that herb. It can be very dangerous if used in improper combinations or if overused. It is also called belladonna, and its therapeutic effects are well known though not well studied. Why, may I ask, do you wish to know? Surely, you have not eaten these berries. They are sweet, but they can be poisonous!"

Fear crossed his face. "Poisonous? I didn't know that. But, if they have positive effects, is it the mixture or the proportion that makes the difference?"

"Well, my good Lord Aubrey, if you—a strong and virile man—ate of these plants, you might experience mild hallucinations, nausea, and even cardiac difficulties—heart problems, I mean. Did someone in your household consume these? I can come take a look, since your physician has so suddenly passed away."

"That would be most appreciated. In fact, it was accidental, I believe. Is that possible? A tea made from local leaves?"

"No one with any experience would brew a tea with belladonna leaves. Not intentionally," she assured him. "Now, it is possible, I suppose, that a child might pick these leaves or berries without recognising the danger and add them to a basket of leaves for making a poultice or a remedial tea, but a knowledgeable nurse would never use them. Is this person now unwell? If so, Lord Aubrey, you must not delay administering the antidote!"

"There is an antidote?" he asked.

"It is not well known, but I have some in my medical bag at my hotel. It is a wonderful powder made from an African bean, found only to my knowledge in Old Calabar. When did this occur and to whom? Surely not you! Tell me it was not you!"

"No, not to me, but to someone on our staff," he lied, suddenly wondering why he would reveal such a thing to a total stranger, even one with medical experience. "He has recovered now. I only wondered what to do should it occur again. Our housekeeper, who shares your interest in herbs, is a skilled nurse, and she kept watch over our imprudent patient. Hearing your explanation, I wonder that he was not much more ill. It is a relief, and I shall instruct my uncle's gardeners to remove these plants at once."

"That would be wise," she said, inwardly pleased. "You spoke of your uncle earlier. Is he in Glasgow then? For I know that your home, Lord Aubrey, lies closer to that of my parents and grandparents. Wait—don't tell me, for I believe I know! Was not your mother, the late Countess, sister to the Duke of Drummond?"

"She was, and yes, we are guests of my uncle whilst on our shopping tour. My cousin has only recently inherited his title, and I am helping him to rediscover his Scottish roots."

"How generous of you," she purred. "And it strikes me now that there is a strong resemblance betwixt you and your newly titled cousin. You are both quite tall and, if I may be so bold, also quite handsome. Your hair is much lighter, though, and your eyes are more like a clear lake, whilst Lord Haimsbury's, from what I can recall, hint of the sea. I find yours the more pleasing, if I am not being too forward."

What was it about this woman that both delighted and alarmed Paul? He was trying to keep a clear head, but her emerald eyes had him enchanted. "You are too kind by far. You said your medical bag is at your hotel? Where, if I may ask, are you staying?"

"Cranston's," she replied. "It is quite nice, and their tea room has the most delicious pastries. I fear my figure will not survive if I remain there much longer."

"I know that hotel," he said. "And your figure could not be more perfect," he heard himself say. "May I call on you tomorrow?"

She managed a pretty blush, followed by a coquettish smile. "I shall look forward to it, Lord Aubrey."

He rose, for his mind now wondered about Elizabeth, and his instincts nagged him to engage in the task at hand: finding William Trent before he found them. "Ten tomorrow morning?" he asked.

"That would be a bit early. I have the funeral at nine. May I meet you for luncheon?"

"Is one tomorrow afternoon better?"

"Perfect," she answered. "I shall be happy to continue our medical discussions. You are having your shoulder tended now, I hope."

"Yes," he answered, suddenly realising the seductive danger of such beautiful hands upon his bare skin. He pushed the imagery away as he kissed her hand. "If you will excuse me for now, I must make certain our tailor friend has not bought out the entire shop."

She laughed, inwardly forced but subtle enough to fool a willing victim. As he walked away, she withdrew a mirrored compact from her purse and pretended to check her face. Behind, she could see the shadow of William Trent and one other—their great Prince—such an honour to have him near!

Well done, her prince told her, the deep, silken voice reaching into her mind. *Very well done, Lorena, but do not press. If he suspects, you will lose your chance with the earl.*

She closed the compact, and returned it to her bag. Inside, she saw her weapons: a small derringer which served when all else failed and, alongside it, the belladonna and opium mixture, which she had secretly infused into a kettle of water, two nights past. She hoped to have no need of it where the earl was concerned. His magnificent body would be so nice to manipulate, and she preferred her prey fully conscious and screaming.

The Crown Luncheon Room sat directly across from MacCallum's on Argyle Street, and it was to a small, private room that Charles had taken Elizabeth. She seemed preoccupied, looking around her as they shared tea together.

"So many people," she said.

"Which is why I asked for a private room, Princess. What troubles you?"

"It strikes me that William might suddenly appear from any-where. Foolish, I know, but my earlier courage begins to fail me, Charles."

He reached for her hand, his eyes on hers. "Look then at me, Beth, and trust in my guardianship. I will not permit him to harm you again—not ever. You know that, surely?"

"I do know it, but sometimes I wonder if he is not more than a man—more than…" her voice trailed off, and he could see dark thoughts cloud her sweet face. "You wished to speak to me more privately. This quiet room may be our best chance, but what is it you wish to say that cannot be overheard, Charles?"

"Perhaps, I wish only to declare my love for you," he said ca-sually, wondering if his true purpose for speaking to her might not be better postponed for a time when her thoughts were not fixed upon fear.

"And is that your declaration?"

Charles nearly said all that was in his heart, but so much he'd learnt from the meeting with the inner circle members now made him wonder if perhaps his love was truly what she most needed. It certainly was all that he needed, but Redwing clearly *wanted* a match between himself and Elizabeth. Would marrying Paul keep her safer?

"You know my feelings," he said, gazing at the earl's ring upon her hand.

"I do—or I believe I do. Now that you and Paul have become friends and even cousins, have your feelings altered?"

"If anything, my darling friend, my beautiful Princess, my feel-ings have grown deeper roots than ever I'd thought possible. Beth, I would marry you today, now, if you would have me. Do you not know that? Yet, I am all too aware that your intent has always been to call my newfound cousin your husband. If that is your true desire, then I shall find a way to be happy for you both, though I would never find love again."

She grew silent for a moment, twisting the ring as if it burnt her skin. "If I said yes, that I would marry you, what then? Could you face your new cousin? Could I? And yet, Charles, there is grow-ing within my mind, something new—a dreamy connexion which I am unable to understand." Her lower lip trembled, a tiny move-ment he'd seen so many times before, and he longed to comfort her.

"Charles, this strange memory will consume me, if I do not reconcile its truths. It is to my shame that I cannot tell you. You would think me mad."

Her hands were twisting now, as if some horrid thought plagued her. Sinclair took her hands to help calm her, noticing that they trembled. "My darling, you can tell me anything. Anything. If it helps, I, too, have something to tell which most would say makes me mad."

"Did you hear anything, Charles? That night in the cottage?"

"I thought you had no memory of that night," he said, for she had denied knowing much of that wild night's dangers. He had hoped the drugs had made this true.

"That is what I told everyone at the castle, for I am not sure that it was not all a dream. I do remember you, carrying me in your arms and laying me upon a soft bed. And I think a woman spoke, and she gave us tea. She called me your wife. But surely that was a dream, and in many ways, a wonderful one."

"If I said it was not a dream, would it cause you to worry?"

"Are you saying it happened?" she whispered, her eyes wide.

He nodded, keeping careful watch on her face. "It did. Elizabeth, if you can bear it, I shall tell you all that occurred that night, beginning with our arrival at Drummond Castle."

She thought about this for a moment, her breath becoming more rapid, but she squeezed his hand and nodded. "Yes. I think I can bear it, if you are with me. Tell me, Charles. Please."

"Very well, but I shall stop if I see it distresses you. Our balloon escape had left both you and Paul exhausted, and I believe your mind had been forced to recall things beneath the abbey—in that devilish place—that you have long tried to forget. Your foot, too, pained you and drained your energies, and Paul's wound continued to bleed, which I know terrified you."

She nodded once more. "Yes, it did. Though, to be honest, I remember very little of our mad journey. I do recall Mr. Reid showing me landscapes that only a hawk or an eagle might see. So magnificent, yet dizzying!"

"Yes, you often complained that the heights went to your head, but they did so to mine as well. I'm no aeronaut, I fear. Reid is more acclimated to that rarified air than I, nor shall I ever be. He is a brave and faithful friend, and I look forward to buying him his own balloon one day, now that I can afford it."

She smiled. "A just and well-earned reward. But what after?"

"We came to the castle late on the next evening, and your grand-father had marshalled his forces to meet us at our landing, and they conveyed us all to our rooms that night. Once he knew that you and Paul were being tended, and that Paul's injuries did not threaten his life, James gave me my reading assignment: a box filled with papers that Mr. Kepelheim had collected revealing my true history and con-nexion to James and to Paul—and even to you, my darling. I cannot tell you how this worked on my mind, Beth! And bless the Lord's provision that it did, for it was because I could not rest, but thought to walk that night, that I discovered Dr. Lemuel's malicious intent."

"I remember nothing of that," she said. "Unless a vague notion of movement in a carriage counts as memory."

"I wish you had no memory at all of his deeds, darling. Lemuel was blackmailed into abducting you, and I believe his purpose was to hand you over to William or to his agent. Paul wanted to go after you, but his injury had made him weak, so James—the dear man whom I may now call Uncle—put me upon his swiftest horse and sent me into the night to rescue you."

"My Captain," she said softly as she clutched his hands. "You are so brave! And yet, I fear when you risk your life."

"Your life, little one, is a life worth the risk," he replied, kiss-ing her small hand. "But though I have always felt at home in the saddle, the ride was a wild one. The full moon shone upon the road as I followed the carriage's dusty path, eventually catching it thanks to Clever Girl's sure-footedness and unfailing heart. And when I confronted him at last, Lemuel confessed his guilt, believing his complicity somehow sensible, given his sorry state and secrets. You need not know them, just know that he meant to murder me and hand you to some unseen person. But as I stood there, not ten feet from the man's front door, someone else shot him! And he fell at my feet, dead."

"What?" she exclaimed, keeping her voice as low as possible, but believing she now knew why he had wanted to conduct this con-versation in private. "Did you see the assassin?"

"I did not. With this killer nearby, I realised our only chance was to flee, but the moon hid within the cloudy night, and I lost all sense of direction. You could not walk, and I feared taking you into unknown paths with my poor sense of our location. Knowing we might not make it back to the castle before the same or even another marksman found us, I thought it better to return Clever Girl to the duke as our messenger, so I sent her flying over the hills. I then took charge of the doctor's horses and carriage, turning back toward what I hoped would be our salvation. I was completely out of my depth. The heaths and hillsides all look alike to my London eyes, and with no moon to guide me, nor seeing the castle in the distance, I must have turned left when it was right I had wanted, and we became entirely lost."

"Oh, my poor Captain! How terrifying for you!"

"I am only glad you were not awake to see my face, for I was terrified, Beth, for you. I had no idea what drug Lemuel had given you, or if you would ever awaken again. I only thought to find the castle and hope. And then, ahead, I saw a farm with a small light burning. I stopped, knocked upon that weathered door, and found—or so I had thought—a refuge from the night. The couple welcomed us, once we told them we were guests at the castle, and the husband told me we had strayed far to the south. He promised to draw me a map the next morning at dawning, and he and his wife offered to let us sleep in their son's small cottage until then. The horses had gone as far as they could without rest, so I had no choice but to accept. The wife, when she saw your injury, understood why you had fainted, or so I had told her. She saw, too, the ring upon your hand—and seeing it and perhaps my honest emotions—she asked if we were newlyweds. I told her yes, Beth. And though the idea of it is more than welcome to my heart, I did it so that they would permit us to remain together. I would not have allowed you to sleep unguarded. Not then. Not that night. Not ever, if my fondest wishes could come true."

She closed her eyes, her hands still in his own, and those slender hands had begun to tremble once more.

"Shall I go on? I fear this drags at your brave heart, little one."

She found her composure and nodded. "Yes. Speak until I stop you. I think I know where this is headed, and Charles, I am suddenly very afraid."

"Then, dearest, let us wait until you are stronger."

"No. I must know. I must have these misty memories verified."

He shook his head. "No, not now. We shall speak more of this later, darling. We have already left our friends too long without us, and it may not be wise to leave Paul unguarded."

Her chin flew up, her eyes moist, but her expression defiant. "Do you mean William? Do you think he would—would hurt him, here, in so public a venue?"

"I think a devious man would use softer ammunition to inflict new wounds. I hope I am wrong, but I find it curious that this Dr. MacKey has so conveniently come into his life, and that she has already drawn him from your side. I do not say this to alarm you, for Paul's heart and affections where you are concerned are ever true, but I have seen many evil women in my line of work, and that one wears the look of a predator."

She considered this, and he could see that his words troubled her. "Yes, she does bear that look. In truth, my experience with such women is rather sparse. My entire life has been spent with family, but there is something unsettling about this doctor. Hers is a look I have seen before, though I cannot recall where. Very well. We shall postpone our conversation for now, but promise me that you will return to it as soon as possible, Charles, for it grows upon me, this memory—this strange dream."

"Tonight then," he said. "If you will give me your hand after supper, we shall take a walk in the moonlight and speak more."

"Yes," she agreed. "Tonight."

CHAPTER TWENTY

Evening fell at the castle, and the duke was glad to see his nephew's wound healing nicely and colour returning to the young earl's face. The company had gathered for supper, and the new marquess sat opposite Elizabeth with Kepelheim to his right. The earl sat beside the duchess with the duke at the head. A muscular young man named Algernon Dryden had also joined the castle's guest list along with Malcolm Risling, who sat to Kepelheim's right near the duke with Dryden opposite twixt the earl and Drummond. Both men had served as agents with the circle for over a decade. Dryden was their expert on munitions and artillery but also served as Kepelheim's assistant, whilst Risling provided expertise in ancient languages and semiotics. Dryden and Risling had arrived just after noon, and both listened attentively to the conversation.

"Any sign of Trent?" Drummond asked as he sliced into that evening's roast beef and rosemary potatoes.

"No, sir," Sinclair replied. "But it would have been foolish for him to show himself in the open. It makes me wonder if there was another reason that we were lured to Glasgow this morning," he added, glancing at his cousin.

Paul had said little, but his cousin's suggestion that their trip to the city had been for a darker purpose disturbed him. "I fear that Charles may be right," he replied with a frown. "We met someone there, and though she seemed harmless enough, a serendipitous meeting with a physician with ties to Briarcliff now strikes me as contrived."

The duke's dark brows shot up. "A woman doctor, you say? Now that is interesting. Who is she and how is she tied to your estate?"

"Assuming she was honest, her family is from Glencoe."

"And her name?" the duke pressed.

Beth had been quiet since their return, and Sinclair noticed she ate little. "Is everything all right, Princess?" he asked her.

Elizabeth took a sip of water. "Yes, I suppose so. Grandfather, this woman calls herself Lorena MacKey, and she made quite an impression on my cousin. Did she not, Lord Aubrey?"

The earl's face pinked slightly with embarrassment. "She struck me as singular," he said vaguely.

"Singularly attractive?" the duke asked.

"Singularly educated," Aubrey replied quickly. "Anyone else ready for wine?" he asked, rising suddenly.

Beth stood as well, setting aside the serviette she'd held on her lap, but her balance shifted strangely as she pushed the chair out of her way, and she nearly fell. The earl caught her in his arms, and everyone rushed to make sure she had not been injured. "Darling, are you ill?" Aubrey asked. "You should not have gone into town this morning. It's too soon after all that's happened."

She seemed unsteady, and he gently assisted her back into the chair. Her eyes were unfocused, and Sinclair knelt beside her. He touched her face. "You're warm, Beth. I fear our cousin is right. You should not have gone shopping this morning. Perhaps, you should retire early."

"No, I'm all right," she argued. "Just a slight headache. I am sorry, Mr. Dryden, Mr. Risling. I am not ordinarily such poor company."

The artillery expert bowed, for all the men now stood politely. "You are as beautiful and gentle as ever, Duchess. But if you have been ill, then..."

"Not ill," she said. "As I'm sure my grandfather has told you, it has been an adventurous few days. Something I'm not as accustomed to as you brave men of the circle. If you will excuse me, I shall follow Charles's advice and see if a short nap might help. Do forgive me for ruining supper, Grandfather."

"Never ruined, Princess. Not with your beauty to enhance the meal." The duke called for Laurence to fetch Mrs. MacAnder, who entered now with her medical bag. "Mrs. Mac, give our girl a once-over, won't you? Charles, do you mind helping Beth upstairs?"

"I can walk on my own," the duchess protested, but Sinclair put his arm around her nonetheless.

"Lean on me," he whispered sweetly. "I shan't be long," he told the men. "I look forward to hearing the latest news from London," he finished as he led Beth out of the dining hall.

MacAnder followed, her hand on the duchess's small wrist as they walked. "Your pulse is a bit quick, my lady," she said. "I noticed you'd eaten very little. Was the food not to your liking? I can have Mrs. Calhoun make up something else, if you wish."

"I'm just not hungry, Mrs. MacAnder. We had a rather large luncheon in Glasgow."

Charles kept his arm around her waist as they navigated the long hallways toward the main staircase. "It's true," he explained. "We enjoyed a delicious meal at a place called The Royal."

The housekeeper's face widened into a grin. "Aye, that's the place to eat if you're a man who likes good, stout food. I imagine many o' your policemen friends would enjoy Mrs. McGregor's fare, sir. Is she still the manageress?"

"She is," Sinclair answered as they neared the staircase. "In fact, we dined near a table of her regulars. A party of veterans from the Glasgow Highlanders regiment. Riflemen who served alongside the Royal Scots Fusiliers at the Battle of Inkerman in '54. Brave men."

"Aye, I know that group of men and that battle. I was there with my late husband and the duke, though he had to leave soon after."

"Really?" the detective asked. "I'd hear your stories when you've the time, Mrs. Mac. Beth, can you climb? I could carry you, if you wish."

Her colour had improved a bit, but she still seemed unsteady on her feet. MacAnder answered for the duchess. "I'd not want her to fall, sir. Do you mind?"

"Not in the least," he said, lifting her easily into his strong arms and mounting the steps. She'd chosen to leave her drawing room sleeping quarters in favour of the small apartment she used as her own whenever at the castle.

"I'm in here," the duchess said as Sinclair reached the first door beyond the landing. "I think Grandfather's put you in the apartment opposite. My father's former rooms."

"Yes, so he said," the marquess answered as he followed the housekeeper into the beautiful suite.

"Sir, if you wouldn't mind carrying her into the bedchamber," MacAnder asked. "It would make it easier, just in case. Once there, I'll look after her. My lady, your foot looks a bit swollen still. I'll make you a mugwort and potato poultice. It should ease up soon after."

He carried her through the connected private parlour and set her upon the bed. "There you are. Mrs. MacAnder, would you mind fetching the duchess a pitcher of cool water?"

The housekeeper smiled knowingly. "I'd be happy to do so, Lord Haimsbury. And I'll need to find my dried herbs, too—to add a tincture to the poultice you know. I might be away for fifteen minutes or more."

Charles waited until the good-hearted housekeeper had left them and then he sat beside Elizabeth on the bed. "She's a kind woman. Beth, is it something I've said?" he asked, taking her hand gently. "You've not been yourself since we left the tea room. I fear that our conversation upset you."

She sat back against the cushions of the bed, and he could see tears playing at the corners of her dark eyes. "No, Charles, you've said nothing wrong. It really is a headache, and I suppose the foot is beginning to bother me. That's why I nearly stumbled at the table downstairs. A little sleep will help."

"Darling, if you're not feeling well, we could postpone our talk until tomorrow. You've been through much the past few days, and I don't wish to push you too quickly."

She looked worn out, and her eyes appeared weary to Sinclair, but she offered a genuine smile nonetheless. "Truly, Charles, it's only a mild headache. Nothing more. Let me rest for an hour, and then after, you and I can view the loch from the rose gardens along the western cliff."

He longed to kiss her properly, but chose instead to kiss her fingertips lightly. "One hour," he whispered. "An eternity. Rest now, my darling. But if you change your mind..."

"I won't. And I shall be counting the minutes of that hour, even as I dream, Captain."

He kissed her hands and left, shutting the door and tripping happily down the staircase, the taste of her skin lingering upon his lips as they widened into a delighted smile. As he made the turn toward the main flight of the case, he found the duke waiting, concern blazed across his tanned features. "She's fine, sir," he assured his uncle. "Her foot's bothering her, that's all, but she's in good hands."

"I can see that," Drummond replied with a wink. "We're all getting together for a drink, lad. Come, join us. She'll keep."

The detective offered his uncle a broad smile. "But will I?" he asked, noting a bright twinkle in Drummond's eye. "So, is this an informal meeting?"

"It is, if you've the time," his uncle said, perceptively. "I've told Paul and the others to meet us in my library. I'd like us all to go over Matthew Laurence's findings together, and Risling's brought some items from London he wants us to see."

As their number was small, the duke chose to convene the meeting in a small parlour just off the private library, where his Irish setters, Molly and Max, slept near the fire. "Come in, Charles," he said to Sinclair. "Paul, fetch us all some brandy, won't you?"

The earl located several filled crystal decanters in a nearby cabinet and poured four glasses of the brandy and then a sherry into a fifth. "Risling, I remember that you like claret, but this brandy is superb. And I know our armoury specialist has never met a sherry he doesn't like. Particularly that brunette one in Marseilles. Oh, wait, I suppose our tailor will also want some," he said as the door opened. "Martin, brandy or sherry?"

"Do you have any more of that lovely port we had last night?" he asked the duke, who nodded. "Oh, good. Then, I shall be happy to have more of that, Lord Aubrey. It has such a lovely bouquet. Is our butler joining us?"

The earl searched through the large liquor cabinet, turning at this question. "I think Matthew wanted to gather up all the evidence he collected this morning. From what he's told me, I fear our trust in Lemuel was far more foolish than previous thought. James, I don't see any of the port. Shall I go to the cellars?"

Charles had been watching the earl curiously, and he now began to laugh. "My, my, Cousin! This is all too much! To think that a peer of the realm is happy to serve as wine steward is quite more than I'd ever expected when I first entered your world ten years ago."

"I'm not sure how to take that," Aubrey complained with a mischievous grin. "I'm quite good at choosing wines, actually. I worked in a Spanish vineyard once as part of an assignment. You'd be surprised at how accomplished I am at discerning the chemical properties of fermentation."

"I've no doubt about it now," Charles replied with a smile. "But I must tell you that when I first learnt that the young girl in my keeping was in fact a duchess and the 'Paul' fellow she kept asking for a viscount, I had quite a different picture of you in my mind."

Aubrey handed the glasses to the men and then sat. "Martin, I've given you sherry for now. Once my cousin is finished telling us all how peerage classes should behave, I shall fetch you that port, though I'll probably have to decant it first."

At this last, Sinclair burst into loud laughter, and soon all the men laughed so hard that they wiped their eyes of happy tears. "Truly, Cousin," the marquess told them, "I am so very glad that the Stuart men are nothing like how I pictured you. I've met far too many peers in my life, most of them lower ranking, of course, but invariably they are pig-headed and self-absorbed. Many believe themselves above the law, and most see Whitechapel as a recreational extension of their men's clubs, rather than home to hard-working individuals who unload their expensive wines, Argentinian beef, Indian spices, and Spanish fruits. The docks of the east end feed the fatted cats of the west, and they receive very little compensation for it. I feared Beth's family would be the same, and I am so very happy you are the opposite. It makes me feel as if I can actually fit into this family. Truly, Paul, James. I could not be happier."

The men clinked glasses, and the duke raised his high. "I shall toast to that, Nephew. To never being a fatted west end cat."

Sinclair began to laugh once more, and he raised his own glass. "And to knowing the chemical properties of fermentation. No doubt that long mop of hair is part of the secret."

The earl swiped at his auburn locks, pulling the hair behind his right ear. "The ladies love it, Cousin," he said with a wink. "Is that not true, Malcolm?"

Risling, who wore his hair longer than even the earl's, shook his head. "Leave me out of this, else I shall have to relate the tale of the amorous cow, and I doubt you want that known, Aubrey."

The earl's left brow arched. "You would do that? Well, despite my friend's imputations, Charles, women find it quite romantic. Very Jane Austen. You should give it a try."

Charles sat forward, ready to challenge this, but the door opened again, and the butler entered, carrying a large canvas bag, which he set next to the duke. "Sir, forgive me for interrupting, but if you and your guests are ready, I shall be happy to offer my report."

The duke looked at his nephews. "Paul, why don't you pour our agent a glass of brandy?"

Laurence stepped forward. "Please, sir, allow me to do that."

Drummond stood, placing a hand on Matthew's arm. "Sit down, son. Right now, you're a circle member not a butler. We're all equal in this service."

Aubrey poured the young man a drink and set it before the startled servant. "James is right, Matthew. Now, what did you find? Were you able to locate the farm?"

The butler nodded toward the canvas bag. "The items we uncovered are all inside there, sirs. The farm, I fear, is a loss for the most part. Both the Campbells were dead. Shot. And the barn and other buildings set afire."

Charles picked up the bag, opened it, and began to explore the contents. "Shot at close range?" he asked. The butler nodded. "Executed, no doubt," the detective continued. "Just as Lemuel was executed. Redwing is eliminating any and all evidence, which means they fear that we might discover their ultimate aim in all this. The Campbells seemed genuinely kind, but clearly they were complicit in some way. Did you find anything else at the farm?"

"We found wolf tracks, Lord Haimsbury. Running circles all 'round the smaller of the two cottages. And strange symbols written upon the exterior walls and beneath the windows. The fire obliterated most of it, but I've drawn what I could discern from the remains."

He handed the marquess a small book containing his notes and sketches. Charles thumbed through the pages and stopped at one with several pencil drawings, his brows pinching together as he concentrated. "These remind me of old cuneiform texts I studied back at Cambridge."

The tailor reached across, setting his glass of sherry to one side. "May I?" he asked. Sinclair handed him the book, and Kepelheim peered at the curious writing. "Oh, yes, I've seen their like as well. You have a good eye, Superintendent—I call you that, of course, for we now follow the skein of crime, do we not? These are indeed cuneiform, and whilst I know a bit, I am no expert. Malcolm, what do you think? Have you come across these in your studies?"

Risling took the pages, and held them up to the light. "I've seen all of these at one time or another as symbols upon stele and a variety of jar seals. Mr. Laurence, where did you find this one?" he asked, pointing to a star-shaped sketch.

"Beneath the window of the smaller cottage, sir. There were many wolf tracks leading up to the window and away from it, mixed in with bootmarks. Small bootmarks."

"A child's?" Sinclair asked.

"Perhaps, sir," he answered.

"A woman's, then?" Sinclair suggested, and the Londoner's face grew serious.

Risling continued. "If the bootmark is a woman's, then this takes on a very interesting aspect. This symbol is a rare one, and I've seen it several times, but most recently just today. And you won't like hearing where I found it, gentlemen."

The pencil drawing showed an eight-pointed star within a circle, centred by a circumpunct. "Where was that, Risling?" the duke asked.

"Here, sir."

The others gasped, but Charles did not seem surprised. "Let me guess," the detective said. "You saw it at the southwestern entrance."

Malcolm Risling's mouth opened in shock. "Why yes! How did you know, sir?"

"Because that is the door from which the doctor abducted Beth, most likely because no one would wonder why he parked his carriage there, since Beth's temporary invalid room lay within that wing. Also, the guards kept watch upon the front entry but not the southwest, I noticed."

"No longer," the duke assured them. "We're adding twenty extra men from Briarcliff. I wired Paul's butler Henry earlier today, and they arrive tomorrow morning. The entire estate will be watched now."

"Good," Sinclair remarked. "I imagine any group of men under the earl's tutelage will be formidable indeed. Despite his hair." Everyone laughed, and the detective smiled. "But to return to our speculation, if this symbol is part of some ritual, then perhaps Lemuel thought to protect his mission by inscribing the image on the ground. I assume that's where you found it."

"Yes, it is," Risling replied. "Superintendent, your intuition is matchless. Your reputation as a consummate investigator is well-earned. Yes, after we arrived, the duke told us about the abduction, so when I had a moment, I walked through that area to see if there might be any images. Redwing often uses these ancient symbols, as you say, Lord Haimsbury, to protect a mission or enhance its power."

"What does this image indicate?" Sinclair asked. "I fear my experience with semiotics at Cambridge was scant."

"It is a representation of the goddess," Risling said simply.

"Which goddess is that?" the duke asked.

"That is an excellent question, sir. There are many names for the same fallen entity, but also many individual goddesses. This particular symbol is a call to one that has been worshiped for as long as mankind has walked upon the earth. She's been called Ishtar, Astarte, Anath, Isis, Venus, Aphrodite, even Diana. She may also be the same entity the Celts worshiped as the Morrigen, though the connexion is slender. Some call her a goddess of war, but others of love. It is difficult to say what the purpose was here, but since it is well known that our battle is against Redwing, I doubt if it is war, for that aspect is ongoing."

"Love then," Drummond said, glancing at Sinclair. "And if it is love, then how are we to interpret this?"

Risling shrugged. "I'd imagine, since from what you've told me, the intent was to force our new marquess and the duchess together, that the purpose lies beyond love."

"What do you mean?" Sinclair asked, casting a glance at his cousin. "What lies beyond love?"

Malcolm finished his sherry with a sigh. "You're right, Lord Aubrey. This is very good. Perhaps one of the best I've had in many a year. Sherries are sweet and seductive, my lords, as is the goddess to her pagan acolytes. Her idea of love is hardly what Miss Austen would consider romantic. It is one of seduction, control, and power. Redwing has but one goal that relates in any way. They desire an heir to inhabit, one born from the line of the twins. That is their purpose for using this symbol. Monday night was a full moon. It was, in fact, a specific full moon known to the pagans and witches as a 'blood moon'. Its power when associated with the goddess assures fertility and a son to those who conjoin beneath her light. Redwing not only wishes for our duchess to marry a particular cousin, but they wish to ensure that a son is born of that union. I believe this symbol was meant to ensure their success."

Aubrey's good humour faded completely, and he jumped to his feet, pacing. "Fertility?" he asked, glaring at Charles. "Blood moon? Is there more to this tale than we know? Why would this ritual involve fertility?"

Sinclair felt like vomiting. "I cannot say," he whispered, his eyes riveted to the duke's face. "Both Elizabeth and I had ingested some hallucinogenic agent, but if that symbol was made by Lemuel, then it supports his connexion to Redwing. As I told you after Mr. Laurence rescued us and returned us here, my failure to protect Beth is my own. I take all blame. All of it. If anything happened whilst she and I were drugged, then that also is my fault."

"A curious statement," Aubrey replied. "But..."

"But nothing, Paul," the duke interrupted. "We are merely guessing now, which is self-destructive at this point. For all we know, Lemuel left that symbol there to set us to fighting. We'll speak no more of this now. Matthew, what else lies inside that bag?"

The earl swallowed his anger and touched his cousin on the shoulder. "Forgive me, Charles. I am out of sorts, but even so, there is no reason to take it out on you. I thank the Lord that you and Beth survived that night uninjured. And you mustn't assume any blame. Redwing is the perpetrator of this evil, and you merely fell into their carefully laid snare."

"Paul, you needn't apologise. I understand how you feel. I wish it could have turned out otherwise, that it could have been you riding to her rescue, but..."

"But at least Sinclair kept her safe and got her away from Lemuel," the duke finished for him. "Charles, you are to be thanked, and I know Paul feels the same. Risling, didn't you tell me that you had news from London?" he asked, trying again to change the subject.

"I do, sir, but that will keep. Are there more items Mr. Laurence wishes to show us?"

"There are, sir. Once we learnt all we could from the farm, we rode to Dr. Lemuel's home. We found a number of things that may tell a story. Inside the bag, Lord Haimsbury, you'll find several sheets of writing paper."

"Ah," Sinclair replied as he continued to look through the canvas bag. The detective held up the rubbings of the door from Lemuel's home. "What are these, Risling? Not cuneiform, but they look oddly familiar."

Laurence explained. "They're charcoal rubbings taken from the doctor's front door, sir. I noticed carvings upon the wood and thought this a good means of duplicating them."

Aubrey stood behind his cousin, overlooking his shoulder and peering at the papers. "That one's a pentagram. The others are less clear. Circular patterns of some kind. Perhaps...a nautilus? Strange, given Beth's nickname for you, Cousin."

Dryden finished his brandy and cleared his throat. "What nickname is that, sir?"

"She calls him Captain. Has since '79. Apparently, our little duchess sees my cousin as the embodiment of the mysterious Captain Nemo."

"I've never quite understood the connexion," Charles admitted. "She told me I looked lonely when she first met me, which in truth, I was. However, I think this image is supposed to represent the golden mean, which appears also in nautilus shells. The perfect proportion of creation. 1.618, also called a Fibonacci spiral or *Phi*. It is a pattern repeated again and again, throughout God's creation. A sign of order and incomparable beauty."

The duke joined his nephews and gazed at the rubbings. "This imagery crops up over and over where Redwing is concerned," Drummond told the men, "and they care little for God's true design. They seek to counter his order with their own seeds of chaos. Knowing Lemuel's true colours now, I fear these carvings you found, Laurence, may be part of another or perhaps the same ritual."

"You may be right, Uncle. I've seen these same images elsewhere—and recently," Sinclair responded. "Beneath the abbey at Branham. Why would Lemuel carve such demonic images? Even if he was mixed up with some ritual, why put them on his own door?"

Kepelheim reached over and took two of the pages. "Perhaps it is a charm against detection or to attract power. This one is a spiral labyrinth. I've seen its like in some of the old books, and I'm sure Malcolm has as well. These circular mazes were quite popular during the Druidic period and even earlier. Charles, you asked me at Branham about the older maze beneath the current one. I believe its contour is much like this image. I wonder what we're supposed to take from all this."

Aubrey sighed and returned to his own chair. "Is it a ritual? Matthew, did you learn anything about the doctor's personal life, outside of these strange carvings?"

"All that I found upon his person is contained in the small drawstring bag, sir. Yes, that one, Lord Haimsbury," he continued as Charles held up the black bag.

Sinclair looked inside. "A calling card, a sovereign, and a pen. I've seen these pens at the stationers in Harrods. Very expensive. They're from America, actually. A man carves them one at a time." He unscrewed the cap and a slip of paper fell out. "Well, hello," the superintendent whispered as he unrolled the small bit of paper. "It's in code. Written in very small handwriting. Block letters, possibly to disguise the writer. You know, I think it's a Vigenere Cipher."

"You are familiar with codes?" Kepelheim asked. "Oh, wait, silly me! Of course, you are! Tops in Mathematics, but you also studied encryption at Cambridge, did you not?"

Sinclair laughed. "Martin, did you examine my entire record whilst dogging my steps?"

The tailor smiled and nodded. "Perhaps, and if I may say so, Charles, you've cause to be proud of your time at Cambridge. All your dons and professors considered you quite a scholar with a logician's mind. Save for one don, that is."

"The French tutor?" he asked, smiling.

"Yes, but in your defence, he seemed quite the snob to me."

Sinclair picked up the pen. "Languages were never my strong suit, but numbers, now that is different. This code is a tough nut to crack, though; primarily because there's so little of it. It may require a key word to decrypt. Wait, perhaps not." He used the pen to scribble on one of the sheets of paper, copying out the message, crossing out letters and then entire words.

Meanwhile, the duke took the calling card and read out the name. "Hannibal Alexander, Esquire? Now, why is that familiar?"

The tailor sat forward. "I'm not sure, Duke, but it strikes me as familiar as well."

Dryden spoke. "I imagine you're thinking of Hannibal Alexander, the shipping tycoon, sir. New York based. Runs a fleet of steamships that are reputed to be the fastest in the world."

"Ships that transport what, Mr. Dryden?" Charles asked, looking up from his puzzle.

"Whatever will sell and make him more money," came the agent's reply. "Passengers, of course, though Alexander's line boasts only three luxury liners, but also foodstuffs, merchandise, chemicals, weaponry. Even slaves."

"That is disturbing," the tailor noted.

"That is the truth of the world," Sinclair responded darkly as he finished with the pen.

"Charles, have you uncovered something?"

The detective had begun to stare at the page. "Perhaps. Though it makes no sense. Here's what I get: *Hermetic upon syon sum.* Assuming I'm right, would Hermetic refer to Hermes? And 'sum' is Latin, of course. First person singular of the irregular verb 'to be', is it not? Am I missing something?"

Paul took the page and stared at the strange phrase. "Might this hint at the Hermetic orders so popular these days amongst the poets and writers? The Golden Dawn, perhaps? Taken together with the Fibonacci spiral Matthew found near the cottage, and the spirals carved on Lemuel's door, perhaps it does."

"But why mix up such a word with a Latin verb, unless it is a clumsy reference to the Lord, the Great I Am," Kepelheim pondered aloud. "Perhaps there is a second layer. Here, Charles, let me see it a moment."

The tailor's hand took up the pen and began to scribble out many copies of the translated phrase. He then began to cross out letters as he rearranged them.

Sinclair gasped. "It's an anagram!"

The tailor smiled as he completed the phrase's rearrangement. "Assuming that the original message also has four words like your translation of the code, then it would read: *Your prince summons you.* Oh, my. Who is this prince? The prince of darkness?"

Charles's dark brows rose in arched dismay. "I pray it is not. Hamish and Maggie Campbell both mentioned that many of their neighbours believed Lemuel in league with the devil, that he'd been touched by Satan in some way, but I thought them superstitious. Perhaps, the belief is due to more than just the man's bizarre appearance. Matthew, did you find anything else? Anything relating to his ties to Redwing?"

"Nothing else, sir. And the shooter seems to have left little behind other than imprints of his right boot."

"Is there a maker's mark of any kind?" the detective asked. "Did you measure it?"

"It is ten and one quarter inches long precisely, sir, from tip to back of heel. But no marks that I could perceive in the mud. It had rained the previous morning as it often does here in the autumn, but not enough for the ground to receive a deep enough imprint to discern any markings. I am sorry, sir."

Sinclair smiled. "Mr. Laurence, your investigative techniques surpass that of many police detectives I know. You've nothing to apologise for. The boot measurement aids us, however. That would fit a man of six feet or taller. A rarity in most families, ours aside, since my cousin and I are both well over that, and our esteemed uncle is one inch beyond it." He looked at the tailor. "Is that not so, Martin?"

"You are correct. In my line, I have cause to measure many a man's height, and it is rare indeed to find one who rises to six feet. The Stuart and Sinclair bloodlines are a beautiful exception to that rule."

"We are exceptional in many ways, I'm learning, though I shall keep my short hair, Cousin," he told the earl with a wink. "So, was Lemuel summoned by this prince?"

"I'd say the answer to that is yes, Charles," Kepelheim posited. "The traitor told you that he'd abducted the duchess because of what? Blackmail? That doesn't ring true if one considers the carvings and this strange message. No, I think Solomon Lemuel was compromised long ago."

Sinclair turned the pen over and over in his hand. "I wonder if these pens are used by other agents in Redwing to deliver messages. Hiding the slip of paper into the cap is a secure and simple means of transporting important information without using a telegraph. As I said, these pens are quite expensive, so they might even be reused." He turned toward his cousin. "I say, Paul, might we also use this to send false messages to known Redwing assets?"

"That is a very good idea, Cousin," the earl said, taking the pen from Sinclair. "I wonder how many of these pens are imported into England each year. I'd wager that number is small, if he carves them one at a time. I'll have one of our New York agents look into the company. What's the name again, Charles?"

"Waterman, I think. E.L., or maybe L.E. Waterman. I nearly bought one of these last time I was in Harrod's, but at the time its price was well beyond my budget. Now, I could buy an entire box without so much as blinking," the detective answered. "You have agents in New York?"

"Of course," Aubrey said easily. "The circle has agents in just about every country, but we have over a hundred in America. Matthew, you've done some really, excellent work here. Fine work. Martin, could you and Malcolm look through our books for images like these rubbings to make sure we've not missed something? I'd like to know if the door is another message board of sorts."

"I shall get on it this evening."

Malcolm Risling had brought a small leather satchel along, which he now opened. "The duke mentioned earlier that I'd brought a few items with me from London, but first, Lord Haimsbury, allow me to extend my condolences on the loss of your friend, Sir Robert Morehouse."

"Thank you, Mr. Risling. Seldom do crimes shock me, but this took me by complete surprise. Is the Yard still calling it suicide?"

The agent handed several newspapers from a variety of publishers around to his companions. "These are dated from Sunday morning and on, and as you will see from the headlines, most in the press do not believe the reports. That being said, the official government conclusion is suicide by accident."

"What?" Charles asked, dumbfounded. "By accident? Whose hogwash is that? I pray it isn't something Warren said, else I shall have to tender my resignation immediately. Policing requires honest leadership, but that sort of claptrap is beyond all imagining!"

"It is what the Home Office is calling it, sir. Warren has expressed his own doubts in similar fashion to your own, I might add."

Kepelheim thumbed through the pages of both *The Star* and *The Gazette*. "Simon Keepe appears to believe there is subterfuge at the Home Office, Charles. And..." he paused as he turned the page, growing strangely silent as he read to himself for a moment.

"And?" the superintendent coaxed. The newspaper before him lay unopened on his lap but he glanced down now. Seeing the photograph and headline, he snatched it up and also began to read. "Why that gossiping old maid!" he murmured. "James, does your paper also include this trash?"

The duke had been quietly reading to himself as well, and he looked up over his spectacles. "If you mean the long article about your interesting relationship with my granddaughter, why yes, it does."

The earl switched from his copy of *The London Daily News* to glance over his uncle's shoulder. "The Policeman and the Peeress," he read aloud. "Oh, and there's a lovely photograph with this caption: Ripper Investigator Charles St. Clair in intimate congress with duchess."

Charles snatched the newspaper from Drummond and slammed it to the carpet. "Damn that infernal reporter! I shall hang O'Brien up by his pencil!"

"Now, now, son," the duke cautioned. "Keep your head. This story's been all over London for the past couple of days. I've just kept you from seeing the papers. Besides, you've had other things on your mind, Charles."

"This tripe doesn't worry you, Uncle?"

"Why should it? Read on, and you'll see what I mean."

Kepelheim retrieved the discarded newspaper and continued. "It's by a man named Michael O'Brien. Apparently, a man who may have to mind his pencil when our marquess returns to London."

The detective sighed, still seething with anger.

"Ah, but the photograph is rather nice. Forgive me, Charles. Yes, well, here is what the article says: 'This reporter witnessed a remarkable event on the morning of Saturday last in Whitechapel. Elizabeth Stuart, Duchess of Branham, a well known and much beloved peeress who only recently returned from France, entered the Leman Street station house—on her own—and immediately commenced a secretive conversation with our own Superintendent Charles St. Clair. The two whispered together, and the stalwart detective referred to the lovely duchess by her Christian name, an assured faux pas. However, since we first reported on this in our Saturday evening special, an astonishing truth has come to light. After sending a telegram of inquiry to the duchess's own family in Scotland, we have learnt that our Charles St. Clair is, in fact, Charles SINCLAIR, heir to the marquessate of Haimsbury and the duchess's own cousin. This may explain not only the abrupt return of the lady from France but also her surreptitious departure from Leman Street on Saturday afternoon in the new marquess's company. Is there a wedding in the wings for Scotland's Stuart dynasty? Stay tuned to future installments to learn the truth as it is revealed to us.'"

"Has Beth seen any of these?" the earl asked. "Perhaps that is why she has been so strange all day."

"No, I've kept all the papers to myself," Drummond replied. "That bit about contacting her family, well, the telegram was sent to me, so you can blame me for letting the cat out of the bag, Nephew. I sent back word that Charles's name was misspelled and that they should check with Scotland Yard to confirm that. Then, I sent a wire to Warren letting him know all about your inheritance. I also sent the same to Salisbury and the queen."

Charles stood near the fireplace soothing the dogs, who had both jumped at his irritated exclamations. "You sent it?" he asked. "Sir, I am sorry for allowing those hacks to print anything that may be misconstrued..."

"It's neither here nor there, son. I'm not bothered by it. Beth's been the topic of many a scandalous press report these past four years. Ask her about the trash written regarding some Hungarian prince—oh, and there's also the supposed elopement with an American rail baron. In fact, Beth's been married off more times than the queen has given birth! All fabrications. The Paris newspapers often made up stories just because she refused to grant interviews, and public fascination there ensured any edition with her name in the headline sold record numbers of copies. Besides, I'm glad your true name is being spoken all across England. I'm proud to call you my nephew."

"You are too kind to me, sir. I shall endeavour to learn from your wisdom regarding our press, but I reserve the right to deal with O'Brien and his American compatriot, Mr. Dam." He glanced at the mantel clock which had begun to chime. "I hope you will forgive me, gentlemen, but I promised to tour the garden with our duchess in a short while, and I hope to write some letters first. With these reports lining birdcages in every household, I owe Lady Martha Morehouse a note of condolence and explanation, and I'd like to write to Reid as well regarding the investigation into Bob's death. I may even extend my thoughts on O'Brien's article to his employer, T.P. O'Connor. Though I've had very little influence on that ambitious man in the past, perhaps my new title will supersede my former one in his eyes. With your permission, sir. I shall see you after my walk with Beth," he said, bowing to his uncle.

The earl looked a bit uncomfortable, but as they had decided to allow Elizabeth to make her own choice regarding her future, he said nothing.

James Stuart waved his hands, the grin widening across his face. "Write your letters, son. "Enjoy the view, but be back for music later. Beth's promised to play for us."

Charles bowed again. "Thank you, sir. Gentlemen."

He left the room, and Martin Kepelheim set aside the newspapers and stood. "My congratulations on a match well played, Duke. Not only did you defuse and thoroughly disappoint the press's ink-spattered salvos, you turned it to your nephew's advantage. This may even put a crimp in Redwing's current plans, for they probably hoped we'd cower after the attempted abduction. Instead, you go on the attack. You are a masterful player, sir."

Drummond laughed. "I've been playing against that foul group for most of my life, Martin—as have you. Oh, I heard back from the queen this afternoon, by the way. She's delighted to hear about Charles. She always had a soft spot for Robby Sinclair, I think. It hit her hard when he died, and only a year after Albert passed away, too. I sometimes wonder which man she mourns the most."

"Wasn't the queen born ten years earlier than the late marquess?" Risling asked.

"Nine actually, but it never seemed to matter to Victoria," the duke remarked. "Charles's father and she were quite close, though she was already married when they met for the first time in '48. Robby was just turned twenty and had inherited his father's title and attended the House of Lords ceremony. A bit of costumery foolishness, if you ask me, but the queen was there, and I can tell you that her eyes lit up like I'd never seen them do! Robby was a gold-plated looker, like his son. She'll no doubt be happy to meet Charles. As I said, she's already expressed great joy that our lad's been found. When we all get back to London, we're in for a round of parties, or my name's not Stuart!"

The tailor laughed. "Then, I shall have to make sure our new marquess is properly attired before those parties commence. And speaking of such, I should probably look through my music, if the duchess is to play this evening. If she is recovered from her headache, I might even convince her to sing. Malcolm, you and I shall peruse the stacks after the musical concert, later. Dryden, I imagine you've brought us news of a more practical kind, judging by the steel boxes the duke's men unloaded from your wagon. I look forward to examining your cargo."

Dryden smiled. "The latest from America, Martin. Whitworth rifles with Davidson telescopic sights, the new Browning model Winchester repeaters, and a new type of explosive that puts TNT to shame. The earl and I will be practicing with them tomorrow morning on the duke's range, if you're up."

"Oh, my! American weapons. How exciting," Kepelheim whispered, feigning foppishness—a mannerism that often disarmed his opponents and had become somewhat of a habit after decades of practise. In truth, Kepelheim could handle many weapons with ease. "I wonder if you and Risling would be interested in helping me choose a light weapon for myself. But first, let's choose a better wine. Matthew, you've come a long way since you first took up Brannan's old spot. Why don't you accompany me to the cellars where we shall all see if there is any more of that delicious port."

Laurence looked to the duke, who nodded, and the butler bowed and followed the tailor and the London men out into the hallway. Once alone, Drummond poured himself another glass of brandy and also one for his nephew. The duke handed the refilled glass to the earl. "Charles and Elizabeth seem to be getting on well."

Aubrey's mood had darkened, but he managed a reply. "Yes, so I've noticed."

"Beth will make her own choice in time, son. Let her have a bit of space, and be generous with Sinclair. This is all new to him, and the newspaper articles only make it worse, which is why I have tried to douse that fire before it begins. Now, tell me more about this woman doctor. Does she seem capable?"

"I expect so," he said vaguely, for his mind still wondered why he had felt so drawn to her considerable charms.

The duke laughed. "So! She is beautiful, is she?"

"I did not say so," Paul protested. "She has a pleasing face. Somewhat tall, I imagine. She certainly seems capable with regard to her art."

"Medicine or bewitchment?" he asked with a mischievous grin. "It's natural to find a beautiful woman attractive, Paul. Elizabeth knows your heart is hers alone. And I know you could never truly be, shall we say, distracted. Not now that you have grown wiser."

Paul shook his head. "Elizabeth knows nothing of that, James. But perhaps I owe it to her to tell all. I do not like keeping secrets. Not from her."

"She would probably forgive you, son, but it would break her heart, I think. She has always seen you as perfect. Do you dare reveal that you are but a man after all?"

He sighed, his head dropping against the high back of the leather chair. "I was certainly foolish then. How do I know I am truly immune to my foolish nature now?"

"Because you are," he said simply. "Which reminds me, I'm bringing Adele here. I've worried that our scattered family is like sheep without a shepherd, so I've sent a letter to Briarcliff, instructing Henry to send her to us tomorrow morning along with the additional men. Our girl will arrive just after eleven."

"Uncle! I am ashamed not to have thought of that! Sweet Adele, my angel. How can I have forgotten her, all alone and far away?"

"You've had much to occupy your mind this past week. Much to distract you, but she will be delighted to find her brother waiting, and I am always happy to hear that child's laughter."

"Was I right—was my father right—were we right in what we did, James?"

"You made the best choice, son. What is past is just that—past. Della loves you, and she is much better off, is she not?"

"I like to think so. I could not abide leaving her there. Not after what happened to her mother."

James sipped the brandy, thoughtfully. "She is with family, and that's what matters. She needn't know the truth, unless you choose to tell it. It is your past, Paul, but your choices impact Beth's present, as well as her future. So, this woman in Glasgow, she's a beauty then?"

"She is, but—she, well, now I don't know what to say. You make me wonder now if I've been a fool."

The duke's black eyebrows shot upward, and he laughed heartily. "You? A fool? Paul, my boy, you are no one's fool! Would Gladstone and Salisbury both have placed the fate of the empire into your capable hands—more than once, I might add—had they believed you a fool? You are a crack shot, a keeper of dark secrets, an erudite man who can box, hunt, spy upon, and kill without remorse anyone who dares to threaten those you love. But you are also a true servant of Christ, who knows his Bible better than most parsons. Son, you are a rare man, and England and our beloved Scotland are both better for your birth."

The earl's shoulder ached, but his heart hurt more. "I wish I found your confidence in me cheering, James, but I feel as if I've made a mess of this from the start. Had I not been wounded during the skirmish outside the train, I'd have been able to go with her to those hellish tunnels, and…"

"And what? Somehow all this would have gone better? Paul, if you had been down there with her, Charles would not have known how to organise an escape. Yes, I know, Kepelheim is a cool head, and his connexions are vast, but yours are intricate and your men are completely loyal to any command you give them. They follow you like they would a prince. All has turned out well, my lad, so let's drink to that and learn from our mistakes. If you want to speak of blame, it was my trust in Lemuel that nearly led to all our ends."

Laurence entered and whispered into the duke's ear, who sat forward and tapped his nephew on the knee. "You've a visitor," he said, standing. "A young woman, I'm told."

"Surely not Adele already?"

"No, but someone you've seen this very day," James remarked. "Show her into the blue room, Laurence. And ask our other guests if they wish to join me in the music room. Whilst we wait upon the piano concert, I'll give a listen to some of those cylinders Elizabeth bought for me today."

"Very good, sir," the young man said and left to follow his orders.

James led Paul out of the drawing room and into the main hallway, where the grand staircase curved upward, past full-length portraits, potted ferns, and mullioned stained glass windows toward the two floors above.

The duke had been a magnificently handsome man in his youth, with a muscular build, not unlike his nephew's, but with black hair and fierce black eyes. He had grown a moustache in the Crimean War, where he served not only as espionage agent but also helped with the Paris negotiations afterward in '56. Once accomplished, he'd been assigned to gather information on the autonomy movements in Wallachia and Moldavia. Upon his return in 1860, his duchess, Elizabeth Elaine Campbell Stuart, the third daughter of the

Duke of Argyll, had demanded he forever keep the moustache, preferring him with the facial hair.

Since her passing in 1875, three months after suffering a stroke, the duke had continued to wear the moustache, salted now with grey, thinking of his beloved bride each time he trimmed it. He thought of her now as he and Paul joined their unexpected guest in the blue room, a magnificently furnished parlour, preferred by the late duchess for its low, deep-seated chairs and cheerful, yellow and white, silk upholstery.

"So, you are Dr. MacKey," the duke said with a wide grin, his hand out to take her own. "I am delighted to make your acquaintance."

She held out her hand and let him kiss it. MacKey wore no gloves, and the duke noticed that her skin smelled of soap and lavender—and one other trace scent, which he could not quite place.

"I am honoured, Your Grace," she cooed. "Please, forgive my impertinence. I know that I am not expected, and that it was thoughtless to show up at your door unannounced, but I simply could not stop thinking of your nephew's shoulder. He told me that your family doctor died quite suddenly, and that only your good housekeeper has been tending it. I have brought my medical bag, and it would ease my mind to make certain that his injury is not serious, and that it is mending as it should."

Paul stepped forward, feeling completely undone. "Lorena, this isn't necessary. It is kind of you, but I am fine and mending speedily."

"My Lord Aubrey, I am the better judge of that, and it would be a disservice to my oath were I not to assure the duke that his gallant nephew is out of all danger."

The duke winked at Paul and again kissed the doctor's hand; another chance to smell the odd scent lingering beneath others more pleasant. "I'll leave you to your patient, then, Doctor. My staff are available should you require anything. Just ring; the bell pull is by the fireplace."

He shut the doors, leaving Paul alone with his beautiful but devious physician.

"Will you sit, Lord Aubrey?" she asked, lifting her medical bag to a table and opening it wide. Inside, Paul could see instruments, powders, bottles, syringes, and tubing, much like any other medical kit he'd seen before.

"Remove your shirt, please," she said simply as if it were a matter completely ordinary. "Please, sir," she added, seeing the reluctance on his face, "I do not bite. If I am to examine your injury, then I must have access to it. Here, let me help you."

She leaned in close and removed the sling, setting it to one side. She then helped him to unbutton his waistcoat, and then release both the waistcoat and shirt sleeve from his left arm, and then the right.

"What have you done to your right palm?" she asked, noticing the cuts where he had smashed the tumbler two nights before. "You must be more careful, my lord! So important a personage cannot risk sepsis of the blood. This will become infected if it is not cleaned again. And it may require stitches. How was this done?"

The earl sat in the room, bare to the waist, his heart beating fast. He wished her examination would end, but he knew his wound did need looking after, and part of him hoped she might ease the pain in his shoulder and help him to sleep.

"You flinch," she said, her practised hands probing the palm first. "So, how did you cut yourself?"

He shook his head, keenly aware of the perfume upon her throat and scarf. She wore a satin dress unlike the one he'd seen that morning. This was more for evening, cut low with bared arms, but she had demurely covered her décolleté with a silken scarf, which rounded her slender throat and ample bosom, making it more noticeable by half.

"I broke a glass," he said, hoping she would probe no further.

"What was in the glass? Water? Wine?"

"Whisky," he said, and she laughed.

"Typical, and so completely in keeping with my image of you, my lord. Scotch whisky. Well, the good news is the alcohol content probably kept your injury from causing mischief, for it may have added a cleansing effect, but it should have been tended earlier. I fear you will have a scar there, and such a shame, for your hands are so very nice."

"It won't be my first scar," he admitted, immediately wishing he'd not said it, for when his ears heard it, the phrase sounded boastful. "I mean only that life brings injury at times. I should have been more careful."

"I understand, my lord. I have a salve which will aid in healing and perhaps prevent a scar, if I may apply it?"

He nodded, and she removed a small jar from the bag and spread a pleasant smelling ointment into his palm. "I want to bandage this, to seal the salve's healing powers within and keep out any agents of mischief." She then wound a gauze bandage around his hand, and finished by tying and knotting it. "There. Now, to that shoulder. You say it was treated by a doctor when first it happened?"

"A doctor of a kind," he explained, not wanting to reveal the truth. "A hunting accident, as you may have guessed. It was a foolish move on my part. Another hunter mistook me and fired."

"A bullet wound! Oh, my, that is different!" she exclaimed, though she knew precisely how he'd been injured and where. "I thought you said it happened—well, no matter." She removed the bandage set there the night before by the housekeeper and shook her head. "Paul, this must have bled a great deal, for it lies close to a major blood vessel. I'm surprised you are even walking about. Why, on earth, were you shopping this morning, when you should have been in bed?"

Her hands probed about the wound, and he gasped in pain as she pushed into the centre. "I am sorry, but pain is a good sign. I had feared nerve damage when I first saw this. Evidently, the bullet passed through cleanly, which is good, as you know I am sure. I see that it has been stitched three times. I take it that the wound re-opened after the first attempts. I wonder if you refused rest even then."

"There's been much to occupy me these past few days, but I've rested whenever I could."

She pulled a chair in front of his, sat into it, and then took his hands in hers, looking deeply into his eyes. "My lord—Paul, my brave and handsome knight—I imagine that you are one of those wonderful men who rescues damsels, and who refuses to sit until all around you are settled, but I tell you that if those around you are to rely upon your good deeds, then you must take better care of yourself. Strength of heart does not always make up for weakness in body. Trust me, I know. My father was a slave to his own foolishness, and he died of sepsis. It was a horrible way to die, and—well, that is why I vowed it would never again happen to one for whom I cared. I enrolled in medical college one month later."

He had watched her eyes and mouth the entire time that she spoke, and he found her words almost hypnotic and her perfume delightful. "Perhaps, you are right, Doctor."

"Lorena, please."

He blinked, wondering how her eyes could be so green. "Lorena. My life is more complicated than I can say, but I promise to be better about resting. Thank you for your kindness."

"How can I do less for the man who rescued my best hat? Now, I shall clean and redress this, and you must promise to rest. I know you said you would join me tomorrow for luncheon, but I cannot— as your doctor—allow that. You need sleep and lots of it. And eat! Your face is pale, and I expect you have eaten little of late. Red wine will strengthen the blood, so choose that instead of whisky for a few days. I shall leave some morphine with your housekeeper. Does she know how to administer it?"

He nodded. "Mrs. MacAnder served as a nurse in the Crimea."

"Then she has witnessed sights more horrible than most in this realm. She must be a fine woman. Very good then. I shall leave that with her, and now I would like to relieve your pain by injecting you. It may hurt a little, but I promise you will sleep well tonight."

Paul did not like the idea of spending another night under the spell of a drug. "I have need for remaining able to awaken easily. It is…"

"Complicated, yes, I can see that it is. Very well. I leave you then with this small bottle of a medicinal which I use myself whenever I have a headache but wish to be alert should a patient require I go out into the night and work. It is a tincture made from a wonderful herb I found whilst in Vienna. A fellow practitioner there grows them, and the plant produces a lovely flower. In fact, it can be made into a fragrance. I wear it even now."

"Is that it? I've been trying to place it, but the scent is new to me. I can discern lavender, I think, but the other is a mystery."

"It is my little secret," she replied, smiling. "I now grow them in a flowerbox near my bedroom window. They love any light, and the blossom is a glorious white, putting on a show even in moonlight."

"You live in London?"

"For now. I seek a practice wherever I might, and I have high hopes. Women doctors are less rare than once they were, and more cities are building hospitals, which means a need for physicians like myself. Now, this liquid is a little bitter. Have you some wine I might mix with it?"

"I am not sure if there is any in here. I doubt it. If you pull the bell rope, one of the footmen will bring you a glass."

"Or two, perhaps?" she suggested as she completed the work on his shoulder.

"Perhaps. Lorena, it is very late, and…"

"Oh, you are right. Quite correct. I am an intruder, and you and your family have plans, no doubt, which I interrupt. I shall ring for the wine and leave the bottle with you. Just one drop in each glass of wine. No more."

Paul shook his head. "No, no, you misunderstand me. Our home is more than an hour from the city by the fastest carriage, and that only when being driven by someone accustomed to the roads. How did you arrive here? Do you have a driver waiting?"

She closed her bag and shook her head, her glossy auburn curls bouncing in the chandelier's glow. "In truth? I rode with a delivery-man who left me at your door. He was passing on his way north, but he said there may be someone else passing by with whom I might find a ride back. I know, it was brazen and quite silly of me. For a woman with a sharp mind, I sometimes leave all common sense behind."

Paul thought this story thin, but his sense of decency could not permit her to go back into the night on her own. "Then you must stay here tonight," he said. "I cannot allow you to risk these danger-ous roads at night, even were there a deliveryman who passes here so late—something which I doubt. Only two nights ago, we heard wolves on the moors, so you would not be safe."

"Stay here? But, Lord Aubrey, how can I do such?" she pro-tested. "I have been bother enough. I shall be fine. I am quite re-sourceful."

"No, Lorena, I will not hear of it. Remain here tonight. I am sure we can find attire to suit anything you should need, and we've plenty room."

"You do at that," she laughed. "All right, if you insist, but I warn you; I shall be a pest when it comes to your medical welfare, so do not be upset if I remove any whisky glasses I may find in your vicinity!"

Paul laughed, unable to resist her charms, as she helped him into his shirt and waistcoat. "Thank you," he said, meaning it. "I'm a bear when it comes to some things, but you have turned me into a lamb."

And lamb is one of my favourite meals, she thought.

By eight, Charles Sinclair had finished writing his letters, so he knocked on the duchess's door.

"Elizabeth?"

No reply.

He knocked once more. Still no answer. "Beth?" he called into the darkened interior.

The layout of the large apartment featured a beautifully finished parlour that led into the connected bedchamber and private bath. The fireplace in the parlour had burnt down to glowing embers, and Beth's bedroom door was ajar. He could hear faint murmurings coming from within. Stepping forward, he peered into the chamber. The duchess lay upon the bed, a coverlet across her hips, and she appeared to be dreaming, though the content of the dream seemed to distress her, for her entire body twitched, and her hands tore at the bedclothes.

Despite propriety, Sinclair rushed forward and sat next to her on the edge of the bed. "Darling, wake up." He touched her hand, and it was like ice. "Beth, please, wake up. You're having a nightmare, I think." She turned, thrashing about, as if panicked. He warmed her hand in his, kissing it. "Elizabeth!" he called out, and her eyes popped open.

"Oh!" she exclaimed, and he could see that her pupils were large, for the moonlight fell across the bed. "What? Where am I?"

"You've been sleeping, dearest. I'm sorry for daring to enter, but it seemed to me that you fought against some nocturnal intruder in your dreams. Are you all right?"

She slowly made sense of her surroundings. "Captain, is that you?" He nodded. Her breathing slowed, and she began to make more sense. "Oh, Charles, it was an awful dream! I was at a masked ball, and this shadowy prince kept asking me to dance. You were there," she added, her dark eyes fixed on his face. "And you kept me safe from him, and there was a strange mirror, but then... Well, I'm not sure now. It's all a bit of a blur already. What time is it?"

"Nearly nine. I think your grandfather and the others await us for a little music, but if you're not up to playing, then perhaps you should go back to sleep. I can make your apologies."

"I've no wish to go back to that dream," she whispered, rising from the bed with his help and then sitting on the edge. "Give me a few moments and I'll join you in the parlour."

He bowed and left, and the duchess splashed water on her face and straightened her raven hair. The night was cool, so she took a tartan shawl from the closet. Exiting the room, she smiled at him. "Ready for our walk, Captain?"

"Darling, you are so very beautiful. And yes, I'm ready."

They left the upstairs, followed the staircase down to the main entry and slipped away into the night. Elizabeth led her champion past several of the duke's sentries, whom she greeted with smiles and thanks. The gravel path was lined with boxwood and ornamental trees and curved around to the south and then westward toward the cliffside. Above them, the moon still seemed round, though it had already begun to wane, and the white face shone down upon the roses that now put on a final show before going to sleep for the winter.

"Do you think much about Whitechapel, Charles?"

He sat next to her on a stone bench, placing a blanket beneath them both and the woolen shawl in Stuart red around her shoulders. "Occasionally, but I've found little time to think lately—at least about things that do not connect to you in some way. Beth, it will be far too chilly here to speak for much longer, for the nights drift toward winter."

"It is not so cold," she assured him. "Not if you keep me warm."

He kissed her hands, enjoying the sweet taste of her warm skin against his lips. He had not stopped thinking of the night at the cottage, and though he'd loved her before far more deeply than ever he could have imagined, the dream, if dream it was, had only intensified his connexion to her. "I would happily keep you warm, every day and every night of our lives, if permitted. But first, you and I must determine exactly what happened—what truly happened—in that cottage."

What he'd learnt from their meeting, regarding the symbols both at the cottage and the castle, worried Sinclair, and though he had no intention of informing Elizabeth, it was becoming clear to him that Redwing's goal had been for her to conceive a child that night. Why on that particular night? Was it because of the so-called blood moon, or was there another reason?

"Beth? Do you prefer not to talk about it?" he prompted, noting her silence.

She looked away, clearly dreading the conversation. "No, Charles, we must, as you say, discern precisely what happened, but will you allow me to speak first? Only please remember I had been drugged with an unknown compound by Dr. Lemuel, a man intent upon what we do not truly know, but here is how I recall it. And, please, my wonderful Captain, remember that these images are like a dream, rising up in a thick mist as I recall them, and yet in some ways they are more real to me than any waking memory."

"Be open and unafraid," he told her. "And once your dreams have seen the light, I shall tell you of my own."

"Agreed. But be patient with me, Charles, for this is difficult to tell. Were you any other man, I'm not sure I could recount it at all, but I have always known that I may trust you completely—even when first we met. Very well. We spoke of the cottage, and I told you that I sensed that you had laid me upon a bed, though I was not sure how or where, or even why, if that makes sense. I see you nodding, so I suppose that it does. The bed was inviting and warm; I do remember that very well. The air was pleasant, filled with the sweet smell of burning wood. A part of me understood that I lay in that bed, and I knew you sat nearby, if that makes any sense. Yet, I had a strange feeling that I walked in a dream, for though I knew myself to be sleeping—or so I thought, again these memories are ephemeral—yet I walked, for I could feel the cool, dew-covered grass beneath my bare feet.

"Music floated upon the very air, played by some unseen hand. No source did I perceive, and yet like sweet, seductive music—a violin, to be precise—this melody whispered into my mind. I felt my body moving, swaying as if dancing to the seductive tune. I wore different clothing in this dream, and as I said, my feet were bare. Behind it all, and this truly makes no sense, I could hear dogs barking—at least, I think that they were dogs. Or wolves, perhaps," she said, beginning to tremble. "I know not which. I only remember thinking that the sound was somehow familiar. And then…" she continued, her face grown suddenly soft as she looked directly into his eyes. "Then, I saw you."

He wanted to speak, but he knew what this confession must be costing her, so he remained silent, holding her hand to give her strength.

"You were there, and you looked more handsome than I'd ever seen you look before. The fire danced in your wonderful eyes, and you seemed to me a prince of the night, and the music grew louder, and the night warmer, and you came to me, kissed me deeply, your hands caressing my...my body, and you moved closer and then—you—you…"

"Be brave, dearest. I am listening, and I make no judgment."

She turned away for just a moment, as if steeling her nerve. "You pulled me to you, and we began to dance in time, our bodies in union, and…oh, Charles, must I say it?"

He took her into his arms, holding her tightly. "No, my love. You needn't say it, for my own dream was the same. The music, the dance, and it was you with whom I danced, though I did not realise it at the time. And wolves howled in the distance all the while. And we shared an intimacy that only a man and wife would share. Is that what you meant?"

She nodded, her eyes downcast. "But that cannot be! Why does my mind tell me that this was *not* just a dream, but what *actually happened* in some mystical way?"

"Because, Beth, I think it did happen. Wait, hear me out," he said, as she pulled away in panic. "Listen. Hush now," he said, drawing her into his long arms and stroking her dark hair to calm her. "I also fell into this dream, this hallucination, whatever you may call it, for you and I had been given some strange soporific mixture, darling—it was in the tea, I believe. I fell asleep whilst keeping watch over you from a chair beside the fire. You slept soundly in that bed, but I *never* came near you—not with my waking will. Not until... Beth, when I awoke I was lying next to you in that inviting bed, and our discarded clothing lay strewn about the floor as if we had tossed them there, but I do not remember doing such a thing. I only remember the dream, and then I awoke to find... Beth, I believe that what you and I both fear, *did* in truth, happen. I should have found a way to fight the drug, fight the enchantment if that is what it was, for I begin to see through that darkened glass St. Paul wrote about so long ago, but I did not resist! Darling, I believe I left all sense behind and behaved like…like a…beast!"

"No, Charles," she whispered, glancing up at him, her dark eyes shining with love. "You could never be that." She sat still as a stone, her head against his chest, and he could feel her tremble. "Charles, I did not resist either. Though, I should have, I did not. What does that say about me?"

He kissed her hair. "Beth, I love you so very much."

"Yes, I know it, Charles, and it makes me happier than you can imagine, for I have loved you for as long as I can remember." She looked up, her eyes wet with tears, but she smiled as she stroked his cheek. "My darling Captain, you have no cause for remorse. You behaved like a wonderful guardian who had been drugged, and who would never have done such in other circumstances," she said gently, though her hands still shook. "Charles, I thought and have thought, since our return to the castle, that somehow it had all indeed, really, truly happened. I do not know what this means; I only know that I love you all the more for it, if that makes any sense. My one regret is that I cannot remember awakening in your warm embrace."

He took her chin, kissing her lips, softly at first, but as she returned his kiss, with greater passion. "Oh, I do love you, Elizabeth! I love you, and it feels right to say it. Yet, I fear what may come of our marriage, should we do such. Paul is a man I should regret hurting, ever. And I know you feel that way, too. And then there is Redwing. Surely their dark hand in all this is obvious, and I begin to wonder if the entire affair—the kidnapping, and perhaps even the mad chase from Branham, were not part of some long, fiendish game meant to end in my marriage to you."

"Can such deceit and foreknowledge exist?" she asked, realising at once how naive the question sounded. "I must tell Paul the truth," she said at last as he held her. "He deserves to know. All of it."

"Yes, dear, I agree, but allow me to do it. If he hates me, then I can live with that, but I would never wish for Paul to have even one dark thought about your purity of heart. I shall speak also with Uncle James, and if he believes it best, then I will retreat as you become my cousin's wife. However, if he sees no harm otherwise, then I intend to fight for you, Beth, if your heart still desires it."

"Desire it? Yes, Charles, it does, and I do! I love you, and I shall for all eternity, my darling. Nothing and no one will ever alter that fact. And whatever Redwing's reasons for forcing us together, whatever their dark plans, I shall not fear them, so long as you are by my side."

He took her hands, helping her to stand, and then walked her back into the southwest entrance, where Laurence had just arrived to find them and bring them into the music room.

In the shadows of the night, where no human could see him, a tall man-shaped being watched, his red eyes glowing from within a spectral face.

Oh, my sweet, young duchess. You follow my plans as if it is your own desire. Trent is a useful tool at times, but soon I shall dispense with him and reveal myself to you, and once the blood of your line and Sinclair's has firmly established itself and is in my control, I shall take you and your beautiful body—all for myself.

CHAPTER TWENTY-ONE
3:30 a.m.

Paul Stuart awoke to darkness. Drowsy beyond his capacity to remain awake, he had bid goodnight to all in the music room and retired to his own upstairs apartment, leaving the company at eleven and falling asleep within moments of shutting off the lamp. Having decided he no longer needed to be treated as an invalid—or rather no longer wishing to be—the earl had forsaken the west drawing room for more familiar surroundings. Elizabeth retired soon after the earl, and her apartment lay just around the corner near the main staircase. Charles slept in a large apartment across the hallway, once occupied by Connor Stuart.

Lorena MacKey, the unexpected guest, had charmed her hosts during their musical evening, though she failed it seemed to bring much good humour to the earl's cousin Elizabeth, despite offering to sing several songs she'd learnt in medical school after visiting a music hall. The men had laughed at the humourous lyrics, but Elizabeth and even Charles—Lorena had noticed with delight—seemed distracted and thoughtful. Beth had played but declined to sing, explaining that her head still hurt somewhat. Instead, the duke had shared his own curious repertoire, though he had no voice for singing, and even the staff had laughed when he offered impressions of a favourite chanteuse he'd once seen in Paris.

Now alone within the moonlit room, the earl's cool blue eyes slowly accommodated to the dim light as he stared at the coffered ceiling. Turning, Paul felt a sharp pain in his shoulder, so he decided to drink more of the doctor's mixture, which stood in a wine glass just where he'd left it, beside his bed on a night stand. He drank the remainder and then set the empty glass back onto the marble-topped table, staring once more at the ceiling of the shadowy room as he waited for the concoction to take effect. Lying there, Paul thought of Lorena and her brash ways, and then he reminded himself that his future lay elsewhere, though he wondered now if Elizabeth's heart still felt the same. Yes, she loved him, but did she love Charles more? He had no answer, and he had promised to wait for Christmas, so wait he would.

Adele.

His sister's name whispered inside his mind as if someone had spoken it.

Adele. Who is Adele?

Again, a voice, as if someone lay beside him, softly entreating him to reveal secrets from his past.

Adele. Precious Della. He would have to tell Elizabeth soon, because she had a right to know that the child whom all believed to be his father's ward, Paul's adopted sister, an orphan whose mother died when she was only two, was in fact Paul's own daughter.

Paris had been the earl's first assignment in the early days with the Foreign Office, and the twenty-two-year-old viscount had traveled *incognito* to accomplish his secret mission. As a spy for the British government, he had assumed an identity as a struggling painter named David Saunders, a reprobate who would do anything for money, living in Montmartre on the Rue Caulaincourt.

To maintain believability, Paul spent countless hours in unsavoury places: gambling houses, brothels, opium dens, illegal boxing rings, and the like. It was in one of the brothels, an upscale *maison close* called *La Chabanais* that he met and befriended a beautiful prostitute named Cozette du Barroux, rumoured to be the favourite of a wealthy banker named Michel Fermin. This banker's connexions to a smuggling ring that specialized in war materiel had not been proven, and it was Paul's assignment to obtain corroboration. However, known only to a handful of inner circle members within the Foreign Office, the viscount also used his time in the French backstreets to pursue information about Redwing.

Despite making every effort to keep his relationship with du Barroux all business, Paul had grown fond of her, for the prostitute's life had taken a bitter road, and he could see that many of her customers, though paying her well, considered her so much dust beneath their expensive shoes. When his assignment was completed, and the banker's secret financials exposed, Paul had visited Cozette one last time to say farewell. She had wept bitterly, pleading with him to take her with him. Knowing such was impossible, the viscount had left her with five-thousand francs in the hope that she might leave that life behind and begin anew.

Two and a half years passed, and Paul returned to Paris for a more 'official' duty, helping to negotiate a treaty fixing import fees betwixt several European nations and England, and whilst there, Fermin, who had left his banking position in disgrace, paid the viscount a visit. It was a tense and unpleasant confrontation, but Paul maintained that he knew nothing of any person named David Saunders. Fermin threatened and probed his enemy's defences, even daring to mention the House of Aubrey's rumoured pursuit of a secret cult known in Parisian circles as *la Bande de la Colombe Bless*ée or the Band of the Wounded Dove. The encounter had nearly come to blows, but realising perhaps that the young viscount outmatched him physically, Fermin had left suddenly, pretending he'd made a mistake.

Unconvinced by the former banker's sudden change of mind, Paul had followed Fermin and discovered him talking with du Barroux regarding a small child in her care. Cozette had lost much of her former beauty in the years since Paul had kissed her goodbye, but she still bore a proud expression in her gaunt face. She appeared ill, and Paul heard her speak of dying soon. Fermin then delivered a terrible blow to the viscount, which haunted his nights for weeks, by revealing to Cozette that her child's father, a man named David Saunders, for whom she had spent two years searching in vain, was in truth a devious and manipulative liar with great wealth—in fact, a titled Scottish lord!

Paul's guilt nearly overwhelmed him, but he remained faithful to his mission, completing it just before Christmas. Whilst preparing to return to London, he decided he could not leave Paris without visiting his daughter and asking her mother's forgiveness. His intent was to set them both up in a small house and make sure they wanted for nothing, however Cozette's plight proved far worse than ever he might have imagined.

He called on du Barroux in her tiny apartment, for she had lost her home at *Le Chabanais* as soon as she refused to seek an abortion, and a fallen woman who is pregnant is no longer a commodity but a hindrance to a proprietress. She was very ill, nearly out of her mind with fever, her health failing. She had caught a chill whilst walking, she had insisted to him, but Paul recognised the signs of advanced consumption. He summoned the finest doctors, but the disease had already ravaged her poor lungs, and Cozette would soon die.

Deciding that he could not simply abandon her again, nor the child she told him was his very own, Paul took them both to a beautiful, private home in the countryside and kept them with him until Cozette's death six weeks later. The woman explained that she had tried to find him when she learnt she had fallen pregnant, but his garret was empty, and she found no one who would tell her where David Saunders had gone. Her deep love for him made it impossible to destroy his child, so she had supported little Adele as best she could, using up every franc he had left with her to make sure the child wanted for nothing. The wicked Fermin had discovered her secret, and promised to find Saunders for her, if she would but give him a description.

After burying Cozette, Paul departed Paris with his daughter, and though no one in government or the police made the connexion, three days later, Monsieur Fermin's bloated, lifeless body was found floating in the Seine, his neck broken. The death was ruled a suicide.

The girl, Adele Marie, was a miniature of her father, with Paul's soft chestnut hair that fell down her back in beautiful little waves and his clear blue eyes and dimples. He had missed Christmas with his parents, but when he explained the truth to his father, Lord Aubrey had welcomed the child with open arms, making her his legal ward and adopting her as his own. Because of the strong family resemblance, some did whisper, but it was assumed that it was the father's indiscretion that had led to an addition at Briarcliff. No one had suspected it was the son's.

Now, as he thought about sweet Adele, grown tall and nearly eleven, he resolved to tell Elizabeth all.

Charles had not yet fallen asleep. After the others had retired, the newly titled detective spent several hours talking with the duke and Kepelheim about the inner circle, learning the fine details of recent activities, including all that the circle knew about William Trent and Duchess Patricia's murder. Now, though physically exhausted, he lay awake pondering his own part in a centuries old plan.

Who am I really? A policeman? A peer of the realm? A royal heir?

Dressed in Connor Stuart's nightshirt and a paisley patterned, silk dressing gown, he finally despaired of trying to sleep and left his bedchamber, walking into the large private parlour of the late earl's apartment. Over the fireplace mantle, hung a portrait of Elizabeth, painted when Beth was very young, perhaps three or four. Scattered throughout the room, Sinclair found numerous photographs of Elizabeth at various stages of early childhood, including one as an infant, taken at her christening. He held the hand-coloured image, his eyes misting over as he thought of the possibilities of making Elizabeth his wife—and of one day, perhaps, having a son or daughter with her. His heart ached, fearing the dream was but an illusion, a fantasy.

Setting the photograph back onto its position of honour near a large leather chair, Charles's mind switched into detective mode, and he began to wonder just what sort of man Connor Stuart had been. The books upon the shelves covered a broad range of topics: science, mathematics, geography, politics, and warfare, but also poetry, medicine, biographies, and numerous volumes on history.

"Apparently, Cousin Connor, you were a well-read man," he said aloud. "Beth seems to have inherited your love of books."

As he thumbed through various volumes, he discovered a wall-safe, hidden behind a set of six books titled *Peter the Great and the Expanding Russian Empire*. Charles had learnt to crack safes during his years of policing, so he tried his hand at the three dial strongbox, and after several attempts, its movements finally yielded to defeat. Opening the door, the detective found an envelope, written on the outside with the disturbing legend, "For my father, should anything happen to me."

Looking at the portrait of his beloved Elizabeth, Charles felt a sudden stab of anxiety. Her father had penned this strange phrase and secured this envelope sometime before November 1876. Had he, too, been given a premonition of his own demise, or was there another reason for this precaution?

Not sure whether or not he should be doing so, Sinclair's investigative instincts at last overcame his doubts, and he opened the envelope, finding a note in cipher. He spent several minutes trying to decode the message, but it was far more complicated than the Redwing missive from earlier, apparently requiring a keyword, and since he had no idea what the inner circle's key might be, he placed the envelope with its strange contents into his pocket, intending to speak with the duke and Kepelheim about it the following morning.

Turning away from the bookshelves, Sinclair opened a magnificent, hand-carved mahogany wardrobe. Inside, he found several, beautifully tailored suits. "I wonder if Martin made these," the marquess whispered to himself as he explored the cedar-lined interior. Recalling the portrait of the earl back at Branham, Charles could picture the handsome Scotsman wearing these tartans, tweeds, and silks. Trying on one of the suitcoats, he glanced at himself in the mirror. The fit was an inch too large in the waist, slightly long in the arms, but overall looked quite nice. Without thinking, he put his hand in the pocket and found a much-used briar.

"So Connor Stuart smoked a pipe," he mused. "Strange that Beth said she didn't like pipe smoke as a girl. Now, what is this?" he said aloud, his left hand finding a small key. It looked like it might fit a suitcase or perhaps a strong box. "What other secrets might you have had, Cousin?"

Assuming the key fit a lock nearby, he decided to search for something within the room that it might fit. Besides the bookcases, the parlour also held a large desk. The top drawer contained a small, combination lap desk and folding blotter, so the detective removed it and set it aside. Beneath the blotter, he uncovered a small, locked diary. Charles placed the key into the lock, and it turned easily.

"Perhaps, I shouldn't..." he whispered to himself. "No. It is too intrusive. I'll speak to Uncle James about it tomorrow." He placed the small diary and its key within the deep right pocket of the dressing gown and continued his search. The third drawer on the right held a selection of stationery engraved with 'Drummond Castle' and the duke's crest, but he also found several sheets with a different crest and 'Connor Stuart, 6th Earl of Kesson' printed across the top.

Deciding he'd start making notes about his discoveries, Sinclair began to look for writing paper. Not wishing to use any of the engraved pages, he shut that drawer and opened the topmost on the left, finding envelopes, a variety of penny and halfpenny postage stamps, and a few coins. Beneath the envelopes he found a stack of blank stationery. Taking several of these sheets, he closed the drawer, took the blotter, an ink pen, and a bottle of ink and sat into the leather chair. He set the ink bottle onto a small smoking stand and opened the blotter.

To his surprise, it contained a letter, apparently written but not posted, many years earlier. A letter written by Connor Stuart. Sinclair considered whether or not he should take the letter to the duke, but his natural curiosity won out, and he decided to read it first.

23 November, 1876

Patricia,

I shall keep this short, for I doubt that you have any desire to read more than a few lines from me. Suffice to say that I know everything. The man in Paris, the secret meetings in Hampton, and even your indiscretions in our own bed! I never deceived myself into thinking you loved me as much as you loved Ian, but I did imagine you held me in some esteem. I have been thoroughly disabused of that notion.

I plan to speak to my attorney tomorrow in Glasgow, and I intend to seek full custody of Elizabeth. She will never, I repeat never be permitted to witness your infidelities with that man, nor will I allow her to be in danger of any kind. I do not trust William Trent. I've had him investigated, Trish. He is Redwing. I know you have no desire to hear about circle matters, but can you not at least care enough about our daughter to protect her from the enemy? I've not yet said anything to my father, but I will.

Elizabeth knows, Trish. She knows. I do not yet comprehend how she discerned it, but she's having nightmares again, and the blame lies squarely upon your shoulders. There was a time when I could not have imagined not loving you—but in truth all love in my heart for you has died. You murdered it. I will not permit you to ruin Elizabeth's life in like manner.

I will not press for any financial settlement, but if you think you will marry Trent once our divorce is final, then think again. If you do, I shall see to it that you are stripped of your title and lands and all will immediately pass to Elizabeth. There is a morals clause in your father's will that you probably do not recall. He placed it there because of your infatuation with Ian. I shall not hesitate to seek enforcement of that clause if you so much as become engaged to Trent.

Do not put this to the test, Patricia, for you will lose. –Connor

Sinclair stared at the extraordinary letter, feeling completely stunned. Though he imagined no one awake at this hour, he knew he would never rest until he'd told someone about this, so he decided to seek out Kepelheim rather than the duke. He dressed and found his way to the tailor's rooms, knocking softly.

To his surprise and relief, the door opened quickly.

"Come in, friend Charles. I'd thought it might be you. Perhaps, you read my mind, eh? Come in!"

"Thank you, Martin. I didn't wake you, did I? If you're sleepy, just kick me out..."

"No, no, my dear friend. You find me awake and contemplative. Apparently, that is your current state as well. Sherry? You look as if a small glass might do you a world of good."

Charles entered the cosy parlour connected to the guest room suite and dropped into one of two forest green chairs near the cheerful fire. "Yes, thank you. In truth, Martin, I rarely drink, but oftentimes this past week I find myself in need of what Mrs. Alcorn calls a 'stiffener'. My mind cannot rest."

"Of course, it cannot," the tailor agreed, pouring two small glasses of an *oloroso dulce* and handing one to the detective. "Think how different your life is suddenly! You left Whitechapel with naught but the clothes upon your back and love in your heart and suddenly you find yourself heir to a huge estate and a peer of the realm. A high ranking one, at that. Haimsbury is the oldest marquessate in our kingdom."

"Really? I'd no idea."

"Most don't, but those who study such matters are keenly aware of it, as is Her Majesty. And there is another matter that the duke has been discussing with me, regarding his successor, being as you are the elder nephew. Can you imagine yourself a duke, my friend?"

Charles gulped the spirit down and held out the glass for a refill. "A duke? Perhaps, I need more than a stiffener. Isn't Paul his heir, or perhaps Elizabeth?"

"Beth wants no part of another ducal title, so yes, Aubrey is the current heir, but as I say you are the elder nephew, and your uncle has told me that he hopes you will accept it. The earl only agreed to being named as heir because there was no one else at the time. James has discussed it with the earl in private, and I understand that he seemed quite relieved. Paul prefers to keep his chains as light as possible, and titles and lands can weigh one down. But you have a look about you that speaks of more than just an unexpected inheritance. Tell me, Charles, what has happened?"

"You know I'm staying in Connor's old rooms."

"Yes. The duke had wanted you to stay there from...well, from the moment he knew you were on your way. He's looked forward to welcoming you back into the family for many years."

"Has he?" Sinclair asked, the impact of the tailor's words hitting his heart.

"Indeed, he has. My investigations into you began long ago, as I'm sure you now realise. The duke, you see, thought you looked familiar when he first met you in '79."

"How can that be, Martin? James had not seen me in almost twenty years, and only then as a small boy. I'd changed dramatically in those years."

"Yes, that is so, but even I was startled when first I saw you in person. Not on the train, of course. I'd been shadowing you for many years. With so many of us within the circle dogging your steps, Charles, I'm surprised you did not notice us sooner!"

Sinclair laughed, sipping at the wine. "It doesn't speak well for a policeman, does it? When you saw me you were startled, what do you mean?"

The tailor leaned back in the chair and cleared his throat. "It was that summer, I think, when the duke assigned me the task of looking into your background. I decided to commence my investigation by following you so that I might learn your routine and observe your friendships. Since you'd never met me or even seen me, I doubted you would notice a nondescript tailor, but still I kept a low profile as best I could, which made it difficult to see your face without risking your seeing my own. Though you knew me not, I had no doubt of your capabilities, my friend. Like your cousin, you have a mind for faces, so I kept mine from you. I suppose it was the following year when I finally found myself in a position to assess your face without your seeing mine. With a careworn hedge betwixt us, I stood as close to as I am now, and I had five minutes or more to examine the lines of your face. I was surprised you did not hear me gasp, for in truth I did."

Charles smiled. "Why?"

"It is your eyes. Do you recall my mentioning them on the train?"

He laughed, swirling the spirit in the glass. "I do. You said you had a fabric that would work well with my eyes. I'll admit to wondering what you meant by it, Martin."

Kepelheim laughed softly, twisting his greying moustache. "Yes, well, your eye colour is unique, you see. I have never seen its like in any other face. Man or woman."

"Blue eyes are hardly uncommon in England. In fact, they are more common than brown. Ask any booking sergeant. One of the boxes he has to tick each time is eye colour. Blue outpaces brown by a factor of three."

"How very interesting! I'd not known that, but it makes sense, I suppose. Many of our forebears in England came from German and Danish stock, did they not? The Celts, however, often have dark eyes like Elizabeth. Your father had brown eyes, did you know that?"

"No. I've not yet seen any images other than the photographs, but none that's been coloured. Do I resemble him?"

"Yes, very much," the tailor said. "You and Paul have a similar appearance, of course, but you look a great deal like your father. When I saw you that first time, full in the face, it struck me that you were a wonderful echo of Robby Sinclair. Such an energetic and erudite man and a thorn in the side of Redwing, I can tell you that. Your eyes are an interesting combination of both your parents."

"How so?" Charles asked.

"I dabble in painting, and I can tell you that if one took your mother's beautiful and unique blue eye colour and added a tiny bit of yellow to it, you'd arrive at yours. Brown eyes are but variations of yellow, you know."

"Beth calls them sea blue eyes."

"And so they are," the tailor agreed. "Azure is one way to describe them, but they are almost a turquoise shade. I had not seen eyes that colour since last I saw you, Charles, and that day, when I saw your eyes and your uncanny resemblance to Robby Sinclair, I knew we had at last found you. Yet my intuition and claims of eye colour mixing were not enough for the duke. I had to find the legal proofs, and so now we have. Had we told you long ago, how might it have changed your path, I wonder?"

He thought about this, finishing the sherry. "I'd probably still be married," he said at last. "Amelia would never have left a marquess, no matter how little she loved me in the end. And she'd be alive." His mood grew somber as Charles pondered this.

The tailor leaned forward and touched the younger man's forearm. "One cannot alter the past, my friend, but we can move forward from the present as best we may. Keep your mind focused upon that. The duke chooses to do that daily. When you and your mother disappeared, I thought your uncle would go into a dark despair from which no man can emerge, but he has come out the other side of that darkness into this beautiful, bright present."

Charles's eyes grew moist. "I cannot tell you what that man means to me, Martin. I've admired the duke for nearly a decade, but learning that he is my uncle is the second greatest gift I've ever received."

The tailor smiled. "I think I can guess what the first greatest gift is, my friend. Elizabeth, no?"

The marquess nodded, his eyes bright. "She is, Martin. I love her more than life. I suppose that is one reason this letter is so disturbing."

"Letter?" the tailor asked, reaching out as Sinclair removed the sheets from his jacket pocket and handed them to Kepelheim. "Where did you find this?"

"In a folding blotter inside the late earl's desk, but I also found this," he said, handing the coded message to the older man. "It was locked inside a hidden safe."

"Hidden?" Kepelheim asked, a smile playing at the corners of his mouth. "It seems your detective instincts never truly take a rest. But how did you open it?"

It was the detective who now smiled. "Let's just say it isn't my first time opening a strongbox. Cracking a dial safe is easy for a mathematician."

The tailor laughed heartily, wiping at his eyes. "Oh my, yes! I should imagine it would be. Your father would have been quite proud of you, Charles. He, too, had a mind that loved solving puzzles and equations. It was he designed our first cipher. This one looks similar to that early key." The tailor squinted at the strange symbols. "My eyes are not what they used to be. Can you hand me those spectacles, Charles? Over by the lamp."

The marquess found the gold-rimmed *pince-nez* and handed them to the tailor, who settled them onto his bulbous nose. "Yes, it is indeed the code created by your father and the late earl. They were great friends, you know. Let's see." He stared at the note for many minutes, his brows squirming with the effort. "No, I shall have to find my old key to make sure I do not mistranslate it, but I believe it speaks of matters that relate to you and Redwing."

"To me? Why would Beth's father write about me?"

"The late earl loved you like a son, Charles. As I say, he and your father were quite close, and Connor often visited you."

Sinclair sighed. "I wish I could remember that. But why would he mention me in a message with such an ominous phrase written upon its envelope?"

The tailor's eyes grew serious. "As I said, I do not wish to mistranslate it, so allow me to offer further explanation tomorrow, once I've consulted with the duke."

"Very well, but what about the letter that he wrote to Beth's mother? It is not in code. I cannot believe no one else has found it until tonight. Why did he not mail it?"

"Perhaps, Connor thought better of it after penning it."

"I doubt it, Martin. Read it."

The tailor's silvery brows pinched together as he scanned through the distressing missive. "So, he did plan to divorce her," he muttered.

"You knew about this?" Sinclair asked, dumbfounded.

"I suspected it. It is the date of this letter that most concerns me, Charles. It is the day that Connor was attacked by the wolf."

Sinclair's eyes widened, and his face paled. "I might need another drink."

In another part of the castle, Elizabeth also found herself unable to rest. The dreams she and Charles had shared were shadows of a real liaison, memories of an actual event. She had given herself to him, and by doing so, offered a once in a lifetime gift she had always thought would be Paul's.

She wondered if the earl now slept, if his shoulder gave him pain, and she considered knocking on his door, but she could not bring herself to go to him, not yet. Instead, getting out of bed, she slipped a long robe of royal blue satin over top her silk and lace night dress, and then took a candle to light her path down the grand staircase to the main level. She was after a book to read, perhaps a Jules Verne.

As she entered the upstairs hallway, she could hear a woman speaking to Lord Aubrey. It was Lorena MacKey, who stood near the earl's door, asking if he needed something to help him sleep. Hearing Paul's reply, that he had already consumed all of the wine mixture, MacKey spoke something else—whispered and inaudible, something that sounded almost like chanting—then turned to find Elizabeth looking at her.

"Oh! Your Grace, I hope I didn't wake you," Lorena said, briskly walking toward the duchess. She spoke in hushed tones, as if joining in a conspiracy. "I had worried that the earl's medicine would have worn off, so I asked if he needed an additional dose. Are you all right? Does your foot pain you? I have a mild soporific in my bag."

"No, it is much improved. Thank you for your concern. I am simply restless. I thought to find a book in my grandfather's library."

"Oh, a book is such a good idea! Do you mind if I join you?"

"Not at all," Elizabeth replied, glad to have the chance to sound out the woman privately. "The stairs are not the most even. It's often so with these old castles, so watch your feet. The guest library is in the west wing, so we've a bit of a walk."

"How exciting," Lorena whispered, holding her own candle high as they walked down the long flights to the flagstone floor of the foyer. "Now where? I'm completely lost."

"Follow me. We shall go to the right here, and then through the grand gallery."

"Oh yes, I think Paul—I mean the earl—took me through there last night. It's the very long room filled with lots of chairs and beautiful old paintings, correct?"

"Yes. Those ancestral faces used to stare down at me whenever I came here as a little girl, and I was convinced their eyes watched my every move."

MacKey had borrowed a nightgown from Elizabeth, since she had arrived with no baggage, and as the doctor stood six inches taller than the duchess, the fit was sufficient but not precise. "Thank you for allowing me to wear your beautiful things. This nightgown is finer than anything I could ever afford, though it is a trifle short, but then I have dreadfully long legs. When I was little, my friends called me 'stork legs'. Not very flattering, but as I've grown and rounded a bit, I find men appreciate them, so it's not so bad."

Elizabeth had spent little time with female friends in her life. As the only child of two high-ranking peers, but especially a child in the constant protection of the inner circle, her life had seldom taken her to homes outside her own family.

"Do women say such things when alone?" she asked, hoping to engage MacKey in open conversation, which may reveal a hidden motive for her sudden appearance in Glasgow the previous morning and subsequent arrival at the castle later on.

"I suppose we do," Lorena answered as they entered the grand gallery. "This place is rather spooky at night with just a small candle for illumination. I see what you mean about the eyes!"

"That is my great-great-grandfather," she said, indicating a full-length portrait of a boy in satin breeches standing next to a large chestnut horse. "He was, oh seven I think, when that was painted. James Paul Ian Stuart, the 8th Duke of Drummond. The family uses the same names a lot. I suppose that's often the case in old families. You grew up in Glencoe, did you not?"

"My parents did," Lorena replied, slowing her pace a bit. "Is that Paul?" she asked, pausing before a full-length portrait showing the earl at twenty-one in full kilt and kit, standing next to a large stone fireplace.

"Yes," Beth answered, smiling as she recalled the painting's ceremonial hanging. "The duke had this commissioned when he named Paul his heir."

The doctor looked at the painting as if willing it to life. "He is to be the next duke?" she asked. "Won't you inherit?"

"I could, but my grandfather preferred to offer it to Paul after my father died. I saw no point in having two ducal titles."

The doctor considered this for a moment, her eyes on the portrait. "Paul is a very handsome man, and he's changed very little in twelve years. But what if he leaves no heir? Then, to whom would it pass, if not to you?"

Beth had no desire to even imagine Paul's death, but she assumed the doctor must have asked for some surreptitious reason, so the duchess put aside her natural tendency toward introspection and answered openly. "Well, I imagine the title would then pass to Lord Haimsbury, since he is also the duke's nephew. You know, it occurs to me that Scottish law might actually consider him the first heir, before Paul, as Charles is older by a few months."

"Really? But, how does all this work? Can the duke dictate succession, or does the queen decide? I know very little about peerage laws, Your Grace."

They stood before the portrait, and Elizabeth found herself nearly overwhelmed by guilt as she gazed at Paul's trusting face. She took a moment to reply, and MacKey seemed to sense her prey's troubled heart.

"Are you all right, Duchess?" she asked, though she felt certain that the little mouse's sudden silence had much to do with the night in the cottage. "You grow pale. Perhaps, you should sit down. I'm told you suffered from a migraine last evening."

Beth shook her head and gathered her courage, moving away from the portrait and continuing through the gallery. "I'm all right, thank you, Doctor. You said your family was from Glencoe?"

MacKey had to work to keep from laughing, for she knew the prince was pleased with her success, but she remained moderately composed, though a smile played at her lips. "Actually, my parents left before I was born, but we visited several times when I was a girl."

They left the gallery and passed into a wide corridor that branched toward the right, leading into the suite of parlours where Beth, Charles, and Paul had slept the first two nights. Rather than follow this hallway, Elizabeth turned left toward a large anteroom that ended in a pair of gleaming white doors, one of them standing open.

"Through here is the guest library," the duchess said as they entered a large, cherry-paneled room containing hundreds of books in dozens of genres. "I enjoy reading these marvelous old history books. Do you like history? Those are on the right there, beneath the dictionaries and other reference books. If fiction is more to your taste, my grandfather has a quite nice selection of recent works. Wilkie Collins's *Moonstone* is there near the top. Dr. Doyle's wonderful new novel *A Study in Scarlet* is already a favourite of mine. *Allan Quartermain* is a nice adventure, and of course there are first editions of Mr. Dickens's books, Miss Austen, the Brontë Sisters, some Thomas Hardy—I believe the duke finds those intriguing. But if you prefer dark tales, then Mary Shelley's *Frankenstein* is here as well as Mr. Stephenson's newest, I see, though I've not read that one yet. I did see the play in Paris though—it is terrifying! What is your preference, Doctor?"

Lorena wandered around the room, touching nearly every shelf that her long arms could reach, her green eyes scanning each spine's title. "Is this the only library?" she asked.

"Well, it's the one I always use. I believe my grandfather also has a private collection, but it's kept locked, and only he and the butler have keys."

"A shame. I've been looking for a rare volume that my mother used to have, but I've not been able to find it. It's a history about old Scottish families."

Beth led her to the reference area, and took down a thick leather-bound book called *Peers of Scotland*. "Is this it?"

"No, I don't think so. This book was very old. Published in the 15th century. My father used to say it was the secret history of Scotland."

Elizabeth replaced the book and sat into one of the armchairs. "Scotland's history is a bloody one, but then that is probably true of many parts of the world. Change brings the need for expansion, and expansion brings more change—both leading to war."

"You don't like change?" Lorena asked, sitting on the settee, her green eyes fixed upon Elizabeth like a cat looking at a small brown mouse.

"I actually do like it. If you visited my London home, you would find it as modern as any government house, but I wonder how far our world will go as we move into this new age. Paul says that Europe is poised for war once again, and that it will certainly erupt within the next thirty years, if not much sooner. Germany and France continue to quarrel, and Russia may pretend to honour her agreements, but Paul insists that both Germany and Russia seek dominion of Europe. He's seldom wrong when it comes to politics.

War, as I see it, is—well, a bit like the eruption of a volcano, which appears without warning, but beneath a seemingly peaceful summit, geological changes have been moving toward that eruption for years, perhaps decades. Civilisation also undergoes silent, creeping shifts. Local crimes, greed, betrayal, lusts, and even lies may lead to larger and larger indiscretions and dark deeds, and soon the world mountain begins to shake with war."

"You are a philosopher, Duchess."

"I am not, or I am not aware of being one. I merely see our world progressing further into political darkness."

"But isn't progress also good?" the predator asked, finding her mouse tastier by the minute. "I mean, women are making their way into the world of men, and I believe we shall have the vote soon. Think what wonderful amendments we shall make to man's law! Were women to join the political machine, then war might be avoided."

"Perhaps," Elizabeth answered. "However, progress is not a neutral state. Though we rush toward a modernized society, I am not certain that all scientific discovery is in fact good, though I see your point. My mother took me to Calcutta when I was a little girl to visit my father. He was serving as governor there, and we stayed for several weeks. Have you ever been?"

The doctor shook her head. "No. Isn't it awfully hot?"

"Yes, it is. India is such a different world from England! I was amazed at how little it took to make people happy—*truly* happy. Water, a day's bread, and the love of family are all we ever truly need, and yet we who are *civilised* strive to accumulate more and more. You will laugh when I say this, but I once told my mother that I wanted to study medicine when I grew up."

"Really? Why didn't you?"

Beth struggled inwardly to maintain her composure, for memories of her mother's broken body still haunted her thoughts and dreams, but she wanted to make a statement—to introduce a lure into the conversation, hoping the doctor would find it tempting and bite. "My mother told me that, though a doctor may heal many people, someone who has the capability and privilege of funding an entire teaching institution has the potential to heal many generations of people whilst providing jobs and education."

This information apparently surprised MacKey, for her guard dropped for a tiny second. Not long, but long enough, for Elizabeth could see a raw and overwhelming emotion on the woman's face: *Desire*. The duchess continued, "That is why I plan to commission a builder to construct such a teaching hospital, one where both men and women with aptitude but little money may learn the art of healing, in Whitechapel."

"Whitechapel? Well, I must say, that is another surprise, Your Grace. Forgive me, I am never clear on my manners in our situation, should I address you as such, or is it Duchess?"

"However you wish, Dr. MacKey. Debrett's will say it must be 'your grace' if the person speaking is not a peer. A peer would usually call me Duchess. Personally, I care not. Call me Elizabeth, if you like."

"That's very kind of you, Duch—I mean, Elizabeth. It's such a beautiful, queenly name. But Whitechapel? Isn't that far from your usual zone of comfort?"

"It is where my mother's body was found when I was a child, and I wish to honour her memory by placing a learning and healing institution where she breathed her last."

The story was mostly true, though Patricia Stuart had not breathed her last on Commercial Street, for she had died on the road from Branham to London. Beth's memory had not yet re-discovered all the true facts of that wild journey, and at that moment, most still remained hidden behind a slowly crumbling wall.

"Oh—I, well, I don't know what to say. That must have been horrible! I am so sorry, Duchess. How old were you?"

"Ten, nearly eleven. It will be ten years next March, in fact. Yes, it was quite, quite horrible."

MacKey thought for a moment, and her emerald eyes suddenly rounded. "Of course! That must be how you met your fiancé!"

Beth stared, completely perplexed. "My fiancé? I am sorry, Doctor, but I do not follow."

"It's all right, I won't tell if it is still a secret. I can tell when two people are in love, and the ring on your hand is clearly an engagement ring. Paul told me that Lord Haimsbury only recently learnt he was the heir and that he is in truth a marquess. That must have been quite a shock for a Whitechapel detective! But then, perhaps that is where the two of you met. If you are building a hospital there, then it makes perfect sense."

Elizabeth had no intention of revealing her first meeting with Charles all those years before, but she felt she must clear up the idea of an engagement. "You have drawn an understandable inference, Doctor, based on our morning activities yesterday, but against all appearances to the contrary, Charles and I are not engaged."

"But it's so clear that Charles loves you, Elizabeth. Why else would he sweep you off to a tea room for a quiet conversation? The ring is beautiful. I'd be proud to wear one like it, though I don't know if I shall ever find the right man."

"I'm sure you will," the duchess replied, wishing to leave off talking about Sinclair for the moment.

"Of course, it's foolish to wish for, but your cousin is certainly dashing, is he not? I regret that it is quite unlikely that I should ever discover myself the heiress to a title, so it is just as unlikely that the earl would ever see beyond my medical bag."

"You find Lord Aubrey attractive then?"

"I find him to be beautiful, remarkable, and a deliciously sensual man! In fact, I would call him a perfect specimen of manhood."

Beth found this line of conversation too intimate and familiar, especially when the subject was a man she had planned for most of her life to marry, but soft interrogation requires being willing to accommodate, her grandfather had once told her. "He is indeed a wonderful man. Has he given you any reason to hope, Lorena?"

The doctor's head tilted, curious that the duchess had suddenly switched to addressing her by her first name. "Perhaps. I cannot tell, since I do not yet know his moods and what is called his means of conveying non-verbal communications, and yet I believe there is a spark there. He is your cousin; do you know if his heart belongs to anyone else?"

"Paul has been my closest friend for all my life. I'm not sure I could make that assessment fairly."

The predator looked deeply into her prey's eyes searching for signs of deception, but the duchess appeared to be speaking her heart. *Good. Very good.* Any woman who loved with all her heart would surely have risen to such bait. Trent and the Prince would be pleased. The belladonna and opium mixture had surely muddled her mind, and it now appeared that it had also erased the earl from the centre of Elizabeth's heart. Indeed, a new king now ruled there—Charles Sinclair, the one with the blood most perfect for their infernal sovereign's goal.

"I will continue to hope," the cat said smoothly. "My father always said I could hope with the best of them."

"Hope is mankind's greatest gift, is it not? Our Saviour Jesus Christ and the salvation He offers us; does that not define hope itself?"

Lorena's face twisted for just a tiny fraction of a second, but her recovery was too late, for Elizabeth now knew that the woman in front of her was a liar and perhaps in league with devils.

CHAPTER TWENTY-TWO
11 October, 9:12 a.m. - Golden Lane, Aldgate

Edmund Reid took his seat amongst the witnesses as the inquest into the death of Catherine Eddowes reconvened. The proceedings at the Golden Lane mortuary had begun the week previous, but due to a call for additional evidence collection, City of London Coroner F. H. Langham had adjourned until today. Sitting next to Inspector Fred Abberline, who had also been called to give testimony, Reid thumbed through his notebook to refresh his memory of the murder.

Eddowes's body had been discovered on 30, September, 1888, at approximately 1:45 pm in Mitre Square by City of London Police Constable Edward Watkins. The forty-six-year-old woman was a mere five feet tall, and wore a black straw hat, a black broadcloth jacket trimmed in imitation fur, a green chintz skirt, and men's lace-up boots. Amongst her meagre belongings, Leman Street's CID investigators found bits of soap, matches, tins of tea and sugar, a cigarette case, and two pawn tickets.

Though discovered on the eastern edge of the square mile, and therefore technically a City Police case, H-Division had been called in to aid, since the case appeared to be yet another in the Whitechapel Murder series, but also because a scrap of the victim's apron, stained in blood, had been discovered in H-Division's jurisdiction near the stairwell of a tenement house on Goulston Street. Not far from the bloody apron, Constable Alfred Long had found a mysterious graffito message written in white chalk that read 'The Juwes are the men that will not be blamed for nothing'.

Superintendent Thomas Arnold stood in the witness box now, relating his involvement with the mysterious message and why it had later been ordered expunged by Commissioner Sir Charles Warren without ever being photographed.

As he listened to Arnold give his account, Reid chewed at his moustache, wondering what kind of man could completely destroy a total stranger—a woman with little to keep her warm, save a bottle of gin. In fact, Eddowes had been in H-Division's lockup on charges of public drunkenness until one o'clock the morning of the murder. Not for the first time, Reid pondered if Eddowes might not still be alive and walking about Whitechapel if they had retained her in custody just one day longer—or had the poor woman always been fated to end in such a pitiable manner?

As the clock ticked toward quarter past, a young police constable stepped up behind Reid and Abberline and tapped both on the shoulders, whispering that they were needed right away at the station house. A disgruntled Abberline turned and asked why, but the lad refrained from answering, which irritated the seasoned detective to the extent that he actually stood and ordered the boy to 'spill it!' Remaining calm, PC Desmond wrote a short note, showing it to both men: *It might be another one. Ripper.*

Fred Abberline's eyes grew wide, and he grasped the constable by the coat collar, and all three men left the proceedings.

Outside, the policemen hastened to step clear of the considerable crowd that had gathered to watch the inquest, including George Lusk and his Vigilance Committee, Fred Best, Michael O'Brien, and Harry Dam of *The Star* and many dozens of reporters from all over London—and as far out as Manchester and York—along with half a dozen well-dressed bankers and businessmen, there for a cheap thrill.

"What makes Detective Constable Harvey think this murder is Ripper?" Abberline asked in a low but strained voice.

The lad kept walking, flanked by his superiors, heading toward a hansom. Dam tapped O'Brien on the shoulder and nodded toward the two inspectors. The American photographer—using the camera he'd recovered from Leman Street—began snapping photographs whilst O'Brien crept close enough to overhear. The reporter took notes quickly, in shorthand.

"We don't know the murder location, but..." the constable said.

Abberline's boots bit into the packed dust, and a passing cart and pony nearly ran him down. "What? How can you not know where the body was found, Mr. Desmond?"

The young man, only twenty years old and just two weeks into his new duties, thought for a moment before answering. "Well, Inspector Abberline, sir, it's just that the body came to us."

"Came to us? What, it flew, did it?"

"No, sir. Of course not, sir, but it—well it was *delivered*."

Edmund Reid interrupted. "Out with it, son."

"A local publican found it in front of our doors, sir. And he rushed in to inform the desk sergeant."

"Did you then arrest this publican?"

"We are holding him for questioning, sir, but he says the body was left by another."

Abberline gaped. "Left by another?"

"Yes, sir. He said a gentleman left it. A tall man, dark hair with a moustache, a fur hat, fancy coat, and a cane."

"That description would fit half the men in London today, did you get nothing more specific?" Abberline asked, noticing the reporters. "Edmund, let's move this into the hansom." The two inspectors joined the constable inside the rented carriage, the thin youngster jammed in between his superiors within the cramped interior.

"All right," Abberline said as the hansom set into motion. "This man with the cane. Do we have anything more?"

"Yes, sir. The publican said the man spoke to him, and then he just disappeared."

"He spoke, this man? What did he say?" Reid prompted.

"The landlord quotes this gentleman as saying, 'Tell Elizabeth I am coming.'"

Abberline threw his hat to the floor of the cab. "Is this your idea of a joke? Because, boy, I am not laughing!"

Reid's face grew pale. "Is that all he said? Think, lad. Every word matters."

"Yes, sir, Inspector Reid. That is all. And, as I have told you, the man then disappeared."

"Disappeared 'round the corner, you mean?" Reid probed.

The boy gulped, knowing they would not believe it. "No, sir. He vanished. Into thin air."

Adele Marie Stuart was a lithe and beautiful female version of her father—or rather the man she knew as her brother, Paul Stuart—and she entered Drummond Castle as if blown upon a summer breeze.

"Paul!" she shouted with peals of laughter as she saw him on the staircase. "Whatever did you do to yourself, brother mine? Oh, your poor, poor shoulder!"

Aubrey jumped down the last two steps and knelt to receive her hugs and kisses. He adored his daughter, but he had always been careful to maintain a brotherly manner, though sometimes it proved nearly impossible. "How this one can giggle, and that smile would break your heart," he said to his uncle, who had already received many hugs and kisses. "Della, my love, you are a treasure!"

Adele kissed Paul once again and then paused for a moment, her face working out a puzzle. "Are you my new cousin?" she asked, seeing Charles descend the staircase behind the earl. "You could be another brother, you know. You look very much like my dear, wounded Paul. I am Adele, and you must be Charles. I was told all about you by Mr. Parks on the drive from the train station in Glasgow."

Sinclair bowed and kissed her hand. "Charmed, dear Cousin. I am indeed that lucky fellow. Your brother has done nothing but talk of you all morning. Though I had expected you to have two heads. Cousin Paul, did you not tell me that Adele has two heads? A lovely feathered hat perched prettily upon each?"

She giggled again, her blue eyes sparkling. "That is silly!" she laughed, pulling him down so she could kiss his cheek. "You are a lovely cousin, and I shall insist you buy me two hats now, one for each head!"

Charles lost his heart, and he picked her up, since Paul's shoulder made it impossible for him to lift his own daughter, though Charles knew nothing yet of that family secret. "You are very light for someone with two heads," he told her with a serious face.

"That's because I keep one on my neck and the other in my pocket," she teased.

"Really?" he asked, patting all around her coat for a pocket head. "I don't think so. I cannot find it, Cousin. Did you perhaps leave it on the train?"

Paul laughed, giving her another kiss as she perched in Sinclair's arms. "Shall I send Parks back to the station to fetch your second head, Della?"

"No, I shall simply manage with one," she said most seriously. "Uncle James, have you got two heads?"

The duke laughed merrily. "Not right now, but I thought I saw a man with three heads just yesterday!"

She burst into a shower of wonderful laughter, and Charles handed her to James, tapping Paul on the arm. "When you've a moment, I'd love a word."

Paul nodded, but seeing Elizabeth's face grow suddenly ashen, he thought again. "Would this evening do?"

Sinclair's back was to the duchess, so he did not see her silent communication. "That will do, thank you. After supper in the duke's library?"

"I'll be there," Paul promised. "Now, little one, or should I say, young lady, for you have grown two feet since last we saw each other, shall we get you settled?"

"Oh, Paul, I've not grown two feet, but two heads!" she corrected, once again breaking into joyous giggles. "And I shall wear both my heads and both my hats for your wedding to Cousin Elizabeth!"

Paul kept smiling, but it was work to do so. Adele's arrival would add strain to all their conversations now.

"And who is this?" asked a woman's voice as she descended the stairs dressed in a bright blue dress borrowed from Elizabeth. The hem rose much higher on Lorena's leg than it did the gown's owner, and it allowed for the borrower's length of ankle to reveal a comely shape.

James set Adele onto the flagstone floor, and she gazed up at the newcomer. "I am Adele Stuart. Are you another cousin?" she asked innocently.

"No," Lorena said, "I am a doctor."

Adele looked puzzled. "But doctors are men with grey beards who smell of soap and quinine," she insisted.

Elizabeth stepped forward, taking Adele's hand. "This is one of a new type of doctor, my darling. Dr. MacKey came to help take care of your brother's poor shoulder. A nasty fall riding. Don't you think he needs another hug for that?"

Adele agreed and threw her arms around her 'brother', not knowing the true depth of affection he held for her.

"Darling, Brother," she said honestly. "You are the best horseman in all the land, but I have never fallen from my pony, and yet you have fallen from your horse. No more horses until you learn to watch better."

Paul agreed, glad for Elizabeth's quick thinking. "I shall always remember to ask your advice first. Now, it is time for luncheon. Shall we go see what Mrs. Calhoun has made for us?"

"Will there be pudding?" she asked, her blue eyes round, dark lashes circling them like two lush fans. "A cake, perhaps?"

"We shall have to wait and see. Why don't you go with Mrs. MacAnder and wash your face and hands, and we shall meet up with you in the dining hall."

She ran to the housekeeper to give the buxom woman a fond hug, and Paul went to Elizabeth and kissed her, his lips lingering for a moment on hers, and he whispered, "I love you more today than ever before, Princess."

She held his embrace, focusing her eyes away from Charles. "I must talk with you before you meet Charles. Please, tell me when, but it must be private."

He released her, his face filled with concern. Had James told her about Adele? Did she know the truth? "My rooms, right after luncheon?"

"Yes, thank you," she said with more seriousness than he recalled her using in many years. She turned toward the staircase just in time to greet Mr. Kepelheim, who had descended with a coat, waistcoat, and two pairs of trousers on his arm, a marking chalk in his top pocket, and his ever-present measuring tape slung 'round his ample neck.

"Lord Haimsbury, I must make a few minor adjustments to your new attire. May we use the blue drawing room, Your Grace?" he asked the duke, whose attentions had returned from thoughts of his young niece.

"Use whatever room you like, Kepelheim. In fact, here's the key to my library; you'll have total privacy there. Not even Laurence enters that room unless I ring the bell, but be quick about it. We cannot keep our young lady waiting, now can we?"

"I should never dream of such a thing!" the tailor called, signaling for the marquess to follow him to the library. Lorena, had been standing in the foyer, just near the turn toward the gallery, and she peered around to see which direction they had gone, and then once the foyer emptied, quietly followed.

Inside the private library, Kepelheim wasted no time in locking the door behind them. "We must find a way to get that witch out of this house!" he cried out, his face becoming florid and pale all at once like a patchwork. "My word, how she lies!"

Charles felt no need to ask who the tailor meant. "The doctor is indeed more than she seems, my friend. I have not spoken to the earl about her, but I hope to heaven he has been putting on a show to lure that woman into setting an obvious trap. And she does it wearing Elizabeth's own clothes," he added, suddenly remembering that was precisely what he had done: taken Elizabeth whilst wearing his cousin's clothing. However, MacKey's intent was purposeful, but his behaviour had been designed by someone else. "There are times, Martin, when I feel as if the past few days are all a strange dream—like a chapter from an old fairy tale."

"And Lorena MacKey is the sorceress in that tale, my friend," the tailor agreed. "Lord Aubrey plays right into her charming and devious hands."

Charles put on the first pair of trousers along with the matching waistcoat and turned as the tailor marked the alterations with the chalk. "Paul has always struck me as discerning, but he may be up against something more powerful than flesh and blood."

"As are we all, my dear friend," the tailor replied with a finger to his nose. "But this woman—she is something to be feared. I would swear that she leaves sulfur in her wake as she prowls about the halls! And, may I tell you what I overheard, purely by chance of course? Last night, after our talk, I found myself restless and happened to be standing in the hallway twixt our apartments sometime after three o'clock this morning, when first one, and then another lady appeared in the dim light. The first was our dear one, but the second of course, was that pretender, sniffing at the earl's door like the predator that she is. You called her that to me only yesterday afternoon, and my friend you are so right in that. Never let your detective's instincts go unheeded, Lord Haimsbury."

"What did she want from Paul at that time of night? Wait, of course, I can guess," Charles said as he slipped his arms into the fashionable suitcoat.

"Oh, my, I suppose anyone with eyes could," Kepelheim said, running the chalk across the garment's shoulders. "She knocked ever so sweetly upon his door to make certain he was sleeping. She claimed she had heard him tossing about, and that she feared he suffered pain, and should she then come in to administer therapeutic aid, or some such duplicitous words. I was half asleep, of course, but the earl said he required no new remedy or visitation, and despite his refusal, this devil woman looked ready to enter, with malicious intent I've no doubt, but her attempted assignation was stopped in its tracks by the appearance of our beloved lady—our remarkable duchess—she had espied the witch!" he exclaimed, and then wiping his brow, pointed to a sturdy table. "Stand there, will you, friend Charles, and let me accomplish my work, so we have our cover complete."

Charles stood upon a heavy iron and ash table whilst Kepelheim marked the trousers, his fingers flying as he spoke. "And then, my ears could not believe it, but the woman she says she is only being a good doctor, or some such excuse, but our Princess, our sweet Elizabeth, she is clearly suspicious, yet I know not whether this doctor can tell it. The duchess says she is restless and would find a book to read in the library, and the doctor says she, too, would find a book much help, so both ladies go to the guest library in the west wing."

"Go on," Charles said, watching the time on the mantel clock. "We must not be too long."

"Yes, and I must not make your hems too long. All right, so. I tiptoe as best and as quickly as my old feet and knees can manage, and I get to the library first—taking the short cut through the dining hall. I slip inside and hide behind the silk screen that sits in the corner by one of those large plants the ladies so love. The palm, I think, or is it a fern? I can never remember my botany."

"The doctor would probably know," Charles said with a faint smile. "But then, she'd also know how to use it in a potion, I imagine. Martin, are we being too harsh on Dr. MacKey? I agree that there is something about her that does not ring true, and her brazen flirtations with Paul concern me, but..."

"But, my generous friend, she will claw out your heart even as she flirts with it! No, this kind the circle has seen many times, but this one—she is more powerful, I think. Have you watched her eyes when she speaks to Lord Aubrey? It's like one of those snakes in India, you know the ones being hypnotised by the street magicians, or whatever they call themselves. Only she is the snake who hypnotises her human prey, and her tongue is as poisonous as her kisses are sharp!"

He finished the marking, and then helped the marquess down to the carpet. "Let us speak no more of any of this outside these walls. The duke is a clever man, and he had this room sealed to make it sound proof to anyone who may linger outside in the anteroom. And there is another secret to this room. Do you see that wonderful portrait of our dear one as a little girl? There in the corner by the dictionaries?"

Charles nodded, admiring the large painting. The pose showed Elizabeth standing inside that very room, beside the great fireplace, wearing a black velvet skirt with a white silk blouse, a Stuart tartan shawl about her small shoulders. Two Jack Russell terriers played at her feet, and her dark eyes seemed fixed on the dogs as she laughed. "What was she then, Martin? Five? Six?"

"Seven, I think," the tailor said. "She's always been petite, of course, but see how she smiles? I was here when this was being painted, you see, so I can tell you that Elizabeth spent that entire Christmas laughing. Well, nearly all of it. She'd come here with her father, for Duchess Patricia had decided to spend the holiday with a cousin in France."

"Really?" the detective asked. "Martin, perhaps I am suspicious due to my profession, but given Connor's letter, is it possible that this holiday was but an excuse for the late duchess to meet Trent? It breaks my heart to learn the truth about their marriage. Elizabeth has told me several times just how close the two of them were, and how the entire family celebrated together at Branham each Christmas."

"So she likes to remember," the tailor said mysteriously. "Forgive me, Charles, but there is much that the sweet duchess does not recall clearly. I've told you before that her mind has been tampered with, and though we've not enough time for me to explain fully, let me tell you this. Redwing has managed to manipulate Elizabeth often in the years since her birth. We've tried to protect her, but all too often, the enemy's schemes have caught us unawares. That Christmas, when she posed for this painting, was filled with both joys and terrors. It was the first time we saw the wolf, but not the last."

Sinclair removed the marked coat and waistcoat and changed into the second pair of trousers, which Kepelheim had finished that morning. "A perfect fit," the tailor remarked. "You begin to look like the peer of the realm that you are, my friend. I've also finished the waistcoat that matches, but the coat requires another night's work. If tonight you again find yourself unable to sleep, then perhaps I will sew whilst you and I talk, eh? Now, what was I saying?"

"The wolf. You said it first appeared that Christmas."

"Yes, so it did, but I think our dear one had seen it before—as had her father, for both seemed particularly shaken by it. Connor became very protective of Elizabeth after seeing the wolf on the moors, and much of her mirth disappeared, and she began to suffer terrible nightmares and migraines."

"Like the ones Connor mentions? Martin, Elizabeth suffered from both a migraine and a nightmare only last evening."

"A nightmare, really?" the tailor asked. "Did she admit this to you? She is often somewhat reticent when it comes to discussing the spirits haunting her. But she did retire with the headache after supper," he added. "Forgive me, Charles. I know you are in love with Elizabeth, and it seems to me that she returns that feeling. Did she readily admit the dream to you? If so, its content may prove vital."

"In a way. I knocked upon her door after I left the library, and when she did not answer after several attempts, I entered the bedchamber. I could hear her muttering as if in a dream, so I wanted to check on her. It took several attempts to waken her, but she opened her eyes at last, and they were filled with terror. Once she calmed, she told me she'd dreamt of attending a masked ball and that a shadowy prince kept asking her to dance, but that I rescued her."

Kepelheim smiled as he folded up the garments. "How telling. She looks to you for such rescue, I believe. Our Elizabeth does not offer her trust or her heart easily, Charles. The fact that you have won both says much about your strength of character."

Donning his coat, the detective gazed at the portrait, his mind on the beautiful girl he'd met so long before—and the remarkable woman she'd become. "Does she still see the wolf?" he asked, thinking about the massive grey male and picturing Beth as a small child at its mercy. The thought made him shudder.

"Probably. Are you cold, Charles?" the tailor asked as he turned up the sleeves, examining the fit of the earl's borrowed suit coat. "Yes, that is quite a good match for these new trousers. Lord Aubrey's clothing fits rather well, though your shoulders are three-quarters of an inch wider, and each forearm a trifle longer than his. You're also half an inch taller. I shan't tell him, though," he said smiling. "You are lost in thought."

"Was I? Sorry, Martin. I was just thinking of Elizabeth as a child."

"Ah, yes, well, I can see why you might," he said, gathering up his measuring tape and sundries. "You must try to forget that letter, Charles. And never tell Elizabeth about it. If she knew that her mother's affair with Trent began long before Connor's death, it would tear her apart, I think."

"You can trust me, Martin. I only want to protect her. I just don't understand Patricia! How could she fall for a bounder like Trent when she had Connor Stuart as a husband? The man adored her."

"Love is a strange emotion that defies logic and measurement. And only rarely is it an even match. Tell me, Charles, if your wife still lived, would you love Elizabeth any less?"

"In truth, no, I would not, but that is an unfair comparison, Martin."

The tailor's eyes softened. "Is it? Perhaps, to Patricia, Trent embodied all she'd lost in Ian. She'd loved Paul's elder brother dearly, and his death devastated her. She married Connor at her father's insistence, but she never truly loved him. Trent may have offered her another chance for romance. I do not say that I agree with it, but I believe I understand it. My friend, do not think on it today. I have already given the letter to the duke, and he will decide how to deal with its contents. As to the cipher, well, I've decoded that."

"Have you?" Sinclair asked. "What did it say?"

The tailor paused, his mind pondering how best to explain. "I do not have ample time to apprise you of the many events that led up to your father's death and your subsequent disappearance, but the coded message seems to indicate that the late earl knew more about your father's murder than we did at that time."

"His murder? Do you know for certain that it was homicide?" Charles asked, his blue eyes wide.

"Allow me to speak to you more of this later, my friend. I know that the duke prefers he tell you. As to the letter from his son to Patricia, if he feels it might provide important information to our circle, then he will bring it up at the next full meeting, but if not, he will likely remain silent on it. He wishes only to protect Elizabeth."

"I'm only glad she didn't find it," Sinclair said. "The way she laughs in that portrait is how I want Beth to live life from now on, as though nothing drags at her heart. That the sun always shines and no wolves linger anywhere nearby."

"You are so like your father," Kepelheim said proudly. "As I've told you, he and Connor were very close friends. In fact, they were born the same year, two months apart. Both attended Harrow and then Cambridge. I shall tell you more of that another time, but as I started to explain earlier, the portrait of our dear one is actually the access to a secret exit that leads to an underground passage. That passage comes out several miles from here. Drummond is a cautious man, and he needs to be. I've used that exit twice, and once was that Christmas, but we'll have to continue that part of this discussion later. Remind me after supper. For now, we mustn't keep Della waiting, else both her heads will be sad."

Charles smiled, his hand on the tailor's shoulder. "Thank you, Martin, not just for welcoming me in my freshman days with the circle, but also for being a friend to me and to Elizabeth. I count few men as true friend, and you are amongst that small number."

Kepelheim blushed, his greying hair tinging with crimson. "You honour me, Lord Haimsbury. Did the duke tell you that there are portraits of your forebears here and also in London? In the small gallery, on the second floor, you will find a magnificent painting of your father and mother. And, I expect there are portraits in many other locations, for unless I am wrong, your estates are many. As are your enemies, so make sure of everyone on your staff and fortify your secret rooms, as has the duke. He is a man from whom you can learn much."

The tailor unlocked the door, and once open, found—not to either man's surprise—the very woman of whom they had been speaking, bending down as if to buckle a shoe.

"Lord Haimsbury! Mr. Kepelheim, oh, I had not realised anyone was in there. Is that another library? My! But this house has interesting secrets—and so many books. My shoe, it has come undone."

"So it has," Kepelheim noted dryly. "Would that a needle and thread might repair it, but alas, I am no cobbler. Do you require our aid, Doctor?"

She put her foot down, turning it to show off her trim ankles. "No, it seems fine now. Silly of me! Lord Haimsbury, would you help me to find the dining room. I'm all turned 'round now."

Charles left with the serpent on his arm, shooting Kepelheim a quick look as he led her away from the door. Immediately, the tailor locked the library and dashed to find the duke, lest the key mysteriously disappear.

Back at 76 Leman Street, Inspector Frederick Abberline had just arrested a Whitechapel landlord named John Bellingham, for it was the unfortunate publican who had witnessed the arrival and sudden departure of the 'Man with the Cane', as the police now called him. Fred hoped that a swift, successful interrogation would lead to solving the east end murders, and unmask the fiend all now called Jack the Ripper.

"So, where is it you killed her?" Abberline asked again. "We know you did it, Bellingham. Her blood's all over your clothes!"

The middle-aged man with the shock of red hair wiped at his bulbous nose and began to weep. "I tell you, sir, it weren't like that t'all. I were on my way to the Ten Bells to 'ave a talk wif me old barmaid, Sally Tambor. You know 'er, Inspector Abberline, sir. Sally's a dancer now over at the Cambridge. Wif the nice legs an' all."

"Nice legs! I'm sure you'd be the one to notice a woman's legs, Bellingham! We're going through your pub and your rooms above right now, and if we find even a scrap of evidence to tie you to these murders, we shall charge you, and your legs will soon be dangling from several yards of hemp rope!"

"Naw, sir! No' me, sir! All I done was to see this 'ere fancy gent leave the lady's body, just laid it right down, like 'e were puttin' 'er to sleep. I swears it! That man, wif the cane, sir. 'e done it. 'e even bent down like an' kissed 'er, din' 'e?"

Finding the man's continued obstinacy infuriating, Abberline swung a wide arcing, roundhouse punch, knocking the startled publican off his chair and onto the wooden floor.

"You keep lying to me, Sonny Jim, and I'll charge you right now! Admit the story is a lie!"

Bellingham lay on his side, iron manacles around both wrists, his arms reaching toward each other behind his back, chaining him to the sturdy chair. He wept sorrowfully, so much so that even the men in the other cells, who had been taking turns catcalling and shouting for a rope—for the Ripper fiend was much hated in the borough—now grew quiet, perhaps wondering if the real murderer might actually be a supernatural fiend who could disappear into thin air.

"Tell 'em, John!" shouted a tow-headed teen arrested that morning for vagrancy. "We go' a ghost, we do! Don't let Bobby Whiskers 'ere abuse you o' yer rights!"

Abberline turned and glared at the youth, making his point without a word. Then, softening his tone and nodding to two constables to upright the prisoner, the seasoned policeman leaned in close. "Look here, son. We want to make it right for the women of our borough who've lost to the knife and the cut. If there's a toff on our streets taking our women to the grave, then we need a better description than a man with a bloody cane! Did you hear anything else, son? Did he have a watch? A stick pin? A fancy boot? Or better yet a name! Give us that, and we'll see about unlocking those irons."

The publican's face glistened with sweat, and his shirt—not all that clean to begin with—had turned from grey to black. "Look, sir, I…"

"Does he have a name!?"

The man gulped. "He never give me a name, but 'e give me that message, and—no, wait! That ring what 'e wore! Great big silver one, i'n' it? Wif some white bird all enamel-like. The kind o' ring some judge'd wear from one o' them fancy men's clubs. Tha's right. I seen tha' bird afore. Back o' Greasy Johnny's place. Toffs an' all. Comes and goes like they owns it."

"Is that John Kenneth's place? On, uh…, Constable?"

The lad on the right spoke. "Church Street, sir. It's in an alleyway. He's right. We've seen a lot of rich men go in and out. Slum tourists, we figure. A ring like that might stand out even amongst such a group."

Abberline sighed, his mutton-chop sideburns heaving up and down. "Very well, Mr. Bellingham, we're going to look into your story, but if we find nothing, then we start again."

CHAPTER TWENTY-THREE

Luncheon finished with several puddings, including cake and straw-berry jelly, which made Adele stand up and sing. Paul relished every moment with his beautiful child, but the conversation planned with Elizabeth weighed heavily on his heart now. Adele clearly noticed her brother's mood and suggested they all come hear her play her newest music, which she had brought for the occasion. Elizabeth longed to confess her sins to Paul, but how could she disappoint Adele, who only wanted everyone around her to be joyful?

Adele played a Chopin, hardly making any mistakes, and then Beethoven's *Moonlight*, flawless if a trifle slower than needed, and she finished by playing a heart-rending version of Mozart's *Lacrymosa* from the *Requiem* mass—in an easy piano arrangement. All applauded, Paul most of all, and she bowed dozens of times, throwing kisses as if from a stage.

Charles had seen strange looks pass betwixt Paul and Beth, and he feared she planned to speak to the earl regardless of his own insistence that he do so first. Sinclair saw the duchess leave quietly, heading for the upper floors, and when Paul followed and Adele right after, Charles ran to the girl and knelt before her as if to beg.

"Surely you will not leave before playing just one more song for your new cousin? Della, no one has fingers like yours that can play a sonata and gobble up cakes all in one day!"

She burst into peals of laughter again and threw her arms around his neck. "Very well, Cousin Charles, I shall play another little Mr. Johann Strauss, if you like. And perhaps a Brahms, but then, you must play the left hand on the next piece. It's very difficult, and it is all I can manage to play the right."

Charles agreed, and Adele sat once more, her tapering fingers placed in position, her head high, and she began to play a waltz. Her style was fluid, though hesitant in places, but she finished the long piece with a flourish, which brought another round of praise and applause. Next, she played an *Intermezzo* in E Flat by Johannes Brahms, an elegant piece that lasted for over five minutes, and though Charles tried to concentrate on his young cousin's skillful rendition of the beautiful opus, his mind was fixed on what Beth must now be saying to the earl.

As Adele finished the Brahms, and seeing that Paul and Elizabeth had not yet returned, Charles suggested they play their duet. She nodded her head and took his hand, and the pair walked to the grand piano. "This is the one that's difficult for me," Della explained. "The notes move so very quickly toward the end that I get all mixed up."

Sinclair had studied piano for five years at Harrow and three at Cambridge. As a mathematician, he found the instrument beautifully precise, and playing often allowed his mind to work through puzzles and equations. He glanced at the musical selection Adele had chosen, a gypsy csárdás, a traditional Hungarian folk dance that began with a slow tempo but then drove to one more quick-paced, a difficult piece to be sure, but one that—to Charles—seemed deliberately placed. Surely, this was pure coincidence, but all he could think of for a moment was the gypsy music at the cottage and that gut-wrenching sense of panic when he awoke next to Elizabeth. His mind felt pulled back into the dream as violin music echoed in his ears, accompanied by the howling of wolves, and suddenly all blood drained from his face as the room spun and his vision telescoped into blackness.

"Charles," he could hear Adele say, patting his cheeks with her small hands. She sounded far away, as if from some other place and time. "Charles! Cousin Charles, are you all right? You don't have to play the left hand, if you don't wish to. I can try them both."

Kepelheim had jumped from his chair and now stood behind Sinclair, and Charles could hear his Uncle James calling for Mrs. MacAnder and sensed the duke's strong hands joining with the tailor's to help him to a chair. As he sat, his vision cleared momentarily, and he could see Lorena MacKey's face, her green eyes boring into his, and he suddenly knew that *she* had caused it. *Witch*, he thought, realising all at once that she was everything that Kepelheim had said, but perhaps far more. For there was a deep malevolence to her face—as if she had been unmasked—though only for his eyes to see. He could hear her speaking at his elbow, telling Kepelheim to pour cool water, as her hands unknotted his tie and touched his face.

"He's so very warm and his pupils grow black and large. I fear he may have been accidentally poisoned," she said, but he could also hear her thoughts, deep inside his mind.

The room grew hot and close, and his heart pounded in his ears. He heard the violin music again, and the wolves howling all about him, their voices nearly human. The doctor spoke words of medicine and concern to the company with her mouth, but with her thoughts the witch spoke only to Charles, and the words rose above the phantom violin's haunting refrain like a descant.

Do you see now, Lord Haimsbury? Do you dare make your plans against me—against Trent? Our Prince protects us both, and his plans will find fulfillment. Already, he works in your mind. There is nothing you can do to stop our plans. There is no one you could tell who would believe what you now hear me say. You, pitiful human, are an island, deserted and alone. And we shall use her as we wish, for nothing you may do, no plan you devise, no prayer you may speak, can stop us!

Charles thought he perceived a looming Shadow, standing behind the woman, and he tried to gain his feet, reaching out toward it. Was it William? Or the Other, the Prince? He leaned toward it, but suddenly he was falling into blackness, into utter despair, into *hell.*

"Catch him!" he heard Kepelheim cry, just as he blacked out.

Two floors above, in the quiet of Paul's apartment, as Della played the Strauss piece, Elizabeth sat, her face like stone, wondering how to begin her confession. Paul paced about the room, convinced her desire for secrecy was intended to reveal his deception regarding Adele. As his mind raced to all possible outcomes, he suddenly fell to his knees before her and began to tell all.

"Yes, Adele is my daughter," he said before his brain could stop his lips from saying it.

Elizabeth had been summoning up her own courage, but forgot all she had wished to say and stared, her mouth open wide in obvious shock. "What?"

Paul felt a stab to his heart. Had he been wrong? Could it be, she knew nothing? *Too late! Too late!* He paused a moment, and then began to explain. "It was in Paris. My first trip there for the government. Uncle James and an inner circle member who serves in high office there had asked me to learn all I could about a Redwing group that met there on the outskirts of the city. My official mission was to spy upon a banker, but it turned out that the two assignments were actually one. Since my actions could not be served in my own person, I assumed a false identity as an art student, who frequented the low Parisian bars and gambling houses. I called myself David Saunders, an outcast son with predilections for depravity."

"You?" She asked, for she had never considered what unsavoury methods Paul may be forced to employ in the greater world beyond her own. "But that is so dangerous!"

"Beth, darling, that is my life. The life I live apart from you. I have always tried to keep it from you—the truth of how I must live and work—but there it is. As I said, my false identity required me to inhabit areas to which I pray you may never go, for the denizens of these densely packed back streets will pick your pocket and slash your throat for the price of a few centimes. It was into these dark avenues I went, happy to serve my country—and you."

"But, Paul..." she began, stopped by the touch of his lips on her own. He kissed her desperately, longingly for what he feared may be the last time. Then he stood up, pacing as he spoke.

"To follow my primary prey, I had to frequent a house of liaisons, where certain women please men—physically, that is, for pay."

"A prostitution establishment?" she asked, her mind working through this confession as if trying to sift through a dark puzzle.

"The same," he said simply. "I spent many months moving through this benighted society, and in so doing, I formed a strong— attachment—with a woman who worked in one such establishment. Her name was Cozette du Barroux."

Elizabeth wanted to speak, but she knew he had to tell all now, and she waited patiently, doing her best to keep her face calm to help him in his difficult task.

He gazed at her for a moment, seeing the effort she now made on his behalf. Paul longed to sweep her into his arms and take her away to a place known only to themselves and make her his bride, but that would never be, for this confession was sure to part them forever.

"When I had accomplished my mission, I bid Cozette farewell and sailed back to England, not realising that she..." He struggled to say it, but it had to be said. Elizabeth had to have surmised it, for Paul had already admitted that Adele was his own daughter.

"She had conceived your child," she said bravely, but he had no idea that her mind worked not only on his confession and how it would affect their lives, but also on her night with Charles. Had she, too, conceived a child? Was that the dark purpose for what occurred that night? The answer to the riddle?

"Yes," he said, clearly grateful that she said it first. "I did not know, Beth. Not until more than two years later, when I returned as my true self to negotiate a treaty. It was then that I again found myself following the man who had played a central role in my earlier mission. One who then led me to Cozette and her secret. I needn't say more, but when I learnt the truth, that Cozette's daughter was my own, I leased a home for all three of us and stayed with her until— until Cozette died. She had contracted consumption in my absence, and she... She died in my arms," he finished, his voice breaking as tears slid down his cheeks.

Elizabeth rose to her feet, encircling his waist and burying her face in his chest. "Oh, Paul, I am so sorry! But you did honour to her in those final days," she cried, kissing his hands. "I have always known you are a man of great character, and you would have done more had she told you. So you then brought Adele home to be with her family?"

"My father would not allow me to reveal Adele's true parentage, as my own daughter, so he adopted her. Della has no idea."

"And she never shall, unless you think it best to tell her. Paul, my wonderful cousin and friend! I do love you, and now that I know she is yours, I love her all the more for it! I pray her mother sings now with the angels in heaven as she looks upon the pair of you."

He held her as best his wounded shoulder allowed, kissing her hair and face. "I felt certain that you would hate me when you learnt the truth."

"I could never hate you, darling. Never. I think you are wonderful, and nothing would ever alter that."

"You grant me too much praise," he whispered, taking her hands in his. "Beth, tell me truly. Is it Charles you love?"

Charles. It was now her turn for confession, and she prayed for courage to say it quickly. "Now, my darling Paul, you must sit whilst I pace, for I know that my words will hurt you."

She opened her mouth to speak, but no sooner had she done so, than a great commotion erupted from below. Shouts for both her and Paul to come down, accompanied by the rushed footsteps that she knew to be Adele's, and then suddenly the girl burst into Paul's apartment, her small face filled with fear. "He's fainted! Cousin Charles has gone all white, and he's desperately ill!"

Beth and Paul hurried to the main floor, only a few steps behind the flying feet of Adele as she led them into the music room. Mr. Kepelheim, Mrs. MacAnder, and Dr. MacKey stood over the prostrate marquess, checking his pulse and administering medication, as a footman cooled his face with a large, feathered fan.

"See?" Adele said, rushing to James. "He has fainted, and it is all my fault!"

Kepelheim advanced to his friends, his round face filled with deep concern. "He simply collapsed, and we have no idea why. Our doctor is practising her craft, but the marquess remains unconscious. Dear lady, might you see what you can do for him?"

Paul released her hand, and Elizabeth rushed to the couch where Charles lay. "Captain, you must open your eyes! We have our Adele to play for us, darling. Please, touch my hand if you hear me." She kissed his forehead, and it was like ice. "Did he receive a shock?" she asked, looking about the room. "What happened?"

Adele was in tears. "I asked him to play a new song with me, and that is when he fell. Oh, it is my fault!"

Elizabeth considered this for a moment, but it was the tailor who thought to glance at the music. He reached for the sheets, and shuffling through them, he went to the child. "Of course, it is not your fault, Della. Lord Haimsbury has been ill of late, and he must have eaten a bit of pudding that did not settle well. Do you know which music it was that you asked him to play?"

She pointed to the csárdás, which the learned tailor knew to be of Romany origin. "Gypsy music?" he asked aloud. "Oh, I think he could have played this, although it is a difficult piece. Now, now, sweet Della, you must dry your tears. Charles will want you to be laughing from both your heads when he awakes."

"I shall, if that is what will make him better," she said bravely.

"Very good," he said, kissing her hand. "You are a Stuart, through and through." And then, turning to the earl, he drew both him and Elizabeth to one side. "Our friend is in danger if that woman continues to work her spells. Lord Aubrey, can you not find some way to distract her?"

Paul wondered for a moment what Kepelheim could mean, but knowing the tailor's record for nearly always being right in any given circumstance, he nodded, saying aloud, "Mr. Kepelheim, whilst your medical bag is out, I wonder if you might find a stronger remedy for my arm. It has kept me awake much of the night, and I find it now feels numb."

MacKey's head bobbed up, and she left her ministrations and slithered to the earl's side. "Numb? My lord, that is a dangerous symptom. You must allow me to examine you at once."

Paul allowed Lorena to lead him back up the stairs, but his thoughts remained with Elizabeth and Charles. What had she been about to tell him?

Upstairs, Lorena took the earl back into the bedroom where only moments before he had confessed his darkest secret to the woman he loved. Now, a woman whom he had known less than forty-eight hours worked her fingers across his bare chest and shoulders in a manner more like a lover than a physician.

"Can you feel that?" she asked, running her soft hand along his muscled arm. He nodded. "Make a fist for me. Good. You had frightened me, Lord Aubrey. Nerve damage is not uncommon in such a wound, and I despaired that you might never regain full use of your arm, which would be a shame on many counts."

Paul felt that same, seductive power ooze from her words, and he struggled to keep his mind alert and thinking clearly. Had she cast a spell on him? Was she the witch that Kepelheim believed? "I have you to thank if I do," he said sweetly, playing her game. It was very likely Beth's future now lay in the hands of another man, so he must use his own skills to keep this woman from further harming Charles. "I feel a bit weak, though. Is that to be expected? It has been a very trying few days since we came here on Monday."

"Has it?" she asked, clearly probing for information. "Perhaps, it would help you to speak of it. You do look mildly feverish. You might feel better if you lie down, my lord. If you did not sleep well, then your nerves must be ragged. Here, let me help you into bed."

Paul leaned upon the tall woman's shoulder, forcing himself to ignore the seductive scent that played now upon his better judgment.

"It is a comfort to know we have one as skilled as you with us right now," he whispered as she helped him into the cool, silk sheets. "I know you must return to my cousin, but would you remain with me for a few moments?"

She smiled, and her green eyes sparked fire. "I would be pleased to do so, for I worry about you, dear brave Paul."

She kissed his injured right palm as if to soothe it, and then she leaned forward and kissed his face, gently at first, slowly moving her focus from cheek to mouth until her lips won his own.

Despite his desire to keep the doctor occupied, this bold move startled the earl, and he jerked away. "No!" he shouted, instantly regretting the blunder. She clearly wanted to seduce him, but he must play along without letting her win.

"I am sorry," she said, pouting. "I thought…"

"It is my fault," he explained, smoothing over the mistake. "Lorena, I must confess something to you. I may have shown improper familiarity when first we met, for you see, there is an unspoken understanding twixt myself and the duchess."

"Forgive me. I had no idea," she lied. "Elizabeth shows so much attention to your cousin, that I had assumed the ring she wears was his. Now, I am completely embarrassed. I have thrown myself at you shamelessly. It is just that you—well, you seemed unattached, and even interested."

"Will you forgive me?" he asked sweetly, finally in control once more. "My relationship with Elizabeth is rather complicated. She owns my heart, but I'm no longer confident of her affections. I believe they may be shifting toward another."

"She is a fool then," the doctor said as she brushed a lock of chestnut hair from his eyes. "I, however, am not a fool. And though she may govern your heart, I would settle for just a bit of you, my lord, though I know that makes me sound like a great fool myself."

"If so, then you are a beautiful fool," he admitted and meaning it. "Would you agree to give me time?"

"All that you require," she said prettily. "I shall be waiting in the wings, as they say. My heart—and my body eager to be your very own."

She left him then, closing the door, wondering if he truly meant what he'd said. Somehow, it seemed all too easy, but perhaps the earl was a pragmatist, and he found a willing woman better than none at all. No matter! She would happily snap the trap when it was time.

Three days passed, and Charles Sinclair still lay unconscious in a mysterious fever, tended by Martin Kepelheim and Mrs. MacAnder. The experienced nurse had, at first, feared that the marquess had contracted typhus or caught a chill, but nothing she did seemed to help. The only time his fever lessened seemed to be whenever Elizabeth held his hand or bathed his brow, so the duchess remained with him nearly all hours of the day and night, sleeping now and then in a chair near his bedside.

Paul managed to keep Lorena MacKey occupied and distracted by taking her to Glasgow, where they collected her suitcases and enjoyed a day's shopping. Though no one in the house trusted the woman, the duke felt it was wiser to keep her close rather than allow her to operate from a distance, and he suggested to his nephew that her interest in *him* might prove useful to the circle.

On the morning of the fourth day, Kepelheim entered to find the duchess asleep, her head resting against Sinclair's shoulder, her hand holding his. The tailor cleared his throat as he shut the door.

"Oh, Mr. Kepelheim," the duchess said, sleepily. "Is it morning already?"

"It is, dear lady. Mrs. Calhoun has provided a delightful repast in the breakfast room, and your grandfather hopes you will join him for an hour whilst Laurence and I see to our sleeping marquess."

Beth stood, stretching out her aching back. "Perhaps. I am rather hungry, but you will send for me if he awakens, won't you, Martin? I'm not sure how long I've been sleeping, but the last time he stirred was around two this morning. He keeps calling for someone named Albert. I'm not sure who that is."

"Nor am I," the tailor muttered. Kepelheim had brought ice and linen towels as well as alcohol to bathe his patient, and he set these items aside for a moment, turning toward the door as it opened once more. "Ah, Mr. Laurence. I'd hoped you would join us. I should appreciate your help with our patient. Duchess, we must see to Lord Haimsbury's needs, and perhaps…"

"Oh, of course. Privacy. I understand. But you will send for me, if…"

"Should anything change or the marquess awaken, we shall send for you at once, dear lady. Now, take a few moments to nourish your mind and heart, and when you are refreshed, he will be here, clean and perhaps awake. Who knows?"

She leaned down to kiss his lips, wiping at his brow softly. "Darling, I shan't be long. You must come back to us soon, Captain. We miss you so. I miss you."

She kissed him once more and then left, shutting the door. Martin helped the butler to remove the marquess's sleep shirt, turning him as they did so. "He is soaked through again. What can this illness be to cause him such night sweats? The duchess did not mention the room's being overheated; in fact, it seems quite cool in here to me, yet, he is burning up."

"Is it typhus, sir?" Laurence asked as he placed the damp nightshirt into a cotton, laundry bag.

"No, I do not think so, yet, he lingers beyond our reach." Martin applied the cold cloths to his patient's wrists and throat, hoping to lower the fever whilst the butler changed out the bedclothes. "You do that well, Matthew. Has Mrs. MacAnder been training you in nursing care?"

Laurence laughed easily, his coppery brows rising with the corners of his mouth. "She has, sir, but my mum also knew a bit about caring for invalids—not to say the marquess is such, but if he cannot get out of bed, then one must change out the sheets to make him comfortable, is that not so?"

"It is. Medical ministrations are useless without tending to basic comforts. Do we have another sleep shirt for him?"

"The duke suggested using Lord Kesson's Indian pyjamas for the marquess. Just the trousers, though, since he seems so prone to overheating. But would that be appropriate, if the duchess insists on remaining at his bedside?"

"No, probably not. Still, if he is more comfortable, and as you say, the duke suggested it. Yes, I think it is a good idea. Are the pyjamas nearby?"

"I'll fetch them, sir." Laurence left the bed chamber, and the tailor checked his patient's eyes and listened to his heart.

In a few moments, the butler returned and together they dressed the marquess in a pair of dark blue silk pyjamas, deciding to also use the shirt, but leave it unbuttoned. "I think that is a brilliant compromise," the tailor said. "He looks much cooler already."

"He does, sir. The duke asked me if I'd like to travel to London with the marquess when he opens Haimsbury House."

"Really?" Martin asked, closing his medical bag. "I like that idea very much. I've been to that home many times, though not since '60, of course. Such a terrible year that was. It is a magnificent home. Would you serve as butler or as an agent for the circle?"

"That would be up to Lord Haimsbury, sir. He's been very kind to me, and if he asks me to serve, I'd be pleased to say yes to whatever position he requires."

"You're a gentle young man, my friend. Laurence, has Lord Haimsbury spoken at all when you are in here? The duchess has reported our friend crying out at times during the night. Have you witnessed such?"

"Only once, sir. I came in two nights ago to sit with him whilst the duchess stepped out for a few moments. I believe that is when the earl and the doctor returned from Glasgow."

"Ah, yes. I think our sweet duchess was surprised that the doctor returned with her cousin. No matter. The duke is right to keep that witch close by, but it is also good that the earl distracts her whilst our marquess recovers. So, what did he say?"

"Sir?"

"Lord Haimsbury. You said that he spoke."

"Yes, he did, but it made no sense."

"Perhaps, the fever causes him to rave, or perhaps not. Do you recall the words?" the tailor asked.

"I do. He cried out for someone named Albert, but he also said something else. He spoke of wolves, sir. And violin music."

"Wolves? That is disturbing, but it may refer to the wolf pack you and your men took down. And a violin, you say?" The tailor asked, recalling the apparition he and Sinclair had pursued in the east wing at Branham. "Strange. It may all be due to his fever, but I begin to think this illness is spiritual rather than physical. Now that you've completed the bed change, perhaps, you would ask the duke to call a meeting. A prayer meeting, and all members of the household who can should attend. Our Aubrey will have to keep this witch doctor occupied whilst we seek the Lord's guidance and mercies."

"Very good, sir. I shall go to the duke at once."

As the door closed, Kepelheim sat into the armchair left vacant by the duchess, taking Sinclair's pulse. "Where are you, Charles?" he asked. "I fear you stand betwixt worlds now, but if so, then we must pray that our Saviour will keep you safe. Why do you call for your dead son, my friend? I doubt the duchess knows about that sad period of your life, and I shan't explain it. That is for you to do, Charles. Come back to us, my dear friend. Come back."

Charles Sinclair had wandered into a distant, spiritual realm, and there found himself face to face with a dark entity who claimed to know him. The being was very tall and remained shadowed as he spoke, referring to days long lost to Sinclair's waking memory.

"You are still mine," the being told him. "It was I who saved you, who took you from your sick mother—for she had abandoned you— and you lived with me for two years. Do you recall it, Charles?"

Sinclair's mind boiled in the oppressive heat of the place, but he shivered, unable to fetch up the past. "My mother would not have abandoned me. She loved me."

"How do you know that, Charles, if you cannot recall your childhood?" the being asked, his voice deep and resonant but with a strange discordant buzz beneath, as if a million flies lived within him.

"My family is a loving one, so I know my mother would have never left me. She died to protect me."

"Really? If that is what you've been told, then your family lies."

"You are the liar!" he shouted, though his throat was dry as parchment and his tongue thick. "You hide in shadow. Why do you not step into the light?"

"Do you really wish to see me in all my glory, Charles? With earthly eyes? Those eyes would burn in their sockets to behold such beauty. You are little more than a lump of clay, whilst I? *I am starlight!* Yet, I find you interesting—perhaps, even special. I have chosen you, Charles, from all the men of the earth, to usher in a great, new age. I have whispered to you many times. Did you hear my voice when I spoke to you at Branham? Did you see the visions?"

Charles lowered his eyes, refusing to look at the shadow, keeping his mind focused on one thought: Beth. Her welfare. Her future. Her safety.

The hideous shadow began to laugh. "Ah, you think of her, do you? Shall I reveal your future? I showed you that vision when you were but a boy, Charles. Do you recall it?"

"Leave me alone!" he cried out, weeping.

"I have put much effort into your blood, Charles. Many thousands of years of manipulation and marital design. An affair here, a liaison there. A secret prince, a hidden heir, preserved for a future reign. You hold the key to the world, Charles, within your body. You shall remember it all one day. Never fear. And you will help me to establish my kingdom on this earth."

A small boy appeared, standing just outside the bars of Sinclair's cage now, his blue eyes fixed upon the prisoner. "Father," he whispered.

Sinclair's heart nearly stopped, for he recognised the child, an older version of his own dead son, Albert. The boy's skin was charred and black, and his mouth yawned into a gaping oval of accusation. "You murdered me!" he screamed.

"No! Albert! No, I... Son, I tried to keep you safe," the detective wept, reaching out to touch the apparition but failing.

The Shadow began to laugh, and the buzzing became the rush of many winds, as if the million flies had taken flight, and their hellish wings beat together in unison. "Albert had to die, you know. Blood is too precious to waste on an heir who is not suitable. Smallpox came to London for one reason and one alone. To kill your son."

"Leave me alone!" Sinclair shouted, but no sound left his throat, for the heat had closed it, and all he could taste now was blood and bile.

Both the child and the Shadow began to laugh, and Charles looked up to speak, and though his eyes burnt and ached, he perceived a great divide, a monstrous pit of eternal fire. The entity who spoke did so from beyond the pit, as if he dared not cross the yawning chasm.

"Father, help me," the detective whispered. "Help me, please," he prayed, his eyes downcast, the words barely making a sound.

Suddenly, beside the great divide appeared a man, arrayed all in white. Sinclair recognised this beautiful being as the gardener who had awakened him beside the yew trees at Branham. The man turned toward Charles and smiled, and straightaway a gentle, cool breeze fluttered across the prisoner's brow.

"My Lord," the marquess whispered, his eyes fixed on the beautiful protector. "Are you a dream?"

"I am real," the man told him. "And your child is with me. Albert lives, and you will see him again one day. And though you cannot yet recall your own childhood, I promise that you will remember all, Charles. In *my* time. The enemy did not steal your memories. I allowed them to be stored inside your mind for a future time. Do not fear those who walk in darkness. Their judgement is coming, and they know it. Their time grows short."

The shadow cowered behind the brilliant light that emitted from the man in white, and Charles began to strengthen. "Yea, though I walk through the valley of the shadow of Death, I shall fear no evil," he quoted, tears streaming down his cheeks. "Thy rod and thy staff they comfort me." Then as the being's brightness rose upward within the endless cavern, Sinclair felt a rush of strength within him that overcame all his fears. Turning back toward the Shadow, he proclaimed, "You lie, Demon! You have no power over me! No control! Christ the Saviour alone has that power, for His blood covers me!"

"Oh but I do have power over you, Charles. I *made* you!" it screamed, losing all calm for a moment, and then growing kinder— or trying to sound so, it added. "No, Charles, you will remember me one day, and you will come to appreciate all that I have done for you. *And for her.*"

"Not Beth! Not her! You will not touch her! Not ever—not whilst I have breath!" he shouted, realising that his arms could not move, and that he was in fact chained.

"But your human body is so fragile, Charles. I could snuff it out now with but a thought, if I chose to do so."

"Then do it, Shadow! But leave her alone!" Charles gasped, for the searing heat of the place tore at his eyes and lungs, setting them on fire. "Good Father," he prayed once more, his hands clasped together. "I trust in you. Even if I must stay here as a prisoner, even though I would remain forever chained, I could bear it, if you would keep Beth safe."

"You call me Father?" the thing asked with a smile. "That is good."

"No, foul devil! I call for the true Father—in heaven! God Almighty who gave His only begotten Son, Jesus Christ, so that..."

"SILENCE!" it screamed, the piercing wail nearly shattering Charles's eardrums. "NO MORE OF THAT NAME!"

"Christ Jesus, Saviour to all who believe," Charles continued, filled now with an authority not of his own making, standing up, his chains falling away. "It is to the only true King, Lord Jesus, that I go for comfort, for aid, for healing! And every knee shall bow to Him—even yours, foul creature!"

The thing began to howl like a massive, wounded beast, and Charles felt himself rising, the terrible prison disappearing beneath him, and the sweet air rushing past his face brought coolness and relief.

Sinclair opened his eyes, and he found himself sitting in a garden, more colourful, more real, more dazzlingly bright than any on Earth. Before him stood the beautiful, white-haired man, garbed in a gardener's clothing. Charles gazed at the stranger. "It was you," he whispered. "At Branham. In the garden near the maze. You woke me from my dream and... You spoke to me."

The man's hand touched Sinclair's brow, and he heard the kindest voice ever to speak in his ears, as from a Shepherd to a wandering lamb. "Well done, Charles. Trust only in Me. The enemy sought permission to test you, but you have passed that test. Do not fear the infernal realm's plans. I am allowing them to proceed for my purposes. Trust in me, Charles. Trust in my love for you and for your beloved duchess. And for your children."

Sinclair fell to his knees, weeping. "I am not worthy to be here—not worthy to even be in your presence, my Lord," he choked, but again the hand touched his brow.

"You have been bought with a great price, my son," the man said gently. "You are worthy of that price. The Shadow did say one thing that is true. You *have been* chosen, but not for Redwing's devices. I chose you because I love you. I have put you where you are, for my reasons. That false god did not create you. I did. And though the future will bring more tests, if you trust always in me, I promise you that the enemy's designs will fail."

Charles looked up and saw two hands that bore scars in each palm, and he fell upon his face, praising the Saviour. "My God and my King!" he proclaimed, his eyes filled with tears, and a comfort beyond comprehension filled his heart, strengthening it. Charles felt himself pulled as if snapping back to the material world, but the Master's voice echoed in his ears: "Trust in me, Charles. Trust only in me."

It was then, that he opened his eyes to a candle-lit room and found Elizabeth sleeping in a chair nearby. As his reason returned, he knew that he had confronted a demon of the pit, and that Christ's power alone had defeated it.

He said nothing, fearing he might wake her, enjoying the soothing quiet of the darkened room and the beauty of her sweet face. As he watched her sleep, he thought of how he had kept watch over her in the cottage. How he had sworn to guard her safety for the rest of his life. He knew now that it was for this cause that he had been born—that he had survived. The demon had lied. It was not that thing who had saved him as a boy, but Christ alone, for *His* purposes not the enemy's. No longer would he fear the night; for if he and Beth trusted only in Christ Jesus, their risen Saviour would always bring them to the dawn. And one day, to heaven.

"Beth," he called softly, reaching out for her hand.

She moved, sitting up slowly, her dark eyes opening. "Charles?" she called. "Darling, are you back with us?"

"I am, dear one. I have found the strength to fight—in our Saviour's healing touch—and in yours. You look tired. You must go sleep. Tomorrow, I intend to speak to your grandfather, and we may need rest for what is to come."

She kissed his forehead, tears spilling from her eyes as she stroked his dark hair. "I love you, Charles. So very much. Goodnight, my wonderful Captain. Tonight, I shall sleep at last, for you have lain upon this bed for three nights and four long days. It is now nearing midnight, and I am weary, yet much stronger for seeing you smile once more. Tomorrow, we shall speak."

"Goodnight, dear heart," he said as she shut the door. He closed his eyes then and slept the sleep of babes until nearly ten o'clock the following day.

CHAPTER TWENTY-FOUR

19, October, Leman Street, Whitechapel

Fred Abberline stood inside Reid's dead room, staring at the woman who'd become their latest guest, five days previously; now identified as Katherine Lamont, a woman of nineteen years, six months, three days. Lamont had been born in Manchester and recently arrived in London, where, her mother claimed, she had found employment with a rich builder who lived in a west end mansion. Lamont had now been officially classified as a murder victim, but not as Ripper. Billingham had also been cleared of all charges, for the present. After going through the publican's lodgings with a fine-toothed comb, it was decided to release him but also to follow him day and night in hopes of discovering if they'd missed anything.

Fred was exhausted. Since the Nichols murder in late August, he'd spent weeks without rest, sifting through sketchy evidence and mountains of bloody clothes, and photographs by the hundreds; all that work, with nothing to show for his efforts. Abberline's longsuffering wife, Emma, rarely went amongst her friends now, no longer happy to spend a pleasant evening playing cards or taking in the theatre, for her companions now hounded her for clues and information and ghoulish details, so that the prim housewife had all but become a shut-in. Fred hated this aspect of the Ripper business. Seven times, he'd chased reporters from his own door, threatening to box the ears of two of *The Star's* nosy hacks, and earning a dressing down from Police Commissioner Sir Charles Warren for his efforts.

"Mr. Abberline, sir," Inspector France called as he ran up the stairs at Leman Street. "We have a lead, sir! At that gambling establishment. A man with a ring matching the landlord's description has been seen!"

Fred threw open the office door, grabbed his hat and coat, and rushed toward France. "Then let us be off, Inspector France. Perhaps, we shall at last meet this disappearing man with the cane."

It took nearly half an hour to reach the laneway that ran behind Church Street and the shadowy establishment known as 'Greasy Johnny's'. Though nearly everyone of the club's patrons recognised Abberline at once, both policemen displayed their warrant cards to the hostess who greeted them with a smile and escorted them into the smoke-filled, upscale interior. The gaming tables and curtain-draped side rooms were populated with well-dressed men and scantily clad women, and a sultry blonde songstress with a single octave range and an aversion to singing on pitch murdered a selection of music hall tunes.

Inspector Arthur France recognised many of the men from the political pages of the *Times* and *Star*, and to his amusement, he also noticed Michael O'Brien in a darkened corner of the main parlour. "Inspector Abberline, sir," he said, pointing toward O'Brien. "Perhaps, we might spend a moment with that gent?"

Fred sighed at seeing the reporter, one of the many he'd chased from his home. "Gent is a rather speculative term when it comes to this one. Allow me, Inspector France. You take names of all the men here, and find out who wears a silver ring with white enameling on it."

Abberline drew up a chair and sat into it, his grey eyes boring into O'Brien's. "Well, well, Michael. Does T. P. O'Conner know that you spend your nights jollying about with Whitehall's finest?"

O'Brien was a slight man with sandy hair and a waxed moustache, and he grinned in response to the inspector's insinuations. "I cover the political beat, do I not, Inspector Abberline? What brings Leman Street's boss to a haven for parliament's entertainment seekers?"

"A little bird," Abberline replied neatly, looking up as a buxom woman brought two drinks. "Nothing for me, girl. And nothing more for our reporter, here. He's returning to Leman Street with me in a few moments."

O'Brien started to object, but Abberline interrupted. "Tell me, Michael, how is it that a roll of confiscated film still managed to be developed—and how did the images on that miraculous roll come to be published in newspapers across London?"

O'Brien smiled, sipping at his drink. "What a surprise, Inspector. You read the London press?"

Fred's brows rose into an arch of accusation and frustration. "I've chewed up men like you for lunch, Michael. Don't test my patience. Sinclair..."

"Ah, yes, the new Scottish marquess, you mean? And how would you even know about our titled detective's bounty save for my words and Harry's remarkable photographs, eh? Readers may want information, but photographs are proof, Inspector. I'm sure even Lord Haimsbury is relieved that my colleague had already switched film rolls by the time the camera was...shall we say, borrowed?"

"You are a menace," Abberline bit back. "And do not think that Lord Haimsbury will show you any gratitude when he returns to London. And now, I imagine, he'll find himself much more influential with certain publishers. I'd keep careful watch on my pay packet, if I were you, Michael. It may contain a redundancy slip soon."

A strawberry-haired woman in a low cut dress sidled over and began to stroke O'Brien's hair just as Arthur France joined them, whispering into his superior's ear. Abberline rose, grasping the reporter by the collar. "It appears we're leaving now, Mr. O'Brien. Say your goodbyes to the lady."

Michael snatched at his hat and smiled at the girl. "Sorry, Sally. Perhaps next time."

France laughed as the energetic Abberline escorted the hack through the doors, past the hostess, and down the narrow staircase. Once outside, the inspector shoved O'Brien into a hansom, and in a moment, the trio were on their way to Leman Street.

As the horse and cab pulled away from the doorway, a tall man emerged from the house, his face lit temporarily by the flash of a match. "Looks like they've uncovered our meeting place, eh?" a second, shorter man remarked. "I heard the younger one asking our proprietor about your ring, my friend. Perhaps, you stand out too much, eh?"

"I stand out only when I wish to do so, Clive. Now, we surely have the remainder of the evening before Mr. O'Brien gives up our secrets, so let us enjoy the tender fruits that await us upstairs. And whilst we do so, we can decide where our next meeting house will be."

The tall man turned and climbed the staircase, his gleaming black boots clicking on the painted wood with each step. Urquhart shrugged and closed the street door, turning back toward the interior stairs. "It's a shame," he muttered as he climbed. "Such a delightfully debauched place to hide. Now ruined."

Friday had dawned in Scotland, and Matthew Laurence commenced his numerous chores by fetching the post bag from the foyer. Taking the bag into his office, the young butler sorted through a collection of invitations, personal correspondence for the duke, letters addressed to the servants and staff, two packages, and four London newspapers. One of these last caught Laurence's attention, for the front page featured a headline he knew the duke would wish to see at once. "Mrs. Calhoun, I'm heading up to waken the duke."

Annalisa Calhoun had already been up for an hour fashioning dough left to rise overnight into loaves, and she wiped her hands on a tea towel as she peered over the butler's shoulder. "Another one?" she exclaimed. "The marquess will not be pleased to read this."

"Indeed, he will not. This may alter their travel plans, now that Lord Haimsbury is recovered. I say, are your cookies burning? Lady Adele will be disappointed if she cannot devour at least half a dozen by afternoon."

The cook checked the oven, glad to see that the young butler had only been joking. "Your sense of humour eludes me sometimes, Mr. Laurence. Will the duke even be awake? Tis not yet seven."

"The duke rarely sleeps past six. I imagine he is awake, yes. Plan to serve breakfast at ten, though. Our company has endured much these past two weeks. I suspect that most will sleep late, so don't worry about tea yet. I shall return in a short while and then take some back up to his lordship."

The butler took the stack of letters, the package, and two newspapers with him and left the kitchen. On his way to the duke's apartment, Laurence met Sinclair, who had apparently just left the private library. "Oh, good morning, sir. I'd no idea anyone was yet awake."

The marquess appeared content and much healthier since recovering, and he paused to offer the butler a warm smile. "The duke and I have been talking. He and I have been awake for over an hour, and we decided to make use of the quiet time. Is that the morning post?"

"It is, sir, and I was cutting through this part of the house to reach his lordship's apartment. He is still in the library then?"

"He is. I can take this in—oh, wait a moment. Let me see that newspaper."

"I'd thought you might wish to see it, sir."

"And I imagine my uncle will also wish to see it. Is that package addressed to the duchess? Give me that as well. I shall explain it to her later. Thank you, Laurence."

"You're most welcome, sir. Shall I bring in tea?"

"Yes, that would be quite nice. Have you any coffee, though?"

"We do, sir. I shall bring both."

The butler bowed and left, and Sinclair returned to the library. "James, I fear that we may have to return to London sooner than planned. There's been another murder in Whitechapel."

Drummond took one of the newspapers and read through the article. "I don't know if you paper includes this, but a witness is claiming the woman was murdered by a disappearing man with a cane."

"Yes, that's in here, too, sir. Tall, well-dressed, wearing gleaming boots. William Trent, you think?"

The duke scowled. "He's trying to lure you back to London, son. Don't let him manipulate you."

"It's my job, sir. The east end is still under my supervision, and I owe it to Reid and Abberline to be there. I know that we'd planned to go to Briarcliff and then Rose House, but I really must leave as soon as possible."

"And Beth?" the duke asked. "Will you leave her here with us and return on your own?"

Sinclair set down the paper with a sigh. "I would prefer she go with me, if at all possible. She knows I intended to ask you for her hand in marriage, but I think she's been unsure of how you would respond."

"Charles, if she loves you—and I can tell you that she does—then that's all that matters. We'll sort it out with Paul. In truth, if you'd not vanished back in '60, you'd have been given the task of looking after and marrying Elizabeth anyway, so it's like we've come full circle. I cannot tell you how overjoyed I was when Kepelheim's letter came with the news of what he'd uncovered about you. I apologise for not telling you sooner, lad, but I didn't wish to get your hopes up before we had all the facts. You know, I noticed your resemblance to Paul ten years back, but I didn't dare think past it. Those bodies we were shown that washed up in Ireland, they looked very convincing, and I'd genuinely thought you dead. Each day I spend with you now, I see more and more of Robby Sinclair in you. Your physical resemblance, of course, but also your mannerisms, and even the sound of your voice."

"Thank you, sir. I wish I could remember my father, but I'm just grateful to the Lord for allowing me to know you. You've become more than an uncle to me, sir. I hope you know that."

The duke's eyes grew misty. "And you're like a son, Charles."

"That means more to me than I can say, sir," Sinclair answered, his own eyes growing bright. "James, are you certain that Paul will accept my marrying Elizabeth? He's loved her for a very long time."

"Aye, he has, but Paul will find other adventures to follow. You two may bear a physical likeness, but your temperaments are vastly different. Paul grows restless if he's not tracking down some killer or spying upon a diplomat. I'd always worried about his ability to remain near to our Beth for very long, but I've no doubts about you."

"I cannot imagine leaving her, sir, not ever," Sinclair admitted, "which is why I would like to take her back to London with me when I go. But may we return to this other matter? The cottage. I know you have said that you understand, but there is another aspect to it that concerns me, especially given Risling's interpretation of the symbols left here and outside the cottage windows."

The duke sighed, reaching for the stack of letters. "Have you mentioned this to Beth?"

"No, sir, but I'm sure it's crossed her mind, too. Should we not marry as soon as possible—just in case?"

"The newspaper stories about your title and those photographs of you and Beth may help us toward that end, son. Well, now this is interesting," he said as he opened an important looking envelope. It was made of fine linen paper with a gold seal on the exterior. "Seems Her Majesty is anxious to meet you, Charles."

"The queen?" he asked, sitting forward. "She mentions me?"

"Aye, she does. Read it for yourself."

Sinclair reached for the expensive notepaper, reading aloud, "'James, just a quick note to thank you for letting me know about the wonderful news regarding Lord Haimsbury. Given the reports in our press, I assume you will be announcing a wedding soon. If it's to take place this year, please, consider a date before December if at all possible, as I leave for Balmoral on the 2nd. I hope to attend and meet Charles in person, and I've already planned a little gift. My best to Elizabeth. Tell her that Eddy will be disappointed, but we'll weather through. – V.'"

The detective's mouth had opened in genuine shock. "The queen wants to attend our wedding?"

Drummond grinned broadly. "And she's given you an excuse to set the date right away, son. She grows weary, I think, and she probably doesn't want to wait. This is her way of choosing the date for us."

"Well, I shan't complain about setting the date for as soon as possible. Of course, I've not yet proposed, officially."

"Then make it soon, son. Now, what's in the package?"

"I'm not sure, sir, but I intend to find out. I know that it's addressed to Elizabeth, but I'd prefer to make certain it is safe before she opens it. You can see that it's been forwarded from Queen Anne House, so I am concerned that this Saucy Jack person may have decided to send her another greeting. You'll notice the original address was written in red ink."

"Aye, I did at that. Was the letter also addressed in red?"

"Yes," he said as he untied the twine that secured the brown wrapping paper. "And thanks to the newspaper reports about Beth and me, this person most likely knows she is here, particularly if this Saucy Jack is a member of Redwing..." he began, but the contents made him stop.

"What is it? Is it from this madman?" the duke asked, leaning forward.

"I don't know, sir. But it contains a photograph of—of my son."

"Albert?"

"Yes, sir. Why would someone send this to Elizabeth?"

"It's a strange puzzle, but I imagine the sender wishes her to know about Albert. You should tell her, Charles, before she learns it from someone else."

He set the box aside, his heart suddenly heavy. "You're right, of course, but it's not a conversation I look forward to having. Especially, if it turns out that she is with child."

"Yes, I understand," the duke replied gently. "Look, son, you do what you think is best. I'll not press. Just know that whatever you decide, Elizabeth loves you, no matter what. Now, let's see about breakfast. Oh, and if you're set on marrying right away, we'll see how quickly that might be arranged, but it's unlikely we can pull it off before you go back to London. That is, if you're set on heading back straightaway. I'd prefer to make a show of it. Redwing's gone to a lot of trouble putting this plan into effect, and I want them to see that we're complying—or at least appearing to do so. Besides, we'd disappoint Her Majesty if we held the wedding up here. I'll write to my friend, Ed MacPherson. He's pastor of the church we attend in London, and he's a good friend. I'll see how quickly he thinks we could put together a wedding. And I'll write to my sister and get her started on the arrangements and invitations—all that. Victoria loves a challenge."

The detective smiled at last. "I could never have imagined where any of this past month would lead, when I received your granddaughter's letter. All right. A big show it is, but first I must propose—and also, we must make sure that Paul agrees. I have grown to love and respect my cousin, and I do not wish to move forward without his approval. I'll send a wire to Abberline saying I shall return as soon as possible."

"Fair enough. I doubt that breakfast will be served before ten at the earliest so let's you and I find the earl and try out Dryden's new rifles."

As Charles left the library, he passed the doctor, who now wore her own clothing. "Good morning, Lord Haimsbury," she said with a glint in her eye. "It's wonderful to see you looking so healthy now, but do not overdo. You could relapse, and none of us would wish for that to happen."

Charles still held the package, so he tucked it beneath his left elbow. "It's kind of you to say so," he replied, wondering if her words contained a veiled threat. "May I speak to you for a few moments?"

MacKey appeared surprised by this. "I suppose so. I had planned on taking a short walk to stimulate my appetite. Would you care to join me?"

The marquess thought for a moment, but he spotted the butler returning to the library with the coffee, and he waved him down. "Laurence would you mind setting this package inside the duke's library for me? And let my uncle know that I'm just going out for a short walk. I'll meet him back here in quarter of an hour, and we can leave for the shooting range then."

"Very good, sir. Shall I keep your coffee hot?"

"Yes, thank you, Laurence. Doctor, shall we?" he said, giving her his arm. In a few moments, the pair arrived in the very garden where Beth had listened to Charles explain about the night in the cottage, and Charles paused near the edge of the cliff. "It's a sharp drop, so mind your feet, Doctor."

"I see that. Very steep," Lorena answered as she peered over the stone fence. "So, my lord, are you content with your new life?"

"My new life?" he echoed. "Oh, the title, you mean. Yes, I suppose I'm getting used to it. May I ask why it is you suddenly decided to strike up a friendship with my cousin?"

She seemed startled by such a blunt question. "Sir?"

Sinclair smiled. "Before I became a marquess, my title was Detective Superintendent, and it still is. You want something from Paul, and I'd like to know what that something is. Do not deny it."

"I merely wish to know him better. He is a handsome man, and it seems to me, Superintendent, that the earl's future is about to change."

Charles considered this strange reply for a moment. "Now, why would you say that? Or is it possible that you have played a part in that change? No, no, Doctor, do not try to leave, for I have observed far more than you might think. I wonder if my cousin would find your part in my fever of interest? Or, if he knows of your attempts to solicit information from the duchess?"

"You observe much," she said, her eyes sparkling in the morning light. "But I wonder just how much you truly know? You think me a heartless woman, don't you, Detective Superintendent?"

"I think you—no, wait. Allow me to reconsider," he said, surprising her. "Lorena, is it possible that you are in over your head? Do you have any idea what fate awaits you once this life is through?" She had not expected him to take this tack, and the doctor grew silent. "Lorena, you are bound for hell, and you know it. Redwing may have convinced you that this fate can be avoided, but I assure you that it cannot. No one may outrun God's judgment. Either you reach the end of this life protected by Christ's blood or you do so naked and alone in your sins. Which would you prefer?"

"Leave me alone," she said, starting to leave, but he caught her arm.

"Lorena, do not wait until it is too late. You think those in the circle are your enemies, but we want only to serve Christ, which means we follow His commands. One of those commands is to love others as we love ourselves."

She laughed. "Oh, so you love me?"

"Christ loves you, and it is my imperative to tell you this. I would be your friend, for it occurs to me that you need true friends. The men and false gods that you serve care nothing about you."

MacKey blinked, all bluster gone. "And you do?"

"I think you are unhappy."

She gazed at him, seeing far more in his face than she'd realised lay there before. "You are different from any man I've ever known. Why is that? What is about you that would cause you to even try to save me?"

"Nothing about me is worthy. Only Christ within me."

"No, no, it is more than that. Yes, I recognise the presence of what you call the Holy Spirit within you. That presence shines from within your eyes, and though most might not see it there, I do. But there is more to you. Our Prince says that you are the chosen one. That your blood has qualities beyond that of any other human. I wonder if your unique nature goes far beyond that, though. Beyond what the Prince imagines."

"Who is this Prince, you speak of, Lorena? Is he flesh or spirit?"

She started to reply, but suddenly, as if her old nature called her back, she shook her head. "Do not ask me! I—I'm no longer able to make choices like one with free will. Now, if you'll excuse me, Lord Haimsbury, I should pack."

"Pack?" he asked, following her back up the path toward the castle. "You would leave us?"

"You and your circle may wish only good things for me, but I have others to whom I must bow, and they have no intention of allowing me to avoid that."

"And what of you, Lorena? Is there not a longing within you to have true peace? To know a life where there is no fear of this Prince? No fear of hell?"

"Why do you care? And do not pretend it is to please your God!"

"You think me so callous that I speak to you of Christ as a tactic? No, Lorena, I do not. I see a frightened woman beneath all your bravado and pretense. I would be your friend, if you would permit me."

"Why? You are in love with the duchess. Why would you befriend me?" she asked, and he could see a change in her demeanor.

"Perhaps, because I see your loneliness and understand it."

She considered this, and when she again looked at him, Charles thought he perceived tears. She wiped at her face, angry with her own emotional display. Forcing a smile, she spoke at last, and her old nature overcame her momentary lapse. "My how gallant you are, Lord Haimsbury. Shall I tell the duchess just how fortunate she is? Shall I send her into a fevered longing for her Captain?"

"Beth is off limits, Lorena."

"Is she?" the doctor asked with a harsh look in her eyes.

He took her arm. "Do not think me overly kind, Lorena. I may wish to honour Christ by telling you of His love, but I will not have you harm Elizabeth."

"Why is that woman at the centre of all men's thoughts? Forgive me, but not all women have such blessings!"

She stormed off, and he chose not to follow. Perhaps, he had overstepped, but the marquess had begun to wonder just why any woman would choose evil over good. Then he thought of Amelia and of his son. Could he tell Beth about Albert? If he did, then he would have to admit his own failure to keep Albert from dying. Would Elizabeth understand, or would she blame him the way Amelia had? The only way to know would be to have the conversation, but once said, it could never be unsaid. With these thoughts in his mind, Charles decided to remain near the cliff and take an hour to think before returning to the house.

CHAPTER TWENTY-FIVE

That evening, as the company finished supper, Adele Stuart announced that she would sing for their evening entertainment. Following the disastrous conclusion to her piano recital, the adolescent had that afternoon asked Elizabeth to play whilst she sang several art songs that her new music tutor, a Mr. Andrew Kettle, had taught her recently. Adele had a lovely soprano voice, and her sweet renditions cheered all in the music room that night. Charles had hoped to speak quietly to Elizabeth that afternoon, but every time he found the duchess alone, someone entered the room, so he had finally decided to wait until everyone had gone to bed. Now, the marquess relaxed and enjoyed every moment and every note of the young lady's concert, but he especially loved watching Elizabeth's dainty fingers flying upon the keys. Realising what an accomplished pianist she was, he hoped now that she would also sing for them.

Paul, looking more like himself with good colour and a smile upon his lean face, kept his eyes fixed proudly upon his daughter. Unaware that Charles had asked the duke for Beth's hand, the earl continued to hope she might come to accept his indiscretion with du Barroux and forgive him completely, and that their engagement would soon be announced. Though Elizabeth had tried several times to speak with the earl privately since the night of his confession, each time something or someone had interrupted, so the earl still lived in complete ignorance of the *dreams* experienced by his love and Charles eleven days before.

James Stuart, Duke of Drummond, was no fool. He'd been quietly observing all the players in the strange company now staying within his home, and he sensed a major shift in the direction of their inner circle. The servants, too, had noticed the rise and fall of mood and melody within the castle walls, and many wondered just what events would occur in the concluding acts.

As Adele sang the final note of Beethoven's *Ich Liebe Dich*, Paul broke into vigourous applause, and Elizabeth rose from the piano bench to give her little cousin a kiss and a hug. "My, my! Your voice has certainly grown since you started with this new tutor," she told her. "Be careful when reaching for those high notes, Della, that you do not sing more sweetly than the birds, for the nightingale may become jealous and cease to sing us to sleep at night."

Adele beamed. "Paul, what did you think?" she asked, skipping toward the man who was in truth her proud father.

"I think that you are an angel," he said joyfully, lifting her up with his right arm and taking her onto his lap. "I must hold you like this whilst I may, for you are growing into a young lady, and you'll not want my hugs and kisses soon, but only those of your young gentleman."

She blushed, and Mr. Kepelheim offered his praise. "Delightful, my dear Adele, simply delightful! But, perhaps we should ask the duchess to sing. Lord Haimsbury has heard you play, Your Grace, but he has not yet heard your elegant soprano. Lord Aubrey, will you exert your considerable influence upon our duchess?"

She looked from Paul to Charles, and both men wore handsome smiles, their faces so similar, yet each one unique. She felt so very happy that night, for all darkness seemed at last far away. Paul set Adele down, and the girl ran to Sinclair, sitting next to him on the sofa.

The earl rose to his feet and took Elizabeth's hands in his, gazing deeply into her dark eyes, his own filled with love and admiration. "Charles, this one sings so beautifully that she will break your heart and mend it all at once. Do sing, Beth."

She let him kiss her cheek, and then she looked to the tailor. "Mr. Kepelheim, do you recall the time that you and I performed together at Lord Salisbury's home?"

Kepelheim's face beamed as he leapt to the piano and twirled his fingers as if limbering them up. "I do indeed, Duchess, and I even recall our repertoire. You see, one allowed *me* to sing as well, Lord Haimsbury, which fulfilled an old dream of mine to tread the operatic boards. Are you in voice for our duet?"

Elizabeth looked surprised. "Surely not the Verdi! Oh, Martin, that is so tragic."

"True, but beautiful when sung by you, and it rends my old heart every time I hear you voice it. Will you sing it with me, dear lady? I am not much of a Germont, but your Violetta would make the most callous man weep."

"Oh, please, do sing it, Cousin Elizabeth," Adele called from her seat next to Charles. "I have not heard you sing in so very long. And my new cousin says he has never heard you."

"Very well," she said at last, "though I cannot promise to match the Royal Opera, so grant me your patience."

Paul smiled proudly as he turned to Charles. "She actually can," he said. "Last June, Beth sang at Salisbury's gala to raise funds to support one of the queen's charities, and the Royal Opera's director asked if she would sing there the next night. She has a splendid voice."

Kepelheim set the scene. "This famous duet is from Act Two of *La Traviata*, of course, and Violetta has been living in peace and happiness with Alfredo, a profligate gambler who is perhaps not the most astute man on earth though he is handsome enough. Alfredo has just left the villa, and whilst the son is away, the father enters, and his demand to poor Violetta is simple: she must give up the great love of her life, so that Alfredo's sister's reputation and chances for marriage may be restored."

The tailor then began playing the music by heart, raising up his quite decent baritone to begin the *Madamigella Valery* that opens the famous duet betwixt the proud and interfering father, Germont, and the desperate woman whom his son loves, Violetta Valery, a courtesan stricken with consumption. As Elizabeth responded with Violetta's shock at Germont's demands that she spurn his son, Charles sat forward to listen more closely, and when she took her turn in the duet to respond with tragic longing, he found himself drawn into the scene as if watching from a gilded opera box. But then, she began the poignant *dite alla giovine*, and her sweet voice and expression nearly broke his heart. She *was* Violetta, trapped between her love for the thankless son and the moral outrage and paternal demands of the overbearing father.

As she sang the final note, Charles could see tears tracking down her face, and her right hand trembled as she clutched at the piano. When the duet finished, the room exploded into applause. All the company shouted approval, and Kepelheim rose to bow, holding up his hands to applaud his Violetta, insisting that she must now sing the *Sempre Libere*, for as amazing as her voice proved that night, she could not leave without singing the most famous aria written for the tragic character.

Kepelheim paused for a moment before looking up at his Violetta.

"Shall we begin with the *E Strano*?" he asked. "I am only passable as a tenor, but I shall endeavour to provide what few lines Alfredo sings, if our company will indulge me."

All laughed, and the tailor commenced with a pounding to the piano, setting up the first line where the lonely courtesan ponders the meaning of her deep and growing love for Alfredo, and as the aria progresses into near madness, she bewails the impossibility of it all, telling herself that for a fallen woman such as she, only depravity and loneliness lie ahead.

Elizabeth lost herself in the music, and for those moments, she embodied Violetta Valery. The imagery was not lost on Paul, who had never before thought of Elizabeth as lonely or tragic, but the connexion to his own guilt for Cozette's painful death now stung with a new brand of vengeance, and he wept silently as his duchess sang. *I am no better than this Alfredo,* he realised. *How could I have treated Cozette with such dispassion? Such arrogance? I should have listened when she begged me to take her with me. I as much as killed her.*

Elizabeth's final note, voiced in a high E flat, soared sweetly in the air as she effortlessly ended the mournful song. Charles rose to his feet, shouting *brava!*, but Paul, drowning in his own sea of guilt, went to Beth and took her into his arms as if struggling to keep her as his own. His face was streaked with tears, and he kissed her sweetly, tenderly.

"Beth, forgive me. I do not deserve you," he whispered, and she began to weep at the brokenness he now displayed. "I bring only heartache to those I love."

Though Charles had no knowledge regarding the root of what now passed between them, it was clear that some new phase of their love had been reached, and his own heart began to dread. He now began to wish he had found a way to propose to her that afternoon. *Is it now too late?* he wondered.

"She is amazing, is she not?" Kepelheim asked Sinclair.

"She is more than that to me," he said, unaware of the duke's insightful gaze upon the scene.

"Well, Charles, you have heard the loveliest voice in all our realm, have you not?" the duke spoke as he crossed the room. "Music is good for the soul, but then so is a moment of quiet now and then. How does a whisky sound? I've a mind to play cards, if you're game."

"Uh, sorry," he stammered, his thoughts diverted suddenly by the duke's gentle prodding. "Cards? Surely, but I must warn you, Uncle, I play to win."

"So I see," the duke said with insight. "Ladies, we shall now adjourn to the guest library for a round of Whist. Would any of you wish to join us?"

Elizabeth, still in Paul's arms, shook her head. "I am completely exhausted, thanks to Maestro Kepelheim's vigourous accompaniment, so I shall retire early. And I believe it is Adele's bedtime as well. Enjoy your game, gentlemen. We shall wish you all goodnight."

She stepped away from Paul after letting him kiss her once more, and then took the girl's hand and led her through the anteroom and into the large foyer, and then climbed the stairs to their apartments.

Paul wiped at his eyes and forced a laugh. "Whist? A woman's game, Uncle. And as much as I love our Violetta, I fear Beth has never done well with cards. Charles, she and I once partnered in a round, and only after all hands were revealed, did it become clear that Beth and I would have won, except she had no idea what her hand actually meant!"

James laughed heartily, tapping Sinclair on the shoulder. "Now, let me clarify this story, Charles, for I was in that game as well. What Paul leaves out of his version of events is that Elizabeth was only six. But since it's all men, we can repair to my library, if you've a mind, gentlemen."

Charles had followed Elizabeth to the door, and he now watched as she and Adele disappeared up the staircase. His heart followed, and his feet longed to do so as well, but he sensed the duke's offer of cards had been meant as a distraction.

"Dr. MacKey," he said, turning back into the room to speak to their mysterious guest, "you've been thoughtful all evening. Perhaps, your card playing will match my own."

Lorena had been quiet, because she had been speaking telepathically to both Trent and the shadowy Prince. Both feared that the renewed attachment betwixt the earl and his cousin may unravel all their carefully designed plans, and their mental conference had determined a need for changing the tack of their secret game.

"I also play to win," MacKey said in challenge to the marquess, "but tonight I must write some letters, including one to my college friend—you remember, the one whose mother had died? My brash arrival here caused me to miss the funeral, and I owe her a note of explanation. I plan to leave on the morrow and return to London. I have truly enjoyed meeting all of you, and especially you, Duke," she said, offering him her hand. "I shall never forget your kindness and how you have made an impertinent commoner feel most welcome in your household."

"We are forever in your debt," the duke replied. "Without your ministrations, Paul's wound may have worsened, and Charles might not have recovered."

She batted her long lashes coquettishly. "I am only too happy that you have recovered," she told Sinclair for all to hear. "Had I been told when I arrived that you had ingested belladonna, I might have prevented that serious complication by offering the antidote, but I fear the poison had already begun its secretive work by the time of your collapse, and any physician could only hope to counter the effects by treating your fever. In truth, I did little to aid your recovery, merely looked in now and then. Mr. Kepelheim and the duke's housekeeper may take credit for your current state of health."

"I give credit to the true Healer," Charles said. "Our Saviour, Christ Jesus," he replied, still wishing MacKey would abandon her loyalty to a side that would happily toss her into the lake of fire if it served their ends.

She blinked, managing a tiny smile. "Yes. Well, I am delighted you have fully recovered. Goodnight, Mr. Kepelheim. Your Germont was inspired. Thank you all. I shall see you at breakfast."

She turned to go, passing through the anteroom, and Sinclair kept watch to make sure the doctor's steps continued on up the stairs. Once she had disappeared into the upper floor, Charles found himself wondering just what the doctor now planned. "Is it my policeman's nature, Uncle, or is there something disconcerting about our Dr. MacKey?"

The duke agreed, his left brow arched. "She requires watching, which is why I've been pleased to keep her here these many days. We'll want to take note of all addresses on those letters she writes tonight."

He pulled a bell rope and within moments, two footmen appeared along with the butler. "We're adjourning to my private library, Laurence. Would you make sure we are not disturbed, and oh, Laurence," he added before leaving, "Dr. MacKey will be adding a few letters to our post bag sometime before the morning, I should think. I want to know all the addresses on those letters."

"Consider it done, sir," the efficient Laurence replied. "Will you require anything else before retiring?"

The duke thought for a moment. "I guess not, lad. Get some sleep. It's been quiet the past few days, but I've a feeling we're not out of all dangers yet, so see to it that you have men stationed as before."

"Already done, sir."

Charles followed Dryden, Risling, Paul and the duke, turning to Kepelheim as they walked toward the private library. "This isn't a game we're heading to, is it?"

The tailor's face had grown serious. "Hardly. I believe the duke wishes an informal meeting. The duchess never plays cards, and he certainly did not expect Adele to begin a game so late in the evening. And, of course, had the doctor, as she calls herself, accepted your invitation, we would not be going to the private library. No, my dear Marquess, this is not a game at all."

A dense fog rose up along the back alleys of Whitechapel, blanketing warehouses and whorehouses alike. Inside one such, the mistress, a woman with shockingly red hair and a corseted, hour-glass figure, knocked on her girls' doors to roust out any gentlemen who had overstayed their time. Ever intent on improving profits, Dolly Waters, known locally as the Abbess, knocked on Rachel Connor's freshly painted, blue door.

"Rachel? It's been half an hour, luv. That's long enough. Tell your guest he must leave or pay double."

There was no response. Other doors began to open, depositing their customers in various states of dress and undress into the wide, beautifully wallpapered hallway. Two men rushed past Waters, one tipping his hat, and the other shading his drugged and sensitive eyes from the hallway's gas lamps.

"Thank you, gentlemen," she said with a bright smile. "Do visit us again soon, Sir Dennis." She knocked once more. "Rachel! You must bid your gentleman goodnight!"

Again, only silence.

Doing her best to remain calm, but fighting against rising irritation—for the girl had only just started two weeks earlier, and she had already proven stubborn regarding the rules—Waters unlocked the door.

The room stood in darkness, but the Abbess perceived two small pinpoints of light hovering and moving like tiny candles.

"Rachel?" she whispered. "Sir? I must ask you to leave now or…"

The twin candles moved suddenly, growing brighter with dreadful intensity, lighting up the entire room in a hushed glow of crimson.

And *blood*.

And *death*.

As Waters screamed, the eyes—for eyes they were and not candles—disappeared through the window and out into the thick fog.

"*Murder!*" the Abbess shouted, bile rising to her throat and burning there as she ran into the hallway to vomit. "Oh, Gawd! The Ripper! It's the Ripper again!"

She dropped to her knees weeping, for no male customer was to be found within; only her new girl's torn body remained inside the gaily wallpapered room, her legs splayed and carved, eyes gouged out, internal organs ripped from her body and laid across her breast.

And upon the wall behind the bed in large bloody handwriting: *Duchess Violetta, Scotland will not protect you.*

Paul Stuart had been mostly quiet for the hour since their meeting commenced, nodding or shaking his head in response to each topic of discussion, his mind fixed on something, or someone unseen. The duke had been proposing alternative measures they might make to protect Beth and now Adele, but Paul contributed little. Suddenly, as if jolted into action, the earl leapt to his feet, and began pacing back and forth.

"We've been wrong about all of this," he said, all eyes riveted to his face. "We have acted as Elizabeth's guardians since the day of her birth—and I for my part, have done all I felt necessary to keep her safe, and will do so to my dying breath—but James, I think coming here has been a mistake."

Charles wondered if the earl's true regret was ever to have involved his new cousin in Beth's escape. "How so?"

"Is it possible that we were driven to the castle like so many sheep? That the enemy's plan all along was to force us into bringing Elizabeth here? Since our arrival, we've encountered demonic events that seem focused on one thing, one objective: to drive a wedge betwixt Beth and her guardians. Trent is trying to separate her, like a wolf would a wounded lamb!"

Charles began to object, but he could see some truth in the earl's statement. However, it was Kepelheim who spoke.

"I am not family, though you have always welcomed me as such, so it might be easier for me to offer a less romantic viewpoint. Yes, my good friend Aubrey, our duchess has been isolated in some ways, but I would state rather that she has been directed away from you and toward another."

Paul's eyes flashed, and he glared at the tailor with uncharacteristic anger. "And your point, Martin? Am I so poor a watchman for her?"

The tailor took no offence, explaining gently, "I mean no disrespect to your care regarding the welfare of our charge. I wish simply to state what is obvious. The enemy clearly prefers a particular bloodline be united with hers."

Risling nodded agreement. "The symbols left at the castle and the cottage indicate this fact, sirs. The staged abduction was intended to lure Lord Haimsbury into rescuing the duchess. And once rescued, he was to take her to the cottage."

The earl seemed unsatisfied. "And how then did Redwing expect my cousins to arrive at that cottage, Malcolm? How? How would they know that Charles would become lost and seek refuge at the farm? He could just as easily have returned here with her."

Risling smiled indulgingly. "I imagine that was the assassin's purpose. Murder the doctor before Lemuel could reveal too much and frighten Sinclair into returning to the road with a team of ex-hausted horses, requiring a stop somewhere along the road. But we all know that Redwing is capable of controlling situations even 'on the fly', as the Americans might say. No matter where the marquess drove that night, he would invariably have ended up at that cottage."

Charles found this interesting. "Can you explain that, Malcolm?"

Risling took a sheet of paper and began to sketch out a figure. "Spiritual entities interact with time and space in ways unknown to us. Think of the unseen world of the supernatural as a spider's web," he said, drawing out a simple web. "The denizens of this web perceive tugs on a single filament no matter where it might fall, and they move toward it. Now, imagine that same web in more than two dimensions—three, perhaps even four or more. Once Sinclair turned toward the cottage, Redwing's demonic forces were able to move along the timeline web to a point which allowed them to leave the symbols and contaminate the tea, assuming the woman there didn't do it. We must not think the spiritual realm is limited to what we mortals can see and do."

The men grew thoughtful with this insight, and the duke turned to Kepelheim. "Didn't you suggest something along those lines to me years ago, Martin? That Redwing's fallen rulers can either see into the future and divert its path, or else they can alter events that have already occurred? If the enemy can move backward in time, then how can we possibly counter their moves?"

The tailor patiently replied, "I do not believe they can travel backwards very far, sir, if at all. Perhaps a few moments, but I sus-pect that they have limited vision into our future, which actually works quite well with Risling's analogy. A web that reaches across the dimension of time might permit a spiritual spider to detect a tug from a future moment and reach that temporal point to snatch up the hapless prey as it becomes trapped. But ultimately we must put our faith in the Creator of Time, must we not? And with all due respect to Lord Aubrey's concerns, may we put them aside for a moment and consider the items our marquess discovered in the late earl's rooms?"

Aubrey sighed as the tailor removed the letter and small note from his pocket and settled his spectacles onto his nose. "This letter is telling, in many ways," he said, handing the two page missive to the earl. "Charles found it in Connor's desk. After the late earl's death, the duke decided to leave his son's rooms as they were, for sentimental reasons, but perhaps the Lord inspired it. I find it more than interesting that it is our Charles who uncovered this truth. Connor intended to divorce Patricia. We had suspected as much, but now we have the proof. But it is the mention of Trent that is most unsettling and informative."

Paul glanced up from reading the extraordinary letter, handing it back to Kepelheim. "Beth must never see this."

Sinclair nodded. "I agree. It distresses me to read these words, and I have no memories of the late Lord Kesson. Elizabeth would find them more than she could bear, I think."

Paul handed the letter to Risling. "It would tear her apart. But this letter may actually aid us. Connor did not die from a hunting accident, as I'm sure you now know, Charles. He was torn apart by the same massive grey wolf that chased you upon the road. If that wolf is Trent, then he was directly responsible for Connor's death, and this letter indicates a link in an evidentiary chain. Might it be enough to bring him in for questioning?"

Sinclair sighed. "Perhaps, but even if I could convince a judge that Trent is able to turn into a wolf or even control one, most would consider this letter hearsay at best. Connor does not present any evidence for making the claim that Patricia was having an affair with him, nor does he offer evidence that Trent is Redwing. However, he does imply that Beth knows. This would require she testify to what she knows in court. I prefer not to involve her in such matters, if it can be helped."

The duke poured whiskys for everyone. "Nor do I, son. Connor had admitted to me that he thought Trish was having an affair, but he never mentioned Trent. Martin, did you decipher my son's other note?"

"I did, sir, with Mr. Risling's aid. He and I spent all of yesterday scouring through our archives for the old keys, and we finally found one that Connor created in tandem with his good friend, the late Lord Haimsbury. As I've told you, Charles, your father and Beth's were very close friends, and both were brilliant when it came to devising ciphers."

"But you thought you recognised my name in that note," Sinclair replied. "Were you right?"

"Yes, your name is in there. And so is Beth's. Here is what it says. 'Father, you must find Charles. He is alive. I have seen him in London. I will not say where, just in case this is found by our traitor. Redwing also knows, and a man named William Trent has already begun to construct plans involving Charles. Robby's instincts on this were correct. The Sinclair blood is prized, and I've seen their plans to marry his blood to Beth's. Look in Robby's London house. He'd left a cipher there before his death. I know not where, but I'm sure there are clues if you look. Also, I've secreted information in London. If I am killed, you must find Charles. His lost memories are the key to saving Elizabeth. Father, please, if God allows my death, you must keep our Princess safe.'"

The tailor removed his glasses and drank the whisky in one gulp. "I am getting too old for all this," he said, wiping his eyes. "Duke, I am sorry for the heartache this letter brings you, but your son's death must have been a direct result of what he'd uncovered about Redwing's plans. I have said all along that Charles was taken by that foul group for a reason, and it seems Connor believed it as well. Charles, we must unlock your memories, my friend."

Sinclair took Kepelheim's translation and read it through again to himself. "This says that Connor had already found me," he said to himself. "I wonder how. James, I do not know how or why my blood enters Redwing's demonic plans, but I shall do whatever it takes to keep Elizabeth safe. But this mention of a traitor in Connor's note. Could it be he knew about Lemuel even then?" the detective asked.

"Perhaps," the duke replied. "We must find out, for if not Lemuel, then someone else. It is troubling to say the least."

The tailor continued. "It is, and whilst it is true that we must rout out any traitors, it is also true that we must not allow ourselves to forget Redwing's ultimate design! Connor's message confirms that it is our newly titled marquess, Charles Sinclair, that Trent and his ilk wish to unite with Elizabeth. Your place as her protector, Lord Aubrey, will always be needed, and I believe the dear lady would echo such, but—and I know that I am being presumptive here, so please forgive me—but if it is Charles they insist she marry, then would he not be the *safer* choice?"

Paul would hear no more. "No! That is madness, Martin! Assuming this theory is correct, how can we give them what they want? It places both of them in extreme danger. Look what happened to

Robby Sinclair and Cousin Connor! I will not allow Beth to follow that path. Not ever!"

He paused for a moment, and his lean face showed great anguish as he strove to regain control of his heart. "Charles, forgive me. I have come to love you as a cousin and as a friend, but you cannot know what she means to me. When Elizabeth was born, right here in this house, my father placed her into my arms—so tiny, so indescribably beautiful—and he admonished me to care for her as if she were my own. He and Uncle James had already begun teaching me our true history, about the inner circle and about Redwing, because of my elder brother's death. I stood there, twelve years old, and I was told that this infant was to be my bride when she came of age.

"I'm ashamed to tell you how my thoughts and fears often played upon my mind in the coming years. At first, I thought marriage a distant reality and simply watched her grow as any cousin might, but as I matured into manhood, Beth became more like a girl in need of a friend than a lover. I confess that I strayed many times, sowing wild seeds as most men do, but I kept telling myself that Beth would always be there, when I was ready. Watching her fall in love with you, Charles, has been both an agony and an alarm to me. I will not give her over to destruction, and though I would not force myself upon her as husband, it is my hope that she will choose me in the end."

Charles marveled at the young earl's energy and passion. He turned to the duke. "Paul speaks for my heart as well, sir. I would not wish to place Elizabeth in any danger, and if she is safer with him, then I shall agree to that, though I think you know, Uncle, that it would forever tear out my heart. Still, should Paul and Elizabeth marry, I shall remain their friend and do all within my power to keep both of them safe."

Kepelheim turned now to the two cousins. "My Lord Aubrey, my new and dear friend Lord Haimsbury, it has been clear for many days that you both wish Elizabeth as bride, but is it not our enemy's hopes that now dictate her future? No, no, my friends, permit me to finish before you speak again. Think of how the enemy has maneuvered to place Elizabeth into Lord Haimsbury's life—even murdering her mother so that she might be forced to put her hopes in you, Charles, at so young and tender an age. Certainly, this was the true purpose behind that mad drive described to us by our sweet duchess; a long journey taken by Trent in dark of night, all to place poor Patricia's body where our policeman friend might find it.

"Then, how is it this most recent business began? A note signed by—what was it now?—'Saucy Jack' is delivered to her very door in a way that shows the enemy has gained easy access to Queen Anne House, which then causes her to fly—to whom? *To Charles.* This sent us to Branham and thence to our sanctuary here, but is it such, really? No, it was never a sanctuary, but a carefully constructed trap!

"Even before we left Branham, Trent or someone in his cabal had already threatened Dr. Lemuel with exposure, and that only by agreeing to effect the dear lady's drugging and abduction could he be assured of their silence. And why? For ransom? Nay, not so. The purpose of his crime was to force Charles to become her sole defender. That, friend Paul, is why you were wounded—to prevent you from being able to rescue her. You are an excellent marksman, but I saw the man who shot you, and I fear he would have killed you, had that been his intent. No, it is the union of Charles and Elizabeth that Redwing wants! Their bloodlines merged into a son—that is what the enemy most desires. It is the final move in a long and treacherous game."

"That is precisely why we must not let that happen!" Paul shouted, slamming his palm against the table. "Martin, how can you suggest we do so?"

The tailor placed a reassuring hand on the earl's right shoulder. "Because, my dear friend, to best guard our treasure, we must be present to do so. Is that not right? Beth's safety requires that someone she trusts and who stands against Redwing be always near her. The best way to accomplish this is in the person of husband. If we give them what they want, then Charles will be there to act as ever-present guardian, but if we insist on preventing it, then who can tell what dangers they will inflict upon her, upon Charles, upon you? They have already shot you to remove you from her side, what more might they do?"

"I have no fear for myself," he said bravely.

"This is true, for I have seen it many times," the tailor continued. "And I know that you would gladly die to keep her safe, but I would speak of something else—another danger that may not have occurred to you. Adele."

Paul had not expected this. "What? How could she be a danger?"

"She is not one consciously, but her presence here acts as a distraction to you and places the good Lady Adele within the enemy's reach. Forgive me again, but though I suspect you've said nothing to Charles, it is vital that he understand that Adele is not only your adopted sister. She is also your daughter."

1:13 a.m.

Elizabeth awoke to darkness. She had slept deeply, without dreams, for which she was grateful, and outside her room, she could hear a soft tapping at the window. Assuming it to be a tree branch in the wind, she rose from her bed and walked to the mullioned panes. No branches stood nearer than a foot away, so she opened the window to see what might have caused the sound.

Outside, the moon had waned to half her form, but even that soft light in so isolated a world as the Drummond estate lit up the landscape, casting long, deformed shadows across the statuary, exterior buildings, and sloping hills. Her window opened out onto the main entrance, so Beth could see the long gravel drive and the carriage park nearest the front doors. Six men stood sentry there each night—or had been until tonight—but Beth could see no one patrolling the area, and she wondered if the duke may not have altered his usual strategy for some reason.

Then she saw her.

It was Adele's slender form, clad only in her nightdress, walking along the rocky path toward the moors beyond. Della had been prone to sleepwalk as a small child, so Elizabeth feared shouting, but rather threw on her robe and—barefoot—ran out her door and down the stairs as quickly as she could. She hoped to find a footman or one of the other men standing guard in the foyer, but the entire main floor area was empty, and the great oaken doors to the front stood open wide. And it had begun to rain, a sudden downpour that quickly gathered into silvery puddles along the gravel path.

Without further thought, Elizabeth ran out the front toward Paul's daughter, terror filling her mind as she wondered where all the men had gone.

"Della!" she shouted, no longer concerned about waking her from a dream. "Adele!"

As Beth reached her at last, the girl turned, her blue eyes open and glazed. "Mother?" the girl said, reaching out.

Beth threw her arms around her. "Della! Wake up, darling!"

The girl blinked, the heavy rain dripping from her curls and soaking into her thin clothing. "Cousin Beth?" she asked mechanically. "Where is Mother? I saw my mother."

"You've been sleeping, dear. Come, let's return to the house."

Both turned back toward the doors, but their path was now blocked.

Before them, stood a huge grey wolf with crimson eyes.

Instantly, Della screamed—the high-pitched sound piercing the night as it echoed against the clouds overhead. In response, the gigantic wolf lunged forward several yards, close enough now for Beth to see its hot breath hang like a misty ghost upon the cool night air.

"Darling, you must do as I say. Exactly as I say. Get behind me," Beth instructed, praying someone inside had heard the child's loud scream. Though she knew it not, the meeting had only just adjourned in the soundproof library, otherwise, no one inside would have heard.

The girl moved behind her cousin.

"Good," Elizabeth said evenly. "Now, I am going to turn 'round, very slowly. The wolf will also move, I pray, and as it does, it will clear your path to the front door. Now, I want you always to stay behind me, and when I say run, Della, you must do so, as quickly as you can, all the way into the house without stopping. Do you understand?"

Terrified into near paralysis, the girl's arms held tightly to Elizabeth's waist, but she nodded and whispered, "Yes. I will run—but you must run, too!"

Beth knew the wolf had come here for her, luring the girl into danger in order to force the duchess into coming outside, so it was her hope that it would leave Adele alone.

"I shall run, but do not look back or wait for me, darling. Focus only on the door when you run, and if the wolf follows, you must shut the door behind you!"

"But..." she objected.

"Do as I say, Della. I shall be fine."

All this time, Elizabeth had very carefully kept her eyes locked on the wolf's intense red-eyed gaze, and she had slowly turned it so that it now faced the house, as she had hoped, putting as much distance betwixt Adele and the creature as possible, and clearing the child's escape to safety.

Adele now stood thirty feet from rescue, and Beth prayed silently before telling her to run.

"All right, Della. Be brave, darling. Turn very slowly now until you are facing the door." She paused, listening as the girl's bare feet turned on the gravel. "Are you facing it?"

"Yes," the girl replied, her entire body trembling.

"All right, get ready to run at my command."

Elizabeth blinked for a second, took a deep breath, and then focused all her energies upon the wolf's red eyes.

"Now, Della, run!"

Della's legs blurred into motion, and gravel flew as her small feet dug into the muddy path toward safety.

Beth stood her ground, holding the wolf's gaze, daring it to move. Her small hands shook, and her heart pounded as the rain soaked her night clothes and robe, but she raised up her arms and challenged the supernatural predator. "I will not surrender; do you hear me? I know who you are, I know *what* you are, and I will *not* allow you to hurt *anyone* I love! You may devour me, but you will not harm that child whilst I have breath! May our Lord Christ help me now, *I will not!*"

The wolf stared at her for the briefest of moments and then suddenly lunged forward, its massive teeth bared to tear into her flesh. Beth shut her eyes, expecting to feel its fetid breath and sharp fangs upon her neck as she fell to her knees, but instead two strong arms swept her into a desperate embrace as a hailstorm of bullets flew past, all hitting their target.

Not daring to open her eyes now, her breath came and went in great pants, and Elizabeth slowly realised it was Charles who held her, and that he had carried her to safety within the castle.

Half a dozen rifles and pistols belched fire, smoke, and powder, rising like a vengeful fog, and she heard Adele screaming again and again, because Paul, who had raced toward Elizabeth alongside Charles, now stood directly in front of the animal, his pistol nearly empty, hot blood drenching his clothing and boots.

The great wolf lay still, its massive body riddled with black gashes and holes, but Paul bent down and fired the final round, point blank, into its enormous skull. Slowly, the earl returned to the castle, dropping the empty weapon onto the flagstones as he passed through the doors, and then wrapped his arms around his child, smothering her with kisses.

The earl looked up at Charles, who still carried Elizabeth, for she had now fainted, and he said softly, "Charles, you are right. Kepelheim is right. If we fight them, they will kill her. Take Beth, Charles. Please. Take her, and marry her. I am only a danger to her now. And to my Adele."

CHAPTER TWENTY-SIX

The following morning, Elizabeth slept late, Adele at her side, for the girl had refused to sleep elsewhere. As the duchess awoke, she could hear raised voices downstairs, and it was clear that her grandfather was upset with someone. Turning to Paul's daughter, who slept peacefully despite the previous night's events, Elizabeth kissed her and rang the bell for the young woman who had been serving as her maid. The door to the hallway opened.

"Yes, my lady?" asked a young woman wearing a black muslin dress with a long white pinafore and cap. "Shall I set out your clothes for breakfast?"

"Not yet, Agatha. Can you tell me what is happening downstairs?"

The young woman was in her twenties and had lived on the estate her entire life, working first in the kitchens, and then rising through the ranks to become an upstairs maid, and now hoped to serve as a lady's maid permanently. "Well, my lady," she whispered so as not to wake Adele, "it's the post bag, I believe. After all of last night's madness, begging your pardon, well, his lordship has been calling all over the house. More than that, I do not know."

"Well, I suppose I'll need to find out more then. Would you hand me that shawl there, please? I'll just wrap it around my nightdress and slip down. Oh, and if you'd draw me a bath, I would love to soak for a bit. I shall be back in a few moments."

She rose, wearing a cotton nightdress trimmed in eyelet lace. Still barefoot, she wrapped the tartan shawl about her shoulders and crept down the stairs until she could observe her grandfather, Paul, and the butler in a huddle.

"When did she leave, man? Did no one see her?" the duke asked, tossing the post bag to the butler, clearly angry.

Laurence remained calm, as was his way.

"Before even Cook was awake, sir. We believe sometime in the night. No one saw her depart, but it is likely that she made her escape using one of our horses when all our attentions were upon the wolf. Black Button is gone, sir, along with her saddle and halter."

Beth sat on the step, listening and watching, her mind replaying what had happened the previous night. The 'woman' must surely be Dr. MacKey, though why she would ride out into a rainstorm Beth could not fathom, unless it was to escape danger. Had the doctor known about the wolf's plans? Why had she suddenly left off her strange pursuit of the earl?

"Spying, Princess?"

Beth jumped at the voice, turning around to find Charles behind her on the staircase. He sat down, joining her on the steps.

"Last night. That was the bravest thing I've ever seen in my life," he said softly.

"Paul, you mean? Facing down that wolf? It was. But he might have been killed."

"No, Beth. Not Paul. He's accustomed to danger, and he was armed. I meant you. I cannot tell you how terrified I was when we ran to the foyer after hearing Adele's scream—and thank God that she did scream!—and there you stood. You had nothing to use as a weapon except faith, but you placed yourself twixt Adele and mortal danger. I have never felt such terror nor such marvel all at once in my life."

She leaned against him, glad to feel his strong arm around her. "If it looked like bravery, then you did not see my face. I was petrified, Charles. I know it sounds mad, but I—I had seen that wolf before. As a girl. And that was all I could think of then. That it was *him*. The same—I don't know, entity. The Shadow Man who used to speak to me with his thoughts. Did you kill it? Is it really dead?"

He kissed her hair and held her close. "We saw it go down, all of us; but once we had made sure you'd not been injured—for you had fainted, and I know few men who would not also have done so, my darling—then Laurence and the duke and a few others went out to examine it, but I tell you this truly: the wolf was not there."

She shivered. "Not there? Oh, how I wish it had been there, Charles! Then it would be possible to put this thought out of my mind. It is a demon, I believe. And it takes many forms."

"Trent," he said, for that was the conclusion all the men had drawn, based on Connor's message.

"No. Not William. It cannot be William."

He started to ask what made her so certain, but Paul and the duke came up to the steps, for they had heard Elizabeth's voice.

"Princess, if you're strong enough, we must talk," the duke said. "Charles, would you bring her into the breakfast room?"

Charles helped Beth to her feet, noticing she wore no shoes. "Do your feet hurt? I noticed some of the rocks had left small cuts."

She shook her head. "My feet took a little bruising, but I plan to soak them this morning, if I have time. I've a feeling we're all about to travel."

He held her hand as they walked toward the breakfast room, a sun-drenched space with many windows and a large oak table with carved legs shaped like great palm fronds, laden now with bread, fruits, cheeses, and blue and white china.

The duke came in and drew Elizabeth into his arms, tears in his dark eyes, holding her as if he dared not let go. "Princess, I thought last night that I would lose you forever! Do not *ever* do that again! Oh, but you made me proud, lassie. Della would surely be dead now if you'd not been there. I think that doctor may have drugged our guards, for all had fallen into a mysterious sleep. They're fine now, though all nurse headaches. But that witch has left us, thank the Lord!"

"I'm glad of that," she answered, kissing him on the cheek. "The wolf—Grandfather, I'd seen him at Branham, I think—and perhaps also here. I used to believe it all a childhood nightmare, but now I remember him. When I saw Adele in danger of that beast, I could not do anything else," she said simply. "But wait, what else has happened? You look very worried. Is it about the mailbag?"

"Sit, Princess. Let's eat our last meal here, and then we must all pack. Charles, this came for you in the morning post. It's a telegram, and it's not good news."

Everyone sat and two footmen served a variety of hot dishes, which the men devoured. Elizabeth had no appetite, but she managed a bit of bread and a cup of tea.

"You should eat, Princess," the duke said. "I don't know how much food we'll have on the train, since we've not given Armstrong much notice."

"The train? Then we are leaving."

"For London. As soon as we can pack and reach Glasgow."

"It's a shame Mr. Reid could not convey us in that beautiful airship," Kepelheim said, digging into a plate of potatoes and sausages. "The view from the air must have been breathtaking!"

Charles set down the telegram and looked at the company, his handsome face now lined with worry. "Paul, have you seen this?"

The earl nodded. "Yes. And for the record, I was against telling Beth, but I was outvoted."

"What did you not wish me to know, Paul?" she asked.

The earl nodded toward Charles. "His telegram. It comes from Inspector Reid. But not to say he is on his way with the Queen of the Meadow. Rather he sends a message. One, I fear, was left for you, darling."

"For me? I don't understand."

Charles sat next to her and took her hand in his. "Beth, in most circumstances, I would vote with Paul, but after seeing you last night, I know how brave your heart is. And I believe you are safest when you are given full information. Last night, a young prostitute was found murdered in Whitechapel. I will not go into detail, for Reid gives little information, other than to record a message found at the scene. It reads thusly: *Duchess Violetta, Scotland will not protect you.*"

Her face grew pale, but she did not tremble. "I had expected as much," she said, surprising them all. "We have been watched all along, and we have been pointed this way and that. No more, gentlemen. No more. Last night, seeing that *thing*, that demonic creature threaten Adele was his first mistake. That fallen angel has tortured and tempted me since I was but a girl, and I grew up terrified that one day, he might consume me, but now he has dared to show his claws and teeth to another girl, another child. I will not permit Adele to live as I have. No, gentlemen. We take this battle to him now! How dare he snarl at me like I am his prey? No more will we hide. No more will we defend only. We must devise an offensive, and that offensive begins today."

Charles broke into applause, and Paul joined him.

"Princess," the earl said, "you are the bravest of us all. Woe to our enemy, for he has severely underestimated you, as have we, and I ask your forgiveness for that. And though I had originally thought to speak to you in private regarding this, I shall do so rather here, now, before all our company. For that is what we are. The Company of the Duchess. Beth, I have served as your knight errant all your life, and I had hoped that soon the ring you have been generous enough to wear would be shown to all as representing our love and our promise to each other."

She had gone quiet, fearing what he might say next. "Paul, I…" she began, but he stopped her, moving around the table to sit next to her.

With himself on one side and Charles on the other, the earl continued. "Beth, it's become clear to me that though you love me, and I know you would live with me as wife for the rest of our lives, that your heart now looks to another. No, don't speak, darling. Not yet. I have already said all this before these good men, but you should hear it from me. I will continue to serve as your knight whenever needed. I will love you with all my heart until I die, but—but, I relinquish your heart and any pledge you have made to me, and I give both to the man you truly love. To Charles Sinclair, my cousin and my best friend on this earth."

She had no idea what to say. "Paul, I... I don't understand."

The duke rose, too, kissing his granddaughter's hand. "Princess, we all know that it is Charles who has won your heart. In fact, he has already asked me for your hand, and I have given it—with one requirement, that he vows he will always love and protect you. I think I can safely say that he will not disappoint."

Charles fell to his knees now, taking her hands in his, his sea blue eyes moist and shining. "Elizabeth Georgianna Regina Stuart, would you do me the honour of becoming my wife?"

Beth could hardly believe her ears. "Is this not a strange setting for a proposal of marriage?" she asked, looking at her clothing. "Here I sit, wearing a simple nightgown and shawl, and no shoes! Would you have such a shabbily dressed bride, Lord Haimsbury?"

"To me, Beth, you look like a queen, and yes, I would. Please, say yes."

"Yes," she whispered, her eyes glistening with tears. "Oh, my wonderful Captain, yes!"

He took her into his arms, and for the first time, in front of all their stalwart company, Charles gave her his heart openly, and they kissed, knowing that the joy they now felt might soon fall into tears, for their future—and the future of England and the world—was mobile, and Redwing watched.

END BOOK ONE

TO BE CONTINUED IN
THE REDWING SAGA, BOOK TWO:

BLOOD RITES

WWW.THEREDWINGSAGA.COM

ABOUT THE AUTHOR

Science, writing, opera, and geopolitics are just a few of the many 'hats' worn by Sharon K. Gilbert. She has been married to SkyWatchTV host and fellow writer Derek P. Gilbert for nearly twenty years, and during that time, helped to raise a brilliant and beautiful stepdaughter, Nicole Gilbert.

The Gilberts have shared their talents and insights for over a decade with the pioneering Christian podcasts, *PID Radio, Gilbert House Fellowship,* and *View from the Bunker.* In addition to co-hosting SkyWatchTV's flagship interview program and *Sci-Friday* each week, Sharon also hosts *SkyWatch Women* and *SkyWatch Women One-on-One.* She and Derek speak several times each year at conferences, where they love to discuss news and prophecy with viewers, listeners, and readers.

Sharon's been following and studying Bible prophecy for over fifty years, and she often says that she's only scratched the surface. When not immersed in study, a writing project, or scouring the Internet for the latest science news, you can usually find her relaxing in the garden with their faithful hound, Sam T. Dachshund.

Learn more about Sharon at her website: www.sharonkgilbert.com.

BOOKS BY SHARON K. GILBERT

Ebola and the Fourth Horseman of the Apocalypse (non-fiction)

Winds of Evil (fiction)

Signs and Wonders (fiction)

The Armageddon Strain (fiction)

Contributing Author:

God's Ghostbusters (non-fiction)

Blood on the Altar (non-fiction)

Pandemonium's Engine (non-fiction)

I Predict (non-fiction)

When Once We Were a Nation (non-fiction)